D0405032

The Lost Steps

BY ALEJO CARPENTIER

The Kingdom of This World
The Lost Steps
Explosion in a Cathedral
The Chase

The Lost Steps

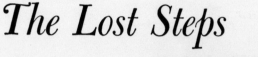

Alejo Carpentier

TRANSLATED BY HARRIET DE ONÍS

THE NOONDAY PRESS

Farrar, Straus and Giroux

NEW YORK

Note

Even though the site of the first chapters of this book does not call for any specific location; even though the Latin American capital and the provincial cities that appear later on are mere prototypes to which I have not given a local habitation because the elements which make them up are common to many countries, I feel called upon to make it clear, to satisfy the reader's natural curiosity, that beyond the place called Puerto Anunciación, the landscape reproduces the very precise vision of little-known and rarely, if ever, photographed places.

The river in question, which, earlier in the book, might be any great river of America, specifically becomes the Orinoco in its upper reaches. The location of the Greeks' mine might be not far from its confluence with the Vichada. The passage with the triple incision in the form of a *V* marking the entrance to the secret channel really exists, with the sign, at the entrance of the Guacharaca Channel, some two hours' sail up the Vichada. It leads, through vaulted roofs of vegetation, to a village of Guahibo Indians whose wharf lies in a hidden cove.

The storm took place at a spot that might be Raudal del Muerto. The Capital of the Forms is Mount Autana, with its air of a Gothic cathedral. From this point on, the landscape becomes that of the Great Savanna, a vision of which is to be found in different portions of Chapters iii and iv. Santa Mónica de los Venados is what Santa Elena del Uariren might have been in the early days of its founding, when the easiest way to get to the young city was a seven-day trip from Brazil up a turbulent river. Since then many such settlements have sprung up—still without geographic location—in distant regions of the American jungle. Not long ago two famous French explorers discovered one of them, of which nobody had heard, which bears a striking resemblance to Santa Mónica de los Venados, one of whose inhabitants' experience was that of Marcos.

The chapter of the Conquistadors' Mass took place in a Piaroa village close to Mount Autana. The Indians described in episode XXIII are Shirishanas from the Alto Caura. An explorer made a recording—the record forms part of the archives of Venezuelan folklore—of the dirge of the shaman.

The Adelantado, Montsalvatje, Marcos, Fray Pedro, are personages every traveler encounters in the great theater of the jungle. They all represent a reality, as does the myth of El Dorado, which is nourished by the deposits of gold and precious stones. As for Yannes, the Greek miner who traveled with the *Odyssey* as his sole possession, I should like to say that I have not even changed his name. I might add that, along with the *Odyssey*, he admired above everything else in the world the *Anabasis* of Xenophon.

A. C.

The Lost Steps

Chapter One

*And thy heaven that is over thy
head shall be brass, and the earth
that is under thee shall be iron.*

—DEUTERONOMY XXVIII, 23

I/ Four years and seven months had passed since I had
seen the white-pillared house, with the austere pediment
that gave it the severity of a courthouse; now, among the
furniture and decorations, whose positions never varied, I
had the distressing sensation that time had turned back. The
claret curtain beside the wrought-iron lantern; the empty
birdcage next to the rose trellis. In the background, the elms
that I had helped to plant during the first enthusiastic days
when we had all lent our hands to the common enterprise;
alongside the scaly treetrunk, the stone bench that echoed
woodenly under my heeltaps. To the rear, the river walk,
with dwarf magnolias and ornate New Orleans-style iron
fencing. Now, as on the first night, I walked under the
portico, listening to my steps' hollow ring, and took the

shortcut through the garden to where the groups of branded slaves, the women with the skirts of their riding habits over their arms, and the ragged, wounded, clumsily bandaged soldiers were awaiting their cues in the shadows stinking of varnish, of felt, and of the same old frock coats with new sweat added to old.

I stepped out of the light just in time, for the hunter's shot sounded and a bird fell to the stage from the second drop. My wife's crinoline swooped past my head—I was standing exactly where she made her entrance, crowding the already narrow passageway. So as to be less in the way, I went to her dressing-room, and there time and the present flowed together, everything bearing witness to the fact that four years and seven months do not go by without taking their toll. The laces of her costume for the climax had grown dingy; the black taffeta of the dance scene had lost the stiffness that had made it rustle like a whorl of dry leaves at every curtsy. Even the room's walls looked bedraggled, with repeated traces of fingermarks in the same places, and revealed their long association with make-up, withered flowers, and disguise.

As I sat on the couch that had turned from sea-green to mold-green, I realized with a shock how hard it must have become for Ruth to bear this prison of lumber and contrivance, with its air-swung bridges, its string cobwebs, its artificial trees. In the opening days of the run of this Civil War drama, when we had all been trying to help the young author working with a company just out of the experimental theater, we had foreseen at most a run of twenty nights. We were now giving the fifteen-hundredth performance, and the actors—whose contracts included an indefinitely renewable clause—had had no chance for escape since the play had come under professional management, turning the generous, youthful enterprise into a big-business venture. For Ruth this play had become a Devil's

Island instead of an escape mechanism, a gateway to the multitudinous world of the Drama. Her brief fugues in the wig of Portia, the draperies of one of the Iphigenias, brought her little relief, for under each costume the eyes of the spectators sought the familiar crinoline, and in the voice pretending to be that of Antigone they heard the contralto tones of Arabella, who was on stage at that moment, learning correct Latin pronunciation from Booth by repeating the phrase *"Sic semper tyrannis"* in a scene that the critics had called astoundingly intelligent.

It would have taken the genius of a tragedienne such as the world has never seen for Ruth to rid herself of the parasite that was sucking her blood, that occupant of her very body, grappled to her flesh like an incurable disease. There were times when she longed to tear up her contract. But in the profession one paid for such rebellious acts with long periods of "leisure," and Ruth, who had begun to say her lines when she was thirty, now found herself crowding thirty-five and repeating the same words, the same gestures, every night of the week, every Sunday, Saturday, and holiday afternoon, not to mention summer tours. The success of the play was slowly effacing its interpreters, who, in their unvarying costumes, were aging before the eyes of the audiences. The day after one of them had died one night of an infarct shortly after the curtain descended, the others in the company had appeared at the cemetery in a display of mourning which gave them—probably without their even being aware of it—something of the air of a daguerreotype. Growing more embittered, increasingly unsure of really triumphing in a career that she instinctively loved in spite of everything, my wife had been caught in the automatism of her enforced work just as I had been caught in that of my job. Earlier she had at least tried, in a search for inspiration, to protect her temperament by a continuous review of the great roles she hoped to interpret some day: Nora, Judith, Medea, Tessa. But this illusion had succumbed to the melancholy of the monologue declaimed before the mirror.

Unable to work out any normal arrangement for meshing our lives—an actress's hours are not those of an office worker—we had finally wound up sleeping apart. Late on Sunday morning I used to get into her bed for a while, fulfilling what I regarded as a husband's duty, though without ever knowing whether I was really interpreting Ruth's desires. Probably she, too, felt obliged to maintain this weekly practice to honor the obligation she had assumed by signing our marriage license. As for me, I was motivated by the thought that I should not neglect an urge I was in a position to satisfy, thus silencing for a week certain twinges of conscience. The fact was that our embrace, though somewhat flat, retightened each time the links loosened by our unparallel lives. The warmth of our bodies restored, like a brief return to the home of our early days, a kind of intimacy. We watered the geranium that had been neglected since the previous Sunday; we moved a picture; we cast up household accounts. But the bells of a near-by carillon soon reminded us that the prison shades were closing in. When I left my wife on the stage for her matinee, I had the feeling that I was returning her to a prison in which she was serving a life sentence. The shot rang out; the stuffed bird fell out of the second drop; the Living-Together of the Seventh Day had come to its end.

Today, however, there had been a change in the Sunday rule as a result of the pill I had swallowed toward daybreak to get to sleep quickly—I could no longer drop off the way I used to by just covering my eyes with the sleep shade Mouche had recommended. When I woke up, I noticed that my wife had left, and the confusion of underwear hanging out of open dresser drawers, theatrical make-up tubes tossed into the corner of the room, compacts and bottles thrown everywhere, told me of an unexpected trip.

Now, followed by applause, Ruth was coming off stage and hurriedly unhooking her basque. She shut the door behind her with a kick of her heel which, through repetition, had dented the wood. The crinoline, which she pulled off over her head, billowed from wall to wall on the carpet. As she emerged from the lace, her pale body attracted me like something new and pleasant, and I was about to caress her when her nakedness disappeared under velvet slipping over her head and smelling like the contents of a ragbag my mother kept in the back of her mahogany wardrobe when I was a boy.

I felt a flash of rage at the stupid profession of make-believe which was always coming between our bodies like the angel's sword in the legends of the saints, rage at the drama that had divided our house, driving me to the other one whose walls were decorated with astral figures, and where my desire always found a warm welcome. And to think that it had been to help this career in its difficult early days, to increase the happiness of the one I then loved so much, that I had deflected my destiny, seeking material security in the job that had made me as much of a prisoner as she was. Now, with her back turned, Ruth was talking toward me into the mirror while smearing her mobile face with grease paint. She was explaining that after this performance the company was leaving immediately on a tour to the other coast and that for this reason she had brought her luggage to the theater.

She asked me absent-mindedly about the preview of the film the night before. I was going to tell her about its success and remind her that the end of this work meant the beginning of my vacation, when there was a rap on the door. Ruth got up, and I saw before me once more the woman who had stopped being my wife to become the leading lady: she tucked an artificial rose into her waist and, with a gesture of excuse, walked toward the stage, on which the Italianate curtain had just opened, stirring a breeze that smelled of dust and old wood. She turned toward me again as though saying good-by and entered the dwarf magnolia path.

I was not in a mood to wait till the next intermission, when she would change from velvet to taffeta and spread new make-up over the old. I went back home, where the disorder of the hasty departure was still the presence of the absent one. The shape of her head was indented into the pillow; on the night-table stood a half-empty glass of water with a sediment of green drops, and a book open at the end of a chapter. My hand touched a spot still damp with spilled lotion. A sheet torn from the calendar pad, which I had not noticed before, told me of the unexpected trip: "Kisses, Ruth. PS. There's a bottle of sherry in the desk." I had a desolate sense of loneliness. This was the first time in eleven months that I had found myself, except when asleep, without something that had to be done right away, without having to dash for fear of being late somewhere. I was far from the excitement and confusion of the studios, in a silence unbroken by mechanical music or megaphone voices. Nothing was hurrying me and, for that very reason, I felt a vague threat hanging over me.

In that room deserted by the person whose perfumes were still floating in the air, I found myself disconcerted at the possibility of talking to myself. I caught myself in a whispered dialogue. I went back to bed and, staring at the ceiling, summoned up my last years, seeing them pass, autumn to Easter, blizzard to sticky asphalt, without time to live them, knowing by the signs in a restaurant window that the wild ducks were back, that oysters were in season, or that it was chestnut time. Sometimes my awareness of the passing of the seasons came from the red paper bells that appeared in store windows or the truckloads of pine trees whose smell transfigured the streets for a second or two. There were gaps of weeks in the chronicle of my existence, seasons that left with me no real memory, no unusual sensation, no enduring emotion; days when every gesture left me with the obsession that I had done the same thing before under identical circumstances —that I had been sitting in the same corner, that I had been telling the same story, looking at the schooner imprisoned in the glass of a paperweight.

When my birthday was celebrated among the same faces, in the same places, with the same song sung in chorus, the thought invariably struck me that the only difference between my previous birthday and this one was the extra candle on the cake, which tasted exactly like the last one. Ascending and descending the hill of days, with the same stone on my back, I kept going through a momentum acquired in jerks and spasms, but which sooner or later would end on a date that might be on this year's calendar. But to evade this, in the world that was my lot, was as impossible as trying to revive today certain epics of heroes or saints. We had fallen upon the era of the Wasp-Man, the No-Man, when souls were no longer sold to the Devil, but to the Bookkeeper or the Galley Master.

Realizing that rebellion would be futile after an uprooting that had made me live two adolescences—one left across the sea and one that had ended here—I saw no way of finding any freedom except in the disorder of my nights when any excuse sufficed for abandoning myself to repeated excesses. By day my soul was sold to the Bookkeeper—I jeered at myself—but the Bookkeeper did not know that at night I fared forth on strange journeys through the mazes of a city invisible to him, a city within a city, with dwellings like the Venusberg and the House of the Constellations for erasing the memory of day when a vicious caprice aroused by drink took me to secret apartments where personal identity was left at the door.

Because I was chained to my technique among clocks, chronographs, and metronomes in windowless, artificially lighted rooms lined with felt and soundproofed, my instinct, when at dark I found myself in the street, was to seek pleasures that would make me forget the passing of the hours. I drank and took my ease, turning my back on the clocks until drink and ease laid me low beside an alarm clock in a sleep that I tried to thicken by covering my eyes with a black mask that must have given me, while I slept, the look of a masked bandit in repose.

The bizarre image put me into a good humor. I tossed off a big glass of sherry, determined to silence the one who was thinking too much in my brain, and the effects of the previous evening's drinking were revived by the wine. I stood at the window in Ruth's room, where her perfumes were being dispelled by a penetrating smell of acetone. Summer had arrived behind the haze glimpsed as I woke up, ushered in by ships' sirens calling to one another from river to river above the skyscrapers. Overhead, into the thinning mist, rose the peaks of the city: the patinaless spires of the Christian churches, the dome of the Greek Orthodox church, the large hospitals where White Eminences officiated beneath classical entablatures designed by those architects who, early in the century, sought to lose their way in an increase of verticality. Solid and silent, the funeral parlor with its multiple corridors seemed a reply in gray—with a synagogue and concert hall between—to the huge maternity hospital whose bare façade displayed a row of identical windows that I used to count on Sunday mornings from my wife's bed when topics of conversation ran low. From the asphalt pavement rose a bluish haze of gasoline laced with acrid smells from garbage cans in courts where an occasional panting dog lay like a skinned rabbit, trying to find a cool spot on the hot floor. The carillon was hammering out an *Ave Maria*.

I was seized by an unwonted curiosity to know which saint was being honored that day. "June 4, St. Francis of Carraciolo," said the Vatican edition of the volume in which I once studied the Gregorian chants. He was completely unknown to me. I looked up the book of the Lives of the Saints, printed in Madrid, from which my mother used to read to me during pleasant minor ailments that kept me away from school. It said nothing about Francis Carraciolo. But I happened to open to a section with a series of devout titles: *Rose receives visits from heaven; Rose wrestling with the Devil; The miracle of the Image that Sweats.* And a border festooned with Latin words: *Sanctæ Rosæ Limanæ, Virginis. Patronæ principalis totius Americæ Latinæ.* And these impassioned verses of the saint, addressed to the Spouse:

> *Ah me! My beloved,*
> *Who detains him?*
> *The hour is past, noon strikes,*
> *But he comes not.*

A painful bitterness filled my throat at the evocation, through the language of my infancy, of too many things. Unquestionably, this vacation was making me soft. I drank the rest of the sherry and turned back to the window. The children playing under the four dusty fir trees in the Model Park left their gray sand castles from time to time to look wistfully at the street urchins swimming among scraps of old newspaper and cigarette stubs in the water of a municipal fountain. It gave me the idea of going to a swimming pool to get some exercise. I was bad company for myself in the house. I looked for my bathing suit without being able to find it in any of the closets. Then it occurred to me that it would probably be healthier to take a train and get off somewhere in the woods to breathe the pure air.

I was on my way to the station when I stopped in front of the Museum, where an exhibit of abstract art had just opened, advertised by mobiles hung on rods, their fungi, stars, and wooden bows whirling in an atmosphere that smelled of varnish. I was about to walk up the stairs when I happened to notice that the bus to the Planetarium had stopped close by. A visit there suddenly seemed to me urgent to gather ideas for Mouche's redecoration of her studio. But as the bus was slow in starting, I finally got out and began to walk aimlessly, unable to choose among so many possibilities, stopping at the first corner to look at the drawings a cripple, his breast covered with war medals, was sketching in colored chalks on the sidewalk.

The disordered rhythm of my days interrupted, manumitted for three weeks from the enterprise that in return for feeding me had already bought several years of my life, I did not know what to do with my idleness. The sudden rest seemed to have made me ill. I walked the streets without knowing where I was, torn among subliminal desires. I was tempted to buy that *Odyssey*, or the latest detective stories, or, better still, the *Comedias Americanas* of Lope de Vega displayed in Brentano's window— for the sake of the language I never used, though I could multiply only in Spanish, and add by the "and so many to carry" method. But there, too, was *Prometheus Unbound*, which suddenly made me forget the world of books: its title was too closely linked to that old project of a composition which (after a prelude concluding in a great

chorale of brasses) had got no farther, in Prometheus'
opening recitative, than that defiant shout of rebellion:

> . . . *regard this Earth*
> *Made multitudinous with thy slaves, whom thou*
> *Requitest for knee-worship, prayer, and praise,*
> *and toil, and hecatombs of broken hearts,*
> *With fear and self-contempt and barren hope.*

The truth was that now that I had time to stop in front
of the stores after months of ignoring their existence, they
had too much to say to me. Here was a map of islands
bordered with galleons and mariner's roses; there, a treatise on orthography; farther on, a picture of Ruth in bor-
rowed diamonds advertising a jeweler. The recollection
of her trip filled me with a sudden irritation; it was really
she whom I was now pursuing, the one person I wanted
to be with this sultry afternoon whose sky was darkening
behind the monotonous flicker of the first electric signs.
But once again a script, a stage, distance came between
our bodies, which no longer found the joy of first knowledge in the Living-Together of the Seventh Day.

It was too early to go to Mouche's house. Disgusted at
having to pick my way among so many people going in the
opposite direction and tearing off tin foil or peeling oranges
with their fingers, I wanted to go where there were trees.
I had got clear of the people returning from the ballparks,
miming in their discussions the sports they had seen, when
a few cold drops touched the backs of my hands. After an
interval whose length escapes me now—because of the
seemingly brief course of a process of delay and recurrence
which I could not have suspected at the time—I recall those
drops falling on my skin in pleasurable pinpricks as though
they had been the first announcement—which I did not
understand at the time—of the encounter. A trivial meet-

ing, in a way, as all meetings whose true significance becomes clear only later in the web of their implications appear to be. The origin of everything would have to be sought in the cloud that burst into rain that afternoon with such unexpected violence that its thunderclaps seemed those of another latitude.

II/ The cloud had burst into rain as I was walking behind the great concert hall along that stretch of sidewalk which offers no protection whatever to the passer-by. I recalled that an iron stairway led to the musicians' entrance, and as I knew some of those who were going in, it was no problem for me to get to the stage, where the members of a famous choral society were gathering by voices to take their places on the platform. With his knuckles, a kettle-drummer was testing his drums, which were too high-pitched because of the heat. Holding his violin with his chin, the soloist was striking B flat on the piano, while the horns, bassoons, and clarinets went on in that confused simmer of scales, trills, tuning, which precedes the actual notes.

Every time I saw the members of a symphony orchestra seated behind their music racks, I waited impatiently for the moment when time should cease to pile up incoherent sounds and fall into an organized framework in response to a prior human will speaking through the gestures of the Measurer of its Passing. The latter was often obeying decisions made one century, two centuries ago. Inside the covers of the score were set down in signs the orders of men who, though dead in ornate mausoleums—or their bones lost in the dreary disorder of some potter's field—still held author's rights on time, imposing the measure of motion and emotion on future men. It sometimes happens, I thought to myself, that these posthumous powers suffer a decline or, on the contrary, are strengthened, depending on the taste of different generations. Thus, on the basis of performance, one could prove that in certain years the greatest beneficiary of time had been Bach or Wagner, whereas Telemann or Cherubini had had lean pickings.

At least three years had passed since I had attended a symphony concert; when I left the studios I was so saturated with poor music used for detestable purposes that it seemed absurd to let myself become engulfed in time almost objectified by being subjected to the demands of fugue or sonata form. For that very reason I savored the pleasure of the unexpected at finding myself brought, almost by surprise, to the dark corner of the bass viols, where I could watch what was happening on the stage that rainy afternoon whose muted peals of thunder seemed to rumble over the puddles of the near-by street. After a silence finally broken by a gesture, a light fifth came from the horns, winging into triplets from the second violins and violoncellos, above which two descending notes stood out, as though fallen from the first violins and violas, with a reluctance that soon became anxiety, desire for flight, in the face of the onslaught of a suddenly unleashed force. . . .

I got up in disgust. Just when I was in the best frame of mind to hear music, after ignoring it for such a long time, *this* had to burst forth, swelling now to a crescendo behind my departing back. I might have known it when I saw the chorus coming on stage. Still, it might have been a classical oratorio. If I had known that the Ninth Symphony was on the music racks, I would have kept on through the downpour. If there was some music I could not stand because of its association with childhood sicknesses, still less could I bear the *Freude, schöner Götterfunken, Tochter aus Elysium*, which I had avoided *ever since*, the way one averts one's eyes for years from certain objects that recall a death. Besides, like many of my genera-

tion, I detested everything that smacked of the "sublime." Schiller's *Ode* left me as cold as did the Last Supper
at Montsalvat and the Elevation of the Grail. . . . Now I
found myself in the street again, looking for a bar. If I had
to walk very far to find a drink, I would soon be in the
grip of a depression I had experienced before, which made
me feel as though I were trapped in a locked room, exasperated at being unable to change anything in my life,
always subject to the will of others, which barely left me
free each morning to choose my breakfast meat or cereal.

I began to run, for the rain was pelting down. As I
turned the corner, I crashed head-on into an open umbrella. The wind snatched it from the hands of its owner,
and it was flattened under the wheels of a car. The sight
was so funny that I let out a roar of laughter. And just
as I was expecting an insult, a cordial voice called me by
name: "I was looking for you, but I had lost your ad-
dress." And the Curator, whom I had not seen for over
two years, was telling me that he had a present for me—
a wonderful present—in that old start-of-the-century house
with its dirty windows and graveled flower beds standing out like an anachronism in that neighborhood.

The unevenly collapsed springs of the armchair now
tormented my flesh like a hair shirt, forcing me into an
unwonted air of repose. In the familiar mirror with its
heavy rococo frame crowned by the Esterházy coat of
arms, I saw myself sitting stiffly like a child taken visiting.
Cursing his asthma, crushing out a cigarette that was choking him to light up one of stramonium, which made him
cough, the Curator of the Museum of Organography
trotted about the little room crowded with cymbals and
Asiatic tambourines, making our tea, which was fortunately to be accompanied by Martinique rum. Between
two shelves hung an Incan *quena;* on his desk, waiting
to be catalogued, lay a sackbut of the time of the Conquest

of Mexico, a beautiful instrument whose bell was a Tarascan head with silver scales, enamel eyes, and open jaws that turned a double row of copper teeth on me.

"This belonged to Juan de San Pedro, royal trumpeter to Charles V, and one of Hernán Cortés's famous riders," the Curator explained, tasting the tea. Then he poured out glasses of liquor with the remark—comical in view of the person to whom it was addressed—that a little alcohol from time to time is a thing for which the body feels an atavistic gratitude because man, in all ages and climates, has always found a way to invent intoxicating beverages.

As it turned out, the present he had for me was not on that floor, and a slow-moving deaf servant was sent for it. I looked at my watch, feigning sudden alarm at the recollection of an appointment. But my watch, which I had not wound the night before—as I now remembered—the better to accustom myself to the reality of my vacation, had stopped at twenty minutes past three. In an anxious tone I asked what time it was, but was told that it did not matter, that the rain had prematurely darkened the June afternoon, one of the longest of the year. Leading me from a *Pangelingua* of the monks of St. Gall to the first edition of a vihuela tablature, passing over a rare copy of the *Oktoechos* of St. John Damascene, the Curator was trying to soothe my impatience, which was roweled by my anger at having let myself be led to this floor, on which I no longer had anything to do among all those jew's-harps, rebecs, flageolets, loose frets, splinted violin necks, and little organs with burst bellows, which I saw all piled together in the dark corners.

I was just on the point of saying firmly that I would come back some other day for the present, when the servant returned, taking off her rubbers. What she had brought for me was a half-cut record without label, which the Curator put on a phonograph, carefully selecting a

fiber needle. Anyway, I thought to myself, the suffering
won't last long, not more than two minutes to judge by
the grooving. I had turned away to fill my glass when I
heard behind me the warble of a bird.

I looked in astonishment at the old man, who was smiling with a gentle, fatherly air as though he had just made
me a priceless gift. I was on the point of speaking, but he
enjoined silence on me, pointing a finger at the disk. Now
something different was surely coming. But no. We were
at the middle of the cutting, and that monotonous warbling continued, broken by brief pauses that all seemed of
the same duration. It was not even the song of a very
musical bird, for I could not identify the trill, the porta-
mento, and it had only three unvarying notes whose timbre
had the sonority of Morse code in a telegrapher's cabin.
The record was almost finished, and I could not understand where the vaunted present of my former teacher
was, nor imagine what a document that could be of interest only to an ornithologist had to do with me.

The ridiculous audition came to an end, and the Curator,
transported by a joy I was at a loss to understand, asked
me: "Do you realize? Do you realize?" And then he explained to me that the warbling was not that of a bird,
but of an instrument of fired clay with which the most
primitive Indians of the hemisphere imitate the song of a
bird before they set out to hunt it—this in a possessory
rite to make the hunt propitious.

"It is the first proof of your theory," the old man said
to me, almost embracing me, as a fit of coughing choked
him.

And just because I understood only too well what he
was trying to tell me by means of the record (which was
playing again), I was filled with a growing irritation to
which the two drinks I had tossed off added fuel. The bird
that is not a bird, with a song that is not a song, but a

magical imitation aroused an unbearable resonance in my breast, bringing back the memory of the work on the origins of primitive music and organography I had done such a long time before—it was not the years that frightened me, but the futile rapidity of their passing.

Those were the days when the war had interrupted the composition of my ambitious cantata on *Prometheus Unbound*. After I got back I *felt* so different that the finished prelude and the first draft of the opening scenes had been left where they were, packed away in my closet while I let myself drift into the techniques and drudgery of the movies and radio. In the specious enthusiasm I put into defending those arts of the century, insisting that they opened up unlimited vistas to the composer, I was probably trying to assuage my feeling of guilt toward the work I had abandoned, and to justify my association with a commercial enterprise after Ruth and I had destroyed with our fugue the existence of a fine man. After we had drained the hours of amorous anarchy, I quickly became convinced that my wife's vocation was incompatible with the type of life I aspired to. I had tried to make her absence during performances and seasons more endurable by undertaking something that could be done on Sundays and holidays without that fixity of purpose creative work demands.

Thus I had discovered the house of the Curator, whose Museum of Organography was the pride of a time-hallowed university. Under this very roof I had made the acquaintance of the elementary percussion instruments— hollow trunks, lithophones, animal jawbones, rattles, and anklets—from which man had drawn sound in the protracted days of his emergence on a planet still bristling with gigantic skeletons, on his ascent of the road that would lead him to the *Mass of Pope Marcellus* and *The Art of the Fugue*. Moved by that peculiar form of laziness which consists in bringing great energy to tasks not precisely those we should be doing, I went wild over the methods of classification and the morphological study of those objects of wood, of fired clay, of kitchen copper, of hollow reeds, of gut and goatskin, the original forms of methods of producing sounds which persist down the ages beneath the marvelous varnish of Cremonas or in the sumptuous theological Panpipe that is the organ.

Disagreeing with the accepted ideas on the origins of music, I had begun to elaborate an ingenious theory that explained the beginnings of primitive rhythmic expression as an attempt to imitate the movement of animals or the songs of birds. If we bore in mind that the first cave drawings of reindeer and bison were hunting magic—a means of taking the quarry by previous possession of its image—I was not too far afield in my belief that the elementary rhythms were those of trot, gallop, leap, warble, and trill imitated by the hand on a resonant surface or by the breath in a hollow reed.

Now, watching the revolving disk, I felt a kind of rage at the thought that my ingenious—and perhaps correct—theory was being relegated, like so many other things, to a dream attic, and that the daily tyrannies of the world I lived in would not allow me to complete it. Suddenly the arm was lifted from the groove. The clay bird stopped singing. And what I had most feared happened: the Curator, cornering me affectionately, asked me how my work was coming on, saying that he had plenty of time to listen and to discuss it with me. He wanted to know what I had brought to light, my new research methods, and to hear my conclusions about the origins of music on the basis of my theory of *mimetism-magic-rhythm.*

Pinned down and unable to escape, I began to lie, inventing difficulties that had interfered with the progress of my work. But, my technical vocabulary being rusty, I made ridiculous mistakes, got the classifications confused,

could not recall basic information that I knew perfectly
well. I tried to take refuge in bibliographical references,
only to learn through my interlocutor's ironic corrections
that specialists had already discarded them. And while I
was grasping at the feigned need of examining certain
primitive songs recently recorded by explorers, I could
hear my own voice echoing with such lying resonance
from the copper of the gongs that I completely bogged
down in the middle of an unforgivable *gaffe* in organographic terminology.

The mirror showed me the rueful face of a cardsharper
caught with marked cards up his sleeve, my own face at
the moment. I looked so disgusting to myself that, suddenly,
my shame turned to rage, and I vomited a flood of obscene
words at the Curator, asking him how many he thought
could make a living today from the study of primitive
musical instruments. He knew how I had been uprooted
in my early years, dazzled by false values, led into the
study of an art on which only the worst hucksters of tin-
pan alley battened, dragged for months as an army interpreter through a world in ruins, and then tossed back on
the asphalt of a city where poverty was harder to bear
than anywhere else in the world. I knew from having lived
it the Calvary of those who wash out their only shirt at
night, walk through the snow in shoes without soles, chain-
smoke, and cook in a closet, finally becoming so obsessed
by hunger that the one thought in their mind is eating.
That was as sterile a solution as selling the best hours of
your life from sunup to sundown.

"Besides," I screamed at him, "I am empty. Empty!
Empty!"

Impassive, aloof, the Curator looked at me with complete coolness, as though he had been expecting just such
an outburst. I began to talk again, but in a hoarse voice,
the words rushing out in a kind of gloomy exaltation.

Like the sinner who empties into the confessional the dark sack of his iniquities and lusts, deriving from talking ill of himself a kind of pleasure that verges upon self-abomination, I painted for my teacher, in the foulest colors, with the blackest dyes, the uselessness of my life, its tumultuous days, its reckless nights.

As though they were coming from the lips of another, from a judge I carried within me without knowing it, and who made use of my own faculties to express himself, my words took such hold upon me that it frightened me to realize, as I listened to myself, how hard it is to become a man again when one has ceased to be a man. Between the I that I was and the I that I might have been the dark abyss of the lost years gaped. We lived together in one body, he and I, upheld by a secret architecture that was already—in our life, in our flesh—the presence of our death. In the being circumscribed by the baroque frame of the mirror the Libertine and the Preacher, those basic figures of every edifying allegory, of every moral with an example, were at that moment holding forth.

Fleeing the glass, my eyes moved toward the bookcases. But there, in the Renaissance Musicians corner, beside the volumes of *Psalms of Penitence*, as though deliberately put there, I could read the title, stamped on the leather binding, of *Rappresentazione di anima e di corpo*. The succeeding silence, which the Curator allowed to lengthen into bitterness, was like the falling of a curtain or the putting out of lights. Suddenly he made a strange gesture that made me think of an impossible power of absolution. He got to his feet and, picking up the telephone, called the president of the university that housed the Museum of Organography. To my growing surprise, and without daring to raise my eyes from the floor, I heard him reciting my praises. I was described as the very collector who was needed to secure certain examples still missing from the collection of aboriginal American musical instruments, in spite of the fact that it was already unique in its wealth of documents. Without making special mention of my skill, my teacher stressed the fact that my physical resistance, tested in the war, would make it possible for me to carry on the search in areas that older specialists would find it extremely difficult to reach. Besides, Spanish had been the language of my infancy.

Each reason that he adduced must have made me grow in the imagination of his invisible interlocutor, conferring on me the stature of a young Von Horbostel. With growing dismay, I discovered that I was being entrusted with the task of bringing back, among other unique idiophones, a cross between a drum and a rhythm-stick which Schaeffner and Curt Sachs knew nothing of, and the famous jar with two openings fitted with reeds which had been employed by certain Indians in funeral rites that Father Servando de Castillejos had described in 1651 in his treatise *De barbarorum Novi Mundi moribus*. This was not listed in any organographic collection, though the survival of the tribe that had made it roar ceremoniously, according to testimony of the friar, implied the continuity of a custom recently noted by explorers and traders.

"The president is expecting us," said my teacher.

All of a sudden the idea struck me as so absurd that I felt like laughing. I tried to find some polite way out, alleging my present ignorance, my remoteness from all intellectual activity. I insisted that I knew nothing about the latest methods of classification, based on the morphological evolution of instruments and not on how they sound and are played. But the Curator was so bent on sending me where I had not the slightest desire to go that he resorted to an argument to which I could make no reasonable objection: the job in question could be easily done during my vacation. Was I going to sacrifice to my love of bar-floor sawdust the opportunity to sail up a marvelous river?

I was left without any valid reason for turning down his offer. Lulled into security by a silence that he took for consent, the Curator went into the next room to get his coat, for the rain was now pelting the windowpane. I seized the opportunity to run away. I wanted a drink. The only thing that interested me at that moment was to get to a near-by bar whose walls were covered with pictures of race horses.

III/ There was a note on the piano from Mouche telling me to wait for her. To kill time I began to finger the piano keys, striking meaningless chords, resting my glass on the last octave. The place smelled of paint. On the rear wall, above the grand piano were beginning to come clear the sketched-in figures of the Hydra, the Ship *Argo*, Sagittarius, Berenice's Hair, which would soon give my friend's studio a distinction that translated itself into money. After much scoffing at her astrological pretensions, I had had to accept the evidence of the business in horoscopes she had established, which she handled by mail, mistress of her own time, occasionally, with the most comic solemnity, granting a personal interview as a great favor.

Thus, from Jupiter in Cancer and Saturn in Libra, with information culled from curious treatises, paint pots and inkwells, Mouche drew up Maps of the Future that traveled to remote parts of the country adorned with zodiacal signs that I had helped her dignify with *De Cœleste Fisonomiea, Prognosticum supercœleste,* and other high-sounding Latin phrases. People must be very uneasy over the state of things—I used to think to myself—to consult the astrologers so often, to study the lines of their palms so carefully, the strokes of their handwriting, shivering at the menace of unpropitious tea leaves, reviving the oldest divining techniques because they no longer know how to read the future in the entrails of sacrificial beasts or the flight of birds.

My friend, who believed firmly in veiled mediums, and who had acquired her intellectual formation in the great Surrealist bargain basement, found pleasure as well as profit in scanning the heavens in the mirror of books, juggling the beautiful names of the constellations. It was her present method of writing poetry: her only other attempt, with words pasted on plaquettes illustrated with photomontages of monsters and statues, had left her disillusioned—after the first thrill of the smell of printer's ink had worn off— about the originality of her inspiration.

I had met her two years before, during one of Ruth's many professional absences, and though my nights began or ended in her bed, few words of love had passed between us. At times we quarreled fiercely, then embraced furiously, while our faces, so close that we could not see each other, exchanged insults which the reconciliation of our bodies gradually turned into coarse praise of the pleasure we were experiencing. Mouche, who was very restrained, even chary, with words, at such moments employed the language of a streetwalker, which called for a reply in kind, these dregs of language sharpening our delight.

It was hard for me to tell whether it was really love that bound me to her. She often irritated me with her dogmatic devotion to ideas and attitudes that she had picked up in the cafés of Saint-Germain-des-Prés, and after futile arguing about them, I would leave her house determined never to go back. But by the next night the mere thought of her crudities melted me, and I returned to her flesh, which had become necessary to me, for I found in its depths that imperious, selfish animality which had the power to change the nature of my perennial fatigue, transferring it from the nervous to the physical plane. When this happened, I sometimes knew that kind of sleep, so rare and so longed for, which weighed down my lids after a day in the country, those all too few days of the year when the smell of trees pervaded my whole being and left me as though drugged.

Bored with waiting, I furiously attacked the opening chords of one of the great romantic concertos; but at that very moment the doors opened, and the apartment was filled with people. Mouche, whose face was flushed, as it became when she had been drinking a little, had just come from dinner with the man who was painting her studio, two of my assistants, whom I had not expected to meet there, the interior decorator from the floor below, who was always trying to find out all she could about other women, and the dancer who was working on a ballet based solely on clapped rhythms.

"We've got a surprise," my friend said gaily. And a projector was quickly set up with a copy of the film that had been shown the night before, and whose success was responsible for my immediate vacation.

Now, with the lights out, the images were reborn before my eyes: the tuna-fishing, the admirable rhythm of the nets and the desperate leaping of the fish hemmed in by black boats; the lampreys peering through the holes of their rock towers; the lazy, enveloping movement of the octopus; the arrival of the eels, and the vast coppery vineyard of the Sargasso Sea. And then those still lifes of snails and fishhooks, the forest of coral and the hallucinative battle of the crustaceans, so skillfully enlarged that the lobsters looked like horrific armored dragons. We had done a good job. The best passages of the score were heard again, with its liquid *voix céleste* arpeggios, the flowing portamenti of the *ondes Martenot,* the surge of the harps, the frenzy of xylophone, piano, and percussion instruments in the combat sequence.

Three months of arguing, discouragement, experiment, and flare-ups had gone into the making of the film, but the results were astounding. The script itself, written under the supervision of our studio by a young poet in collaboration with an oceanographer, was a model of its kind. And as for the montage and the musical direction, I could find no grounds on which to criticize my work. "A masterpiece," Mouche said in the dark. "A masterpiece," the others chorused.

When the lights were turned on, they all congratulated me, asking for the film to be run off again. And after the second showing, guests arrived and I was asked to show it again. But my pride dwindled each time my eyes, after a new review of what we had done, reached the "End," ornate with seaweed, which served as the colophon of that model achievement. One truth soured my first satisfaction: all that the grueling effort, those pretensions to good taste, that technical skill, choice, and co-ordination of my collaborators and assistants, had brought forth, when all was said and done, was a publicity job ordered from the studio for which I worked by a Fisheries Association engaged in fighting a chain of co-operatives. A team of technicians and artists had worn themselves out weeks and weeks in dark studios to produce this celluloid product, whose sole objective was to attract the attention of certain important clients to the profits of an industrial undertaking designed to stimulate the daily consumption of fish.

I seemed to hear the voice of my father, in the tone of the dreary days of his widowerhood, when he was so given to quoting from the Scriptures: "That which is

crooked cannot be made straight; and that which is wanting cannot be numbered." That verse was on his lips for
every occasion.

The words of Ecclesiastes left a bitter taste in my mouth
as I thought how the Curator, for example, would have
shrugged his shoulders at this labor of mine, probably con-
sidering it on a level with skywriting or an advertisement
for pie mix so well drawn that it made the mouth water.
He would put me in a class with those who defaced the
landscape, signboard-painters or medicine-show barkers. But
—I thought to myself angrily—the Curator belonged to
a generation of men who saw things in terms of "the sublime," who sought love in the boxes at Bayreuth, in the
musty shadows of faded red velvet. . . . People were coming in, their heads intersecting the light of the projector.

"It's publicity that develops techniques," shouted a
Russian painter sitting beside me (as though he had read
my mind) who had given up oil for ceramics.

"The mosaics of Ravenna were nothing but advertising,"
said the architect who was so enamored of the abstract.
New voices emerged from the darkness: "All religious
painting is publicity. . . . Like certain of Bach's cantatas.
. . . The *Gott der Herr, ist Sonn und Schild* comes from
an actual slogan. . . . The cinema is teamwork; frescoes
should be done by a team; the art of the future will be
the art of teamwork."

Still others came in with bottles, and the conversations
began to break up. The painter was showing a series of
sketches of maimed and flayed figures that he planned to
reproduce on his trays and dishes, like "anatomical plates
with depth," which should symbolize the spirit of the
times.

"True music is nothing but the calculation of frequen-
cies," said my assistant recorder, tossing his Chinese dice on
the piano to show how a musical theme could be hit upon

by chance. We were all talking at the top of our lungs when an energetic "Halt!" flung from the doorway in a bass voice froze everyone in an incipient gesture, a half-articulated word, a puff of cigarette smoke, like figures in a wax museum. Some were halted in the down-beat of a step; others with glasses in the air, halfway between table and lips. ("I am I. I am sitting on a sofa. I was about to strike a match on the emery of the box." Hugo's dice re-called the verse of Mallarmé. But my hand was about to strike a match without conscious order. Therefore I was asleep. Asleep like all those around me.) Another order from the new arrival rang out, and each finished his phrase, gesture, suspended step.

It was one of the many exercises to which X.T.H.—we never referred to him except by his initials, which habit had transformed into the name *Exteeaych*—submitted us to "wake us up," as he said, and bring us to a realization and analysis of what we were doing at the moment, how-ever trivial. Inverting for his own use a philosophical principle we commonly employed, he used to say that anyone who acted "automatically was *essence* without *existence*." Mouche had become professionally enthusias-tic over the astrological aspects of his teaching, an approach that was very suggestive, but which, in my opinion, be-came too involved with Oriental mysticism, Pythagorean-ism, Tibetan tantras, and God only knows what else. But Exteeaych had managed to impose on us a series of prac-tices derived from the Yoga asamas, making us breathe in a certain way, measuring the length of inhalations and exhalations by "matras." Mouche and her friends hoped thereby to arrive at greater control over themselves and at the acquisition of powers about which I had my doubts, especially in people who drank every day as a defense against despair, fear of failure, self-contempt, the shock of a rejected manuscript, or simply the harshness of that city of perennial anonymity amid the crowd, that place of relentless haste where eyes met only by accident and the smile on the lips of a stranger was a build-up for some kind of a proposition.

Exteeaych now went to work curing the dancer's sick headache by the laying-on of hands. Dizzy with so much talk that ranged from existentialism to boxing, from Marxism to Hugo's attempt to modify the piano's sonority by putting bits of glass, pencils, tissue paper, and flower stems under the strings, I went out to the terrace, where the afternoon's rain had washed Mouche's dwarf lindens clean of the layer of summer soot from the smokestacks across the river. I had always been vastly amused by these gatherings, with their kaleidoscope of ideas passing swiftly from the Cabala to Anxiety by way of someone's plans to start a farm in the West to foster group art by raising Leghorns or Rhode Island Reds. I had always loved those leaps from the transcendental to the eccentric, from Elizabethan drama to Gnosticism, from Platonism to acupuncture. I had even planned to take down these conversations on a tape recorder hidden behind the furniture. Such recordings would prove how vertiginous is the elliptical process of thought and language. In these mental gymnastics, in this acrobacy of culture, I would find, besides, the justification of many moral aberrations that would have seemed to me detestable in other people.

But the choice between one group of men and another was not too difficult. On the one hand were the hucksters, the merchants for whom I worked during the day, who were capable of nothing but spending what they had made in diversions so stupid, so devoid of imagination, that I could not help feeling myself a different breed of cat. On the other hand were those gathered here, happy at having found a few bottles of liquor, fascinated by the Powers that Exteeaych promised them, always bubbling over with high-flown projects. In the implacable setup of the modern city, they were carrying out a form of asceticism, renouncing material well-being, suffering hunger and privations in exchange for a dubious self-realization in their work. Yet that evening those men wearied me as much as those whose aim is volume and profit. And it was because, deep down in my heart, the scene in the Curator's house had had its effect, and I was not taken in by the enthusiasm with which the publicity film, which had spelled so much work for me, was hailed. All those paradoxes about publicity and teamwork in art were nothing but ways of shaking off the past, attempts to justify the exiguousness of individual accomplishment.

I was so dissatisfied with what I had done, because of the meretriciousness of its ending, that when Mouche came over to me with facile praises, I abruptly changed the conversation, telling her about my afternoon's adventure. To my amazement she threw her arms around me, exclaiming that the news was formidable, for it corroborated a dream she had had in which she saw herself flying among great saffron-colored birds—which could only be interpreted as *journey* and *success, change of residence*. And without giving me time to set her straight, she held forth on the desire for escape, the call of the unknown, chance encounters, in a tone which revealed the influence of the Arrow-Pierced Rowers and the incredible Floridas of the *Bateau ivre*. I quickly cut her short, telling how I had run away from the Curator without accepting the offer.

"But that is absolutely idiotic," she exclaimed. "You might have thought about me."

I pointed out to her that I did not have the money to pay for her trip to those remote regions, and that the university was willing to pay the expenses of only one person. After an unpleasant silence, during which her eyes took on a disagreeable, offended expression, Mouche began to laugh. "And to think we have the painter of Cranach's *Venus* here!"

Then she explained her luminous idea. To reach the habitat of the tribes who played the drum-rhythm-stick and the funerary jar, we would first have to go to the great tropical city famed for the beauty of its beaches and its colorful folk life. What we could do would be to stay there, making an occasional trip to the near-by jungles, enjoying ourselves as long as our money held out. Nobody would be around to know whether I had followed the itinerary mapped out in my duties as collector. And on my return, for the sake of my reputation, I would turn over a number of "primitive" instruments—scientific, accurate—perfectly designed on the basis of my sketches and measurements by our friend the painter, who was wild about the primitive arts and was so devilishly clever at copying and reproducing that he earned his living faking masterpieces, carving fourteenth-century Catalan virgins, complete with faded gilt, wormholes, and cracks. His greatest triumph had been selling the Glasgow Museum a Cranach *Venus* that he had painted and aged in a couple of weeks.

Her plan seemed to me so low, so shameless, that I turned it down in disgust. The university arose in my mind with all the majesty of a temple whose white columns I was asked to defile with dung. I held forth at length, but Mouche was not even listening to me. She went into the studio to announce our trip. The news was received with shouts of joy. And, without paying any attention to me, she dashed from one room to another in a gay bustle, pulling out suitcases, taking down and putting back clothes, making up the list of things she had to buy. In the face of such insolence, which was more offensive than contempt, I left the apartment, slamming the door. But the street was particularly depressing that Sunday night, already revealing the Monday blues, the cafés deserted by those who were thinking about the next morning and fumbling for their door-keys by the light of the street lamps that cast glimmers of quicksilver on the wet pavement.

I did not know what to do. At home what I would find was the disorder Ruth's departure had left: the shape of her head on the pillow, the smells of the theater. And when the alarm went off, the pointless awakening would follow and the fear of meeting the person who emerged from myself and waited for me each year on the threshold of my vacation. The person full of reproach and bitter upbraiding whom I had glimpsed hours before in the Curator's baroque mirror, ready to rake over the old ashes. The need to check the sound-track equipment and arrange for new soundproofed rooms at the beginning of each summer favored this meeting, which meant only shifting the load, for when I threw down my Sisyphean stone, my *Doppelgänger* climbed on my still-lacerated back, and I could not tell whether, at times, I did not prefer the weight of the granite to the weight of the judge.

A mist drifting in from the waterfront hung over the pavement, refracting the street-lights to rays that pierced as with pinpricks the drip from the low clouds. The iron gates of the movie theaters were closed, and the floors of the long vestibules were littered with torn tickets. Farther along I would have to cross the deserted street with its chilly lights and ascend the ramp toward the shadowy chapel over whose grille I would run my fingers, counting its fifty-two bars.

I leaned against a lamppost, thinking of the three empty weeks ahead of me, too short to undertake anything, whose days would slip past embittered by the sense of lost opportunity. I had not made one move to bring about the proposed mission. Everything had dropped into my lap, and I was not responsible for the exaggerated evaluation of my abilities. After all, it was not going to be a penny out of the Curator's pocket, and as far as the university was concerned, it would be hard for its scholars, gone gray among books, and without direct contact with jungle craftsmen, to discern the fraud. In the last analysis, the instruments described by Fray Servando de Castillejos were not works of art, but the products of a primitive technique that still existed. Museums treasured more than one doubtful Stradivarius, so it could hardly be a major crime to falsify a savage drum. The instruments they wanted could be old or modern. . . .

"This trip was written on the wall," Mouche said when she saw me come back, pointing to the figures of Sagittarius, Argo, and Berenice's Hair, their yellow outlines clearer now that the light was dimmer.

In the morning, while she was visiting the various consulates, I went to the university, where the Curator, who had been up since early morning, was repairing a viola d'amore in the company of a lutanist wearing a blue apron. As he looked at me over his spectacles, he showed no surprise at my coming.

"Congratulations!" he said, without my being sure whether he was congratulating me on my decision or whether he guessed that if at the moment I could think halfway straight, it was thanks to the drug Mouche had given me when I woke up.

I was soon escorted to the office of the president, who had me sign a contract and gave me both the money for my trip and a list of the main objectives of the task assigned me. Somewhat bemused by the rapidity with which the arrangements had been made, and lacking any very clear notion of what might be in store for me, I was taken to a large empty room, where the Curator asked me to wait for a minute while he went to the library to greet

the dean of the Faculty of Philosophy, just returned from
a congress in Amsterdam. I noticed with satisfaction that
the gallery was a museum of photographic reproductions
and plaster casts for the use of History of Art students.
Suddenly, the universality of certain images—an impressionist nymph, the mysterious regard of Mme Rivière, a
family by Manet—carried me back to the far-off days
when I had endeavored to assuage the sufferings of a disillusioned traveler, of a pilgrim frustrated by the profanation of the Holy Places, in the almost windowless world
of the museums.

Those had been the months when I visited the shops of
craftsmen, the opera, the gardens and cemeteries that
evoked romantic vignettes, before I accompanied Goya in
the clashes of the *Second of May*, or followed with him
the *Burial of the Sardine*, whose disturbing masks suggested
drunken penitentes, devils in a morality play, rather than
the garb of merriment. After an interlude among Le Nain's
peasants, I had plunged full into the Renaissance in the
portrait of some *condottiere*, one of those mounted on
horses that seem of marble rather than flesh, against columns hung with banners. There were times when I liked to
sojourn among medieval burghers, drinking deeply of their
mulled wine, who had themselves painted with the Virgin
whom they were honoring—to keep the gift on record—
carving suckling pigs, setting their Flemish cocks fighting,
and slipping their hands into the bosoms of waxy-skinned
wenches who, rather than lewd doxies, seemed lasses making merry of a Sunday afternoon, free to sin again after
absolution by their confessors.

An iron buckle, a crown bristling with hammered points,
carried me back to Merovingian Europe, black forests,
lands without roads, migrations of rats, wild animals
brought slavering with fury to the city square on fair
day. Then there were the stones of Mycenæ, the funeral

pageantry, the coarse pottery of a hardy, adventurous Greece before its own classic period, reeking of bullocks spitted over flames, of carded wool, of dung, of the sweat of rutting stallions. Thus, step by step, I came to the display of scrapers, axes, flint knives, where I stood rapt in the twilight of the Magdalenian, the Solutrean, the pre-Chellean, feeling that I had reached the frontiers of mankind, the limits of possibility, like the edge of the flat earth, where, according to certain primitive cosmographers, heaven, too, could be discerned below by peering into the sidereal vertigo of infinity. . . .

Goya's *Cronos* brought me back to our own time, by way of huge kitchens ennobled with wine cellars. The Mayor lighted his pipe with a coal, the kitchen scullion scalded a hare in a caldron of boiling water, and, seen through an open window, the spinning women chatted in a courtyard shadowed by an elm. Viewing these familiar images, I asked myself whether, in bygone days, men had longed for bygone days as I, this summer morning, longed for certain ways of life that man had lost forever.

Chapter Two

Ha! I scent life! —SHELLEY

(*Wednesday, June 7*)

IV/ For some minutes now, our ears had been telling us that we were coming down. Suddenly the clouds were above us, and the plane wavered, as though distrustful of the unsteady air that suddenly let it fall, picked it up again, left one wing unsupported, and then handed it over to the rhythm of invisible currents. To the right rose a range of moss-green mountains blurred by rain. Beyond, in the bright sun, the city lay.

The reporter who had the seat next to mine—Mouche was stretched out asleep on the seat behind—was talking to me with a mixture of contempt and affection about that helter-skelter capital, anarchic in its layout, without style, whose first streets were becoming visible beneath us. In order to go on growing along the narrow stretch of sand cut off by the hills where Philip II had ordered fortifications built, the inhabitants had been waging a war of centuries against shoals, yellow fever, insects, and the immobility of the cliffs of black rock that rose, to one side and the other, unscalable, stark, polished, like aerolites thrown by some celestial hand. Those useless masses towered among the buildings, the spires of modern churches, aerials, old bell-towers, nineteenth-century domes, falsifying the reality of proportions, establishing a scale of their own, like constructions designed for some unfamiliar use, the work of an unimaginable civilization lost in remote night.

For hundreds of years a struggle had been going on with roots that pushed up the sidewalks and cracked the walls. When some rich property-owner went to Paris for a few months, leaving his residence in the care of lazy servants, the roots took advantage of songs and siestas to arch their backs, putting an end in twenty days to Le Corbusier's best functional designs.

They had done away with the palm trees in the suburbs laid out by the best city-planners, but the palms reappeared in the patios of colonial houses, giving a columnar air of boundary lines to the main avenues—drawn with the points of swords by the founders of the primitive city. Dominating the teeming business and newspaper district, the marble banks, the luxuriousness of the Stock Exchange, the whiteness of the public buildings, under a perennial dog-day sun rose the world of Justice's scales, caducei, crosses, winged spirits, flags, trumpets of Fame, cogwheels, hammers, and victories, all proclaiming in bronze and stone the abundance and prosperity of the city, whose legislation was exemplary on the statute books. But with the rains of April the sewerage system proved inadequate, and the main squares became flooded, so snarling up the traffic that vehicles had to be detoured through unfamiliar neighborhoods, where they knocked over statues, got stuck in dead-end streets, or ran over the sides of gullies that were never shown to foreigners or important visitors, being inhabited by people who went about all day half-dressed, strumming the guitar, beating the drum, and drinking rum out of tin jugs.

Electric power extended everywhere, and machinery throbbed under leaky roofs. Techniques caught on with amazing ease, certain procedures being accepted as a matter of course when they were still being cautiously tried out in countries with older histories. Progress was reflected in the close-clipped lawns, the pomp of the embassies, the multiplication of loaves and wines, the smugness of the merchants, whose senior members dated back to the terrible days of the yellow-fever mosquito.

Nevertheless, something like a baleful pollen in the air —a ghost pollen, impalpable rot, enveloping decay—suddenly became active with mysterious design, opening what was closed, closing what was open, upsetting calculations, contradicting specific gravity, making guarantees worthless. One morning the ampoules of serum in a hospital were found to be full of mold; precision instruments were not registering correctly; certain liquors began to bubble in the bottle; the Rubens in the National Museum was attacked by an unknown parasite immune to sprays; people stormed the windows of a bank where nothing had happened, whipped to a panic by the mutterings of an old Negro crone whom the police were unable to find.

When such things happened, one invariable explanation was accepted by all who were familiar with the secrets of the city: "It's the Worm!" Nobody had ever seen the Worm. But the Worm existed, carrying on its arts of confusion, turning up when least expected to confound the most tried and trusted experience. Moreover, lightning storms were frequent, and every ten years hundreds of

houses were destroyed by a hurricane that began its circular dance somewhere out at sea.

By this time we were flying very low, lining up the
runway, and I asked my companion about the huge, pleas-
ant-looking house surrounded by terraced gardens whose
statues and fountains descended to the shore. I was informed that the new President of the Republic lived there,
and that I had missed by only a few days the celebration,
with parades of Moors and Romans, of his ceremonious
inauguration. But the handsome residence was now disappearing from sight under the left wing of the plane.

Then came the pleasant return to earth, the bumping
over solid ground, and the filing out to the customs office,
where one answered questions with a guilty expression.
Dizzy with the change in atmospheric pressure, waiting
for officers who seemed in no hurry to examine the contents of our luggage, I was thinking that I was not yet
used to finding myself so far from my familiar haunts.
And at the same time there was something like a recovered light, the smell of hot esparto grass, of sea water
that the sky seems to permeate to the depths of its green,
and the breeze that carries the stench of rotted crustacea
from some coastal shoal.

At dawn, while we had been flying through dirty clouds,
I had regretted having undertaken the trip; I had felt like
getting off at the first stop and flying back as quickly as
I could and returning the money to the university. I felt
trapped, kidnapped, an accessory to some shameful crime
in that flying cage, with a rhythm in three changing tempos, its motors fighting an adverse wind that flung a driz-
zle against the aluminum wings at intervals. Now a strange
voluptuousness was lulling my scruples. And a force was
slowly invading me through my ears, my pores: the language. Here once more was the language I had talked in
my infancy; the language in which I had learned to read

and sol-fa; the language that had grown rusty with dis-use, thrown aside like a useless instrument in a country where it was of no value to me.

Esto, Fabio, ¡ay dolor!, que ves agora. This, Fabio . . . There came back to me, after long forgetting, this verse, cited as an example of the use of the interjection in a little grammar put away somewhere with a picture of my mother and a blond lock of my hair cut off when I was six years old. And the language of this verse was that of the signs on the stores I could see from the windows of the waiting-room, laughing and deformed in the jargon of the Negro porters, caricatured in a *¡Biva el Precidente!*

I pointed out these mistakes of spelling to Mouche with the pride of one who, from now on, would be her guide and interpreter in this unknown city. This sudden sense of superiority over her dispelled my last scruple. I was not sorry I had come. And a possibility I had not thought of before occurred to me: somewhere in the city the instru-ments I was commissioned to collect must be for sale. It was unthinkable that someone—a seller of souvenirs, an explorer tired of roaming—would not have thought of making a good thing of objects so highly prized by for-eigners. I would find a way to get in touch with this some-body, and then I could silence the kill-joy I carried within me.

The idea seemed so good that when finally we were riding toward the hotel through the streets of the poor quarters, I ordered the car to stop on a hunch that we might have struck the very place I was looking for. It was a house with ornate iron grilles, old cats in all the windows, and on whose balconies puffy dusty-looking parrots drowsed like a mossy growth over the greenish façade. The old-junk dealer and antiquarian had no knowl-edge of the instruments I was looking for, and tried to call my attention to other objects, a big music box, in which gilded butterflies mounted on hammers played waltzes and redowas on a kind of psaltery. Pictures of flower-crowned nuns taking their vows stood on tables covered with glasses resting in hands of carnelian. One of the Saint of Lima emerging from the calyx of a rose in a joyous swirl of angels shared a wall with bullfighting scenes.

Mouche took a fancy to a sea-horse she found among the cameos and coral seals, though I pointed out to her that she could find one like it anywhere. "It is Rimbaud's black *hippocampe*," she answered, paying the price of that dusty, literary object. I should have liked to buy a filigree rosary of colonial design in a glass case, but it was too expensive for me, as the cross was set with real stones.

As we left the shop, with its mysterious sign, *Rastro de Zoroastro*, my hand grazed a pot of sweet basil. A rush of emotion came over me at this encounter with the perfume I remembered on the skin of a girl—María del Carmen, the daughter of the gardener—when we played house in the back yard under the shadow of a spreading tamarind while my mother ran through some new habanera at the piano.

(*Thursday, the 8th*)

V/ My startled hand fumbled on the marble-topped night-table for the alarm clock that perhaps was ringing back up on the map, thousands of miles away. And it took a few seconds, as I stared out at the square through the Venetian blinds, to realize that my habit—my morning routine, back there—had been mocked by the triangle of a street vendor. Then came the piping of a scissors-grinder, strangely mixed with the melismatic call of a gigantic Negro carrying a basket of squids on his head. The trees, rocked by the morning breeze, showered white fuzz over the statue of one of the fathers of the country whose carelessly tied bronze neckcloth gave him a certain resemblance to Lord Byron while his manner of presenting a flag to invisible revolutionists recalled Lamartine. In the distance the bells of a church were ringing out one of those parochial rhythms produced by swinging from the bell-ropes, the electric carillons of the fake Gothic towers of my country being a thing unknown here.

Mouche lay asleep across the bed, leaving no room for me. At times, bothered by the unaccustomed heat, she tried to kick off the sheet, but only succeeded in getting her legs more entangled in it. I took a long look at her, somewhat put out by the fiasco of the evening before. A sudden allergy, caused by the odor of an orange tree whose perfume floated up to our fourth floor, had made impossible those physical delights I had promised myself for that first night together in a new climate. I had finally quieted her with a sleeping-pill, and had adjusted my black mask to help me forget my disappointment in sleep.

I looked out through the blinds again. Beyond the Governors' Palace, with its Grecian columns supporting a baroque cornice, I recognized the Second Empire façade of the theater where, for lack of more popular entertainment we had forgathered, under great crystal chandeliers, with the draped marbles of the Muses flanked by busts of Meyerbeer, Donizetti, Rossini, and Hérold. A curving stairway with rococo urns on the balustrade had led us to the red velvet salon, with golden dentils edging the balconies, where, under the lively chatter, the orchestra could be heard tuning up. Everybody seemed to know everybody else. The laughter ran along the boxes, from whose warm shadows emerged bare arms, hands putting into motion such survivals from the past century as mother-of-pearl opera glasses, lorgnettes, and feather fans. There was a kind of soft, powdered abundance to the flesh emerging from the *décolletages*, the uplifted bosoms, the shoulders that evoked the memory of cameos and lace corset-covers.

I had hoped to be amused by the extravaganzas of opera presented in the grand manner of bravura, coloratura, fioritura. But the curtain had already gone up on the garden of Lammermoor Castle, and the outmoded scenography with its false perspectives, its claptrap, its trick devices had failed to arouse my irony. On the contrary, I felt myself yielding to an indefinable charm, a fabric of vague, remote memories and partly remembered longings. This great velvet rotunda, the generous *décolletages*, the lace handkerchief warmed in the bosom, the thick hair, the sometimes overpowering perfume; this stage where the singers, against a prodigious vegetation of hanging backdrops, profiled their arias with their hands clasped to their hearts; this complex of traditions, manners, attitudes, which could no longer be revived in a great modern city, was the magic world of the theater as my pale, ardent great-grandmother might have known it, she of the sensual yet veiled eyes, gowned in white satin in the portrait by Madrazo which filled my childhood dreams before my father fell on hard times and had to sell it.

One afternoon when I had been alone in the house I had discovered in the bottom of a trunk an ivory-bound book with a silver clasp in which the lady of the portrait had kept her diary. On one page, under rose petals that time had turned the color of tobacco, I found the ecstatic description of a *Gemma di Vergy* sung in a theater in Havana that must have been the counterpart of the one I was seeing tonight. Negro coachmen in high boots and cockaded silk hat no longer waited at the door; the lanterns of corvettes did not rock in the harbor; nor would the performance conclude with a musical interlude. But there in the audience were the same faces flushed with pleasure at the romantic performance; the same lack of attention to everything but the stars' arias; as soon as the music became unfamiliar, it served only as a background for a vast machinery of meaningful looks, vigilant glances, whispers behind fans, smothered laughs, gossip, flirtations, feigned disdain, whose rules I did not know, but which I watched with the envy of a child looking at a masked ball to which he has not been invited.

At intermission time Mouche flatly stated that she could not take any more of it, for according to her, it might have been "*Lucia* as seen by Mme Bovary in Rouen." Although there was something to what she said, I felt suddenly irritated by her habitual self-sufficiency, which made her adopt an attitude of hostility the moment she came into contact with anything that did not bear the stamp of approval of certain artistic circles she had frequented in Europe. She felt contempt for the opera not because something about it really grated on her very limited musical sensibility, but because it was one of the taboos of her generation. My subtle allusion to the Parma Opera in the days of Stendhal failing of its purpose to get her to go back to her seat, I left the theater in a huff. I felt the urge to start a quarrel with her to get the upper hand of a type of reaction that could spoil the best pleasures of this trip for me. I wanted to spike beforehand certain criticisms I could see coming, recalling the conversations, loaded with intellectual prejudices, that went on in her house.

But we were soon confronted with a far darker night than that of the theater, a night that awed us with the quality of its silence, the solemnity of its star-studded presence. Any transient noise momentarily shattered it. Then it would coalesce again, filling halls and doorways, dense in the seemingly uninhabited open-windowed houses, weighing down the deserted streets with their heavy stone arcades. A sound rooted us where we stood, amazed, and we had to walk forward and stop several times to make sure of the wonder: the echo of our footsteps could be heard from the opposite sidewalk. In a square before a nondescript church, all shadows and stucco, there was a fountain of Tritons where a woolly dog stood on its hind legs drinking with a delightful lapping sound. The pointed hands of the clocks were in no hurry, and they marked time with a measure of their own in old belfries and municipal façades. Downhill, in the direction of the sea, the hubbub of the modern quarter of the city could be sensed; but for all the flashing of neon signs, the insignia of night haunts, it was clear that the real city, its soul and body, revealed itself in the habits and stones of this section.

At the end of the street we came upon an old house with a wide portico and moss-covered roof, whose windows stood open, showing a drawing-room adorned with old pictures in gold frames. Pressing our faces against the grille, we could make out, beside an impressive general in shako and epaulets, a delicate painting of three ladies taking the air in a landau and a portrait of Taglioni with little butterfly wings at her waist. The lights of a rock-crystal chandelier were burning, but there was not a sign of a human presence in the corridors leading to other lighted rooms. It was as though preparations had been made a century before for a dance to which nobody came. Suddenly, from a piano to which the tropics had given the tone of a spinet, came the flowery prelude of a waltz for four hands. A breeze rippled the curtains and the whole drawing-room seemed to fade out in a whirl of floating tulle and lace.

The spell broken, Mouche announced that she was tired. Just as I was being carried away by the charm of the night, which brought out, as in a palimpsest, the meaning of certain faded memories, she cut short my enjoyment of a peace in which time had ceased to exist, and which might have led me to an unweary dawn. Overhead, above the roof, the stars were perhaps tracing the vertices of Hydra, Argo,

Sagittarius, Berenice's Hair, facsimiles of which adorned Mouche's studio. But it would have been a waste of time to ask her, for, like myself, she was ignorant of the exact position of any of the constellations except the Big and Little Dippers. Now, as I thought how ridiculous this ignorance was on the part of a person who made her living from the planets, I couldn't help laughing as I turned toward her. She opened her eyes without awakening, looked at me without seeing me, gave a deep sigh, and turned toward the wall.

I was tempted to go back to bed, but then I thought it would be a good thing to take advantage of her sleep to set out on my search for native instruments—the idea obsessed me—as I had decided to do the evening before. I knew that she would call my determination naïve, to say the least. So I dressed quickly and left without awakening her.

The sun, drenching the streets, reverberating off the windows, spinning shimmering threads over the water of the pools, was so strange and new for me that to face it I had to buy myself a pair of dark glasses. Next I tried to orient myself toward the neighborhood of the old colonial house, in the vicinity of which I felt there would be secondhand stores and strange shops. I set out up a street with narrow sidewalks, stopping here and there to look at the shop signs, which brought to mind handicrafts of bygone days: the flowery letters of *Tutilimundi*, the *Bota de Oro*, the *Rey Midas*, the *Arpa Melodiosa*, and the swaying planisphere of a secondhand-book dealer. On one corner a man was fanning the flame of a brazier over which a haunch of veal was roasting, studded with garlic, its fat sputtering into acrid smoke as he basted it with marjoram, lemon, and pepper. Farther off, sangaree and pineapple juice were for sale, and fried fish redolent of oil.

Suddenly the breath of bread just out of the oven poured through the gratings of a basement in whose half-light men, white from their hair to their sabots, were singing. I stopped in delighted surprise. I had long forgotten this morning presence of flour back there where bread, kneaded God only knows how and where, brought in by night in closed trucks as though it were some shameful thing, had ceased to be the bread one breaks with one's hands, the bread the father hands around after he has blessed it, the bread that should be received with a gesture of gratitude before breaking its crust into the broad bowl of leek soup or sprinkling it with oil and salt to recover a taste which, more than the taste of bread with oil and salt, is the old Mediterranean taste already on the tongue of Ulysses' comrades.

This new meeting with flour, the discovery of a window displaying pictures of mulattoes dancing the *marinera*, made me forget what I had set out to look for in these strange streets. Here I stopped before the execution of the Emperor Maximilian; there I leafed through an old edition of Marmontel's *Les Incas*, whose illustrations had a touch of the Masonic æsthetics of *The Magic Flute*. I listened to "*Mambrú se va a la guerra*" sung by children playing in a courtyard where the fragrance of boiled custard floated. And, attracted by the morning cool of an old cemetery, I wandered in the shade of its cypresses among tombs that lay forgotten among the grass and bluebells. Some of the graves displayed, behind glass dimmed by mold, daguerreotypes of the occupants who lay beneath the marble: a student with feverish eyes, a veteran of the Frontier Wars, a laurel-crowned poetess. I was looking at the monument to the victims of a river flood when the air, somewhere, was torn like a piece of waxed paper by the report of machine guns. Probably the students of a military academy at target practice. Silence followed, and the cooing of the doves puffing out their breasts as they circled the Roman urns was resumed.

Esto, Fabio, ¡ay dolor!, que ves agora,
campos de soledad, mustio collado,
fueron un tiempo Itálica famosa.

I repeated again and again these verses, fragments of
which had been coming to my mind ever since I had arrived, and which finally emerged complete in my memory when the crackle of machine guns began again, louder
this time. A boy ran past, followed by a barefoot, terrified
woman carrying a basket of wet clothes in her arms, who
seemed to be fleeing some great danger. Somewhere behind
the walls a voice cried out: "It's begun! It's begun!" A little uneasy, I left the cemetery and started back toward the
modern part of the city. I quickly noted that the streets
were empty and that the stores had closed their doors and
rolled down their iron shutters with a speed that boded no
good. I was reaching for my passport, as though the letters
stamped between its covers had some magic power, when
an outcry pulled me up short, now really frightened, behind a pillar. A screaming mob, spurred by fear, was pouring out of one of the avenues, knocking down everything
in its path to get out of the range of heavy gunfire.

It was raining broken glass. Bullets were rebounding from
the metal lampposts, making them vibrate like organ pipes
hit by a rock. The snap of a high-tension wire cleared the
street, whose asphalt caught fire in spots. Near me a peddler
of oranges fell on his face, dropping his fruit, which rolled
out, flying into the air at the impact of a low bullet. I ran to
the nearest corner, taking refuge in an arcade from whose
pillars hung lottery tickets left behind in their vendor's
flight. Only a bird market separated me from the rear of
the hotel. I decided to run for it after a bullet just missed my
shoulder and perforated the window of a drugstore. Leaping over crates, stepping on canaries and hummingbirds,

knocking down cages of terrified parrots, I finally made it to one of the service doors that had been left open. A toucan, dragging a broken wing, came hopping after me, as though seeking my protection. Perched on the handlebar of an abandoned tricycle, a haughty macaw sat all alone in the middle of the deserted square, taking the sun.

I went up to our room. Mouche was still asleep, her arms around a pillow, her nightgown around her hips, her feet tangled up in the sheet. My mind at rest about her, I went down to the hall to find out what was happening.

The talk was of revolution. But this meant little to one who, like myself, was completely ignorant of the history of the country aside from its Discovery and Conquest and the voyages of several friars who had made mention of the musical instruments of its primitive inhabitants. So I began to ask questions of those who, judging from their excitement and from the amount they talked, seemed well-informed. But I very soon saw that each one gave his own version of events, referring by name to personages who meant absolutely nothing to me.

Then I tried to find out the position, the objectives of the conflicting groups, without any better results. Just as I thought it was clear that it was a movement of Socialists against Conservatives, of Communists against Catholics, the cards were shuffled, positions were reversed, and the name-dropping began all over again, as though what was taking place was a matter of persons rather than parties. I repeatedly found myself plunged by my ignorance into what seemed episodes of Guelphs and Ghibellines because of the air of a family affair about the whole thing, a fight between brothers, a quarrel between people who had been friends the day before. When, following my customary line of reasoning, I tried to figure out what would seem a typical political conflict of our epoch, I found that I was dealing with something more akin to a religious war. Because of an incredible chronological discrepancy of ideals, the conflict between the conservatives and those who seemed to represent extremist tendencies gave me the impression of a kind of battle between people living in different centuries.

"That's very acute," replied a lawyer wearing an outmoded frock coat, who seemed to accept what was going on with surprising calm. "You must remember that we are accustomed to living with Rousseau and the Inquisition, with the Immaculate Conception and *Das Kapital.* . . ."

Just then an agitated Mouche appeared. She had been awakened by the sirens of ambulances speeding past in mounting numbers, cutting through the bird market, where, meeting the seeming obstacle of the piled-up cages, the drivers slammed on their brakes, skidding into the last of the mockingbirds and troupials. At the disagreeable prospect of being shut up in the hotel, my girl became enraged at the events that had upset all her plans. In the bar the foreigners had organized irritable card and dice games washed down with drinks while they growled about half-breed states that always had a ruckus on tap.

At this point we learned that several of the waiters had disappeared from the hotel. We saw them go by a little later under the arcades across the street, outfitted with Mausers and bandoleers. When we saw that they were still wearing their white service jackets, we joked about their military bearing. But as they reached the first corner the two who were marching ahead suddenly doubled over, hit in the belly by a spray from a machine gun. Mouche gave a cry of horror, clasping her hands over her own middle. We all backed away in silence to the end of the foyer, unable to take our eyes off that prostrate flesh on the reddened pavement, indifferent now to the bullets that were still finding their mark in it, stamping new designs of blood on the white drill. The jokes we had been making a few minutes before now seemed contemptible to me. If they died in these countries for reasons I could not understand, that did not make death any less death. In the rubble of ruins in which I felt no conqueror's pride, I had more than once stepped on the bodies of men who had died in defense of convictions no worse than those upheld here.

Just then several tanks—from our war surplus—rolled by, and when the chatter of their ammunition belts died away, it seemed that the street fighting had taken on new intensity. In the vicinity of Philip II's fortress the reports at moments were fused in a solid din that made it impossible to distinguish single explosions, shaking the air with a steady burst that sounded nearer or retreated according to the wind, like the pounding of a heavy sea. At times, however, there came a sudden pause. It seemed that everything was over. The sound of a sick child's crying, the crowing of a rooster, the slamming of a door, could then be heard. Then suddenly there came the chatter of a machine gun, and the uproar began all over again, always underscored by the earsplitting wail of the ambulances. A mortar had just gone into action near the old Cathedral, an occasional shell striking the bells with a sonorous hammer stroke.

"*Eh bien, c'est gai*," remarked a woman standing near us in a deep, musical voice, with a husky accent, who introduced herself as a Canadian and a painter, the divorced wife of a Central American diplomat. I took advantage of Mouche's having somebody to talk with to have a quick one to make me forget the presence of those corpses stiffening there on the sidewalk. After a cold lunch that held no promise of coming feasts, the afternoon hours slipped by with amazing speed, what with reading that left no memory, card games, conversations carried on with the mind elsewhere, all to cover up a general uneasiness.

When night came, Mouche and I, shut up in our room,

started drinking heavily to keep from thinking too much of what was going on around us. The necessary detachment finally achieved, we let our bodies take over, and discovered a sharp, new voluptuousness in making love while others about us were playing the game of death. There was something of the frenzy of the lovers in the dances of death in our effort to hold one another closer—to plumb impossible depths—while the bullets whistled past the blinds or buried themselves, snicking off the plaster, in the dome that crowned the building. We finally fell asleep on the pale carpet. And this was the first night for a long time that brought rest without eyeshade or drugs.

(Friday, the 9th)

VI/ The next day, as we could not go out, we tried to adjust ourselves to the reality of a beleaguered castle, a quarantined ship, which events had forced upon us. But instead of sloth, the magic situation that reigned in the streets manifested itself within our protecting walls in an urge to do something. Those having a skill tried to set up a workroom or office, as though to prove to the rest that the show must go on no matter what. On the orchestra platform of the dining-room a pianist executed the trills and mordents of a classic rondeau, trying to coax clavichord sonorities from the piano keys. The members of a ballet company did exercises at the *barre*, while the *première danseuse* practiced slow arabesques on the waxed floor, from which the tables had been moved against the wall. All over the building typewriters clicked. In the writing-room businessmen riffled the contents of their briefcases. Before the mirror in his room, the Austrian *Kappellmeister*, who had been invited to the city by the Philharmonic Society, conducted Brahms's *Requiem* with impressive gestures, bringing a vast imaginary chorus in on its exact entrances. Not a single magazine or detective story or anything readable remained on the newspaper stand.

The doors of a covered patio had been opened, and a group of the lazy was taking sunbaths around a mosaic fountain adorned with potted palms and green porcelain frogs. Mouche went upstairs for her bathing suit. I noticed uneasily that the foresighted among the guests had laid in a supply of cigarettes, stripping the tobacco counter. I walked over to the entrance of the foyer, whose bronze grille was locked. The gunfire had lessened. The rapidity of what firing there was gave the impression that small groups of guerrillas in different quarters were fighting short, no-quarter engagements. Isolated shots came from roofs and terraces. A great fire was burning in the northern sector of the city; some said it was a barracks. As the names that the events seemed to swirl around made no sense to me, I gave up asking questions. I spent my time reading old newspapers, and found a certain pleasure in the news of remote areas—hurricanes, a whale washed ashore, cases of witchcraft. It struck eleven—an hour I had been impatiently waiting for—and I noticed that the tables in the bar were still stacked against the wall. We were then informed that the few waiters who had stayed on the job had left at daybreak to join the revolution.

This piece of news, which did not strike me as being especially alarming, caused real panic among the guests. Leaving what they were doing, they swarmed into the foyer, where the manager tried to reassure them. A woman burst into tears when she learned that there would be no bread that day. At that moment a faucet that had been turned on spat out a gargle of rusty water and then set up a kind of yodel that was echoed in all the water pipes of the building. As we saw the jet that played from the mouth of the Triton in the fountain die away, we realized that from that moment on we had only what water was on hand, which was very little. There came a buzz of talk about epidemics, plagues, which would be terrible in that tropical climate. Someone tried to call his consulate: the telephones had been cut off, and their silence made them so useless, so helpless, that there were those who in their exasperation shook them and banged them against the table to make them talk.

"It's the Worm," said the manager, echoing the joke that had become the explanation of the catastrophic goings-on. "It's the Worm."

And I was thinking how frustrated man becomes when his machines fail to obey him as I looked around for a ladder to stand on at the bathroom window on the fourth floor, from which one could look out without danger. When I got tired of the sight of the roofs, I noticed that something was going on at floor level.

It was as though a subterranean world had suddenly come alive, dredging up from its depths a myriad of strange forms of animal life. Out of the gurgling waterless pipe came queer lice, moving gray wafers, and, attracted by the soap, little centipedes that curled up at the slightest alarm, lying motionless on the floor like tiny copper spirals. Inquiring antennæ, whose body remained invisible, reached suspiciously out of the faucets. The closets were filled with almost imperceptible noises, the chewing of paper, scratching on wood; if a door had been opened suddenly it would have set up a scurrying of insects not yet accustomed to waxed floors on which, when they slipped, they lay motionless, pretending to be dead. A bottle of syrup on a night-table became the objective of a column of red ants. There were vermin under the rugs, and spiders looking through the keyholes. A few hours of neglect, of man's vigilance relaxed, had sufficed in this climate for the denizens of the slime to take over the beleaguered stronghold via the dry water pipes.

A near-by explosion made me forget the insects. I went back to the foyer, where nerves had reached the breaking point. The *Kappellmeister* appeared at the head of the stairs, baton in hand, at the sound of the screaming arguments. The sight of his tousled head, his stern, frowning regard, imposed silence. We looked at him in hopeful expectation, as though he was invested with special powers to soothe our anxiety. Making use of the authority to which his calling had accustomed him, he reproached the alarmists for their pusillanimity and called for the immediate appointment of a committee to make an exact report of the food on hand; if necessary, he, who was in the habit of command, would take charge of the rationing. And to fortify our souls, he concluded by invoking the sublime example of Beethoven's resigning himself to deafness.

Some dead animal was rotting near the hotel, and the stench of carrion filtered through the porthole windows of the bar, the only outside windows that could be safely left open on the first floor, they being above the level of the wainscoting. Since midmorning the flies seemed to have multiplied, buzzing with sticky insistence around our heads. When Mouche got tired of the patio, she came back to the foyer, knotting the cord of her terry robe and complaining that she had been allowed only half a bucket of water to bathe after her sunbath. With her came the almost ugly and yet attractive Canadian painter with the deep singing voice, who had introduced herself to us the evening before. She was acquainted with the country, and took in stride what was happening, saying that the situation would soon be under control, which helped to soothe my friend's irritation.

I left Mouche with her new friend, and in response to

the *Kappellmeister's* appeal went down to the cellar with
the members of the committee to take inventory of the
supplies. We soon saw that with proper care it was possible
to withstand the siege for two weeks. The manager promised, with the help of the foreign employees, to provide a
plain dish for each meal, which we would serve ourselves
from the kitchen. The cellar floor was covered with damp,
cool sawdust, and the penumbra of that underground
storeroom, fragrant with food odors, had a soothing effect.
Restored to good humor, we went to inspect the wine cellar, where the supply of bottles and barrels was large
enough to last a long time. Seeing that we were taking our
time about getting back, the others came down to the cellar, where they found us beside the spigots, drinking from
whatever receptacles we could lay our hands on.

Our report produced a contagious happiness. Decanted
into bottles, the liquor rose up in the building from basement to top floor, and the noise of typewriters was replaced
by that of phonographs. For the majority, the nervous
tension of the past hours had been transformed into a furious desire to drink, as the stench of the rotting flesh grew
more penetrating and the invasion of the insects spread.
Only the *Kappellmeister* was still in a foul humor, breathing
fire and brimstone against the malcontents who, with their
revolution, had spoiled the rehearsals of Brahms's *Requiem*.
In his wrath he referred to a letter in which Goethe had
sung the praises of nature tamed, "forever freed from its
demented and feverish upheavals." "Here, jungle!" he
roared, stretching out his long arms, as when he wrenched
a fortissimo from his orchestra.

The word "jungle" turned my eyes toward the patio
with the potted arecas. I thought Mouche had gone back to
her deck chair; not seeing her in it, I decided that she must
be getting dressed. But she was not in our room either. I
waited for her a moment, and then the liquor I had drunk

that morning on an empty stomach gave me the notion of looking for her. I set out from the bar, like someone tackling an important job, up the stairs that rose from the foyer between two solemn marble caryatids. The addition to the more familiar alcohols of a local brandy that tasted of molasses had turned my face suddenly stiff, and I was weaving between the banister and the wall like a blind man feeling his way in the dark.

When I noticed that the stairs had become shallower against a background of yellow stucco, I realized that I had gone beyond the fourth floor, without the slightest idea where my friend was. But I kept on, sweaty, dogged, with a determination not to be deflected by the expressions on the faces of those who mockingly stepped aside to let me by. I tramped along endless corridors over red carpet as wide as a road, past numbered doors—unbearably numbered—which I kept counting as I went by, as though this were a part of my assigned task.

Suddenly a familiar form brought me up short, confused, with the strange sensation of not having traveled, of always having been *there*, on one of my daily trips, in some abode of the impersonal, the styleless. I knew that red metal fire-extinguisher, with its label of instructions; I had known, for a long time, too, the carpet I was treading on, the modillions of the ceiling, and those brass numbers behind all of which stood the same furniture, equipment, objects, all arranged alike beside a colored view of the Jungfrau, Niagara Falls, or the Leaning Tower. This idea of never having moved sent the numbness from my face to my body. The image of the hive returned, and I felt oppressed, compressed between parallel walls, where the brooms left by the servants looked like tools dropped by a chain gang in flight. It was as though I was serving a horrible sentence that doomed me to wandering for all eternity among numbers, leaves of a great calendar set in the walls—a labyrinth chronology that might be that of my own life, with its unremitting obsession with time, and all in breathless haste that served only to bring me back each morning to the point of departure of the previous evening.

I no longer knew whom I was looking for in that range of rooms where people left no memory of their passing. The thought of the steps I still had to ascend before reaching the floor where there was no more stucco trim or acanthus, only gray cement with patches of gummed tape on the windows to protect the servants from the weather, overwhelmed me. The absurdity of this wandering amidst the superficial brought to my mind the Theory of the Worm, the only explanation for this labor of Sisyphus, with a female stone on my shoulders, to which I was condemned. I laughed at the thought, and this drove from my mind my frenzy to find Mouche. I knew that when she had been drinking she became especially vulnerable to sensual appeal, and though this did not imply a real desire to degrade herself, it could carry her to the verge of the most dubious enticements. But this no longer troubled me, what with the weight of the wineskin my legs were dragging along. I went back to our darkened room and threw myself face-downward on the bed, sinking into a sleep that was soon ridden with nightmares having to do with heat and thirst.

My throat was parched when I finally heard someone calling me. Mouche was standing beside me with the Canadian painter we had met the day before. For the third time I found myself in the presence of that woman with her angular body, whose face with its straight nose jutting from a stubborn forehead gave her something of the air of a statue in contrast to her unfinished mouth, greedy, like that of an adolescent. I asked my friend where she had been that morning. "The revolution is over," was her answer. It seemed that the radio stations were broadcasting the victory of the winning party and the jailing of the members of the previous government. In this country, I was told, passing from power to prison was the normal thing.

I was on the point of giving thanks for the end of our confinement when Mouche added that a six p.m. curfew would be in force for an indefinite period, with severest penalties for anyone found in the streets after that hour. All this mess was going to spoil the fun of our trip, so I suggested returning at once, which would have the added advantage of making it possible for me to report "mission unaccomplished" to the Curator without having to return the money spent on my vain attempt. But my friend had already learned that the airlines were swamped with requests and would not be able to give us space for at least one week. Moreover, she did not seem to me especially put out, and I attributed her acceptance of the situation to that feeling of relief which the solution of any abnormal state of affairs brings.

It was then that the painter, at a word from Mouche, suggested to me that we spend a few days with her at her house in Los Altos, a quiet summer resort whose climate and silversmiths made it a favorite with foreigners, and where, for that reason, police regulations would be lightly enforced. She had her studio in a seventeenth-century house that she had picked up for a song, whose main patio recalled that of the Posada de la Sangre in Toledo. Mouche had already accepted the invitation without consulting me, and was babbling of walks through wild hydrangeas, of a convent with baroque altars, beamed ceilings, and a room where the nuns scourged themselves at the feet of a black Christ before the horrifying relic of a bishop's tongue, preserved in alcohol in memory of his eloquence. I did not answer, unable to make up my mind, not so much because I did not want to go as annoyed at Mouche's taking things for granted.

As the danger was over, I opened the window on a

twilight that was turning into night. It was then that I noticed that the two women had put on all their finery to go down to dinner. I was on the point of making some sarcastic comment when I saw something in the street which interested me far more. A grocery store, with ropes of garlic hanging from the ceiling, which had caught my attention by reason of its odd name, *La Fe en Dios*, was opening its side door to let in a man hugging the wall, a basket on his arm. In a little while he came out with a load of bread and bottles and smoking a freshly lighted cigar. I had awakened with a gnawing need for a smoke, and there was no tobacco left in the hotel. I pointed out what I had seen to Mouche, who had been reduced to smoking butts, and ran down the stairs. At the thought that the store might close, I streaked across the plaza. I had twenty packages of cigarettes in my hands when a fusillade of gunfire began in the nearest side-street. Several snipers, stationed along the inner slope of a roof, were replying with rifles and pistols over the cornice.

The owner of the store slammed the door shut, slipping heavy bars into place. I gloomily sat down on a stool, realizing what a fool I had been to take stock in Mouche's words. Possibly the revolution was over as far as the capture of the key points of the city was concerned; but the cleaning out of rebel nests was still going on. In the back of the store various female voices were murmuring the rosary. The smell of salt cod was getting into my throat. I turned over some playing cards lying on the counter, and recognized the different suits of the Spanish deck: *bastos, copas, oros, espadas,* whose look I had forgotten. The gunfire was now coming at longer intervals. The storekeeper watched me in silence, smoking a cigar under a picture showing the sorry plight of the storekeeper who did business on credit and the sleek prosperity of the one who sold for cash only. The peace that reigned within this house, the scent of the jasmine that grew under a pomegranate in the inner patio, the drip of water filtering through an old earthen water jar, submerged me in a kind of stupor, a sleep that was not sleeping, with nods that jerked me back to my surroundings every few seconds.

The clock on the wall struck eight. The sound of firing had died away. I opened the door a crack and looked toward the hotel. In the midst of the darkness that surrounded it glowed all the portholes of the bar and the chandeliers of the foyer, which could be glimpsed through the grille of the door to the marquee. There came a burst of applause, followed by the first measures of *Les Barricades mystérieuses,* telling me that the pianist was playing some of the pieces he had been practicing that morning on the dining-room piano. He must have had a good many drinks under his belt, for his fingers frequently slipped on the ornaments and grace notes. On the mezzanine, behind the iron blinds, there was dancing. The whole building was celebrating.

I shook hands with the storekeeper and got ready to run for it when a shot—a single one—whined past, a few feet from what might have been the height of my breast. I fell back in utter terror. To be sure, I had been in the war, but my experience as staff interpreter had been something different; the risk was shared by many, and one did not make the decision when to fall back. But here death had almost caught up with me because of my own folly.

More than ten minutes elapsed without the sound of a shot. But just as I was asking myself whether to try it again, there came another report. There was a kind of solitary lookout posted somewhere who every now and then fired a blast from his gun—probably an old breech-loader —to keep the street empty. It would not take me more than a few seconds to reach the opposite sidewalk, but those few seconds were enough for my dangerous game

of chance. By some strange association of ideas, I thought
of Buffon's gambler, who tossed a stick on the floor in the
hope that it would not intersect any of the lines of the
boards. Here the lines were these shots being fired without target or aim, indifferent to my designs, cutting unex-
pectedly through space, and the thought that I might be
the gambler's stick, and that at some point of possible inci-
dence my flesh would intersect the bullet's trajectory, terrified me. The element of fatality did not enter into this calculation of probabilities, inasmuch as it was in my power
to choose whether I would risk losing all to gain nothing.

When all was said and done, I had to accept the fact that
it was not the desire to return to the hotel that was caus-
ing my exasperation at being unable to cross the street. It
was the same thing that hours before, in my drunken
state, had driven me to wander through all those halls.
My present impatience was due to my distrust of Mouche.
Thinking things over here, on this side of the moat, the
hateful gaming board of chance, I believed her capable of
the greatest physical perfidies although I had not been able
to make a single specific accusation against her since we
had known each other. I had no basis for my suspicions,
my eternal doubt; but I knew all too well that her intellectual background, abounding in ideas that justified everything, in reasons that were excuses, could lead her to lend
herself to any new experience, encouraged by the night's
abnormal atmosphere.

I told myself that it was not worth while risking my life
just to get rid of a doubt. And yet I could not bear the
thought that she was there, in that drunken building, free
from my vigilance. Anything was possible in that haunt
of confusion, with its dark cellars and its myriad rooms indifferent to copulations that left no memory. I don't know
how the idea came to me that this riverbed of the street,
which every shot widened, this moat, this abyss that every

bullet made more unbridgeable, was like a warning, the shape of things to come.

Just then something strange happened at the hotel. The music and the laughter were cut short. There was the sound of cries, weeping, shouts throughout the building. Some lights went off, others came on. There was a kind of muted commotion there; panic without flight. The shooting in the side-street started up again. But this time I saw several squads of soldiers with fixed bayonets and machine guns. They advanced slowly, under cover of the columns of the arcades, as far as the store. The snipers had abandoned the roof, and the regular troops were now guarding the section of the street I had to cross. Under the protection of a sergeant, I finally reached the hotel. When the grille swung open and I walked into the foyer, I stood rooted in my tracks: there on a long walnut table turned into a bier lay the *Kappellmeister*, a crucifix between the lapels of his evening coat. Four silver candelabra with vine leaf repoussé held lighted tapers. The conductor had been killed by a spent bullet that struck him in the temple as he stood carelessly by the window in his room.

I looked at the faces around him: unshaven, dirty, shocked out of drunkenness by the surprise of death. The insects were still coming through the drain pipes; there was the sour reek of body sweat. A stench of latrines filled the building. Drawn, haggard, the dancers looked like ghosts. Two of them, still in the tulle and tights of an adagio they had been dancing, sank sobbing into the shadows of the marble staircase. The flies were everywhere now, buzzing around the lights, crawling on the walls, getting entangled in the women's hair. Outside, the carrion was multiplying. I found Mouche collapsed on the bed in our room with an attack of nerves.

"We'll get her to Los Altos as soon as it gets light," the painter said. Roosters were beginning to crow in the patios. Downstairs, the undertaker's paraphernalia was being lowered to the granite sidewalk from a black and silver hearse by men in black.

(*Saturday, the 10th*)

VII/ We got to Los Altos shortly after noon, by a little narrow-gauge train that looked like an amusement-park railway. I liked the place so much that for the third time that afternoon, with my elbows on the railing of the waterfall, I was looking out over what I had acquainted myself with on my earlier walks. Nothing that met the eye was monumental or impressive. Nothing had been transferred to picture postcards or been mentioned in guidebooks. And yet I found in this provincial corner, where every nook, every nail-headed door, spoke of a peculiar way of life, a charm that the museum cities, with their over-admired, over-photographed stones, had lost.

Seen by night, the city became an illuminated strip of a city set upon a mountainside, with visions of glory and visions of hell created out of the darkness by the streetlights. Those fifteen lights, abuzz with insects, had the isolating function of picture illumination or theater spotlights, bringing into full relief the stations of the winding road that led to the Calvary of the summit.

As in every allegory of the righteous life and the wastrel life the wicked are always burning below, so the first light fell upon the tavern where the mule-drivers forgathered, with its rum, corn liquor, and brandy, its card games and bad examples, and drunks sleeping on the barrels at the entrance. The second light swung over Lola's Place, where Carmen, Ninfa, and Esperanza, dressed in white, pink, and blue, sat under Japanese lanterns on a dingy velvet sofa that had belonged to one of the judges of the Royal Tribunal. Caught in the third light, the camels, lions, and ostriches of a merry-go-round revolved, while the hanging seats of a Ferris wheel rose into the darkness and returned from it—inasmuch as the light did not reach to the top—in the time it took the perforated roll of the *Skaters' Waltz* to play itself through. As though fallen from the heaven of Fame, the fourth light whitened the statue of the Poet, the favorite local son, author of a prize-winning "Hymn to Agriculture," who continued his versifying on a marble sheet with a moldy pen guided by the forefinger of a Muse who had lost her other arm. Nothing special took place under the fifth light, except that two donkeys dozed there. The sixth was that of the Grotto of Lourdes, a toilsome construction of cement and stones brought in from a distance, all the more noteworthy if it is borne in mind that before it could be built, a real grotto that existed on the same spot had to be walled up. The seventh light marked a somber pine and the rose that climbed over a doorway that was always locked. Then came the Cathedral, its heavy buttresses emphasized by the shadows under the eighth light, which, as it hung from a high post, illuminated the face of the clock, whose hands had been sleeping for the past forty years on the hour of half past seven, which according to the pious women was that of a not-too-distant Last Judgment at which the hussies of the town would have their accounts settled. The ninth light was that of the Athenæum, seat of cultural acts and patriotic celebrations, with its little museum containing a hook from which the hammock of the hero of the Campaign of the Highlands had been hung for one night, a grain of rice on which several paragraphs of *Don Quixote* had been copied, a portrait of Napoleon typed in *x*'s, and a complete collection of the poisonous snakes of the area in bottles. Closed, mysterious, flanked by two dark-gray Solomonic columns supporting an open compass that stretched from one capital to the other, the Masonic temple occu-

pied the entire zone of the tenth light. Then came the
Convent of the Recollect Nuns, whose shrubbery emerged
blurred under the eleventh light, darkened by too many
dead insects. Then came the barracks, which shared the
next light with a Doric pavilion, whose cupola had been
struck by lightning, but which still was useful for band
concerts where the young people circled, the men in one
direction, the women in another. In the cone of the thir-
teenth, a green horse reared on its hind legs, mounted by
a bronze *caudillo* on whom many a rain had fallen, his
advancing sword dividing the fog into two slow-moving
currents. Then came a dark strip picked out by the winks
of candles or braziers, of Indian huts with their pictures
of the birth of the Child and death-watch scenes. Higher
up, under the last light but one, a cement pedestal awaited
the sagittary pose of the Brave Bowman, who wreaked
death upon the conquistadors, which the Masons and Communists had ordered from a stonecutter to annoy the
priests.

Then followed blackest night. And beyond it, so high
that it seemed not of this earth, the light that illuminated
three wooden crosses, set on mounds of stone, where the
wind swept free. There the illuminated strip of the city
came to an end against a background of stars and clouds,
interspersed with smaller lights that were barely perceptible. All the rest was adobe roofs, which in the shadows
became one with the mud of the mountain.

Shivering in the cold descending from the heights, I
made my way back through the winding streets to the
painter's house. Ever since we had left the capital, I was
finding this woman—to whom I had paid little attention
during the previous days, accepting our chance association
as I would have accepted any other—more irritating by
the minute, because of Mouche's growing admiration for
her. With every hour that passed, what had seemed to me

at the beginning a colorless being was becoming more and more a blocking force. A kind of studied leisure, which lent weight to her words, informed the trivial decisions that affected the three of us with a kind of authority, subdued but nevertheless firm, which Mouche accepted with a humility that was out of character. She, for whom her caprices were law, always found our hostess right, though the minute before she might have been in agreement with me. She was always wanting to go out when I wanted to stay in, wanting to rest when I suggested climbing the mountain, revealing a constant desire to please the painter, watching her reactions, and falling in with them.

It was apparent from the importance Mouche gave this new friendship how much she missed—after such a short time—certain things we had left behind. Whereas the difference of altitude, the transparence of the air, the change of habits, the re-encounter with the language of my infancy, were effecting in me a kind of return—hesitant but already noticeable—to a balance I had long lost, it was evident that she was becoming bored, though she did not yet admit it. Nothing we had seen so far corresponded to what she had hoped to find on this trip, assuming that she had really hoped to find anything.

And yet Mouche had talked intelligently about a trip she had made to Italy before we met. For that reason, as I watched how mistaken or inept her reactions were to this country which took us by surprise, undocumented, without knowledge of its past or the preparation of the written word, I began to ask myself whether her shrewd observations on the mysterious sensuality of windows of the Barberini Palace, the obsession with the cherubim in the heavens of San Giovanni Laterano, the almost feminine intimacy of San Carlo alle Quattro Fontane, with its cloister all curves and shadows, had been anything more than apt quotations sipped from the fountain of clichés and set to the rhythm of the day, from reading, conversations. Her opinions were always in keeping with the æsthetic slogans in fashion at the moment. She became enthusiastic over moss and shadows when that was the thing to do. For that very reason, confronted by something she knew nothing about, a fact that lacked association, a type of architecture that had not been previously discussed in a book, she found herself disconcerted, hesitant, unable to formulate an opinion of any value, buying a dusty *hippocampe* because of literary references when she could have bought an authentic miniature of Santa Rosa with her flowering palm.

As the Canadian painter had been the mistress of a poet well known for his essays on Lewis and Ann Radcliffe, Mouche returned ecstatically to the fields of surrealism, astrology, the interpretation of dreams, with all this carried in its wake. Every time she met a woman who (as she put it) talked her language—and this did not happen too often—she plunged into this new friendship with such utter devotion, such a display of attention, such breathlessness, as finally to exasperate me. These emotional crises did not last long; they would end as abruptly as they had begun. But while they went on, they aroused my worst suspicions.

On this occasion, as on others, it was no more than a hunch, a misgiving, a doubt; there was no real proof of anything. But the gnawing idea had taken hold of me the afternoon before, after the *Kappellmeister*'s burial. When I returned from the cemetery, where I had gone with a delegation of hotel guests, petals of the over-fragrant funeral flowers were still scattered over the floor of the foyer. The street-cleaners were busy carting away the carrion whose stench had been so unbearable during our confinement, and as the legs of the horses, stripped fleshless by the vultures, were too long for the carts, they chopped them up with machetes, and scraps of hoofs, bones, and horseshoes flew among the swarms of bluebottles buzzing about the pavement. Indoors the servants, who had come back from the revolution to normalcy, were putting the furniture in place and polishing the doorknobs. Mouche, it seemed, had gone out with her friend.

When the two of them came back after the curfew had sounded, saying they had been walking about the streets in the crowds celebrating the victory of the winning side, I seemed to notice something strange about them. They showed a kind of chill indifference toward everything, a new self-sufficiency—as of one returning from a trip to forbidden places. I kept a careful eye on them to see if I could surprise some glance of understanding; I weighed each word either one said for a hidden or surprise meaning; I tried to catch them off guard with disconcerting, contradictory questions, but to no avail. My long experience in certain circles, my boasted sophistication, told me that I was behaving like a fool. And yet I was suffering something far worse than jealousy: the unbearable sensation of having been left out of a game that such omission made all the more hateful.

I could not bear the perfidy, the hypocrisy, the mental picture conjured up of this hidden and pleasurable "something" these women might be sharing behind my back. Suddenly my imagination gave tangible form to the most hideous physical possibilities, and in spite of the fact that I had told myself a thousand times that the bond between Mouche and me was a habit of the senses, and not love, I found myself ready to play the role of outraged husband. I knew that when the storm had spent itself and I confessed my tortures to my friend, she would shrug her shoulders, saying that it was too ridiculous to make her angry, and would attribute the "animality" of such reactions to my early years in a Latin American atmosphere. But once

again, in the silence of these deserted streets, my suspicions
had flared up. I quickened my pace to get home as fast
as I could, hoping for, and at the same time fearing, some
concrete proof.

But what I found was something wholly unexpected:
a great hubbub in the studio, accompanied by copious li-
bations. Three young artists had arrived from the capital
a few minutes before, fleeing, like ourselves, from the curfew that shut them up indoors from twilight on. The musician was so white, the poet so Indian, the painter so black,
that they brought to mind the Three Wise Men as they
stood around the hammock where Mouche lay lazily
stretched, answering the questions they asked her as though
playing a part in an Adoration of the Magi scene. The
conversation had a single theme: Paris. And I noticed that
the three of them were questioning her as Christians in the
Middle Ages might have questioned a pilgrim returning
from the Holy Land. They were insatiable in their eagerness to learn every detail of what the leader of such and
such a school, whose acquaintance Mouche claimed, looked
like; they wanted to know if a certain café was still pa-
tronized by this or that writer; if two of them had made
up after a quarrel about Kierkegaard; whether non-repre-
sentational painting still had its former champions. And
when their knowledge of French and English was insuffi-
cient for them to understand what Mouche was telling
them, they cast supplicating glances at the painter, hoping
that she would condescend to translate some anecdote,
some precious phrase whose meaning eluded them.

I cut into the conversation with the malicious intention
of breaking up Mouche's big scene, asking the young men
about the history of their country, the first manifestations
of its colonial literature, its folk traditions; and it was evident that my changing the subject was most distasteful to
them. I asked them, to keep my friend from recovering

the conversational ball, if they had ever been in the jungle. The Indian poet, shrugging his shoulders, answered that there was nothing to see there, and that such trips were for foreigners who wanted to collect bows and quivers. Culture, observed the Negro painter emphatically, was not to be found in the jungle. In the musician's opinion, the artist today could live only where thought and creation were really alive, returning to that city whose intellectual topography was engraved on the mind of his comrades, given, they confessed, to dreaming with open eyes before a *Carte Taride*, whose subway stations were marked by heavy blue circles: *Solferino, Oberkampf, Corvisard, Mouton-Duvernet*. Between these circles, above the tracery of the streets, intersected from time to time by the clear artery of the Seine, ran the routes themselves, crisscrossed like the web of a net.

The Three Young Wise Men would soon land in this net, led by the star shining above the great manger of Saint-Germain-des-Prés. Depending on the color of the day, the topic of conversation would be the longing for evasion, the advantages of suicide, the need to slap the face of corpses or of taking a shot at the first passer-by. Some high priest of delirium would initiate them in the cult of Dionysus, "god of ecstasy and fear, of brutality and liberation; a mad god whose mere sight throws living beings into a state of delirium," though without telling them that the one who invoked this Dionysus, the officer Nietzsche, had had himself photographed on one occasion in *Reichswehr* uniform, sword in hand, and helmet on a console table of Munich style, like a prophetic prefiguration of the god of horror whom reality would unleash in the Europe of that *Ninth Symphony*.

I saw them growing gaunt and pale in their unlighted studios—the Indian turning green, the Negro's smile gone, the white man perverted—more and more forgetful of the

sun they had left behind, trying desperately to imitate
what came naturally to those whose rightful place was
in the net. Years later, having frittered away their youth,
they would return, with vacant eyes, all initiative gone,
without heart to set themselves to the only task appropriate to the milieu that was slowly revealing to me the nature of its values: Adam's task of giving things their
names.

That night as I looked at them I could see the harm my
uprooting from this environment, which had been mine
until adolescence, had done me; the share the facile be-
dazzlement of the members of my generation, carried
away by theories into the same intellectual labyrinths, devoured by the same Minotaurs, had had in disorienting
me. I was weary of dragging the chain of certain ideas,
and I felt a lurking desire to say something that was not
the daily cliché of all who considered themselves *au cou-
rant* with things that fifteen years from now would be
contemptuously cast aside. Once again the discussions that
had at times amused me in Mouche's house had caught
up with me. But now, leaning out of the window, over
the stream purling through the ravine, breathing the sharp
air redolent of moist hay, so near the creatures of the
earth crawling through the russet green of the alfalfa with
death in their fangs; at this moment, when night enveloped
me like a living presence, I found certain "modern" themes
unbearable. I would have liked to silence the voices at my
back to catch the diapason of the frogs, the shrill tonality
of the crickets, the rhythm of the creaking axles of a cart
above the Calvary of the Mist.

Furious with Mouche, with the whole world, longing
to write something, to compose something, I left the
house and went down to the bank of the brook to gaze
once more on the stations of the town altarpiece. Above
me a clashing of chords came from the painter's piano.

Then the young musician—his hard touch revealed the presence of the composer behind the chords—began to play. Just for fun I counted up to twelve notes, without a single repetition, until he came back to the E flat with which the tortured andante had begun. I would have bet on it: atonality had reached the country; its formulas were employed here. I kept on to the tavern for a glass of berry brandy. Tightly wrapped in their ponchos, the mule-drivers were talking about a tree that bled when the ax was laid to it on Good Friday, and of thistles that grew out of the bellies of wasps killed by the smoke of a certain wood in the hills.

Suddenly, like a being out of the night, a harpist approached the counter. Barefoot, with his instrument slung on his back, hat in hand, he asked permission to play something. He had come from far off, from a town in the District of Tembladeras, where, as in other years, he had gone to fulfill a vow to play in front of the church the day of the Invention of the Cross. Now what he asked was a glass of good maguey liquor, in exchange for his art, to warm him up. A silence followed, and with the solemnity of one performing a rite the harpist placed his hands on the strings, giving himself over to the inspiration of a prelude to limber up his fingers, which filled me with admiration.

There was a solemn design in his scales, in his recitatives, broken by broad, majestic chords that recalled the grandeur of the organ preludes of the Middle Ages. At the same time, as a consequence of the arbitrary tuning of the village instrument, which limited the player to a range lacking certain notes, one had the impression that all this obeyed a masterly manipulation of the ancient modes and ecclesiastical tones, achieving, by way of authentic primitivism, the most valid objectives of certain contemporary composers. That solemn improvisation recalled the tradition of the organ, the viol, and the lute, discovering new life in the bowels of the instrument, conical in shape, which rested between the player's scaly ankles.

Then came dances. Dances vertiginous in movement, in which binary rhythms ran agilely beneath three-beat measures, all in a modal system that had never been submitted to such tests. I felt like going back to the house and dragging the young composer down by the ear. But at that moment the lanterns and oilskin capes of the night patrol arrived, and the police ordered the tavern closed. I was informed that here, too, the curfew law would be in force for several days.

This unpleasant reminder that our disagreeable—for me, at least—visit to the painter would be even more confining suddenly translated itself into a decision that came to cap a whole process of thought and memories. It happened that the buses going to the port from which one could reach the great southern jungle by river set out from Los Altos. We would not go on with Mouche's hoax, against which circumstances were militating at every step. As a result of the revolution, the exchange value of my funds had skyrocketed. The simplest, the most decent, the most interesting thing to do would be to keep faith with the Curator and the university, carrying out the mission I had been assigned. To make it impossible for me to change my mind, I bought two bus tickets for the next morning from the tavern-keeper. I did not care what Mouche thought; for the first time I felt that it was I who would call the tune.

Chapter Three

*. . . it will be the time when he
takes the road, when he uncovers
his face and talks and vomits what
he swallowed and lays down his
load.*

—*The Book of Chilam-Balam*

(*June 11*)

VIII/   The argument went on until after midnight. All of
a sudden Mouche felt that she was catching cold; she made
me touch her forehead, which felt cool, and complained
of chills. She coughed until she had really irritated her
throat. I went on strapping the suitcases without paying
any attention to her, and before dawn broke we were in
the bus, which was already filled with people huddled in
blankets and with bath towels wrapped around their
necks as mufflers. Up to the very last minute Mouche was
talking with the painter, arranging to meet her in the capital when we returned from our trip, which, at the very
most, would be about two weeks.

We finally began to move over a road that led to the sierra along a ravine so filled with mist that its poplars were but faint shadows in the morning light. I knew that Mouche would pretend to be sick for several hours, for she was one of those who wound up believing what they pretended, so I withdrew into myself, prepared to enjoy everything there was to be seen and to forget about her, though she was dozing with her head on my shoulder, sighing pitifully. Up to that moment the change from the capital to Los Altos had been for me a kind of return, through this renewed experience of ways of life, flavors, words, things, which had left a deeper brand on me than I would have believed, to the years of my childhood, to my adolescence and its first awareness. The pomegranate and the water jar, the playing-card figures, the courtyard with the sweet basil, and the blue door all had something to say to me. But now I was moving beyond the images that had met my eyes at a time when I ceased to know the world only through the sense of touch. As we emerged from the opalescent fog, which was turning green in the dawn, a phase of Discovery began for me.

The bus was climbing, climbing with such an effort, groaning through its axles, plowing through the chill wind, swaying over the precipices, that every slope it left behind seemed to have been achieved at the cost of unspeakable suffering to its whole disjointed frame. It was a sad-looking vehicle, with its red roof, climbing and climbing, holding on by its wheels, steadying itself against the rocks between the almost vertical sides of a ravine. It seemed to shrink in size amid the mountains, which loomed higher —for the mountains were growing. Now that the sun was fretting their peaks, the peaks multiplied, on each side, more pointed, more threatening, like great black axes, their blades turned against the wind that whistled through the passes in an interminable howling. Everything about us magnified its scale to a brutal affirmation of new proportions. After that climb, with its myriad twists and turns, when we thought we had reached the top, another slope rose before us, more abrupt, more winding than the other, between frozen peaks that piled their summits above the previous ones. Doggedly climbing, the bus dwindled to nothing in the passes, more kindred to the insects than to the rocks, pushing itself forward by its round hind feet.

It was now light, and between the frowning crags, harsh as carved flint, the clouds scudded by in a sky buffeted by the wind from the ravines. When, above the black ax-edges, the dividing compasses of the winds, and the still higher steps, the volcanoes emerged, our human prestige came to an end, just as that of the vegetable kingdom had ceased earlier. We were the lowest of beings, silent, benumbed, in a wasteland where all that existed was the presence of gray felt cactus, clinging like a lichen, like a flower of coal, to a soilless surface. Far below we had left the clouds that cast masses of shadow over the valleys; and less low-hanging, other clouds that men who moved among things drawn to their human scale would never see. We were on the backbone of the fabled Indies, on one of its vertebræ, there where the crests of the Andes, sickle-shaped among their flanking peaks, like the mouths of fish gulping the snows, broke and shattered the winds trying to pass from one ocean to the other. We were skirting the craters filled with geological ruins, frightening wells of darkness, or bristling with desolate crags sad as petrified animals.

A silent fear had come over me in the face of this multitude of peaks and abysses. Each mystery of fog, billowing on either side of the unbelievable road, suggested the possibility that depths as profound as the distance separating us from our earth lay beneath its filmy consistency. For from here, from the solid, unmoving ice that whitened the peaks, the earth seemed a different thing, with its animals, its trees, its breezes; a world made for man, unshaken by the nightly bellowing of the organ played by the storms in gulches and chasms. A layer of clouds separated this rocky wasteland from our true earth. Shuddering at the telluric menace that lurked in every form, in these lava slopes, in the shale of the peaks, I noticed with immense relief that the poor, frail thing in which we were traveling was complaining a little less as we began to descend for the first time in several hours.

We were coming down the other slope when the brakes were suddenly jammed on halfway across a little bridge that spanned a stream so far below that its waters were invisible though the boiling of its torrent was deafening. A woman wrapped in a blue poncho was seated on a stone curbing, a bundle and umbrella on the ground beside her. She made no reply when she was questioned, as though she were in a state of shock, trembling, her eyes vague, her lips quivering, her head partly covered with a red handkerchief that had come untied.

One of our fellow passengers went over to her and pushed a bar of molasses into her mouth, pressing hard to make her swallow. As though she understood, the woman began to chew slowly, and little by little her eyes began to focus. It was as though she was returning from a great distance, discovering the world with astonishment. She looked at me as though she knew my face, and got to her feet with a great effort, steadying herself against the curb. At that very moment a distant landslide roared above our heads, churning up the mists that began billowing in puffs from the depths of a crater. The woman suddenly seemed to come to herself; she gave a scream, clutched me, and, almost inarticulate, begged us not to let her die again.

She had come there with people taking a different route who had assumed that she knew the dangers of drowsing off at that height, and it was only now that she realized how near death she had been. With dragging feet she let herself be led to the bus, where she finished swallowing the molasses. When we had descended a little, and the air took on more body, someone gave her a swallow of brandy, and she was soon making light of her terror. Conversation in the bus turned to anecdotes of persons overcome by the altitude, of people who had died in that very pass, episodes narrated as though they were everyday occurrences. Some stated that near the mouth of that volcano disappearing from sight behind the lower peaks eight members of a scientific expedition lay encrusted in ice as in a show window; they had succumbed half a century before. They sat in a circle, in a state of suspended animation, just as death had transfixed them, gazing out from the crystal that covered their faces like a transparent death mask.

We were now descending rapidly. The clouds we had left behind us as we climbed were once more above us, and the mist was breaking up, revealing the still distant valleys. We were returning to man's earth, and breathing was resuming its normal rhythm after being the prick of icy needles. Suddenly a village emerged on a small round butte surrounded by swift streams. It seemed to me astoundingly Castilian in appearance despite its baroque church, its slope of roofs around the plaza into which winding, narrow mule paths debouched. The braying of an ass brought to my mind a picture of El Toboso—with an ass in the foreground —which illustrated a lesson in my third reader, and which had a striking resemblance to the hamlet that lay before me. *"In a village of La Mancha, whose name I prefer not to recall, there lived not long ago one of those hidalgos with lance in rack, ancient buckler, lean nag, and fleet hound. . . ."*

I was proud of my ability to remember a thing it had cost the teacher so much effort to teach the twenty of us. Once

I had known the whole paragraph by heart, and now I could not remember beyond *"fleet hound."* I was exasperated at my lapse, returning again and again to *"village of La Mancha"* to see if the second sentence would come back to me, when the woman we had rescued from the mist pointed to a broad curve on the flank of the mountain we were about to skirt, stating that it was known as La Hoya. *"An olla with more beef than mutton, hash most evenings, eggs and bacon of a Saturday, lentils on Friday, and an occasional squab on Sundays, consumed three quarters of his revenue."*

That was as far as I could get. But my attention was now attracted by the woman who had so opportunely mentioned the word *"Hoya."* From where I sat I could see a little less than half her face, with its high cheekbone under an eye slanting toward the temple and hidden under the emphatic arch of the eyebrow. It was a pure profile from brow to nose, but suddenly, below these proud, impassive features, the mouth turned full and sensual, with lean cheeks rising toward the ear, the strongly modeled lineaments set in a frame of thick black hair held in place, here and there, by celluloid combs. Several races had met in this woman: Indian in the hair and cheekbones, Mediterranean in brow and nose, Negro in the heavy shoulders and the breadth of hips I had noticed as she stood up to put her bundle and umbrella in the luggage rack. There was no question but that this living sum of races had an aristocracy of her own. Her amazing eyes of pure black recalled the figures in certain archaic frescoes that gaze out so steadily, front and profile, with circles of ink painted on their temples.

This association of images brought to mind *La Parisienne* of Crete, and I thought to myself that this traveler of the wastelands and the fog was of no more mixed origins than the races that for centuries had come together in the melting-pot of the Mediterranean. I even asked myself whether certain blendings of minor races, without a transplanting of the parent stock, were not preferable to the fusion of Celts, Negroes, Latins, Indians, even "New Christians," that had taken place on the great meeting-ground of America in that first encounter. For here it had not been the amalgam of related peoples, such as history had fused at certain crossroads of Ulysses' sea, but of the great races of the world, the most widely separated, the most divergent, those which for centuries had ignored the fact that they inhabited the same planet.

The rain suddenly started up in a monotonous downpour, clouding the windows. The return to a quasi-normal atmosphere had plunged the travelers into a kind of stupor. I ate some fruit, and myself prepared to drowse, noticing as I did so that a week after setting out on this journey I had recovered the ability to sleep at any hour, as when I was a boy. When I awoke, twilight was closing in, and we had reached a village of limestone houses mortised to the hillside in the shadow of chilly forests where the cleared fields resembled parentheses in the thickets. From the treetops thick lianas swung over the road, sprinkling it with congealed fog. Lured by the long shadows of the mountains, the night was ascending the slopes. Mouche, exhausted, clung to my arm, complaining that the trip had worn her out with its changes of altitude. Her head ached, she felt feverish, and she wanted to take some medicine and go straight to bed. I left her in a whitewashed room whose fittings were a washbasin and a ewer and went down to the dining-room of the inn, an extension of the kitchen, where a wood fire crackled on a wide hearth.

After a supper of corn soup and a thick mountain cheese that smelled of goat, I was sitting lazy and comfortable in the gleam of the fire, watching the flicker of the flames, when the shadow of a silhouette came between me and them, taking its place across the table. It was the woman we had rescued that morning. She had changed her clothes, and it amused me to observe the details of her toilette. She was neither well nor badly dressed. Her attire was of no period, no time, with its fussiness of drawnwork, gathers, ribbons, in tan and blue, all clean and starched, as stiff as a deck of cards, something out of an old-fashioned sewing-box and a lightning-change artist's trunk. She wore a velvet bow of darker blue pinned to her blouse. She ordered dishes whose names I had never heard, and began to eat slowly, without speaking, without raising her eyes from the oilcloth, as though gripped by some gnawing anxiety.

After a time I began to talk with her, and learned that she would be making a good part of the trip with us. She had come all the way across country, over deserts and highlands, islanded lakes, forests, and plains, to bring her father, who was very sick, an image of the Fourteen Auxiliary Saints which had worked veritable miracles for her family, and which until now had been in the custody of an aunt in a position to display it on better-lighted altars. As we were alone in the dining-room, she went over to a kind of cupboard with drawers which gave off a pleasant perfume of wild herbs and which had filled me with curiosity. Along with bottles of infusions and vinegars, the drawers were labeled with the names of plants. Taking out dried leaves, mosses, and twigs, she crushed them in the palm of her hand and lauded their properties as she identified them by their smell. This was aloes macerated in dew for chest afflictions, and brier rose to make the hair curl, betony for coughs, sweet basil to ward off bad luck, bear grass, angelica root, night-blooming cereus and redbud for ills I cannot recall. She referred to the herbs as though they were beings from a near-by though mysterious kingdom presided over by grim dignitaries.

Through her lips the plants began to speak and describe their own powers. The forest had a ruler, a one-legged tutelary genius, and nothing that grew in the shade of the trees should be taken without payment. When one entered the shadows, looking for the health-giving shoot, fungus, or liana, one spoke a greeting and laid coins at the roots of an aged tree, requesting permission. And on leaving, one bowed deferentially, for millions of eyes were watching every gesture from the bark and the leaves. I could not have said why this woman suddenly seemed to me so beautiful as she threw a handful of pungent herbs into the flames, which brought out her features in strong relief against the shadows. I was about to make some trifling complimentary remark when she brusquely said good-night. I stayed on alone looking into the fire. It had been a long time since I had looked into a fire.

(Later)

IX/   As I sat on before the hearth, I heard faint voices in a corner of the room. Somebody had left an old-vintage radio on among the ears of corn and the cucumbers on a kitchen table. I was about to turn it off when out of that battered box came an all-too-well-known horn fifth. It was the same as that which had made me rush out of a concert hall not many days before. But this evening, beside the logs sending up showers of sparks and the crickets chirping in the dark rafters, this distant rendering took on a mysterious quality. The faceless, anonymous, invisible players were like abstract interpreters of the written notes. The score, falling at the foot of these mountains after flying across the peaks, reached me from some unknown spot with a sonority not of notes, but of echoes answering within me.

Leaning closer, I listened. The horn fifth was already winging into triplets on the second violins and the violoncellos. Two descending notes were suggested, as though dropped from the first violins and the violas with an indifference that suddenly became anxiety, longing for flight in the face of a suddenly unleashed force. And it was, in a rending of storm-tossed shadows, the first theme of the *Ninth Symphony*. I gave a sigh of relief at an affirmed tonality, but a swift muting of the strings, the magic collapse of what had been built up, brought me back to the uneasiness of the phrase in gestation.

After all this time of trying to push it out of my mind, the musical ode was returned to me with the store of memories I was trying in vain to detach from the crescendo that was now beginning, still hesitant and as though uncertain of its way. Each time the metallic sonority of a horn supported a chord, I seemed to see my father, with his pointed beard, jutting his profile forward to read the music open before him, with that peculiar attitude of the horn-player who seems unaware of the fact, when he is playing, that his lips are pressed to the mouthpiece of the great copper swirl that gives his whole person the air of a Corinthian capital. By virtue of that strange mimetism which tends to make oboe-players lean and scrawny, trombonists gay and round-cheeked, my father had developed a voice of copper-toned sonority that vibrated nasally when he showed me, as I sat beside him in a wicker chair, engravings of the forerunners of his noble instrument: Byzantine oliphants, Roman buccina, Moorish *añafiles*, and the silver tuba of Friedrich Barbarossa. According to him, the walls of Jericho could have tumbled down only at the dread sound of the horn, and he pronounced the word with a rolled *r* that took on the weight of bronze as he uttered it.

Trained as he had been in German Swiss conservatories, he upheld the superiority of the horn of metallic timbre, the descendant of the hunting horn that had echoed through the Black Forest, over what was known in French as *le cor*— the word took on a disdainful ring—for he was of the opinion that the technique taught in Paris made this male instrument resemble the feminine wood-winds. To prove his point, he raised the bell of his instrument and blasted out the Siegfried theme against the patio walls like Gabriel blowing his trumpet on Judgment Day.

As a matter of fact, a hunting scene in Glazunov's *Raymonda* was responsible for my having been born on this side of the ocean. The assassination at Sarajevo had caught my father in the middle of the Wagner cycle at the Royal Theater of Madrid, and, outraged by the unexpected bellicosity of the French and German Socialists, he had shaken the dust of the decaying Continent from his feet and accepted the position of first trumpet on a tour that brought Anna Pavlova to the Antilles. As the result of a marriage whose sentimental origins had always been obscure to me, my first steps were taken in a patio shaded by a huge tamarind while my mother, supervising the colored cook, sang about Sir Cat, who, seated in his gold chair, was asked if he wanted to marry a wild tabby, the niece of a gray cat.

The prolongation of the war, the slight demand for an instrument whose services were needed only during the opera season when the wintry blasts blew, led my father to open a small music store. Overcome at times by nostalgia for the symphonic groups with which he had played, he would take a baton out of the window, open up the score of the *Ninth Symphony*, and begin to direct an imaginary orchestra, imitating the gestures of Nikisch or Mahler, singing the whole work with the most deafening reproductions of percussion instruments, basses, and brasses. My mother would quickly close the windows so that people would not think he had gone crazy, though with traditional Spanish wifely meekness she accepted as good, strange as it might seem, whatever this husband of hers did, he who neither drank nor gambled.

In his baritone voice my father had always given a noble phrasing to this ascending movement of the coda, mourn-

ful, at once funereal and triumphant, which was now beginning upon a chromatic tremolo in the depths of the
bass clef. Two quick scales broke into the unison of an
exordium wrenched from the orchestra as though by
blows. Then silence, a silence quickly seized upon by the
rejoicing of the crickets and the crackling of the embers.
But I was waiting impatiently for the opening shock of the
scherzo. And I let myself be carried away, captivated, by
the devilish arabesque painted by the second violins, removed from everything that was not music, when the
doubling by the horns, with its peculiar sonority, in-
jected into the Beethoven score by Wagner to correct a
copyist's error, carried me back to my father's side in the
days when *she* was no longer with us, with her blue velvet
workbasket, who had so often sung me the adventures of
Sir Cat, the ballad of Mambrú, and the lament of Alfonso
XII for the death of his Mercedes: *Four dukes bore her,
Through the streets of Aldaví.* The evenings then were de-
voted to the reading of the old Lutheran Bible that my
mother's Catholicism had kept hidden in the back of a closet
for so many years.

Downcast by his widowerhood, embittered by a loneliness that found no solace in the street, my father finally
broke all his ties to the noisy, tropical city where I had been
born, and left for North America, where he started up his
business again, with very little success. The maxims of Ecclesiastes, of the Psalms, became associated in his mind with
unforeseen longings. It was then that he began to talk to me
about the workingmen who listened to the *Ninth Symphony*. His failure on this continent was turning more and
more into homesicknesses for a Europe seen from the
heights, in moments of apotheosis and rejoicing. This so-
called New World had become for him a hemisphere without history, alien to the great Mediterranean traditions, a
land of Indians and Negroes peopled by the offscourings of

the great nations of Europe, not to mention the boatloads of prostitutes shipped out to New Orleans by tricorned gendarmes to the sound of fifes—this last detail seemed to me reminiscent of a well-known opera.

In contrast he devoutly evoked the memory of the lands of the old continent, conjuring up before my wondering eyes the University of Heidelberg, which I could only see as green with old ivy. In imagination I moved from the lutes of the angelic concert to the famed blackboards of the Gewandhaus, from the contests of the minnesingers to the concerts of Potsdam, learning the names of cities whose mere spelling called up in my mind mirages in ocher, in white, in bronze—Bonn—in swansdown—Siena. But my father, for whom the affirmation of certain principles comprised civilization's supreme achievement, made a special point of the sacred respect in which the life of man was held there. He spoke to me of writers who, from the quiet of their studies, could make monarchies rock without anyone daring to interfere with them. The memory of "*J'accuse*," of Rathenau's campaigns (consequences of Louis XVI's capitulation to Mirabeau), always wound up with the same conclusions on the manifest course of progress, gradual socialization, collective culture, and the workingmen who, in his native city, in the shadow of a thirteenth-century cathedral, spent their leisure hours in the public libraries, and on Sunday, instead of listening like dumb brutes to Mass—science was supplanting superstition—took their families to hear the *Ninth Symphony*.

Thus I had seen them in my mind's eye since early youth, those workers in blue smocks and corduroy pants, stirred by the breath of genius that flowed from Beethoven's composition, listening perhaps to this very trio, whose heated, enveloping phrase now arose in the voices of the cellos and violas. So great had been the spell of this vision that when my father died I employed the meager funds of my inheritance, the product of the auction of sonatas and scores, to becoming acquainted with my origins. I crossed the ocean one day, persuaded that I was never coming back. But after an apprenticeship of wonder, which I would later jokingly describe as the adoration of façades, came the meeting with realities that contrasted sharply with my father's teachings. Instead of turning toward the *Ninth Symphony*, people's thoughts seemed rather to be fixed on keeping time to the parades that passed beneath hastily cobbled triumphal arches and totem poles adorned with old solar symbols.

The transformation of the marble and bronze of ancient monuments into claptrap wastages of cheap pine, planks for one day's use, and emblems of gilded cardboard, should have served as a warning to those listening to the blaring words of the loud-speaker, I thought to myself. But this did not seem to be the case. Each and every one felt as though he had received the investiture, and many were those who sat upon the right hand of God to pass judgment on those of the past whose only crime had been not divining the future. I had myself seen a metaphysician of Heidelberg playing the bass drum in a parade of young philosophers goose-stepping to vote for those who had made a mockery of everything that could be called intellectual. I had seen the couples, on solstice nights, climb the Witches' Mount to light old votive fires, now utterly meaningless. But nothing had made such an impression on me as this putting on trial, this resurrection for punishment and profanation of the tomb of him who had concluded a symphony with the chorale of the Augsburg Confession, or that other who had cried in that pure voice of his, facing the gray-green waves of the great north: "I love the sea like my soul!"

Weary of having to recite Heine's "Intermezzo," under my breath and of hearing about corpses gathered up in the streets, of coming terrors, of new exoduses, I took refuge, like one seeking sanctuary, in the museums, making long

journeys through time. But when I came out of the museums, things were going from bad to worse. The newspapers
were shrieking for blood. The believers trembled before the
altar when the bishops raised their voices. The rabbis hid the
Torah, while pastors were thrown out of their meeting
houses. Before one's eyes the destruction of the rites and the
shattering of the Word were taking place. At night in the
public squares the students of distinguished universities
made bonfires of books. At every step on that continent
one was confronted by photographs of children dead in the
bombing of open cities, by reports of scholars sentenced to
salt mines, of unsolved disappearances, assassinations, defen-
estrations, peasants machine-gunned in bullrings.

I was astounded, outraged, wounded to the heart by the
difference between the world my father had sighed for and
the one whose acquaintance I was making. Where I sought
the smile of Erasmus, the *Discourse on Method*, the
spirit of humanism, the Faustian aspiration, and the Apollo-
nian soul, what I found was the *auto-da-fé*, the court of
some Holy Inquisition, the political trial that was merely a
new form of ordeal. One could no longer view a famous
carved pediment, a campanile, gargoyle, or smiling angel
without hearing it said that they were forerunners of pres-
ent-day philosophies and that the shepherds of the Nativity
adored something that was not really what lighted up the
manger. The age was tiring me. And it was dreadful to
think that there was no escape outside the mind from that
world without hiding-places, amid that nature subdued for
centuries, where the almost total synchronization of life had
concentrated all struggle around two or three problems
raised to white heat. Speeches had taken the place of myths;
slogans of dogmas. Bored with clichés forged in iron, with
expurgated texts, with teachers dismissed from their posts,
I turned once more toward the Atlantic with the idea of retracing my route.

Two days before I left I found myself studying a dance of death whose motifs were set forth upon the beams of the ossuary of Saint-Symphorien in Blois. It was a kind of rustic courtyard overgrown with weeds, impregnated with ages of sadness, above whose pillars there was spelled out, once more, the endless theme of vanity, all is vanity, of the skeleton beneath the lustful flesh, the rotted rib-case beneath the priestly chasuble, the drum beaten with two femurs in a xylophonic concert of bones. But here the poverty of the stable surrounding the eternal Example, the presence of the roiled, muddy river, the proximity of farms and factories, the pigs grunting like those of St. Anthony, at the foot of skulls carved on wood grown greasy with centuries of rain, gave a strange force to this reredos of dust, ashes, nothing, setting it in the midst of the present. And the kettledrums in the Beethoven scherzo took on a gloomy resonance now that they were associated in my mind with the vision of the ossuary of Blois. When I emerged, the afternoon papers informed me that war had broken out.

The wood was now embers. On a hillside, beyond the roof and the pines, a dog howled in the fog. Detached from the music itself, I returned to it by way of the crickets, listening for a B flat that already sounded in my ear. And now, at the quiet invitation of bassoon and clarinet, came the admirable melody of the adagio, so profound in the modesty of its lyricism. This was the only passage of the symphony whose slow measures my mother—more given to habaneras and opera arias—had managed to play at times from a transcription for piano she had found in one of the shop drawers. On the sixth beat, placidly ending in an echo of the wood-winds, I was just coming from school, after running fast to slide over the poplar seed-pods that covered the sidewalks.

Our house had a broad porch of whitewashed columns standing like a stairstep among the neighboring porches, one above another, all cut by the rising plane of the sidewalk leading to the Church of Jesús del Monte, which towered above the roofs, its terrace of trees encircled by railings. The house had formerly belonged to people of quality; its furniture was heavy, of dark wood, with deep wardrobes and a crystal chandelier whose prisms turned to little rainbows under the last rays of sun filtering through the blue, white, red lozenges that encircled the archway of the living-room like a great glass fan. My legs stuck out stiffly as I sat back in the rocking-chair, too tall and broad for a child, and opened the abridged grammar of the Royal Academy which I had to review that afternoon. *Estos, Fabio, ¡ay dolor!, que ves agora* . . . read the example that had come to my mind not long ago. The colored cook, amid the soot of her pots, was singing something that had to do with the days of the colony and the mustaches of the Civil Guard. As usual, the F sharp of the piano my mother was playing had stuck.

At the back of the house there was a room whose window grille was covered by a squash vine. I called to María del Carmen, who was playing among the potted palms, the roses, the carnation seed-beds, the callas, the sunflowers in the patio of her father, the gardener. She crawled through the hole in the hedge and lay down beside me in the laundry basket that was the ship of our travels. We were enveloped by the smell of esparto grass, rushes, hay, of this basket delivered each week by a sweaty giant named Baudilio, who devoured huge plates of beans.

I never got tired of hugging María del Carmen. The warmth of her body filled me with a delicious laziness I should have liked to prolong indefinitely. As lying still like that bored her, I quieted her by telling her that we were at sea and that we were soon going to reach the dock, which was that trunk with rounded lid, covered by bright-colored tin, to whose handle the boats tied up.

I had been told at school about dirty things that go on between men and women. I had indignantly refused to listen, knowing that they were disgusting inventions of the big boys for teasing the little ones. The first day they told me about it I was ashamed to look my mother in the face. I now asked María del Carmen if she wanted to be my wife, and as she answered yes, I squeezed her a little tighter, imitating the sound of a ship's siren so she would not go away from me. I found it hard to breathe, my heart throbbed, and yet this discomfort was so agreeable that I could not understand why, when the cook surprised us there, she got mad, dragged us out of the basket, threw it up on a cupboard, and said I was too big for such games. But she did not tell my mother, to whom I went to complain and who told me it was time to study. I went back to the abridged grammar, but the scent of rush, willow, and esparto grass haunted me.

At times this scent wafted back from the past became so strong that it made me tremble. Tonight I encountered it anew, there beside the cupboard of wild herbs, as the adagio ended on four chords pianissimo, and a ripple, perceptible over the air, ran through the chorus about to enter. I sensed the energetic gesture of the invisible conductor opening the way for Schiller's *Ode*. The thunder of bronzes and kettledrums unleashed, later to echo itself, served as the framework for the summing-up of the themes already stated. But these themes were broken, maimed, twisted, merged into a chaos that was the gestation of the future, each time they attempted to express, affirm themselves, become once more what they had been.

This type of symphony in ruins, which at this point cut across the entire symphony, would furnish a dramatic accompaniment—the thought was the fruit of my professional deformation—for a documentary retracing of the roads I had traveled as military interpreter at the end of the war.

They were the routes of the Apocalypse, winding between walls so shattered that they seemed the letters of an unknown alphabet; roads with holes filled in with pieces of statuary, which crossed unroofed abbeys, marked by headless angels, turning off before a *Last Supper* that howitzer shells had exposed to the weather, to debouch into the dust and ashes of what for centuries had been the greatest library of Ambrosian Chant.

But the horrors of war are the work of man. Every period has left its own etched in copper or in the dark shades of a mezzotint. What was new here, unprecedented, modern, was that cavern of horror, that ministry of horror, that preserve of horror whose acquaintance we were to make as we advanced: the Mansion of Shudders in which everything bore witness to torture, mass extermination, crematories, all set in walls spattered with blood and ordure, heaps of bones, human dentures shoveled up in the corners, not to mention even worse deaths accomplished coldly by rubber-gloved hands in the neat, bright, aseptic whiteness of operating-rooms. Two paces away, a sensitive, cultivated people—ignoring the smoke pall of certain chimneys from which, shortly before, prayers howled in Yiddish had risen—went on collecting stamps, studying the racial glories, playing Mozart's *Eine kleine nachtmusik*, reading Hans Christian Andersen to their children. This, too, was new, sinisterly modern, terrifyingly unprecedented.

Something gave way in me the afternoon I emerged from the abominable park of iniquities, which I had made myself visit to prove that such things could exist, with my mouth dry and feeling as though I had swallowed lime. I could never have conceived such total bankruptcy of Western man as that to which that residue of horror bore witness. As a child I had been terrified by the stories told of the atrocities committed by Pancho Villa, whose name was associated in my memory with a hairy, nocturnal vision of the

Devil. "*Culture oblige*," my father would say as he looked at the newspaper photographs of the firing-squad executions, voicing with this slogan of a new chivalry of the spirit his faith in the ultimate rout of evil by learning. A Manichean after his own fashion, he saw the world as a battlefield where enlightenment, represented by the printed word, was engaged in a struggle to the death with the dark forces of benightedness, the breeding-ground of every form of cruelty among those who lived without benefit of university, music, and laboratory. Evil, in his mind, was personified in this *guerrillero*, who, as he lined his enemies up against the wall, revived, after the lapse of centuries, the exploits of the Assyrian prince blinding his prisoners with the lance point or the savagery of the crusade that entombed the Albigensians in the caves of Mont Ségur. The last redoubt of evil, from which the Europe of Beethoven had freed itself, was on the Continent without History.

But after the sight of the Mansion of Shudders conceived, created, organized by people who knew so many noble things, the bullets of Pancho Villa's *dorados*, the cities breached house by house, the wrecked trains among the cactus and maguey, the rifle fire on moonlit nights, seemed to me gay pages from a novel of adventure filled with sunlight, feats of horsemanship, virile prowess, clean death upon sweated saddle leather, or clasped in the arms of a camp-follower who had borne her child by the roadside. And the worst of it was that on the night of my encounter with the most cold-blooded barbarism of history, the assassins, the caretakers, those who carried away the blood-soaked cotton in buckets, and those who made entries in their black oilcloth-bound notebooks, began to sing after supper in their prison hangar. Sitting up in my cot, brought wide awake by my amazement, I had heard them singing the same music as the chorus now brought to its feet by the director's distant baton:

Freude, schöner Götterfunken,
Tochter aus Elysium,
Wir betreten feuertrunken,
Himmlische, dein Heiligtum!

At last I was hearing the *Ninth Symphony*, the reason for my previous journey, though, to be sure, not under the circumstances my father had described. "Joy! The most beautiful divine gleam, daughter of Elysium, drunk with your fire we enter, O celestial one, your sanctuary. . . . All men shall be brothers where you spread your gentle wings." Schiller's verses, with their unconscious irony, wounded me. They represented the goal of centuries moving steadily toward tolerance, kindness, mutual understanding. The *Ninth Symphony* was the gracious, humane philosophy of Montaigne, the cloudless blue of Utopia, the essence of Elzevir, the voice of Voltaire raised in the Calas trial. Now there rose, swelling with joy, the "All men shall be brothers where you spread your gentle wings," as on that night when I lost faith in those who lied when they talked of their principles, quoting, like the Devil, Scripture to their purpose. To take my mind off the Dance of Death that was overwhelming me, I had let my comrades in arms drag me along with them to their taverns and brothels. I began to drink like them, sinking into a kind of soddenness that stopped short of complete drunkenness and enabled me to conclude the campaign without being taken in by words or deeds.

Our victory left me vanquished. I was not even surprised the night I spent in the prop-room of the theater in Bayreuth, amid a Wagnerian fauna of swans and horses suspended from the roof, beside a moth-eaten Fafnir who seemed to be trying to hide his head under my invader's cot. It was a man divested of hope who returned to the great city and made for the first bar to armor himself against ev-

ery idealistic weakness. The man who tried to bolster himself up by stealing his neighbor's wife, only to return, when
all was said and done, to the loneliness of an unshared bed.
The man who went by the name of Man, and who, only
the morning before, had been willing to trick the person
who had trusted him, bringing him fake instruments. . . .

This *Ninth Symphony* suddenly began to bore me with
its unfulfilled promises, its Messianic pretensions underscored with the carnival repertoire of the "Turkish music"
so cheaply employed in the final prestissimo. I did not wait
for the majestic *"Tochter aus Elysium! Freude, schöner
Götterfunken!"* of the finale. I turned off the radio, wondering how I had been able to listen to almost the whole
work, even forgetting myself at moments when the associa-
tions were not too overpowering. My hand reached for a
cucumber, whose coolness seemed to come from inside the
peel; the other closed around a green pepper, breaking the
skin for the juice that fell so deliciously on the tongue. I
opened the herb cupboard, taking out a handful that I
sniffed deeply. The last embers, black and red like something alive, still glowed in the fireplace. I looked out of the
window. The surrounding trees had disappeared in the
mist. The goose in the courtyard took its head out from under its wing, opening its bill noiselessly, without quite wak-
ing up. A fruit fell in the night.

(*Tuesday, the 12th*)

X/ When Mouche came out of her room shortly after
daybreak, she looked more tired than when she had gone to
bed. The discomforts of a day's travel over rough roads, a
hard bed, early rising, the hardships her body had to endure,
had induced a kind of pallor of her whole personality. She
who had been so sprightly, the life of the party in the disorder of our nights *back there*, was the living image of

boredom here. The glow of her skin seemed dimmed, and from her kerchief locks of blond hair escaped which had taken on a greenish cast. Her disagreeable expression made her look amazingly old and haggard, gave an ugly droop to her mouth, which because of the bad light and poor mirror she had not been able to make up properly.

To entertain her at breakfast, I told her about our fellow traveler I had talked with the night before. Just then the woman came in, shivering and laughing at herself for it; she had gone to wash at a near-by spring with the women of the house. Her hair, twisted in braids around her head, still dripped water over her pale face. She spoke to Mouche as though she had known her all her life, asking her questions that I translated. By the time we got into the bus, the two women had worked out a language of gestures and isolated words by which they managed to communicate. Mouche, already tired again, rested her head on the shoulder of Rosario—we had found out her name—who listened to her complaints about the discomforts of the trip with a maternal solicitude in which I could detect a touch of irony. Happy at being temporarily relieved of the burden of Mouche, I was in a gay frame of mind, with a whole seat to myself. That afternoon we would reach the river port where the boats set out for the jungle of the south, and as we wound around the mountainsides, downgrade all the way, we moved toward sunnier hours.

We stopped now and again at quiet, pleasant villages surrounded by increasingly tropical vegetation. Flowering vines, cactus, bamboo began to make their appearance; a palm tree rose in a courtyard, spreading its fronds over the roof of a house where the women sat in the shade with their mending. Such a heavy, steady rain began to fall at noon, lasting until late afternoon, that I could not see a thing through the drenched panes. Mouche took a book out of her bag. Rosario, imitating her, produced one from her bundle, a volume printed on cheap paper, pure trash, its gaudy cover displaying a woman covered with a bearskin or something that resembled it, in the arms of a splendid knight at the entrance to a cave, while a gazelle looked on benignly: *The Story of Genevieve of Brabant.*

The contrast between this and the best-seller Mouche was reading struck me forcibly. I had put the book down after the third chapter, depressed by a kind of melancholy shame at its obscenity. Opposed as I am to all sexual restraints, to all hypocrisy in things of the body, nevertheless I am irritated by any writing or language that degrades physical love with mockery, sarcasm, or vulgarity. It seems to me that in his mating man should share the element of play that characterizes animals in heat, giving himself up joyously to his pleasant occupation in the knowledge that seclusion behind closed doors, the absence of witnesses, the mutual search for pleasure excludes everything that might give rise to irony or jest—certain physical difficulties, the animal quality of certain unions—in the embraces of a man and woman who cannot see themselves as others see them. For this reason I find pornography as intolerable as certain bawdy stories, double meanings, words metaphorically applied to the sexual act, and I am revolted by a type of literature greatly in vogue in our day which seems to have as its objective the degradation and distortion of all that might contribute, in hours of difficulty and discouragement, to a man's finding compensation for his failures in the affirmation of his virility, achieving his fullest realization in the flesh he divides.

I was reading over the two women's shoulders, establishing a kind of counterpoint between the saccharine and the bitter. But I soon had to give up the game because of the speed with which Mouche turned the pages and the pace at which Rosario read, her eyes traveling slowly from the beginning to the end of the line, her lips moving silently as she spelled out the words, following stirring adventures in words not always in the order she would have chosen. There were moments when she paused, with a gesture of indignation, over some infamous tribulation unhappy Genevieve had suffered; then she went back to the beginning of the paragraph, doubting that such wickedness could be. And then she went back over the lamentable episode once more as though dismayed by her own helplessness in the face of the evidence. Her face mirrored a deep anxiety, as Golo's wicked designs became manifest.

"Those are tales of other days," I said to draw her out. She turned around, startled to discover that I had been reading over her shoulder.

"These books tell the truth," she answered.

I looked at Mouche's book, thinking that if what it related in words that the worried publisher had had to omit in various places was true, not on that account had it achieved—for all its efforts—the obscenity that Hindu sculptors or humble Incan pottery-makers had raised to a level of authentic grandeur.

Rosario closed her eyes. "What these books tell is the truth."

For her Genevieve's history was very probably something real, something that was happening in a real country as she read it. The past eludes the grasp of those ignorant of the trappings, the setting, the props of history. She probably saw the castles of Brabant as the great ranches she knew, which often had crenelated walls. The hunt and the chase were the custom of the country in these lands where deer and wild boar were followed by the pack. As for the style of dress, Rosario's vision was probably that of certain early Renaissance painters who presented the figures of the Passion in the attire of their own day, hurling down to the pit of hell Pilates in the robes of a Florentine judge. . . .

Night closed in, and the light became so dim that everyone withdrew into himself. After a long ride through the darkness, we rounded a hill suddenly and came out upon the illuminated expanse of the Valley of Flames.

I had already been told, during the trip, of the town that had sprung up here in a few weeks when oil began to gush from the marshes. But the news had not prepared me for the fantastic sight that grew with every turn of the road. A bare plain was the setting for a vast dance of flames crackling in the wind like the flags of some divine conflagration. Run up by the escaping gases of the wells, they fluttered, came together, swirled, coiled around themselves, free and yet joined to the exhaust pipes—the flagstaffs of this hive of fire, this tree of fire, which emerged from the ground, flying yet unable to fly, a whistle of enraged reds. The air momentarily transformed them into lights of death, maddened firebrands, to bring them together in a cluster of torches, in a single red-black trunk that took on a fleeting resemblance to the human torso. But suddenly the burning body writhed in yellow convulsions, became a burning bush, teeming with sparks, all aroar before it licked hungrily toward the city as though to wreak punishment on its sinful dwellers. Alongside this chain of pyres the pumps worked on, tireless, monotonous, the pistons having the look of great black birds in profile, sinking their beaks isochronously in the earth like woodpeckers boring trees.

There was something stubborn, obsessive, malefic in these silhouettes, which burned but were never consumed, like salamanders born of the flux and reflux of the fires that the wind whipped horizonward into waves. They seemed to call for names befitting devils, and I was amusing myself, dubbing them *Flacocuervo, Buitrehierro, Maltridente*, when our journey suddenly came to an end in a courtyard where black pigs, reddened by the reflection of the flames, wallowed in pools of water iridescent with oil. The dining-room of the inn was filled with men talking at the top

🐦 *The Lost Steps*

102

of their lungs as though choked by the fumes of the grilling
meat. With their gas masks still hanging around their necks,
without having changed their work clothes, they looked as
though gouts, splashes, stains, the blackest exudations of
the earth, had settled on them. They were all drinking
heavily, holding the bottles by the necks, and the tables
were covered with cards and chips.

But suddenly the games were interrupted and the players rushed toward the courtyard with a jubilant shout.
Transported by some mysterious conveyance, women appeared in evening dress and high-heeled slippers, with
bright ornaments in their hair and at their necks. Their
presence in that slime-filled back yard flanked with stalls
seemed to me nothing short of magic. The sequins, the
beads, the trimmings of their dresses reflected the light of
the flames, which gave new emphasis to their finery with
every shift of the wind. Carrying bundles and suitcases,
these scarlet women rushed busily among the dark men
with a jabbering and gabbling that sent the donkeys into a
panic and awoke the sleeping hens on the rafters. I learned
that the next day was the festival of the patron saint of the
town, and that these women were prostitutes who traveled
about all year, from one place to another, from fairs to
processions, from mines to pilgrimages, making the most
of the days when men feel generous. Their route was that
of the church spires, and their fornications observed the
saints' calendar—St. Christopher, St. Lucy, the Blessed
Dead, the Holy Innocents—in ditches, beside cemetery
walls, on the beaches, or in the cubby-holes of rooms with
washbasins on the dirt floors in the backs of taverns.

What most amazed me was the welcome these women
received from the upright citizens, without the least sign of
contempt on the part of the decent women of the house,
the wife and the young daughter of the innkeeper. It
seemed to me that they looked upon them as clowns or

gypsies or amusing lunatics, and the kitchen maids laughed as they watched them jump, in their evening dresses, over the pigs and the puddles, some of the miners helping them with their bundles to speed up matters. It occurred to me that these wandering prostitutes we had come upon, in this our modern world, were kin to those trollops of the Middle Ages who journeyed from Bremen to Hamburg, from Antwerp to Ghent, at fair time, to relieve masters and journeymen of their evil humors, giving comfort on the side to some pilgrim from Compostela in return for being allowed to kiss the cockleshell emblem of his distant travels.

After they had collected all their baggage, the women made their noisy entrance into the dining-room. Mouche, all wonderment, urged me to follow them to get a good look at their dresses and hair-dos. She, who until that moment had been contemptuous and bored, was transfigured. There are people whom the presence of sex brings to life. Indifferent, complaining since the night before, my friend came awake in the murky atmosphere that had sprung up around her. According to her now, these prostitutes were *formidables*, unique, the like of which no longer existed, and she moved closer to them. Rosario, seeing her seat herself on a bench beside the table where the new arrivals had gathered, looked at me in surprise, as though trying to tell me something. To avoid an explanation that she would probably not have understood, I picked up our luggage and set out to find our room. The writhing flames gleamed above the courtyard walls.

I was trying to figure out how much I had spent these last days when it seemed to me that I heard Mouche calling me in a terrified voice. In the mirror of the wardrobe I saw her pass, at the other end of the hall, as though running from a man who was pursuing her. When I reached them, the man had her by the waist and was trying to push her into a room. When I hit him, he turned swiftly, and his punch threw me against a table covered with empty bottles, which fell with a crash. I threw my arms around my opponent, and we rolled on the floor, fragments of glass biting into our hands and arms. After a short struggle, in which I was left powerless, I found myself between the man's knees, flat on the floor, while two broad fists rose, poised to fall on my face like hammers. At that moment Rosario rushed into the room, followed by the innkeeper. "Yannes!" she cried, "Yannes!" grabbing him by the wrists. The man slowly got to his feet as though ashamed of what had happened. The innkeeper was explaining to him something that in my nervous excitement I could not catch. My opponent looked sheepish. He was saying to me in an apologetic tone: "I not know. . . . It was mistake. . . . She should have said she had husband."

Rosario wiped my face with a cloth wrung out in rum. "It was her fault. She was there with the others."

The worst of it was that it was not the man who had hit me whom I was furious with, but Mouche. It was just like her to have gone and sat down with the prostitutes. "Nothing has happened . . . nothing has happened," the innkeeper announced to the spectators crowding into the hall. And Rosario, as though really nothing had happened, made me shake hands with the other man, who was babbling excuses. To calm me completely, she told me about him, saying she had known him for a long time, that he was not from this place, but from Puerto Anunciación, the town near the Jungle of the South, where her sick father was waiting for her and the miraculous scapulary. The name she used, Diamond-Hunter, made me suddenly interested in my erstwhile mauler. A few moments more, and we were at the bar with half a bottle of brandy inside us, the stupid fight forgotten. Deep-chested, slender-waisted, with something of the look of a bird of prey, the miner had a

face, shadowed by a line of beard, which might have
stepped out of an arch of triumph in the energy and vigor
of its profile.

When I found out that he was Greek—which explained
his complete omission of articles when he talked—I was on
the point of asking him, as a joke, if he was one of the
Seven against Thebes. But just then Mouche strolled over,
her air indifferent, as though she had no idea why our
hands were all cut up. I made some veiled reproaches that
did not begin to express my irritation. She seated herself
across the table, paying no attention to what I had said, and
began to look over the Greek—who was now so respectful
that he moved his bench away, not to be too close to her—
with an attention that seemed to me a deliberate challenge
at such a time. To the apologies of the Diamond-Hunter,
who called himself a "damn-fool brute," she answered that
the incident was of no importance. I looked at Rosario.
She was watching me out of the tail of her eye with a kind
of ironic gravity that I was at a loss to interpret. I tried to
begin some kind of conversation that would get us away
from what had happened, but I could think of nothing to
say.

Mouche, meanwhile, had moved closer to the Greek
with such a tense, provocative smile that my temples began
to throb with rage. We had just got out of a mess that might
have had serious consequences, and here she was, trying
her wiles on the miner who half an hour earlier had taken
her for a prostitute. This attitude was so literary, so much a
part of the spirit that glorified sailors' taverns and foggy
waterfronts, that she suddenly struck me as being an utter
fool in her inability to throw off the clichés of her generation when confronted with any real situation. She had to
pick out a *hippocampe* rather than an article of colonial
handicraft because of Rimbaud; she had to scoff at a ro-
mantically staged opera which truly caught the fragrance

of the garden of Lammermoor; and she could not see that
the prostitute of the novels of Evasion had been transformed here into a mixture of a carnival wench and a St.
Mary of Egypt without odor of sanctity.

I looked at her with what must have been such a strange
air that Rosario, fearful that I was going to start up the
fight again because I was jealous, stepped into the breach
to placate me with a phrase that was a cross between prov-
erb and epigram: "When a man fights it should be to de-
fend his home." I do not know what Rosario meant by my
"home"; but she was right if she was trying to say what I
thought I understood: that Mouche was not my "home."
On the contrary, she was that loud and willful woman the
Bible speaks of whose feet abide not in her house.

The phrase threw a bridge across the table between
Rosario and myself, and at that moment I felt the bond of
a sympathy that perhaps would have suffered to see me defeated again. Moreover, with every hour the girl was taking on stature in my eyes as I noticed how she established
links with her surroundings. Mouche, on the contrary, was
proving utterly alien, revealing a total lack of adjustment
between herself and everything around her. An aura of
exoticism was thickening around her, creating a distance
between her and the others, between her acts, her behavior,
and the norms of conduct here. Little by little she was turning into something foreign, incongruous, eccentric, which
attracted attention in the same way the turbans of the am-
bassadors of the Sublime Porte aroused wonder at the
Christian courts.

Rosario, in contrast, was like a St. Cecilia or St. Lucy
back in her rightful setting in a restored old stained-glass
window. With the passing of morning into afternoon and
afternoon into evening, she grew more authentic, more
real, more clearly outlined against a background that affirmed its constants as we approached the river. Relationships became established between her flesh and the ground

we were treading, relationships proclaimed by sundarkened skins, by the similarity of the visible hair, by a
unity of forms giving the common stamp of works from
the same potter's wheel to the waists, shoulders, thighs that
were praised there. I felt myself more and more drawn to
Rosario, who grew more beautiful by the hour—in contrast to Mouche, who was receding into the distance she
had created—and everything she said or expressed seemed
right to me. And yet, as I looked at her as a woman, I felt
myself clumsy, awkward, realizing my own strangeness in
the face of an innate dignity that seemed invulnerable to
the easy approach.

It was not only the broken bottles that were raised here
to form a wall of glass that spoke a warning to the hands;
it was the thousand books I had read and of which she
knew nothing; it was her beliefs, habits, superstitions, ideas
of which I knew nothing and which, nevertheless, formed
the basis for vital beliefs as valid as my own. My formation, her prejudices, all that she had been taught, all that
she valued, at that moment seemed to me irreconcilable
factors. I kept telling myself that none of all this had any
bearing on the ever-possible coupling of the body of a
man and a woman, and yet I knew that an entire culture,
with its deformations and taboos, separated me from that
forehead behind which there was probably not the haziest
notion of the fact that the earth was round or of the position of the different countries on the map. This came to
me as I recalled her beliefs about the one-legged deity of
the woods. And as I saw the little gold cross she wore
about her neck, I thought to myself that the only common
ground of understanding we might have shared, our faith
in Christ, had been abandoned by my paternal forebears
long before, ever since they, Huguenots expelled from
Savoy by the revocation of the Edict of Nantes, had gone
over to the *Encyclopédie* in the person of one of my great-
grandfathers, a friend of Baron Holbach. They had pre-

served the family Bibles without any longer believing in their content, but because of a certain poetic quality they possessed. . . .

Another shift of miners invaded the tavern. The scarlet women emerged from the back rooms, tucking away the earnings of their first round. To put an end to the ambiguous situation that was making those of us at the table uneasy, I suggested that we take a walk down to the river. The Diamond-Hunter seemed embarrassed by the insinuating attentions of Mouche, who, without listening to him, made him relate his adventures in the jungle in such halting French that he was never able to conclude a phrase. He seemed relieved at my suggestion, bought some bottles of cold beer, and led us down a straight street that was swallowed up in the night far from the glare of the fires.

We soon reached the bank of the river, which ran in the darkness with the vast, steady, deep sound of a mass of waters dividing the land. It was not the noisy chatter of the slender streams, nor the splash of falls, nor the cool purling of brooks I had so often heard by night on other banks. It was the steady drive, the genesial rhythm of a descent beginning hundreds and hundreds of miles upstream in union with other rivers that had come from still farther away with all the volume of their cataracts and springs. In the darkness it seemed as though the water, which was always pushing water, had no other bank, and that from now on the sound of it would drown everything to the ends of the earth.

Walking along in silence, we came to a cove—more like a backwater—which was a graveyard of old beached ships with rudders adrift and decks noisy with frogs. Among them was an ancient sailer of noble cut, with a figurehead in carved wood representing Amphitrite, her bare breasts emerging from sails folded back like wings. We stopped near the hull, almost under the figure that seemed to be flying over our heads. Lulled by the cool of the night and the monotonous sound of the moving waters, we sat down with our backs against the gravel bank. Rosario let down her hair and began to comb it slowly, with a gesture so intimate, so indicative of the hour of sleep, that I did not venture to speak to her. Mouche, on the other hand, kept up her silly chatter, asking the Greek questions, receiving his answers with shrill laughter, without seeming aware of the fact that the elements of the setting in which we found ourselves made up one of those unforgettable stage designs rarely encountered. The figurehead, the flames, the river, the abandoned boats, the constellations—nothing that met the eye seemed to touch her. I think this was the moment when her presence began to weigh on me like a load that grew heavier each day.

(*Wednesday, the 13th*)

XI/ Silence is an important word in my vocabulary. Working with music, I have used it more than men in other professions. I know how one can speculate with silence, measure it, set it apart. But then, sitting on that rock, I was living silence: a silence that came from so far off, compounded of so many silences, that a word dropped into it would have taken on the clangor of creation. Had I said anything, had I talked to myself, as I often do, I would have frightened myself.

The sailors down below were cutting grass for the stud bulls that were traveling with us. Their voices did not reach me. Without thought of them I looked out over the vast savanna, whose boundaries dissolved in a faint circular darkening of the sky. From my vantage point of rock and grass, I took in, almost in its totality, a circumference that formed a perfect, a complete part of the planet on which I lived. I no longer had to raise my eyes to find a cloud: those motionless cirri, that seemed as though they had always been there, were within reach of the hand that shaded my eyelids. Here and there in the distance a thick, solitary tree stood out, always flanked by a cactus like a tall candelabrum of green stone, on which unmoving, heavy hawks rested like heraldic birds. Nothing makes a noise, nothing collides with nothing, nothing moves or vibrates. When a fly in its flight crashed into a spider web, its buzz of horror took on a sound of thunder. Then the air grew calm again from horizon to horizon, without a sound.

I had been there more than an hour without moving, knowing how futile it was to move when one was always at the center of that which was contemplated. Far, far off, a deer appeared among the rushes by a spring. It paused, its head nobly poised, so motionless against the flat surface that it had something of the air of a monument, a totemic symbol. It was like the mythical ancestor of men not yet born; like the founder of a clan that would convert its antlers, fastened to a pole, into coat of arms, hymn, standard. Catching my scent on the breeze, it moved off with measured step unhurriedly, leaving me alone with the world.

I turned toward the river. So vast was its stream that the torrents, the whirlpools, the falls that perturbed its relentless descent were fused in the unity of a pulse that had throbbed, from dry season through rainy season, with the same rests and beats since before man was invented. We were embarking that morning, at dawn, and I had spent long hours looking at the banks, without taking my eyes for too long from the narration of Fray Servando de Castillejos, who had brought his sandals here three centuries ago. His quaint prose was still valid. Where the author mentioned a rock with the profile of an alligator high on the right bank, there it was, high on the right bank. Where the chronicler spoke with amazement of seeing gigantic trees, I had seen gigantic trees, descendants of his trees, sprung up in the same spot, housing the same birds, blasted by the same lightning.

Within the range of my vision, the river entered through a kind of cut, a rent in the western horizon; it broadened out where I was sitting until the opposite bank became a greened blur of trees, and it emerged as it entered, splitting the dawn horizon to empty on the other slope, where the proliferation of its innumerable islands began, a hundred leagues from the ocean. Granary, source of waters, pathway, it had no regard for human activity, set no value on individual haste. Rail and road had been left behind. One traveled with the stream or against it. In either case one had to adjust to immutable rhythms. Here man's travels were governed by the Code of the Rains. I noticed that I, to whom the measuring of time was a mania, shackled to the metronome by vocation and to the clock by profession, had stopped thinking of the hour, gauging the height of the sun by hunger or sleep. The discovery that I had not wound my watch made me laugh out loud, alone there on that timeless savanna. A covey of quail rose around me; the captain of the *Manatí* called me aboard with shouts that sounded like chanteys, arousing caws on every side.

I stretched out again on the bales of hay under the broad canvas awning, with the bulls on one side of me and the Negress cooks on the other. The sweating Negresses, singing as they pounded garlic in a mortar, the rutting bulls, and the acrid smell of alfalfa blended into an odor that left me as though intoxicated. Nothing about that smell could be called agreeable. And yet it invigorated me as though in truth it fulfilled a hidden need of my organism. I was like the peasant who returns to his ancestral fields after years in the city and breaks into tears as he sniffs the manure-laden breeze. It reminded me—I just remembered—of the back yard of my childhood: there, too, were a sweating Negress pounding garlic and singing, and cattle grazing near by.

And above all—above all!—there was that willow basket, the vessel of my voyages with María del Carmen, which smelled like the alfalfa in which I was burying my face with almost painful emotion.

Mouche, whose hammock was swung to catch the breeze, was talking to the Greek miner, and knew nothing of that spot, which was like an attic and a cubby-hole. Rosario, on the contrary, often climbed up to that pile of bales, undisturbed by an occasional shower filtering through the canvas and cooling the new-cut hay. She would stretch out some distance from me, smiling as she buried her teeth in a fruit. I admired the courage of this woman who, without hesitation or fear, was making a trip that the directors of the Museum for which I worked considered a hazardous undertaking. This unflinching temper of women seemed common there. In the stern a mulatto whose body was that of a young girl was bathing, pouring buckets of water over her flowered nightdress. She was on her way to meet her lover, a gold-prospector, at the headwaters of an almost unexplored tributary of the river. Another, dressed in mourning, was going to try her luck as a prostitute—with the hope of rising from prostitute to kept woman—in a village near the jungle, where famine is not uncommon during the flood months.

I regretted more and more having brought Mouche on this trip. I would have liked to strike up an intimacy with the crew, eating their sailor's fare, which they thought too coarse for refined palates, getting to know those strong-limbed resolute women better, and drawing out their stories. But most of all I would have wished to be free to know Rosario better, whose deeper being eluded the probing procedures I had used up to that hour in my dealings with women, whom I found pretty much alike. At every step I was afraid of offending her, annoying her, taking too many familiarities with her, or making her the object of attentions that might seem to her silly or unmanly. There were moments when it occurred to me that these interludes among the cattle pens, where nobody could see us, called for a determined move on my part; everything seemed to invite it, and yet I lacked the courage.

Nevertheless, I noticed that the men on board treated the women with a kind of rough and ready fellowship that seemed to please them. But these people had their rules, their code of behavior, of which I was ignorant. Yesterday when Rosario saw a shirt I had bought myself in one of the best shops in the world she began to laugh, saying that such garments were for women, not men. When I was with her I was always afraid of seeming ridiculous, a fear that could not be conjured away by the thought that "they don't know," for here they were the ones who knew. Mouche was unaware of the fact that though I pretended to keep an eye on her, if I acted as though I cared whether she talked to the Greek or not, it was because I imagined that Rosario felt it my duty to watch over the woman who was my companion on the trip. There were times when it seemed to me that a glance, a gesture, a word, whose meaning eluded me, was an invitation. I climbed up on the bales and waited. But it was then that I waited in vain. The rutting bulls bellowed, the Negresses sang to excite and tantalize the sailors, the smell of alfalfa intoxicated me. Temples and sex throbbing, I closed my eyes and fell into the idiotic frustration of erotic dreams.

At sundown we tied up to a makeshift pier of piles driven into the mud. As we came into a village where the talk was of wrangling and lassos, I realized that we had come to the Lands of the Horse. First of all, the smell of the circus ring, of sweaty withers, which the world has known so long, proclaimed the culture of the neigh. It was the dull thud of the hammer telling of the presence of the black-smith, still busy with anvil and bellows, painted with a dark palette, in his leather apron, by the glow of the hearth. It was the hiss of the white-hot iron plunged into the pail of cold water, and the song that kept time to the driving of the horseshoe nails. And then the nervous prancing of the newly shod feet, fearful of slipping on the stones, and the bucking and rearing mastered by skilled reins for the benefit of the girl at the window with a ribbon in her hair. With the horse the saddler's art had reappeared, with its aroma of leather, the smooth cordovan, the harness-makers at work amidst pegs adorned with cinches, stirrups, embossed saddle-trees, and Sunday bridles with silver-studded headstalls.

A man seemed more a man in the Lands of the Horse. He became once more the master of age-old skills that had brought his hands into direct contact with iron and hide, which had taught him the arts of breaking and riding, developing physical prowess that he could display on holidays before women filled with admiration for the powerful knee, the mastering arm. The male sports were reborn of breaking the screaming stallion, throwing the bull by the tail—the animal of the sun—and laying its arrogance in the dust. A mysterious solidarity was established between the animal with well-hung testicles which covered its female deeper than any other and man, whose symbol of courage was what the sculptors of equestrian statues modeled and cast in bronze or carved in marble, that the spirited steed might go surety for the Hero astride him, lending propitious shade to the lovers who held their trysts in the city parks.

Crowds of men were gathered in the houses where many horses drowsed in the shade of the sheds; but where a single horse waited in the night, half hidden in the underbrush, its owner removed his spurs more quietly to enter the house where a shadow awaited him. I observed with interest that after having been the most prized possession of the man of Europe, his machine of war, his vehicle, his messenger, the pedestal of his heroes, the ornament of his friezes and arches of triumph, the horse had written new chapters of his glorious history in America. It was only in the New World that he still carried on to the full and on so vast a scale his age-old activities. If the Lands of the Horse had been left blank on the maps, as happened with unknown lands in the middle ages, they would have whitened the fourth part of the hemisphere, bearing witness to the mighty presence of the horseshoe in a region where the Cross of Christ had entered by the horse, not dragged at its heels, but aloft, carried on high by men who were taken for centaurs.

(*Thursday, the 14th*)

XII/ We resumed our voyage with the full moon, for the owner had to pick up a Capuchin friar at the port of Santiago de los Aguinaldos on the opposite bank of the river, and wanted to shoot a particularly rough rapids in the morning, leaving the afternoon free to do some trading. This being accomplished with masterly handling of the rudder and poling over some of the rocks, I found myself at midday in an incredible city in ruins. The long, deserted streets were flanked by empty houses, the doors rotted away, leaving only the jamb or the crossbar, the mossy roofs fallen through in the very middle, following the collapse of the rooftree gutted by termites and blackened by empty wasp combs. The pillars of a porch held up the remains of a cornice split by the roots of a fig tree. There were stairways without beginning or end, as though suspended in space, and latticed balconies that hung from window frames open to the sky. White campanula vines hung an airy curtain over the vast expanse of rooms that still preserved their cracked tile floors, and there were the old golds of *aromo* bushes and the red of poinsettias. Cactuses with arms like candelabra swayed in the halls as though held in the hands of invisible servants. There were toadstools on the doorstep and thistles in the fireplaces.

Trees scaled the walls, burying their claws in the cracks in the mortar, and a burned church still displayed various buttresses, archivolts, and a monumental arch on the point of collapse, on its tympanum still to be discerned, in dim relief, the figures of a celestial concert, with angels playing the bassoon, the theorbo, the organ, and the maracas. This so amazed me that I was going back to the boat for pencil and paper to make sketches for the Curator of this rare organographic example. But just then came the sound of drums and shrill flutes, and several devils appeared around a corner of the plaza, headed toward a miserable church of brick and plaster across from the one that had burned down. The faces of the dancers were covered with black cloth, like those of the penitentes of certain Christian brotherhoods; they advanced slowly, in little skips, behind a kind of leader or master of ceremonies who could have played the role of Beelzebub in a Passion Play, of the Dragon, or the King of Madmen, with his devil's mask of three horns and pig's snout.

A kind of fear came over me at the sight of those faceless men, as though they were wearing the veil of parricides; at those masks, out of the mystery of time, perpetuating man's eternal love of the False Face, the disguise, the pretense of being an animal, a monster, or a malign spirit. The strange dancers reached the door of the church and pounded the knocker a number of times. They stood for a long time before the closed door, weeping and wailing. Then suddenly the double doors were noisily flung open, and there in a cloud of incense was St. James the Apostle, the son of Zebedee and Salome, riding a white horse borne on the shoulders of the faithful. At the sight of his crown of gold, the devils fell back in panic, as though seized by a fit, stumbling against one another, falling, rolling to the ground. Behind the image a hymn began, the ancient sonority of sackbut and hornpipe helped out by a clarinet and a trombone:

> *Primus ex apostolis*
> *Martir Jerosolimis*
> *Jacobus egregio*
> *Sacer est martirio.*

The bell rang its full swell, several boys sitting athwart the bell gable pushing it with their feet. The procession wound slowly around the church, led by the nasal falsetto of the priest, while the devils, feigning the tortures of exorcisement, shrank back in a groaning group from the aspersions of hyssop. When all was over, the figure of St. James the Apostle, he of the *Campus stellæ*, shaded by a canopy of moth-eaten velvet, disappeared into the temple, whose doors closed with a bang on a flickering wave of lights and candles. Whereupon the devils, who were left outside, began to run, laughing and leaping, turned from devils to clowns, disappearing among the ruins of the city, shouting lewdly through the windows, asking whether women still gave birth there.

The faithful dispersed. I stayed on alone in the middle of the gloomy plaza, whose flagstones had been pushed up and cracked by the roots of the trees. Rosario, who had gone to light a candle for her father's recovery, soon appeared in the company of a bearded Capuchin who was to embark with us, and introduced him to me as Fray Pedro de Henestrosa. With few words, in a slow, sententious tone, the friar explained to me that it was the singular custom here to bring out the figure of St. James on the feast of Corpus Christi, because shortly after the founding of the town the image of the patron saint had arrived on the afternoon of that day, and the tradition had been observed ever since. We were soon joined by two Negro guitar-players, with their instruments swung across their shoulders, who complained that this year the celebration had been nothing but hymns and processions, and they were never coming back.

I learned then that this had formerly been a city of replete coffers, rich in furnishings, in cupboards filled with cambric sheets. But the repeated lootings of a long civil war had ruined its mansions and estates, covering its hatchments with ivy. Those who could emigrated, selling their manor houses for whatever they would bring. Then came the scourge of plagues arising from rice fields which, no longer cultivated, had gone back to swamp. This time death finally handed the mansions over to the grass and the termites, paving the way for the destruction of arches, roofs, and thresholds. Today it was nothing but an abode of shades in the shade of what had once been the rich city of Santiago de los Aguinaldos.

I listened with interest to the missionary's account, thinking of the cities ruined by the Wars of the Barons, smitten by the plague, when the guitar-players, whom Rosario had asked to entertain us with some music, began to pluck their instruments. Suddenly their song carried me much farther than the scenes I had been evoking. Those two black jongleurs were singing ballads telling of Charlemagne, of Roland, the Bishop Turpin, the treachery of Ganelon, and the sword that cut down the Moors at Roncesvalles. By the time we reached the dock, they were recalling the tale of certain Infantes of Lara, which was unknown to me, but whose archaic flavor was moving in that setting of crumbling, lichened walls like those of ancient, deserted castles.

We cast off as the twilight was lengthening the shadows of the ruins. Leaning on the rail, Mouche remarked that the sight of that ghost city could compare in mystery, in supernatural suggestion, with the best that the greatest of modern painters could have conceived. Here the themes of fantastic art were three-dimensional; they could be felt,

lived. They were not imaginary constructions or cheap
poetic claptrap: one walked through real labyrinths, one
ascended stairs that broke off at the landing, continued by
a railing without balustrades that disappeared in the night of
a tree. Mouche's observations were not stupid; but as far as
she was concerned, I had reached the saturation point at
which a man who has tired of a woman is bored even
when she says intelligent things.

With its cargo of bellowing bulls, coops of chickens, pigs
running about the deck under the hammock of the Capuchin and getting tangled up in his rosary of seeds, the song
of the Negress cooks, the laughter of the Greek diamond-
hunter, the prostitute in her mourning nightgown bathing
in the prow, the guitar-players making music for the sailors
to dance, this ship of ours made me think of Bosch's *Ship of
Fools*. But a ship of madmen now taking off from a shore
that defied ubication; for though the roots of what I had
seen were grounded in styles, reasons, myths I could identify, the final result, the tree that had sprung up on this soil,
was as disconcerting and new as the huge trees that began
to hide the banks, and which, in groups at the entrance to
the channels, stood out against the setting sun—with something of the rotundity of low hills about their foliage and
something of dogs' muzzles about their tops—like councils
of gigantic baboons. I recognized the elements of this
scenography, to be sure. But in the humidity of this world,
the ruins were more ruins, the vines pried loose the stones
in a different way, the insects had other tricks, and the devils were more devils when Negro dancers groaned beneath
their horns.

An angel and maracas were not in themselves new. But
an angel playing the maracas carved on the tympanum of a
burned church was something I had never seen anywhere
else. I was asking myself whether perhaps the role of these
lands in the history of man might not be to make possible

for the first time certain symbioses of cultures, when I was interrupted in my reflections by something that aroused an echo in me of something both very near and very remote. Standing beside me, Fray Pedro de Henestrosa, in honor of Corpus Christi Day, was chanting in a low tone a Gregorian hymn printed in neumes on the yellow, wormholed pages of a *Liber Usualis* of long ago:

> *Sumite psalmum, et date tympanum:*
> *Psalterium jocundum cum citara.*
> *Buccinate in Neomenia tuba*
> *In insigni dei solemnitatis vestræ.*

(Friday, June 15)

XIII/   When we reached Puerto Anunciación, the humid city that for hundreds of years has been carrying on a stalemate war with the jungle, I realized that we had passed from the Lands of the Horse to the Lands of the Dog. There, behind the outlying roofs, the vanguard of the still-distant jungle had posted its sentinels, magnificent trees having the air of obelisks rather than trees, still scattered, apart from one another, towering above the vast expanse of mangroves, whose creeping feracity could wipe out a trail in one night. There was no place for the horse in a pathless world. And beyond the green expanse that cut off the south, trail and track disappeared under such a weight of branches as to make the passing of a rider impossible. The Dog, on the other hand, whose eyes are at the height of a man's knees, sees everything lurking under the treacherous fronds, in the hollow of the fallen trees, among the rotting leaves; the Dog, with tense muzzle, twitching nose, registering danger in rising hackles, has observed over the ages the terms of his first alliance with Man. For it was a pact that joined Dog and Man here, a mutual complementing of powers which made their relation a brotherhood.

The Dog brought to the bargain those senses which had atrophied in his hunting companion—the eyes of his nose, his moving on four feet, his useful disguise of an animal among the other animals—in exchange for the spirit of enterprise, the arms, the oar, the walking upright that the other contributed. The Dog was the only being that shared with Man the benefits of fire, assuming, by this approach to Prometheus, the right to take Man's side in any war against Animals. For this reason, that city was the city of the Bark. In hallways, behind the window grilles, under the tables, the dogs stretched, sniffed, scratched, watched. They sat in the prows of the boats, ran about the roofs, watched the roasting meat, were present at all meetings and collective acts, went to church. Bearing witness to this was an old colonial ordinance, which nobody was interested in enforcing, ordering the beadle appointed for that purpose to drive the dogs out of the temple "every Saturday and on the eve of all feasts." On nights when the moon was full the dogs gave themselves over to its adoration with a vast chorus of howls which was no longer interpreted as presaging some calamity, but whose sleep-banishing effects were accepted with that resigned tolerance with which one accepts the tiresome rites of relatives who practice a different religion.

The place known as an inn in Puerto Anunciación was an old barracks with cracked walls, its rooms opening on a muddy courtyard where big turtles were penned in case food should run short. Two canvas cots and a wooden bench constituted the furnishings of our room, with a piece of looking-glass held on the back of the door by three rusty nails. As the moon had just come up above the river, after a brief pause the howling antiphony of the dogs had broken out again—from the towering silvered trees of the Franciscan mission to the islands drawn in black—with unexpected responses from the other bank.

Mouche, who was in a wretched humor, refused to accept the fact that we had left electricity behind us and that we were in the age of the kerosene lamp and the candle, and that there was no drugstore at which she could replenish her stock of cosmetics. My friend was shrewd enough to hide the constant care she lavished on her face and her body, so those who did not know her would think her above such feminine vanities, unworthy of an intellectual, implying thereby that her youth and her natural beauty were attraction enough. Familiar with her tactics, it had amused me to watch her time and again from the bales of grass, observing with wicked irony how often she examined herself in her compact mirror, frowning with annoyance. What surprised me now was that the very substance of her body, the flesh of which it was made, seemed to have faded since the morning of that last day of navigation. Her skin, roughened by the hard water, had reddened, revealing areas of coarse pores around her nose and temples. Her hair had taken on the look of tow, greenish-blond in color, streaky, making evident how much its normal coppery hue owed to the careful use of tints.

Under her blouse, stained by strange oils that dripped from the sails, her breasts seemed less firm, and the polish peeled off nails broken by constantly having to grab for support on a deck stacked with buckets and barrels on that floating barn which was our boat. Her eyes, hazel and beautifully flecked with green and yellow, reflected a state of mind that was a mixture of boredom, fatigue, disgust, and an underlying rage at not being able to voice her fury over this voyage she had set out upon with such high literary rejoicing. Because the evening of our departure—I recalled it now—she had dragged out the familiar "desire for evasion," ascribing to the great word "adventure" all the implications of invitation to the unknown, flight from the familiar, chance meetings, the vision of the Incredible

Floridas of Rimbaud. Up to now, as far as she was concerned—for she remained indifferent to the emotions that afforded me daily delight, bringing back sensations that had been buried since childhood—the word "adventure" had meant being shut up in a hotel in the city, landscapes of monotonous and repetitious grandeur, seeing one thing after another without a thrill of any sort, the accumulated fatigue of nights without lamps to read by, and of sleep, when it finally came, interrupted by the rooster's crow.

Now, hugging her knees, indifferent to what her tumbled skirt might reveal, she rocked herself gently on the cot, sipping brandy from a tin pitcher. She talked of the pyramids of Mexico and the Incan fortresses—which she knew only from photographs—of the stairways of Monte Albán, and the adobe villages of the Hopis, lamenting the fact that in this country the Indians had erected no such wonders. Then, employing the language of "those in the know," categorical, interlarded with the technical jargon of which our generation is so enamored—and to which I give the name of "the economist tone"—she began to draw up an indictment of the way the people here live, their prejudices, their superstitions, the backwardness of their agriculture, the shortcomings of their mining, which, naturally, brought her to the surplus value and the exploitation of man by man.

Just to be contrary, I said that the thing that impressed me most on this trip was the discovery that there were still great areas of the earth where people were immune to the ills of the day, and that here, even though many people were contented with a thatched roof, a water jug, a clay griddle, a hammock, and a guitar, a certain animism lived on in them, an awareness of ancient traditions, a living memory of certain myths which indicated the presence of a culture more estimable and valid, perhaps, than that which we had left behind. It was of greater value for a people to preserve the memory of the *Chanson de Roland* than to have hot and cold running water. I was glad to know that there were still men unwilling to trade their souls for a gadget which by eliminating the washwoman did away with her song, thus wiping out ages of folklore at one fell swoop.

Pretending that she had not heard me, or that what I was saying was devoid of all interest, Mouche stated that there was nothing worth seeing or studying here; that this country lacked history or character; and, giving her opinion the quality of a verdict, she spoke of leaving the next day with the dawn, inasmuch as our boat, sailing with the current this time, could make the return trip in a little better than one day.

But now her wishes were a matter of complete indifference to me. And as this was something new in me, when I brusquely told her that I intended to fulfill my obligations to the university, traveling to the place where I could find the instruments I had been sent in search of, she suddenly flew into a rage, calling me a bourgeois. This insult—well I knew—was a hang-over from the days in which many women of her background had proclaimed themselves revolutionaries for the sake of militating in ranks joined by a number of interesting intellectuals, and giving themselves up to sexual indulgences under cover of philosophical and social ideas after having done the same in the name of the æsthetic ideas of certain literary coteries. With her eye always on the main chance, over and above all her pleasures and petty passions, Mouche was my idea of the archetypal bourgeoise. Nevertheless, she applied "bourgeois" as the final insult to anyone who opposed to her criterion anything that smacked of duty or principles, who refused to go along with certain physical indulgences or was concerned with religious problems or a world of order. As my determination to do the right thing by the Curator and therefore by my conscience was a stumbling-block to her plans, such an objective became *ipso facto* bourgeois.

She got up from the bed, her disheveled hair hanging over her face, and lifted her little fists to my temples in a gesture of fury new to me. She screamed that she wanted to get to Los Altos as quickly as she could, that she needed the mountain coolness to get back her strength, that that was where we were going to spend the rest of my vacation. The name of Los Altos filled me with a sudden rage, recalling the suspicious attentions the Canadian painter had lavished on Mouche. And though I had always refrained from using rough words in my arguments with her, that night, finding pleasure in how ugly she looked by the light of the kerosene lamp, I felt a need to hurt her, to insult her, to rid myself of all the old grudges that had accumulated within me. As a start, I began to insult the painter, calling her a name that affected Mouche as though I had stuck a red-hot pin into her. She took a step back and threw the pitcher of brandy at my head, missing me by a razor's edge.

Frightened at what she had done, she turned to me with pleading hands; but my words, now justified by her violence, had broken from their moorings. I screamed that I had stopped loving her, that the sight of her was unbearable, that even her body revolted me.

The impression that this strange voice—which astonished even me—made on her was so frightening that she darted into the courtyard, as though fearing that physical violence would follow the words. But, forgetting about the mud, she slipped and fell into the pool filled with turtles. As she felt the wet shells beginning to heave under her like armored soldiers fallen into a quagmire, she let out a scream of terror which aroused the dogs. To the sound of a universal concert of barking, I brought Mouche back into the room, stripped off her clothes, which reeked of rotten mud, and wiped her from her head to her feet with a coarse, torn cloth. I made her swallow a big drink of brandy, pulled the bedclothes around her, and went out of the room without paying any attention to her calls and sobbing. I wanted, I needed, to get her out of my mind for a few hours.

In a near-by tavern I found the Greek drinking Homerically in the company of a little man with bushy eyebrows whom he introduced as the Adelantado, telling me that the yellow dog beside him, which was lapping beer from a cup, was a very unusual animal answering to the name Gavilán. The miner rejoiced at the workings of fate which had so effortlessly brought me into contact with a person rarely seen in Puerto Anunciación. Despite the vast area of the jungle—he explained to me—embracing mountains, abysses, treasures, nomad peoples, the remains of lost civilizations, it was, nevertheless, a world compact, complete, which fed its fauna and its men, shaped its own clouds, assembled its meteors, brought on its rains. A hidden nation, a map in code, a vast vegetable kingdom with few entrances. "Sort of like Noah's ark, where all the animals of the earth could fit, but with only one small door," the little man added.

To penetrate this world, the Adelantado had had to find the keys to its secret entrances: he alone knew of a pass between two trees, the only one within a circumference of fifty leagues, leading to a narrow stairway of stones by which it was possible to descend to the vast mystery of immense telluric baroques. He alone knew of the withe footbridge under the cascade, the postern gate of brush, the entrance to the cave of the prehistoric stone carvings, the hidden trail that led to practicable passes. He could read the code of broken twigs, incisions on treetrunks, the branch not fallen but placed. He would disappear for months, and when least expected would emerge with his trophies through an opening in the vegetable wall. Sometimes it was

a load of butterflies, or lizard skins, sacks filled with heron
feathers, live birds that uttered strange whistles, or pieces
of anthropomorphic pottery, poetic household articles,
rare basketwork that might take the fancy of some for-
eigner. Once he had reappeared after a long absence followed by twenty Indians carrying orchids. The dog Gavilán owed his name to his ability to catch birds without
disturbing one feather, bringing them to his master to see if
they were of any value for their joint enterprise.

While the Adelantado left us to go into the street to
greet the Tuna-Fisher, who was out on an errand with several of his forty-two natural children, the Greek informed
me in a low voice that it was generally believed that this
amazing personage, in the course of his wanderings, had
come upon a fabulous lode of gold whose location he naturally kept secret. Nobody could explain why, when he appeared with bearers, they returned at once with more
cargo than the needs of a few men justified, including an
occasional breeding boar, cloth, combs, sugar, and other
articles that an explorer of remote routes could hardly
need. He turned aside all questions on the matter and
quickly herded his Indians back into the woods without
letting them linger around the settlement. It was said that
he was probably working the lode with the help of out-
laws or with prisoners of war he bought from some tribe,
or that he had made himself king of a group of Negroes
who had run away to the forest three hundred years before and who, some said, lived in a stockaded settlement
in which drums could be heard booming day and night.

When he saw the Adelantado coming back, the Greek,
quickly changing the subject, began to talk of the purpose
of my trip. Accustomed to dealing with people moved by
unusual objectives, among them a strange botanist by the
name of Montsalvatje, whom he praised highly, the Adelantado told me that I could find the instruments I was

looking for in the first villages of a tribe that lived three days off by river on the banks of a channel called El Pintado because of the constantly changing color of its muddy waters. When I questioned him about certain primitive rites, he listed all the objects to make music he could recall, imitating, with brandy-stimulated onomatopoeia and the gestures of their players, various hollowed trunk drums, bone flutes, antler and skull horns, funerary roaring jars, and witch-doctor rattles.

We were deep in this when Fray Pedro de Henestrosa appeared to tell us that Rosario's father had just died. Somewhat shocked by the suddenness of the news, and at the same time eager to see the girl, of whom I had heard nothing since we arrived, I set out for the corner where the dead man had lived, along streets down which muddy brooks ran, in the company of the Greek, the friar, and the Adelantado, followed by Gavilán, who never missed a wake when he was in town. There still lingered on my tongue the hazelnut flavor of the agave brandy I had drunk with such relish in the tavern, whose flowery signboard displayed such a delightfully absurd name: *Memories of the Future*.

(Friday night)

XIV/ Death was still at work in that house with its eight grilled windows. It was everywhere, diligent, looking after all the details, making the necessary arrangements, placing the mourners, lighting the candles, taking pains to see that the whole town should find place in the vast rooms with deep window seats and broad doorways, the better to contemplate its work. On a platform covered with old, mildewed velvets stood the coffin, still ringing with hammer blows, studded with heavy, silver-headed nails, just come from the Carpenter, who never erred in his measurements of a corpse, for his photographic memory preserved the dimensions of all the town's living inhabitants. Out of the night came flowers that were over-fragant, flowers of patios, window-boxes, gardens wrested from the jungle—tuberoses and thick-petaled jasmine, wood lilies, waxy magnolias—tied in tight bunches with ribbons that yesterday had graced a dance. In the hall, in the sitting-room, the men stood in solemn conversation while the women prayed antiphonally in the bedrooms, with the obsessive repetition by all of *Hail, Mary, full of grace! the Lord is with thee; blessed art thou among women*. The sound arose from dark corners among images of saints and rosaries hanging from wall brackets, swelling and receding with the regular rhythm of waves lapping the pebbles of a reef. All the mirrors, in whose depths the dead man had lived, were veiled with crepe and cloth.

Various notables—the Rapids-Shooter, the Mayor and Schoolteacher, the Tuna-Fisher, the Tanner—had just filed past the corpse, first dropping their cigarette butts into their hats. At this moment a skinny girl in black let out a shrill scream and fell to the floor as though in a fit. She was carried out of the room. Now Rosario approached the bier. In deep mourning, her gleaming hair combed tight to her head, her lips pale, she seemed to me breathtakingly beautiful. She looked all around her with eyes hollow with weeping, and then suddenly, as though she had received a mortal wound, raised her clenched hands to her mouth and let out a long, inhuman howl as of an arrow-pierced animal, a woman in labor, one possessed, and flung herself upon the coffin. In a hoarse voice broken with sobs, she cried that she was going to rend her garments, tear out her eyes, that she no longer wished to live, that she was going to throw herself into the grave and let them cover her with earth. When they tried to pull her away, she resisted furiously, threatening in mysterious, bloodcurdling words, which seemed those of prophecy or second sight, those who attempted to loosen her fingers from the black velvet. Her throat lacerated by sobs, she spoke of great misfortunes, of the end of the world, the Last Judgment, of plagues and expiations.

They finally got her out of the room half-fainting, her legs limp, her hair disheveled. Her black stockings, which had been torn in her attack of nerves, her recently polished shoes with run-down heels, the toes dragging along the floor, caused me intense suffering. But now another of the sisters was clasping the coffin. Appalled at the violence of their grief, I suddenly thought of the ancient tragedy. In these large families, where each one keeps his mourning garb folded away in the drawer, death is a common occurrence. Mothers who bear many children are familiar with its presence. But these women who shared the customary duties involved in the death agony, who from childhood had helped lay out the dead, cover mirrors, say the appropriate prayers, were protesting against death in keeping with a rite that had come down from remote times. For all this was, primarily, a kind of desperate, defiant, almost magic protest at the presence of Death in the house.

Over the corpse these peasant women were playing the role of a Greek chorus, their hair falling like thick veils over the menacing faces of daughters of kings, keening Trojan women cast like dogs out of their burning palaces. The insistence in this despair, the admirable dramatic sense with which the nine sisters—for they were nine—appeared one after the other in the right and left doors, preparing the entrance of the Mother, who was Hecuba, cursing their bereavement, lamenting the ruin of a house, crying that there was no God, made me suspect that there was something of the theater about all this. A relative standing near me observed admiringly that it was a pleasure to see how these women mourned their dead. Yet at the same time I felt myself caught up, dragged along, as though what was taking place had awakened in me obscure memories of funeral rites that had been performed by men who had been my forerunners in the kingdom of this world. From a crevice of my memory there emerged the lines of Shelley, which seemed to utter themselves, as though entwined in their own meaning:

> . . . *How canst thou hear*
> *Who knowest not the language of the dead?*

The men of the cities where I had lived all my life were unaware of the meaning of these words, for they had forgotten the language of those able to talk to the dead. The language of those who know the final horror of being left alone and divine the anguish of those who beg not to be abandoned in this unknown bourne. When they screamed that they would throw themselves into their father's grave, the nine sisters were carrying out one of the noblest forms of a millenary rite, in observance of which the dead were given gifts and promises impossible of fulfillment, to mitigate their loneliness. Coins were put in their mouths; figures of slaves, women, and musicians were laid about them; they were provided with passwords, credentials, safe conducts for the Ferrymen and Lords of the Other Shore whose fees and requirements were not even known.

I recalled, at the same time, what a sordid, petty thing death had become for the men of my Shore—my own people—big business, bronzes, pomp, prayers that all failed to conceal, beneath the funeral wreaths and the beds of ice, the fact that it was nothing but a business of black-gloved employees, professional solemnity, articles of common use, and hands reaching across the corpse for payment. Some might smile at the tragedy being performed here. But in it one could see the earliest rites of mankind.

I was thinking this when the Diamond-Hunter came up

to me with a meaningful look, saying that I ought to go and find Rosario, who was alone in the kitchen making coffee for the women. The ironic tone of his words annoyed me, and I told him that it seemed an inopportune moment to intrude on her grief. "You go in there and don't be afraid," he said as though reciting a lesson. "It's boldness that sees a man through, even if he comes from different country."

I was on the point of telling him that I did not need such advice, when he added, in a declamatory voice: "As you go into the hall you will see first the queen, whose name is Arete and who comes from the same line as King Alcinoüs." And in the face of my stupefaction at words that had taken me by surprise, he fixed his birdlike eyes on me, said, laughing: "Homer Odysseus," and shoved me toward the kitchen.

There, among water jars standing in their rack, clay pots, and wood fire, Rosario was busily pouring boiling water through a flannel cone stained by years of coffee grounds. The violence of her outburst seemed to have relieved her grief. In a quiet voice she explained to me that the Fourteen Auxiliary Saints had arrived too late to save her father. She then described his illness to me after the manner of a legend, revealing a mythological concept of human physiology. It had all begun with a quarrel with a friend, aggravated by too much sun as he crossed a river, which had brought on a rise of humors to the brain, congested by a draft, which had left half his body without blood, thus bringing on an inflammation of the loins and privates which, after forty days of fever, had turned into a hardening of the walls of the heart.

While Rosario was talking, I moved closer to her, attracted by a kind of warmth that emanated from her body and reached my skin through our clothing. She was sitting beside a huge tub on the floor, her elbows resting on the rim in such a way that the bulge of the vessel arched her waist toward me. The hearth fire shone in her face, bringing out strange lights in her somber eyes. It filled me with shame to feel that I desired her with a longing I had not known since adolescence. I do not know whether that abominable impulse which has given rise to so many fables was at work in me, which makes us desire the living flesh in the presence of the flesh that will never live again. The look with which I divested her of her mourning must have been so hungry that Rosario pushed the tub between us, turning it with a slow movement, like a person clinging to the curb of a well, and rested her elbows on the edge again, but across from me, looking at me from the other shore of a black pool of water, which gave an echo of the nave of a cathedral to our voices.

At times she left me alone, went to the room where the wake was being held, and then, drying her tears, returned to where I was awaiting her with the impatience of a lover. We spoke very little. With a passivity that had something of surrender about it, she let me watch her across the water of the tub.

The clocks began to strike the dawn hour, but it did not dawn. In surprise we all went out to the street, to the patio. In the quarter where the sun should have appeared the sky was covered by a strange reddish cloud, like smoke, like hot ashes, like a dark pollen that had arisen swiftly, stretching from one horizon to the other. When the cloud moved overhead, it began to rain butterflies on the roofs, the water jars, our shoulders. They were little butterflies, deep amaranth in color, striped in violet, which had come together by myriads in some unknown spot behind the immense jungle, frightened, perhaps, driven away, after multiplying frenziedly, by some cataclysm, some awful occurrence, without witnesses or record. The Adelantado told me that these swarms of butterflies were nothing new in the region, and that when they took place the sun was almost blotted out for the whole day. The burial of the father would have to be carried out by candlelight in a day that was night, reddened by wings. In this corner of the world, great migrations were still a fact, like those described by chroniclers of the Dark Ages when the Danube turned black with rats or packs of wolves invaded the market-places of the cities. The week before, he told me, a huge jaguar had been killed in the church portico.

(Saturday, June 16)

XV/ Overgrown by underbrush that had scaled its walls, the cemetery where we buried Rosario's father was a kind of prolongation and dependency of the church, sep-arated from it only by a rude gate and a flagged walk like the shaft of a thick cross with short arms, on whose gray stones have been carved the emblems of the Passion. The church was low, with thick walls, its volume of stone ap-parent in the depth of the niches and the weight of the buttresses, which looked more like abutments of a fortress. Its low, rough arches, the roof of wood with beams rest-ing on rough-hewn corbels, recalled primitive Roman-esque churches. Inside, at midmorning, darkness prevailed, reddened by the flight of butterflies, which still continued between earth and sun. Thus, surrounded by votive can-dles and tapers, the old saints became more like figures on a reredos, in a religious print, each of them plying his tra-ditional trade, so that the whole church resembled a work-shop: St. Isidore with a spade in his hand so that he can dig his pedestal covered with real grass and cornstalks; Peter with a huge key-ring on which a new key is hung every day; George lancing the dragon with such fury that it seems a goad rather than a weapon that he brandishes against the enemy; Christopher holding fast to a palm tree, such a giant that the Christ Child barely reaches from his shoulder to his ear; Lazarus, on whose dogs real hairs have been pasted to make them seem more lifelike as they lick his wounds.

Rich in the powers attributed to them, overwhelmed by demands paid in kind by votive offerings, carried in procession at any hour, these saints took on, in the daily life of the village, a quality of divine officials, of wholesale intermediaries, of celestial bureaucrats always on call in a kind of Ministry of Requests and Complaints. Every day they received gifts and candles that were a kind of rogation for the forgiveness of some one of the major sins. They were entreated; problems of rheumatic attacks, hailstorms, strayed animals were submitted to them. Gamblers invoked them when making a discard; prostitutes lit a candle to them the days when business was good. This, which the Adelantado smilingly recounted, reconciled me to a divine world which, with the fading of the golden legends in metal chapels, the mannered posturings of modern stained-glass windows, had lost all meaning in the cities I came from. Before the black wood Christ, who seemed to be bleeding to death over the high altar, I discovered the atmosphere of a miracle play, of a mystery, of a stirring hagiology that would have impressed me profoundly at one time in an ancient chapel of Byzantine construction, before images of martyrs with scimitars cleaving their skulls from ear to ear, of mailed bishops whose horses' bloody hoofs trampled pagan heads.

At another time I would have lingered in the rustic church, but the darkness of the butterflies which enveloped us was beginning to have the enervating effect on me of an eclipse that had lasted longer than could be endured. This and the fatigue of the night led me back to the inn, where Mouche, thinking it was still night, slept on, her arms clasped around a pillow. When I awoke several hours later, she was not in the room, and the sun had reappeared after the great brown exodus. Happy at having avoided a possible quarrel, I set out for Rosario's house with the vehement hope that she might be up.

Everything there had resumed its normal rhythm. The women, dressed in mourning, went placidly about their duties, following the old custom of going on with life after the normal accident of death. In the patio, full of sleeping dogs, the Adelantado was arranging with Fray Pedro an immediate trip to the jungle. At this point Mouche showed up, followed by the Greek. Her determination to return, so furiously voiced the night before, seemed forgotten. On the contrary, her expression was one of malicious, defiant satisfaction, which Rosario, who was sewing mourning clothes, noticed at the same time I did. Mouche felt called upon to explain that she had met Yannes at the wharf alongside the sailing canoe of a group of rubber-hunters getting ready to sail up the river, avoiding the rapids of Piedras Negras by a detour through a narrow channel navigable at this season. She had asked the miner to take her to see this granite barrier, which had halted all major navigation since the first discoverers had wept with rage in the face of its terrifying reality of boiling whirlpools, engulfing waves, treetrunks jammed in roaring crevasses.

She was beginning to exploit the literary possibilities of the mighty spectacle, and was showing the exotic flowers, a species of wild lily, which she said she had picked alongside the thundering gorge, when the Adelantado, who never paid any attention to anything a woman said, cut short her speech—which he did not understand, anyway —with a brusque gesture. He was of the opinion that we ought to take advantage of the rubber-gatherers' departure and thus cover with less effort a good part of the distance we had to row. Yannes assured us that we could reach his brothers' diamond mine that same night. Contrary to all my expectations, Mouche, at the sound of the words "diamond mine"—probably dazzled by the vision of a cave glittering with gems—gave her enthusiastic approval. She threw her arms around Rosario, begging her to come with us on this easy stage of our trip. Tomorrow we could all rest at the diamond mine. She could wait for us there while we went on with our journey. What Mouche wanted, it seemed to me, was to find out, without risking more than a short trip, what difficulties were in store for us, and to make sure of company back to Puerto Anunciación in case she decided to give up the venture.

Whatever the reason, I was delighted at the thought of Rosario coming with us. I looked at her and met her eyes looking up from the workbasket as though to read my wishes. When she saw my acquiescence, she immediately went to her sisters, whose outcry could be heard in the rooms and at the washtubs protesting that the plan was crazy. Paying no attention to them, she was soon back with her bundle of clothing and a coarse shawl. While Mouche walked ahead of us to the inn, Rosario whispered to me that the flowers my friend had shown us did not grow among the rocks of Piedras Negras, but on a tree-covered island, the site of an abandoned mission, which she pointed out with her hand. I was about to ask for further explanations, but from that moment on she took care not to be alone with me until we were settled in the rubber-gatherers' boat.

After we had poled through the channel, the boat advanced upstream, hugging the bank to avoid the powerful impact of the current. The three-cornered sail, bellying from the mast like that of an ancient galley, reflected the western sun. The landscape in this antechamber of the jungle was at once solemn and somber. On the left bank rose black slate hills streaked with moisture, depressingly sad. Along their slopes lay blocks of granite in the shape of lizards, tapirs, petrified animals. A three-pronged mound emerged from the stillness of a swamp like a barbarous cenotaph, terminating in an oval formation that resembled a gigantic frog about to spring. At intervals basalt rubble-heaps were visible, rectangular monoliths fallen among sparse, scattered shrubs which seemed the ruins of archaic temples, menhir, cromlech, the remains of a forgotten necropolis where all was silence and repose. It was as though some strange civilization of people different from those we know had flourished there, leaving, as they were swallowed up in the night of ages, the vestiges of an architecture designed for unknown purposes.

A blind geometry had taken a hand in the scattering of these perpendicular or horizontal stones, which descended in series toward the river, rectangular series, series like congealed pourings of metal, combinations of both joined by flagged paths set at intervals with broken obelisks. In the middle of the stream islands were like piles of haphazard stones, handfuls of unimaginable pebbles tossed here and there by some fantastic leveler of mountains. And each of these islands revived in me the impact of a fixed idea that had its origin in a strange remark of Rosario's. I inquired somewhat vaguely about the island where the abandoned mission stood.

"It is St. Prisca," Fray Pedro said, blushing a little. "It should be called St. Priapus," chortled the Adelantado to the rubber-gatherers' loud guffaws. From this I learned that for years the tumble-down walls of the old Franciscan mission had been the refuge of those couples who found no place to take their pleasure in the town. It had been the scene of so many fornications that—according to the helmsman—one whiff of the smell of dampness, moss, wild lilies that hung over it was enough to inflame the most austere man, even a Capuchin friar.

I went up to the prow alongside Rosario, who seemed to be reading the story of Genevieve of Brabant. Mouche, who was stretched out on a sack of tonka beans on the deck, and who had not heard the talk, was completely unaware of the fact that something very serious had occurred as far as our life together was concerned. I was not even angry, nor did I feel any desire—at that moment, at least—to punish her for what had happened. On the contrary, in that twilight filled with the music of frogs in the bulrushes, humming with the buzz of the insects that relieved the daytime detail, I felt buoyant, relieved, released by the knowledge of her infamy, like a man laying down a burden borne too long.

On the bank the flowers of a magnolia stood out against the foliage. I wondered where my wife's path was leading her day by day. But her figure was not entirely clear in my memory, it was blurred, faded. The rocking motion of the ship reminded me of the basket that had carried me on fabulous voyages in my childhood. Rosario's arm, close to mine, emanated a warmth that my arm welcomed with a strange and pleasurable prickling.

(*Saturday night*)

XVI/ In the way he builds his house man reveals his lineage. The house of the Greeks was built of the same materials the Indians use for their cabins, and this fiber, this palm frond, this mud and wattle, have established their own norms, based on their coefficient of resistance, as has happened in every type of architecture the world has known. But a slighter pitch to the eaves and an increase in the width of the crossbeams have sufficed to give the gable end the dignity of a façade and to create the architrave. Treetrunks wider at the base than at the top were selected for pilasters in an instinctive desire to imitate the

Doric column. The rocky landscape contributed, too, to this unexpected Hellenic atmosphere. As for Yannes's three brothers, whom I now met, they were replicas, at different ages, of the profile to be found on the bas-reliefs of triumphal arches.

I was told that in a near-by hut, where the goats are penned up for the night, Doctor Montsalvatje, about whom the Adelantado had already told me, was putting in order and completing his collection of rare plants. He came to greet us, gesticulating, talking in a throaty voice, this scientist-adventurer, collector of curare, peyotl, and all the herbal poisons and narcotics of still unknown properties he was studying and experimenting with. Without showing more than a perfunctory interest in who we were, the herbalist overwhelmed us with Latin terminologies designed for fungi never before seen, crushing an example of one of them between his fingers while explaining why he believed the name he had hit upon was suitable. All of a sudden he realized that we were not botanists, and he poked fun at himself, "The Lord of Poisons," and asked news of the world from which we came.

I tried to satisfy his curiosity, but it was apparent from the indifference of those listening that my information interested nobody. What Doctor Montsalvatje really wanted to know was things having to do with the river. He asked Fray Pedro for a quinine tablet. He planned to go down to Puerto Anunciación with his collections of plants on Monday and to return as quickly as possible, for he had discovered a hitherto unknown mushroom whose mere smell induced visual hallucinations and a cactus whose proximity caused certain metals to rust. The Greeks touched their temples, indicating that the doctor had a screw loose. The Adelantado was tickled by the strange sonority he gave to certain native words. The rubber-gatherers, on the contrary, were convinced that he was a great doctor, and talked of how he had relieved an abscess with the point of a nicked knife. Rosario was already acquainted with him, and his verbal incontinence seemed to her natural in a person who rarely had an opportunity to talk. Mouche, who had nicknamed him "Lord Macbeth," and who talked to him in French, finally got bored with his botanical lore and asked Yannes to hang her hammock inside the house.

Fray Pedro took me aside and explained that the herbalist was not really crazy, but that his imagination ran away with him and that in his long solitudes in the jungle he had worked out a lineage of alchemists and heretics which made him the direct descendant of Raymond Lull—whom he stubbornly called Ramon Llull—basing this on the Learned Doctor's obsession with the tree. But the uproar of the arrival and introductions died down as the miners came forward with their wooden trays of goat cheese, the radishes and tomatoes of their tiny garden, the cassava bread, salt, and brandy—perhaps subconsciously recalling the age-old ritual of salt, bread, and wine. And we sat around the campfire, in the ancestral rite of keeping the fire alive at night. Some of us were leaning on our elbows, others sat with chin in hand, the Capuchin enveloped in his habit, the women reclining on a blanket, Gavilán panting alongside Polyphemus, the one-eyed dog of the Greeks, and all watching the flames that spurted from the damp branches, flickering yellow, bursting into blue in a dry twig, while, underneath, the back logs turned to embers. The great upright stones of the slaty incline where we found ourselves took on a strange air of stellæ, milestones, monoliths, forming a stairway whose top steps were lost in the fog.

It had been a hard day, yet nobody wanted to go to bed. We sat there as though hypnotized by the fire, a little drunk with its heat, each lost in himself, thinking without thinking, sharing an animal sensation of well-being, of peace. Soon over the stone-strewn horizon there appeared a chill light, and the moon rose behind a thick, liana-roped tree that began to sing with the voice of all its crickets. Overhead two cawing white birds passed, swooping earthward. The dying fire was mended and the talk began to flow.

One of the Greeks complained that the mine seemed worked out. But Montsalvatje shrugged his shoulders, stating that farther ahead, toward the Great Plateaus, there were diamonds in all the riverbeds. In my imagination, heated by his words, the Herbalist, with his heavy-framed glasses, his sunburned bald head, his thick freckled hands, whose fleshy fingers looked a little like starfish, took on the air of a spirit of the earth, a gnome watching over the caves. He spoke of gold, and all immediately fell silent, because men like to talk of treasure. The Narrator— seated beside the fire, his traditional place—had studied in far-off libraries all there was to be known about the gold of this world. And gradually there emerged, eerie in the moonlight, the mirage of El Dorado.

Fray Pedro smiled scornfully. The Adelantado listened, his face a sly mask, as he threw twigs on the fire. To the plant-collector a myth was always the reflection of a reality. Where men sought the city of Manoa up and down the extent of its vast, phantasmagorical province, there were diamonds in the mud of the banks and gold in the riverbeds. "Alluvial wash," Yannes objected. "That just proves," Montsalvatje went on, "that there is a main lode we know nothing about, a telluric alchemist's laboratory, somewhere in this chain of mountains, with its cascades, which is the least explored area of the planet, on whose threshold we stand. There is what Sir Walter Raleigh called the 'mother lode,' which feeds the endless flow of gravel washed down by hundreds of rivers."

The mention of *"Sergualterale,"* as the Spaniards called him, led the Herbalist to cite the testimony of fabulous adventurers, who emerged from the shadows at the sound of their names to warm their mail and their cotton-wadded coats at the flames of our fire. Here came Federmann, Belalcázar, Espira, Orellana, followed by their chaplains, their drummers and fifers, the necromantic company of algebraists, herbalists, and keepers of the dead. Fair-haired Germans with curling beards, Spaniards from Extremadura, gaunt and goat-bearded, wrapped in the oriflamme of their standards, mounted on horses which, like those of Gonzalo Pizarro, become shod with solid gold the moment their hoofs touch the elusive confines of El Dorado. And, above all, Philip von Hutten, Urre, as the Spaniards called him, who, one never-to-be-forgotten afternoon, looked down in wonder on the great city of Manoa with its magic battlements, silent with amazement in the midst of his men. The news ran like wildfire, and for a century a grim struggle went on with the jungle, expeditions that ended in tragic failure, wandering in circles, eating saddle leather, drinking the blood of their horses, dying the daily death of St. Sebastian shot through by arrows. This was the story of the known attempts, for the chronicles fail to mention the names of those small groups who had burned their wings in the flame of the myth and left their skeletons in armor at the foot of some unscalable wall of rock.

Standing in the shadows beyond the flames, the Adelantado held out to the light of the fire an ax that had attracted my attention that afternoon by reason of its strange shape. It was the work of a Castilian anvil, with an olive wood shaft that had turned black without separating from the metal. On the handle some rustic soldier had cut a date with knife-point, and the date was of the days of the conquistadors. While the weapon passed from hand to hand, and we eyed it, silent with a mysterious emotion, the Adelantado told us how he had come upon it in the heart of the jungle, in a heap of human bones, beside a welter of helmets, swords, arquebuses, gripped in the roots of a tree that had lifted a halberd to exactly the height at which the absent hands would have held it.

The chill of the ax-blade brought the mystery to the tips of our fingers. And we let ourselves succumb to the world of wonder, eager for still greater portents. There arose beside the hearth, conjured up by Montsalvatje, the medicine men who healed wounds with the magic incantation of Bogotá, the Amazon Queen, Cicañocohora, the amphibious men who slept at night in the bottoms of the lakes, and those whose sole nourishment was the scent of flowers. We accepted the Carbuncle Dogs that bear a glittering jewel between their eyes, the Hydra that Federmann's men had seen, the bezoar stone, of miraculous properties, found in the entrails of deer, the Tatunachas, whose ears can cover as many as five persons, or those other savages with ostrich claws for feet—according to the unassailable account of a saintly abbot. For two centuries the blind pilgrims along the route to Santiago had sung the wonders of an American Harpy, to be seen in Constantinople, where it had died raging and roaring. . . .

Fray Pedro de Henestrosa felt himself in duty bound to attribute such old wives' tales to the work of the Devil—whereas their source was some friar's solemn relation—and to the human weakness for spreading lies—whereas they were stories told by soldiers. But Montsalvatje assumed the role of Miracles' Advocate, stating that the reality of the Kingdom of Manoa had been accepted by missionaries who set out in search of it during the age of Enlightenment. Seventy years earlier, in a scientific report, a noted geographer had claimed to have caught a glimpse, in the vicinity of the Great Plateaus, of something resembling the fantastic city Urre had gazed upon one day. The Amazon women really existed: they were the women of the men slaughtered by the Caribs on their mysterious migration to the Kingdom of Corn. Out of the jungle of the Mayas there had emerged stairways, boat landings, monuments, temples decorated with unbelievable paintings representing the rites of the fish-priests, the shrimp-priests.

Huge heads suddenly came to light under fallen trees, looking at their discoverers with closed eyes more terrifying, because of their inner contemplation of Death, than if the pupils had been visible. In other places there were long facing Avenues of the Gods, side by side, whose names would remain forever unknown, overthrown gods, dead gods, who for centuries and centuries had been the images of an immortality denied to man. On the shores of the Pacific gigantic designs had been discovered, so huge that people had walked over them without being aware of what they were treading upon, drawn on such a scale as though intended to be visible from another planet by peoples who had kept their records with knotted strings, and had punished with the maximum penalty any attempt to invent an alphabet. Every day new carvings turned up in the jungle; paintings of the feathered serpent were to be found on remote rock walls, and nobody had yet deciphered the thousands of petroglyphs that spoke a language of animal forms, astral symbols, and mysterious designs along the banks of the Great Rivers.

Standing beside the hearth, Doctor Montsalvatje pointed to the distant highlands standing dark blue along the route the moon was traveling. "Nobody knows what lies behind those Forms," he said in a tone that brought back to us an emotion forgotten since childhood.

We all felt an impulse to rise, set out, and arrive before the dawn at the gateway of enchantment. Again the waters of Lake Parima gleamed. Once more the towers of Manoa arose. The possibility that they might exist came alive anew, inasmuch as the myth persisted in the imagination of all those who lived in the vicinity of the jungle—that is to say, of The Unknown. And I could not help thinking that the Adelantado, the Greek miners, the two rubber-gatherers, and all those who each year made their way into the heart of its darkness after the rains, were, in fact, seeking El Dorado, like those who first followed the lure of its name. The doctor uncorked a glass bottle filled with dark stones that gleamed yellow in our hands by the light of the fire. We were touching gold. We raised them to our eyes, the better to see it. We weighed them in our hand with the gestures of an alchemist. Mouche touched one with her tongue to see if it had any taste. And when the ore was put back into the bottle, it seemed that some warmth had departed from the fire and that the night had turned colder. Bullfrogs were bellowing in the river. Suddenly, Fray Pedro smote the ground with his staff and it became Moses' rod, as he raised on it the snake that he had just killed.

(Sunday, June 17)

XVII/ On my way back from the mine I chortled to myself as I thought of the shock in store for Mouche when she saw that the marvelous cave, aglitter with precious stones, the treasure-trove of Agamemnon which she undoubtedly expected it to be, was a riverbed, dug, furrowed, churned up, a mudhole in which shovels had probed, up and down, crosswise, returning twenty times to the spot of their first strike in the hope of having missed, by some deflection of the hand, by a margin of millimeters, the fabled Stone. The youngest of the diamond-diggers talked to me on the way of the hardships of the work, of the daily disappointments, and of the strange fatality that always makes the finder of one big stone return, poor and in debt, to the spot of his discovery. Hope revives each time a fine diamond emerges from the earth, and its water, which can be divined before cutting, blots out the view of jungle and mountains, firing the pulse of those who scrape the coating of mud from their bodies after a fruitless day.

I inquired about the women, and was told that they were bathing in a near-by stream whose pools concealed no venomous animals. Nevertheless, I heard shouts, shouts which, as they came nearer, brought me out of the cabin, startled by the violence of tone and the confusion of the cries.

My first thought was that someone had gone to spy out their nakedness from the bank or had made some insulting proposition. It was Mouche who appeared, her clothes dripping, calling for help, as though fleeing from some terror. Before I could take a step, I saw Rosario, partly covered by a coarse slip, rush over to my friend, throw her to the ground, and begin to beat her savagely with a stick. With her hair loose over her shoulders, vomiting insults, kicking her, beating her with the stick and her other hand, she was the image of such appalling ferocity that we all ran to hold her. She went on struggling and kicking with a fury that expressed itself in hoarse growls, unintelligible words. When I helped Mouche to her feet, she could hardly stand. Two of her teeth were broken, and blood was gushing from her nose. She was a mass of scratches and bruises.

Doctor Montsalvatje led her away to his hut to treat her. Meanwhile we surrounded Rosario, trying to find out what had happened. But now an obstinate silence had come over her, and she refused to say a word. Sitting on a stone, her head hanging, she repeated with exasperating stubbornness the gesture of refusal, which tossed her black hair from side to side over her face, still set in fury. I went to the hut. Mouche lay moaning in the Herbalist's hammock. To my questions she replied that she knew no reason for the attack, that Rosario seemed to have gone crazy, and with this she burst into tears, saying she wanted to go back right away, that she could not stand any more, that the trip was killing her, that she felt as though she was losing her mind.

Only a short time before, such an entreaty, so unusual in her, would have made me do anything she wanted. But now the sight of her body shaken by sobs of despair that seemed real left me completely unmoved, armored by an inflexibility that surprised and satisfied me, as though I were admiring somebody else's strength of will. I would never have believed that, after such long association, I could become completely indifferent to Mouche. When the love I may have felt for her had died down—and I now had doubts about the genuineness of this feeling—the bond of a kindly friendship, at least, might have lived on. But the shifts, the changes, the recapture of buried emotions that had been taking place in me during these two weeks, added to what I had discovered the evening before, made me impervious to her appeals.

Leaving her bewailing her plight, I returned to the house of the Greeks, where Rosario, calmer now, lay curled up in a hammock, her arms over her face. A kind of uneasiness furrowed the brows of the men, though their thoughts seemed elsewhere. The Greeks were too nervous about the seasoning of a fish stew that bubbled in a big clay pot, arguing over the amount of oil, garlic, pepper, all of which sounded off key. The rubber-gatherers were silently mending their sandals. The Adelantado was bathing Gavilán, who had been playing with a rotting carcass, and the dog, infuriated by the jars of water being poured over him, bared his teeth to all who came near. Fray Pedro was telling the beads of his seed rosary. I felt in all of them a tacit solidarity with Rosario. Here the disturbing element, which all of them instinctively rejected, was Mouche. They all sensed that the violent reaction of the other woman had its origin in something that gave her the right to attack with such fury, something the rubber-gatherers, for example,

might attribute to jealousy on the part of Rosario, perhaps
in love with Yannes, and enraged by my friend's insinuating
behavior.

Several hours of suffocating heat went by, with everybody shut up within himself. The nearer we came to the
jungle, the more I noticed in the men a growing capacity
for silence. This might explain, perhaps, the sententious, almost Biblical tone of certain concepts expressed in a minimum of words. The rhythm of speech was slow, everybody
listening and waiting for the other to finish before answering. When the shadow of the rocks began to thicken, Doctor Montsalvatje came from his hut with a most unexpected
piece of news: Mouche was shivering with fever. She had
awakened from a deep sleep and had sat up, but she had
been delirious, and now was unconscious and shaken by
violent chills.

Fray Pedro, wise with long experience, diagnosed the attack as malaria, an ailment not taken too seriously in these
areas. Quinine capsules were slipped into her mouth, and I
sat beside her in helpless rage. Here we were, two days
from the goal of my mission, on the threshold of the unknown, in the proximity of possible wonders, and Mouche
had to succumb like this, the victim of an insect that had
picked her of all people, the person least able to cope with
sickness. It had taken only a few days for a powerful, heart-
less nature to disarm her, wear her out, make her ugly,
break her spirit, and, now, deal her the *coup de grâce*. I
marveled at how swift the defeat had been, like a perfect
revenge of the authentic on the synthetic.

Mouche in this environment was an absurd being, torn
from a future where the forest had been replaced by the
avenue. She belonged to another age, another epoch. For
our present companions, faithfulness to one's man, respect
for parents, upright behavior, the pledged word, honor
that obliged, and obligations that honored were constant,

eternal, inescapable values that admitted of no discussion. The infringement of certain laws meant forfeiting one's neighbor's esteem, though killing when a man had to was not a major crime. As in the most classic of theaters, the personages on this real and visible stage were of a single piece, the Good Man and the Bad Man, the Exemplary Spouse and the Faithful Lover, the Villain and the Loyal Friend, the admirable or the contemptible Mother. The river songs told the story, in ballad form, of the outraged wife who killed herself from shame, of the faithful mulatto who for ten years had awaited the return of the husband whom all had given up for devoured by ants in the depths of the jungle. It was evident that Mouche was out of place in this setting, as I should have realized, if I had wanted to keep my dignity, from the moment she mentioned her visit to St. Prisca island in the company of the Greek.

But now that she had come down with this attack of malaria, if she went back I had to go too, and that meant giving up the task I had undertaken, returning empty-handed, owing money, and shamed in the eyes of the one person whose opinion was precious to me—and all this to play the stupid role of escort to a being I now loathed. Perhaps the torture I was feeling was written on my face; at any rate, Montsalvatje came to my rescue, saying that he would not mind in the least taking Mouche with him the next day. He would find a place for her where she could wait for my return in comfort; to make her go on in the state of debility the attack would induce was out of the question. She was not made for such adventures. "*Anima, vagula, blandula,*" he added ironically. By way of reply I threw my arms around him.

The moon had risen again. There at the foot of a big stone the fire around which the men had gathered in the early evening hours was dying out. Mouche's breathing was more like sighing, and the words she uttered in her fever-

tossed sleep were more like rattles and choking. I felt a hand
on my shoulder: Rosario sat down beside me on the mat
without a word. But I understood that an explanation was
on the way, and I waited in silence. The cawing of a bird
flying toward the river, setting off the crickets in the
thatch, finally decided her.

Beginning in a voice so low that I could hardly hear her,
she told me what I already suspected. The bath by the river
bank. Mouche, with that vanity of her body which she
never missed an opportunity to display, urging her, under
the pretense of doubts about the firmness of her flesh, to
take off the slip that in her rustic modesty she had kept on.
Then the insinuations, the subtle provocation, the display of
nakedness, the praise of the firmness of her breasts, the
smoothness of her belly, the gesture of affection, and the
last step, which suddenly made clear to Rosario an intention that outraged her deepest instincts. Mouche, without
dreaming it, had been guilty of an offense which, for the
women of these parts, is worse than the worst epithet,
worse than insulting the mother, worse than being driven
from home, worse than spitting in the face of the nearest
and dearest, worse than questioning their marital fidelity,
worse than calling them bitches, whores.

Rosario's eyes began to glitter so in the darkness as she
recalled the quarrel that I feared another outburst of violence. I caught her by the wrists to keep her quiet, and with
the sudden movement knocked over one of the baskets in
which the Herbalist kept his dried plants between layers of
caladium leaves. The thick, rustling pile fell on us, enveloping us in perfumes like a mixture of camphor, sandalwood,
and saffron. A sudden emotion left me breathless: this was
almost exactly the smell of the basket of the magic journeys,
the one in which I held María del Carmen in my arms when
we were children, close to the plant beds where her father
sowed sweet basil and mint. My face was very close to

Rosario's, and I could feel the veins throbbing in her hands. Suddenly I saw such longing, such yielding, such impatience in her smile—not so much smile as a frozen laugh, a grimace —that desire hurled me upon her, lost to everything but the act of possession.

It was a rapid and brutal embrace, without caresses, more a struggle to crush, to overpower, than a pleasure-giving union. But when we came to ourselves, limb to limb, still panting, and realized what had happened, a great sense of well-being came over us, as though our bodies had signed a pact that marked a new way of life. We lay upon the scattered plants, aware of nothing but our delight. The moonlight coming through the open cabin door crept slowly up our legs. It was on our ankles, and then it reached the back of Rosario's knees, who caressed me with impatient hand. This time it was she who flung herself upon me, her waist curved in breathless eagerness. But even as we sought a better position, a faint, hoarse voice was spitting insults in our ears, startling us apart.

We had rolled under the hammock, oblivious of the presence of the owner of the voice. And Mouche's head was hanging over us, her mouth twisted, sneering, slavering, her tangled hair, falling over her forehead, giving her a Medusa look. "Swine," she screamed, "swine!" From the floor Rosario kicked at the hammock to quiet her. Soon the voice above us wandered off in the ravings of delirium. The disjoined bodies found each other once more, and between my face and the death-mask face of Mouche, hanging from the hammock, with one arm trailing limp, Rosario's heavy hair fell like a curtain. She rested her elbows on the floor to impose her rhythm upon me. When we once more had ears for what was going on around us, we were completely indifferent to the woman wheezing in the darkness. If she had died that very minute, howling with pain, her agony would not have touched us. We were two, in another

world. I had sown myself beneath the down I stroked with
the hand of the master, and my gesture closed the cycle of
a joyful commingling of bloods that have met.

XVIII/ We got rid of Mouche with the determined ferocity of lovers who have just found one another, still unsure
of the wonder, still thirsting for each other, who would
crush anything that stood in the way of their next coming
together. We put her in Montsalvatje's canoe, wrapped in a
blanket, weeping, almost unconscious, making her believe
that I was following in another boat. I gave the Herbalist
much more money than would be needed to look after her,
pay the expenses of moving her, get her settled, and arrange
for all the treatment she might need, leaving myself with
only a few dirty bills and a handful of coins—which were
worthless anyway in the jungle, where all commerce is reduced to the barter of simple, useful articles such as needles,
knives, awls. In my generosity, moreover, there was a secret rite of propitiating the last scruple of conscience:
Mouche would not have been able to come with us anyway, and so, from the material point of view, I was dis-
charging my last duty. Moreover, it may be that Montsalvatje's solicitude for his patient was based on the secret hope
of making up for months of abstinence with a woman who
was not at all bad-looking. Not only did this thought leave
me completely indifferent, but inwardly I deplored the fact
that the botanist's lack of physical appeal might spoil his
plans.

The boat now disappeared around a bend, and its departure brought to a close one phase of my life. I had never
felt so light, so well installed in my body, as that morning.
The ironic slap on the back that I gave a somewhat crest-
fallen Yannes made him turn to me with a questioning, re-

morseful expression, which was further justification for my hardheartedness. Besides, everyone was aware of the fact that Rosario was—as the saying goes—"bespoken" to me. She swaddled me in attentions, bringing me my food, milking the goats for me, wiping the sweat off my forehead with cool cloths. She hung on my words, my thirst, my silence, or my rest, with a solicitude that filled me with pride at being a man. There the woman "serves" the man in the noblest sense of the word, creating the home with every gesture. For although Rosario and I had no roof of our own, her hands were now my table and the jug of water she raised to my lips, after lifting out a leaf that had fallen into it, was stamped with my initials as master.

"When are you going to settle down with just one woman?" muttered Fray Pedro in my ear, making it plain that he was not being taken in by childish subterfuges. I changed the conversation not to have to confess that I was already married, and by heretical rites, and went over to the Greek, who was collecting his things to follow us up the river. Now that he was convinced that the vein was worked out, and that once more fortune had turned her back on him, he planned another prospecting trip, beyond Caño Pintado, in a mountainous region about which very little was known. He reserved the best place in his bundle for the one book he took with him wherever he went: a cheap bilingual edition of *The Odyssey* bound in black oil-cloth, its pages blotched with mildew.

Before being separated again from the volume, his brothers, who knew long passages of the text by heart, checked the Spanish version on the facing page, reading out fragments in a harsh, angular accent, in which the *u* often becomes *v*. In a little school at Kalamata they had learned the names of the great masters of tragedy and the meaning of the myths, but some obscure affinity of character drew them to the adventurer Ulysses, voyager to enchanted lands, himself no enemy of gold, with the strength of will to ignore the sirens so as not to jeopardize his possessions in Ithaca. When their dog lost an eye in an encounter with a wild pig, they named him Polyphemus in memory of the Cyclops whose lamentable fate they had read a hundred times around their campfire.

I asked Yannes why he had left a land to which he was linked by ties of blood whose remote sources he knew. The miner sighed, and the Mediterranean world became a landscape of ruins. He spoke of what he left behind as though speaking of the walls of Mycenæ, the rifled tombs, the peristyles where the goats drowse. The sea without fish, the neglected Tyrian purple, the decay of the myths, and a great lost hope. Then the sea, the age-old remedy of his people, a vaster sea, on which one could sail farther. He told me that when he saw the first mountain on this side of the ocean, he burst into tears, for it was a harsh, red mountain resembling his own harsh mountains of thistles and nettles. But then he was seized by the lust for precious metals, the taste for trade and distance, which had made his forebears bend so many oars. The day he found the gem he dreamed of, he would build, by the seaside where mountains raise their sharp flanks, a house with a columned porch like a temple to Poseidon.

Once more lamenting the destiny of his people, he opened the volume at the beginning, and recited: "It vexes me to see how mean are these creatures of a day towards us Gods, when they charge against us the evils (far beyond our worst dooming) which their own exceeding wantonness has heaped upon themselves." [1]

That is Zeus talking, he added, and lay the book down,

---

[1] All quotations from *The Odyssey* are from *The Odyssey of Homer* (tr. by T. E. Shaw). New York: Oxford University Press; 1932.

for the rubber-gatherers were bringing in, lashed to a branch, a strange hoofed animal they had just killed. For a moment I thought it was a huge wild pig.

"A tapir, a tapir," shouted Fray Pedro, clasping his hands in amazement as he ran to meet the hunters with a rejoicing that revealed how tired he had become of the manioc gruel that was his regular diet in the jungle. First came the ceremony of lighting the fire; then the scalding and cutting-up of the beast. The sight of the hams, the inner organs, the loins aroused in us the inordinate appetite generally attributed to savages. Bared to the waist, his whole heart and soul in his work, the miner suddenly took on a completely archaic quality in my eyes. His gesture as he threw on the fire several bristles from the animal's head had a propitiatory sense that he could probably explain by a verse from the *Odyssey*. The way of threading the meat on the spit after spreading it with fat, the way of serving it on a board after sprinkling it with brandy, were all part of an old Mediterranean tradition. And when I was served the best filet, for a moment Yannes was transfigured into the swineherd Eumæus. . . .

We had just finished our banquet when the Adelantado rose to his feet and strode down to the river, followed by Gavilán, who was barking fiercely. Two completely primitive canoes—two hollowed-out treetrunks—were coming downstream, guided by several Indian oarsmen. The moment had come to leave, and each of us added his bundles to the luggage. I took Rosario to the cabin, where we had one last embrace on the dirt floor, which Montsalvatje, when he arranged his collections, had left strewn with dried plants that gave off the acrid, enervating perfume we had known the day before.

This time we corrected the errors and haste of our first meetings, mastering the syntax of our bodies. Our limbs were discovering a better adjustment; our arms sought out more adequate positions. From the mutual apprenticeship that this forging of a couple carries with it, a secret language was born. From our delight emerged those intimate words which others may not share, which would be the language of our nights. It was a two-part invention that included terms of possession, thanksgiving, sex declensions, words suggested by the skin, names unforeseen yesterday by which we would call each other when no one could hear us.

That day for the first time Rosario called me by my name, repeating it again and again, as though its syllables had to be molded anew, and in her mouth it took on a sonority so strange, so unexpected, that I was spellbound by the word I knew best when I heard it as though it had just been created. We lived the unmatched joy of thirst shared and quenched, and when we returned to the world around us, we seemed to recall a land of new savors.

I threw myself into the water to get rid of the dried grass that had stuck to my sweaty back, and I laughed as I thought to myself that we were running counter to tradition, for our mating season had fallen in midsummer. But my love was on her way to the dock. We took our leave of the rubber-gatherers, and we were off. The Adelantado, Rosario, and I occupied the first canoe, huddled between the sides. Fray Pedro, Yannes, and the luggage were in the other.

"May we go with God," said the Adelantado as he sat down beside Gavilán, who, looking like a figurehead, sniffed the air. From now on we would be navigating without sails. The sun, the moon, the campfire—at times the lightning—would be the only lights our faces would reflect.

Chapter Four

Will there be only silence, repose at the foot of the trees, of the vines? Then it is well that there be guardians.—POPOL-VUH

(Monday afternoon)

XIX/ After sailing two hours between slabs of stone, islands of stone, promontories of stone, mountains of stone, their geometry combined in a diversity of patterns that no longer surprised, a dense, low-growing vegetation of interwoven grasses punctuated by the swaying, dancing presence of bamboo clumps replaced the stone with the endless monotony of impenetrable greenness. I entertained myself with a childish game suggested by the tales narrated beside the fire by Montsalvatje: we were conquistadors who had set out in search of the Kingdom of Manoa. Fray Pedro was our chaplain, who would hear our confessions if we were wounded in the attack. The Adelantado could well be Felipe de Urre; the Greek, Micer Codro, the astrologer.

Gavilán became Leoncico, Balboa's dog. My role was that of Juan de San Pedro, the trumpeter, who had taken himself a woman in the sack of a town. The Indians were Indians, and though it seemed odd, I had accepted the strange distinction established by the Adelantado, who, without intending the least disdain, said with complete naturalness when recounting his adventures: "We were three men and twelve Indians." I imagined a question of baptism established this differentiation, and this gave an air of reality to the setting of the novel I was forging.

Now the bamboo thickets had yielded the left bank, which we were skirting, to a kind of low colorless jungle growth, with roots extending into the water, which threw up a solid fence, as straight as a palisade, an endless wall of trees standing trunk to trunk at the very edge of the stream, without sign of an opening, without a cleavage, without a crevice. In the light of the sun, which faded to mist over the damp leaves, this vegetable wall continued so long that it seemed the work of man's hands, carried out with theodolite and plummet. The canoe drew closer to this sealed, forbidding bank, which the Adelantado scrutinized with the keenest attention. It seemed impossible to me that we could hope to find anything here, and yet the Indians poled along more and more slowly, and the dog, its back bristling, watched as alertly as its master. Drowsy with the waiting and the motion of the boat, I closed my eyes.

I was startled awake by a shout of the Adelantado: "There is the entrance!"

Two yards from where we were, stood a treetrunk, exactly like the others, neither thicker nor rougher. But there was a sign cut in its bark, three *V*'s, one fitting vertically into another in a design that might have been repeated ad infinitum, but which here was multiplied only in the reflection of the waters. Alongside this tree ran an over-arched channel, so narrow, so low, that it seemed impossible to me that the canoe could enter it. And yet our boat managed to make its way through this tunnel, with so little room to spare that its sides grated against the gnarled roots. Oars and hands had to push aside obstacles and barriers to continue this incredible trip through the submerged undergrowth. A sharp stick fell on my shoulder with such force that it made my neck bleed. The branches rained a vegetable soot on us, almost impalpable at times, like plankton of the air. And there was the continuous moving through vines that irritated the skin, dead fruits, fuzz-covered seeds that made the eyes tear, decayed matter, dust that begrimed our faces. The shove of the prow loosed a nest of ants from a hole in the sand.

But what lay beneath us was even worse than the products of the shade. Under the water great riddled leaves waved like dominoes of ocher velvet, lures and traps. On the surface floated clusters of dirty bubbles, varnished over by reddish pollen, which a passing fin sent drifting off into the eddy of a pool with the wavering motion of a sea cucumber. A kind of thick, opalescent gauze hung over the opening of a rock teeming with hidden life. A silent war was going on in those depths bristling with hairy talons, where everything seemed a slimy tangle of snakes. Strange clicking noises, sudden ripples, the plash of waters told of the rush of invisible beings leaving behind them a wake of murky decay. One felt the presence of rampant fauna, of the primeval slime, of the green fermentation beneath the dark waters, which gave off a sour reek like a mud of vinegar and carrion, over whose oily surface moved insects made to walk on the water: chinch-bugs, white fleas, high-jointed flies, tiny mosquitoes that were hardly more than shimmering dots in the green light, for the green, shot through by an occasional ray of sun, was so intense that the light as it filtered through the leaves had the color of moss dyed the hue of the swamp-bottoms as it sought the roots of the plants.

After sailing for a time through that secret channel, one began to feel the same thing that mountain-climbers feel, lost in the snow: the loss of the sense of verticality, a kind of disorientation, and a dizziness of the eyes. It was no longer possible to say which was tree and which reflection of tree. Was the light coming from above or below? Was the sky or the earth water? Were the openings in the foliage pools of light in the water? As the trees, the sticks, the lianas were refracted at strange angles, one finally began to see nonexistent channels, openings, banks. With this succession of minor mirages, my feeling of bewilderment, of being completely lost, grew until it became unbearable. It was as though I was being spun round and round upon myself to make me lose my bearings before bringing me to the threshold of some secret dwelling. I asked myself if the boatmen knew larboard from starboard any longer. I was beginning to be afraid. Nothing menaced me. All those around me seemed calm, but an indefinable fear out of the dim reaches of instinct was making me short of breath, as though I lacked air.

All this was aggravated by the dampness that clung to clothing, skin, hair; a warm, sticky dampness that permeated everything like a grease, making even more irritating the continuous stinging by flies, gnats, all the nameless insects, masters of the air until the malaria mosquito took over with the twilight. A toad that landed on my forehead gave me, after the first shock, an almost delightful sense of coolness. If I had not known that it was a toad, I would have kept it in the hollow of my hand to hold against my throbbing temples. Now little red spiders were dropping on the canoe. And thousands of spiderwebs hung in every direction, just above the water between the lowest branches. Each time the boat touched against them, the sides became covered with grayish combs, full of dried wasps, bits of wing, antennæ, half-sucked shells. The men were dirty, greasy; their sweat-darkened shirts were befouled with the spittle of mud, resin, sap; from lack of sunshine, their faces had taken on that waxy tinge of the jungle-dwellers.

When we came into a small lagoon that died at the foot of a yellow rock, I felt myself trapped, hemmed in on all sides. The Adelantado called to me a short way off from where the canoes had tied up, to show me a horrible thing: a dead alligator, its flesh rotting, under whose hide swarms of green flies came and went. The buzzing that went on inside the carcass at moments took on the tone of a gentle lament, as though someone—a weeping woman, for instance—was moaning through the jaws of the reptile. I fled from the horror, seeking the protection of my lover. I was afraid. The shadows were closing about us in a premature twilight, and we had no sooner prepared a hasty camp than it was night.

Each of us sought refuge in the cradle-like compass of his hammock. And the croaking of enormous frogs invaded the jungle. The darkness trembled with fears and slithers. Somebody, somewhere, tried out the mouthpiece of an oboe. A grotesque brass set up a laugh in a hidden glade. A thousand flutes of two differently tuned notes answered each other through the leaves. And there were metal combs, saws whining through wood, harmonica reeds, the quavering stridulation of the crickets, which seemed to cover the whole earth. There were sounds like the peacock's cry, belly growls, whistles that rose and died away, *things* that passed beneath us, flat to the ground, *things* that dived, hammered, creaked, howled like children, neighed in the treetops, rang bells in the hollow of a hole. I was dazed, frightened, feverish. The exhaustion of the trip, the nervous tension, had sapped my strength. When sleep finally overcame the fear of the threats I felt on every side, I was on the point of surrender—of screaming my fear—for the sake of hearing human voices.

(Tuesday, June 19)

XX/ When the light came once more, I realized that I had passed the First Trial. The darkness had taken with it the terrors of the night. As I washed my chest and face in a pool of the channel, alongside Rosario, who was cleaning my breakfast utensils with sand, it seemed to me that I was sharing with the thousands of men who lived in the unexplored headwaters of the Great Rivers the primordial sense of beauty, of beauty physically perceived, equally shared by body and spirit, reborn with each rising of the sun. Beauty thus perceived, in such remoteness, brings man the pride of feeling himself the master of the world, the supreme heir of creation. Dawn in the jungle is far less beautiful, from the point of view of color, than sunset. Above a soil that exhales an age-old moisture, above water that divides the earth, above vegetation shrouded in mist, the dawn slips in with the grayness of rain, in a vague clarity that never seems to forecast a clear day. Hours must elapse before the sun, now high, freed by the treetops, can shed a clear ray through the myriad leaves. Nevertheless, dawn in the jungle always renews the intimate, the atavic rejoicing, carried in the blood stream, of ancestors who, for thousands of years, saw in each dawn the end of their nocturnal fears, the retreat of the roars, the scattering of the shadows, the confounding of the ghosts, the confining of evil within its bounds.

With the break of day, I felt called upon to apologize to Rosario for the few occasions to be together which this part of our journey afforded. She burst out laughing, and began to hum what must have been a ballad: "I am the new-

wed wife—Whose tears fall like dew—For the bad match I
have made—Which I can only rue." Her malicious verses,
full of allusions to our enforced continence, were still echoing when, poling once more, we came out into a broad
channel leading to what the Adelantado informed me was
the real jungle. As the water had overflowed its banks,
flooding great stretches of earth, certain of the trees, enveloped in lianas rooted in the mud, had the air of boats at
anchor, while others, of golden brown, prolonged themselves in a mirage of depth. Those of the ancient dead forest, whitened until they seemed more marble than wood,
stood out like the towering obelisks of a drowned city. Behind those which could be identified, the mirity palms, the
bamboos, the nameless vines along the banks, came the lush,
exuberant vegetation, a tangle of lianas, bushes, creepers,
briers, parasite growths, through which an occasional tapir
crashed its way in search of a stream in which to refresh its
snout.

Hundreds of herons, poised on their long legs, their necks
sunk between their wings, surrounded the pools; an occasional vigilant humpbacked male dropped from the sky.
A branch suddenly turned iridescent with the jubilant arrival of a flight of chattering parrots, who cast gaudy
streaks upon the sour lower darkness where every species
was engaged in the age-old struggle to climb over the other,
rise, reach the light, the sun. The exaggerated elongation of
certain weedy palms, the upward stretch of trees that
showed a single leaf at the top of multiple trunks were different phases of an incessant vertical battle, above which
towered the largest trees I had ever seen, trees that left far
below, like creepers, the plants retarded by the shade, and
opened out into an unclouded sky above the fray, their
branches forming unreal aerial boscages that seemed suspended in space, from which hung transparent mosses, like
torn lace.

Sometimes, after centuries of existence, the leaves dropped from one of these trees, its lichens dried up, its orchids were extinguished. Its wood aged, acquiring the texture of pink granite, and it stood erect, its monumental skeleton in silent nakedness revealing the laws of an almost mineral architecture, with symmetries, rhythms, balances of crystallized forms. Washed by the rain, unmoved by the tempests, there it stood several centuries longer until one day a ray of lightning finally cast it down into the shifting lower depths. Thereupon the colossus, unshaken since prehistoric times, crashed, groaning in all its splinters, hurling branches right and left, riven, all carbon and celestial fire, crushing and burning all that lay at its foot. A hundred trees died with it, crushed, uprooted, shivered, bringing down with them lianas that shot upward like bowstrings as they snapped. It came to its end in the age-piled humus of the jungle. From the earth emerged roots so vast, so interwoven that two separate streams suddenly found themselves made one by the work of those hidden plowshares, which emerged from their darkness destroying nests of ants, opening craters that became the instant objective of the ant-eaters, with their threadlike, viscous tongues.

What amazed me most was the inexhaustible mimetism of virgin nature. Everything here seemed something else, thus creating a world of appearances that concealed reality, casting doubt on many truths. The alligators lurking in the depths of the swamps, motionless, jaws ready, seemed rotten, scale-covered logs. The vines seemed snakes, the snakes vines when their skins did not simulate the grains of precious woods, their eyes the markings of moth wings, their scales those of the pineapple or coral rings. The aquatic plants formed a thick carpet, hiding the water that flowed below, mimicking the vegetation of the solid earth. The fallen bark soon acquired the consistency of pickled laurel leaves, and the fungi were like congealed copper drippings sprinkled with sulphur. The chameleons were twigs, lapis lazuli, lead brightly striped in yellow, imitating the splashes of sunlight filtering through the leaves, which never allow it to come through fully. The jungle is the world of deceit, subterfuge, duplicity; everything there is disguise, stratagem, artifice, metamorphosis. The world of the lizard-cucumber, the chestnut-hedgehog, the cocoon-centipede, the carrot-larva, the electric fish that electrocutes from the dregs of the slime.

As we skirted the banks, the shade cast by several ceilings of vegetation brought a breath of coolness to the canoes. But a few seconds' pause sufficed to turn this relief into an unbearable fervor of insects. There seemed to be flowers everywhere, but in nearly every case their colors were the lying effect of leaves at varying degrees of maturity or decay. There seemed to be fruit; but the roundness and ripeness of the fruits were feigned by oozing bulbs, fetid velvets, the vulvula of insect-eating plants like thoughts sprinkled with syrup, dotted cacti that bore tulips of saffron-colored sperm a handspan from the ground. And when an orchid could be discerned, high above the bamboo thickets, high above the *yopos*, it seemed as unreal, as inaccessible, as the most dizzying Alpine edelweiss. And there were the trees, too, which were not green, but dotted the banks with clumps of amaranth or glowed with the yellow of a burning bush. Even the sky lied at times when, reversing its altitude in the quicksilver of the ponds, it buried itself in heavenly abysmal depths.

Only the birds met the test of truth by the frank identity of their plumage. The herons were not lying when they invented the question mark with the curves of their necks, or when, at the call of the male sentinel, they raised their fright of white feathers. Nor the kingfisher with its red top-knot, so small and fragile in that terrible world, whose mere presence was in the nature of a miracle, like the magic vi-

bration of the hummingbird. Everything lied, in that un-
ending shift of appearances and imitations, in that baroque
proliferation of lianas, where the playful howling monkeys
suddenly shocked the foliage with their mischief, their in-
decencies, and their mowing, like overgrown children with
five hands.

And overhead, as though the wonders below were not
enough, I discovered a new cloud world: those clouds so
different, so unique, so lost sight of by man, which still pile
up above the dampness of the vast forests, as rich in waters
as in the first chapters of Genesis; clouds that looked like
worn marble, straight at their bases, and which prolonged
themselves to immense heights, motionless, monumental,
with shapes that were those of the clay in which the form
of the amphora can be discerned after a few turns on the
potter's wheel. These clouds, rarely joined together, were
as though suspended in space, as though a part of the sky,
resembling themselves since time immemorial when they
watched over the separation of the waters and the mystery
of the first coming together of the rivers.

(Tuesday afternoon)

XXI/ Taking advantage of the fact that we had stopped
at noon in a wooded cove so that the rowers could rest and
stretch their legs, Yannes went off by himself to explore a
river-bed where, according to him, diamonds were to be
found. For two hours we had been shouting for him without any answer but the echo of our voices around the bends
of the muddy stream. In mounting indignation at the delay,
Fray Pedro excoriated those who let themselves be blinded
by greed for jewels and gold.

I listened to him with a measure of uneasiness, fearing
that the Adelantado, who was said to have discovered a
fabulous lode, might take offense. But he smiled under his

shaggy brows and asked the missionary in a malicious tone how it was that the chalices of Rome were such a gleam of gold and jewels. "Because it is fitting," answered Fray Pedro, "that the most beautiful materials of Creation should be used to honor their Creator."

Then, to prove to me that if he approved of splendor for the altar he demanded humility of the officiant, he lashed out against the worldly priests, those he termed new sellers of indulgences, dreamers of cardinals' hats, tenors of the pulpit.

"The eternal rivalry between the infantry and the cavalry," remarked the Adelantado, smiling.

"It is evident," I thought to myself, "that a certain type of urban clergy must seem unspeakably lazy, not to say evil, to a hermit who has served a forty-year apostolate in the jungle." In the hope of finding favor with him, I agreed with what he said, adducing examples of unworthy priests and the money-changers of the temple.

But Fray Pedro cut me short: "To talk of the wicked, one must know about the others." And he began to tell me about people I had never heard of, priests torn limb from limb by the Marañon Indians; one Blessed Diego barbarously tortured by the last Inca; Juan de Lizardi, shot through with Paraguayan arrows; and forty friars who had had their throats slit by a Protestant pirate. In a vision the "Doctor of Ávila," St. Teresa, had seen them charge into heaven, frightening the angels with their terrible saints' faces. He spoke of all this as though it had happened yesterday, as though he had the power to move backward and forward in time. "Perhaps it is because his mission is carried out in a timeless setting," I said to myself. But then Fray Pedro noticed the fact that the sun was sinking behind the trees, and he cut short his missionary hagiology to call Yannes again, in a threatening tone, accompanied by the epithets used by herders for a stray animal.

When the Greek finally showed up, the friar's blows with his staff against the stone were such that in a moment we were all huddled in the canoes. When we resumed the trip, I understood the reason for Fray Pedro's anger at the miner's delay. Now the channel was narrowing between banks that were like black cliffs, the harbingers of a different landscape. And suddenly the current flung us into the middle of a yellow river that ran through rapids and whirlpools to meet the Great River, on whose flank it would fasten, bringing it the torrents of one whole watershed of the Great Plateaus. The rush of waters had increased dangerously that day, swollen by rains that had fallen somewhere. Taking over the duties of helmsman, Fray Pedro, resting a foot on each side of the boat, steered the canoes with his staff. But the resistance of the current was tremendous, and night was descending upon us before we were out of the thick of the struggle.

Suddenly there came an uproar in the sky. Under the lashing of a chill wind that raised huge waves, the trees loosed whirlwinds of dead leaves. A cyclone was upon us, and over the roaring jungle the storm broke loose. Everything turned a livid hue. The flashes of lightning came so close together that one jagged ray had not faded before another broke, opening in claws that buried themselves behind newly emerging mountains. The flickering clarity from behind, ahead, each side, cut off at times by the shadowy outline of islands whose tangle of trees rose over the boiling waters, this light of the Last Judgment, of a rain of meteors, filled me with sudden terror as it revealed the presence of obstacles, the fury of the waters, the multiplicity of dangers. There could be no possible salvation for anyone in this tumult that hammered, lifted up, shook our boat.

My reason gone, unable to control my fear, I clung to Rosario, seeking the warmth of her body, no longer as a lover, but like a child clinging to its mother's neck, and I let myself fall into the bottom of the canoe, hiding my face in her hair so as not to see what was going on about us, and to escape the fury that held us in its grip. But it was hard to forget, with a half foot of lukewarm water washing the inside of the canoe from stem to stern. The boats could hardly keep afloat as we moved from eddy to eddy, nosing through the gorges, riding over boulders, tacking quickly to skirt a rapid, always on the verge of capsizing, surrounded by foam, in tortured boards that groaned the length of the keel. And to make matters worse, the rain began. It added to my horror to see that the Capuchin, his beard standing out black against the lightning flashes, was no longer steering the boat, but praying. Rosario, her teeth clenched, protecting my head as though it were that of her newborn babe in a moment of danger, displayed an amazing fortitude. Lying face-down, the Adelantado gripped our Indians around the waist to keep them from being washed overboard, so they could give us the protection of their oars.

The terrible struggle went on for a time that in my suffering seemed endless. I realized that the danger had passed when Fray Pedro once more stood up in the prow, bracing his feet against the sides. The storm was gathering up its last flashes as swiftly as it had brought them, bringing the terrible symphony of its wrath to an end with the chord of a prolonged rumble of thunder, and the night became filled with the rejoicing of frogs from bank to bank. Unwrinkling its back, the river pursued its way toward the distant ocean. Exhausted by the nervous tension, I went to sleep on Rosario's breast. But in a moment the canoe pulled up on a sandspit, and when I found myself once more on solid ground, to which Fray Pedro leaped with a "Thank God," I realized that I had come through the Second Trial.

(*Wednesday, June 20*)

XXII/ After hours of sleep I reached out for a pitcher and drank deeply. When I set it down and saw that it remained level with my face, I realized, though I was only half awake, that I was on the ground, lying on a thin straw mat. There was a smell of wood smoke, there was a roof over my head. I then recalled the landing on a spit, the walk toward an Indian village, the feeling of exhaustion and chill which had led the Adelantado to make me down several swallows of a powerful brandy, to which they give the name *stomach fire* and which I accepted only for its restorative powers.

Behind me, several Indian women were kneading cassava bread, their breasts bare, and their genitals covered by a brief white loincloth fastened around their waist by a string that passed between their buttocks. From the palm-frond walls hung bows and fishing and hunting arrows, blowguns, quivers of poisoned arrows, gourds of curare, and trowels shaped like hand mirrors, which I learned later were used to macerate a seed of intoxicating effect inhaled in powder form through a tube made of a bird's breastbone. Opposite the entrance three thick fish, reddish-violet in color, were roasting on a grill of interwoven branches, over a bed of coals. Our hammocks hung out to dry revealed to me why we had been sleeping on the ground.

With aching limbs, I stepped out of the cabin, looked, and stood speechless, my mouth filled with exclamations that did nothing to relieve my amazement. Beyond the gigantic trees rose masses of black rock, enormous, thick, plummet-sheer, which were the presence and the testimony of fabulous monuments. My memory had to recall the world of Bosch, the imaginary Babels of painters of the fantastic, the most hallucinated illustrators of the temptations of saints, to find anything like what I was seeing. And even when I had hit upon a similarity, I had to discount it immediately because of the proportions. What I was gazing upon was a Titans' city—a city of multiple and spaced constructions—with Cyclopean stairways, mausoleums touching the clouds, vast terraces guarded by strange fortresses of obsidian without battlements or loopholes whose role seemed to be to guard the entrance of some forbidden kingdom against man. There, against a background of light clouds towered the Capital of Forms: an incredible mile-high Gothic cathedral, its two towers, nave, apse, and buttresses situated on a conical rock of rare composition touched with dark iridescences of coal. The belfries were swept by thick mists that swirled as they broke against the granite edges.

In the proportions of these Forms, ending in dizzying terraces, flanked by organ pipes, there was something so not of this world—the mansion of gods, thrones, and stairs designed for some Last Judgment—that the bewildered mind sought no interpretation of that disconcerting telluric architecture, accepting, without reasoning, its vertical, inexorable beauty. The sun was casting quicksilver reflections on that impossible temple suspended from heaven rather than resting on the earth. On different planes, defined by the light or shadow, other Forms could be distinguished, belonging to the same geological family, from whose edges hung cascades of a hundred falls that finally dissolved in spray before they reached the treetops.

Almost overwhelmed by so much grandeur, I brought my eyes back to my own level after a moment. Several huts fringed a pool of black waters. A child came toward me, balancing on unsteady legs, to show me a tiny bracelet of peonies. There, where big black birds with orange bills strutted, a group of Indians appeared, carrying fish threaded on a stick through the gills. Farther off, several mothers were weaving, their babies clinging to their nipples. At the foot of a big tree, surrounded by old women pounding

milky tubers, Rosario was washing my clothes. In the way
she knelt beside the water, her hair loose over her shoulders,
the rubbing stone in her hand, she took on an ancestral silhouette that brought her much closer to these women than
to those whose blood, in generations past, had lightened her
skin. I understood why this woman who was now mine had
given me such a sense of *race* that day beside a mountain
road when I saw her return from death. Her mystery emanated from a remote world whose light and time were unknown to me.

All about me everyone was busy at his own work in a
harmonious concert of duties that were those of a life moving to a primordial rhythm. Those Indians, whom I had always seen through more or less imaginary reports that
looked upon them as beings beyond the pale of man's real
existence, gave me the feeling here, in their own setting, in
their own surroundings, that they were complete masters
of their culture. Nothing could have been more remote
from their reality than the absurd concept of savage. The
fact that they ignored many things that to me were basic
and necessary was a far cry from putting them in the cate-
gory of primitive beings. The superb precision with which
this one put an arrow through a fish, the choreographic air
with which the other raised the blowgun to his lips, the
finished technique of that group as it covered the framework of a longhouse with palm fronds, revealed to me the
presence of human beings who were masters of the skills re-
quired on the stage of their existence.

Under the authority of an old man so wrinkled that he
had not an inch of smooth skin left, the young men went
through a rigorous discipline in the handling of the bow.
The dorsal muscles of the men were powerfully modeled
by the handling of the oar; the pelvises of the women were
designed for motherhood, with wide hips that framed a
broad, high pubis. Certain profiles had a stamp of singular

nobility that came from the aquiline nose and the thick hair. Moreover, their bodily development was in keeping with their functional needs. The fingers, prehensile instruments, were strong and rough; the legs, made for walking, were sturdy-ankled. The skeleton was enveloped in efficient flesh. At any rate, here there were no useless callings like those I had plied for so many years.

Thinking all this, I was walking toward Rosario when the Adelantado appeared at the door of a hut, calling me with joyful shouts. He had just come upon what I was seeking on this trip, the objective and end of my mission. There, on the ground beside a kind of brazier, lay the musical instruments I had been commissioned to find. With the emotion of the pilgrim who reaches the shrine for sight of which he has journeyed on foot through twenty unknown lands, I laid my hand upon the fire-ornamented stamping tube with cross-shaped cover through which the rhythm cane passed in the most primitive of drums. I saw the ritual maraca pierced by a feathered branch, the deer-horn trumpets, the decorated rattles, and the clay conch to call the fishermen in the swamps. There were the sets of Panpipes in their original capacity of ancestors of the organ. And, above all, with that unpleasant solemnity which characterizes everything touching upon death, there stood the jar of uncouth, sinister sound, reminiscent of the hollow echo of the tomb, with the two reeds let into its sides just as in the book that described it for the first time.

After concluding the barter that put into my possession that arsenal of objects created by man's noblest instinct, I felt as though I had entered upon a new phase of my existence. My mission was accomplished. In exactly fifteen days I had achieved what I set out to do and, with justifiable pride, I savored the delights of duty's reward. To have secured that roaring jar—a magnificent specimen—was the first outstanding, noteworthy act of my life to that moment.

The object grew in my esteem, linked to my destiny, wiping out, in that moment, the distance between myself and him who had entrusted me with the task, and who perhaps at that moment was thinking of me, examining some primitive instrument with a gesture similar to mine.

I stood silent for a time that my inner satisfaction made measureless. When I returned to the notion of reality, like a sleeper awakening, it was as though something within me had ripened, taking the strange form of one of Palestrina's great counterpoints, which echoed in my head with the majesty of all its voices.

As I stepped out of the hut to look for lianas to use as ropes, I noticed that a strange excitement had upset the rhythm of the village life. Fray Pedro was moving about with the speed of a dancer, going in and out of the hut followed by Rosario and a twittering group of Indian women. Opposite the door he had spread over a log table a worn-out lace cloth mended with threads of different thickness, and two jars crammed with yellow flowers. Between them he stood the black wooden cross he wore about his neck. Then from a scuffed, brown leather bag he always carried with him, he took out the liturgical objects and ornaments —some of them badly dented—rubbing the rust from them with his sleeve before arranging them on the altar. I observed with growing surprise the Chalice and the Host taking their place on the Altar; the Purificator unfolded over the Chalice, and the Corporal-cloth laid between the two ritual candles. All this, in a place of this sort, struck me as absurd and touching.

Knowing that the Adelantado looked upon himself as an emancipated soul, I shot him an inquiring glance. As though it was quite a different matter having little to do with religion, he told me that a Mass had been promised as an act of thanksgiving during the storm the night before. He approached the altar, where Rosario was standing. Yannes, a man of icons, went past me muttering something about Christ being one. The Indians watched from a distance. The headman of the village, a mass of wrinkles among his necklaces of teeth, stood halfway between them and the altar in an attitude of respect. The mothers quieted their children's cries.

Fray Pedro turned toward me: "My son, these Indians refuse baptism. I should not like them to see you indifferent. If you don't want to do it for God, do it for me." And, resorting to the most universal of all arguments, he added, in a harsher tone: "Remember that you were in the same boat, and you, too, were afraid." There was a long silence. Then: "In the name of the Father, the Son, and the Holy Ghost, Amen."

My throat became painfully dry. Those ancient, unchanging words took on a portentous solemnity in the midst of the jungle, as though coming from the hidden galleries of primitive Christianity, from the brotherhood of its beginnings, taking on anew, beneath these trees which had never known the ax, a heroic meaning antedating the hymns intoned in the naves of the triumphant cathedrals, antedating the belfries towering aloft in the light of day. *Sanctus, Sanctus, Sanctus, Dominus Deus Sabaoth* . . . The pillars here were treetrunks. Over our heads hung leaves that hid dangers. And around us were the Gentiles, the idol-worshippers, gazing upon the mystery from a narthex of lianas.

Yesterday I had amused myself with the thought that we were conquistadors searching for Manoa. It suddenly came to me that there was no difference between this Mass and those Masses which the seekers for El Dorado had listened to in similar wildernesses. Time had been turned back four hundred years. This was the Mass of the Discoverers who had just set foot on a nameless strand, who planted the emblems of their Sunwise migration before the astonished gaze of the Men of Corn. Those two—the Adelantado and Yannes—kneeling on either side of the altar, gaunt, sundarkened, the one with the face of a peasant of Extremadura, the other with the profile of a bonesetter recently registered in the records of the Clearing House, were soldiers of the Conquest, used to a diet of jerked beef and all things rancid, scourged by fevers, bitten by vermin, praying with the air of donors, beside their helmets resting on the rank grass.

Miserere nostri Domine miserere nostri. Fiat misericordia —intones the chaplain of the Expedition, in an accent that puts a stop to time. Perhaps this is the year of grace 1540. Our ships have been buffeted by a tempest, and the friar is telling us, in Biblical tone, how such a great movement sprang up on the sea that the ship was filled with water; He was sleeping, and His disciples came to Him and awoke Him, saying: Master, Master, we perish. And He said to them: Why do you fear, men of little faith? Then He arose and rebuked the wind and the raging of the water, and they ceased and there was calm. Perhaps it is the year of grace 1540.

But no. The years are subtracted, melt away, vanish, in the dizzying backward flight of time. We have not yet come to the sixteenth century. It is much earlier. We are in the Middle Ages. For it was not the man of the Renaissance who carried out the Discovery and the Conquest, but medieval man. The volunteers for the great enterprise did not march out of the Old World through gateways whose columns were copied from Palladio, but under Romanesque arches, the memory of which they carried with them when they built their first churches this side of the Ocean-Sea, on the blood-stained foundations of the *teocalli*. Under the Cross, complete with pliers, nails, and lance, they marched to battle against those who employed similar implements in their sacrifices.

Medieval, too, were the devil dances, the grotesque processions, the dances of the Peers of France, the ballads of Charlemagne, which lived on so persistently in the many cities we had recently passed through. And the amazing truth suddenly came to me: since the afternoon of Corpus Christi in Santiago de los Aguinaldos, I had been living in the early Middle Ages. An object, a garment, a drug belonged to another calendar. But the rhythm of life, the methods of navigation, the oil lamp, the cooking-pots, the prolongation of the hours, the transcendental functions of Horse and Dog, the manner of worshipping the Saints, all were medieval, like the prostitutes who traveled from parish to parish on feast days, like the lusty patriarchs, proud to acknowledge their forty children by different mothers clamoring for their blessing as they passed by.

I realized that I had been living with burghers who were mighty trenchermen, always hungering for the flesh of the serving maid, whose jolly life I had so often envied in museums; I had carved suckling pigs with charred teats at their tables, and had shared their fondness for the spices that made them seek new routes to the Indies. A hundred paintings had familiarized me with their red tile-floored houses, their huge kitchens, their nail-studded doors. I knew their way of carrying money in bags at their waists, of dancing without touching their partners, their fondness for stringed instruments, for cockfights, for getting roaring drunk around a big joint. I knew the blind and crippled of their streets, the poultices, ointments, and balms with which they assuaged their aches and pains. But I knew them under the varnish of museums, as testimony of a dead past, irretrievably lost. When, behold, this past had suddenly become the present. I could touch and breathe it. I now saw the breathtaking possibility of traveling in time, as others travel in space. . . . *Ite missa est, Benedicamus Dominum, Deo Gratias.* The Mass was ended, and with it the Middle Ages.

But dates were still losing figures. In headlong flight the years emptied, ran backward, were erased, restoring calendars, moons, changing centuries numbered in three figures to those of single numbers. The gleam of the Grail has disappeared, the nails have fallen from the Cross, the money-changers have returned to the temple, the Star of Bethlehem has faded, and it is the year 0, when the Angel of the Annunciation returned to heaven. Now the dates on the other side of the year 0 are back—dates of two, three, five figures—until we are at the time when man, weary of wandering about the earth, invented agriculture, when he established his first villages alongside the rivers and, needing greater music, passed from the rhythm-stick to the drum, which was a wooden cylinder with burned ornamentation, invented the organ as he blew into a hollow reed, and mourned his dead by making a clay jar roar. We are in the Paleolithic Age.

Those who issued the laws here, those who had powers of life and death over us, those who had the secrets of food and poisons, those who invented the skills, were men who used stone knives and stone scrapers, bone fishhooks, bone arrowheads. We were intruders, ignorant outlanders—late arrivals—in a city born in the dawn of History. If the fire the women were now fanning was suddenly to go out, we would be unable to rekindle it if we had to depend on our own unskilled hands.

(*Thursday, June 21*)

XXIII/ I now knew the Adelantado's secret. He had confided it to me the previous day beside the fire, taking care that Yannes should not hear us. They talked of his gold mines; they believed him to be the king of a colony of runaway slaves; they said that he had a harem of women in the forest, and that his stealthy journeys were so his women would never see other men. The truth was much more beautiful. When it was succinctly told to me, I was amazed at the prospect no one of my generation—I am sure of it—had ever before conceived.

That night in the shed, to the gentle creaking of our hammock ropes, I whispered to Rosario, through the meshes, that we would go on for several days with our trip. Instead of the objections I feared—fatigue, discouragement, or just wanting to get back—she was in hearty agreement. It did not matter to her where we went, nor whether the lands we visited were near or remote. For Rosario the idea of being far away from some famous place where life could be lived to the full did not exist. The center of the universe for her, who had crossed frontiers without a change of language, who had never dreamed of the ocean, was where the sun at midday shone on her from overhead. She was a woman of the earth, and as long as she walked the earth, and ate, and was well, and there was a man to serve as mold and measure, with the compensation of what she called "the body's pleasure," she was fulfilling a destiny that it was better not to analyze too much, for it was governed by "big things" whose workings were obscure and, besides, were beyond man's understanding. That is what she meant when she said that "it is not good to think about certain things."

She called herself *Your woman*, referring to herself in the third person: "*Your woman* was asleep; *Your woman* was looking for you." And I found in this reiteration of the possessive a firmness of concept, an exactitude of definition, which the word "wife" never gave me. *Your woman* was an affirmation that preceded all agreement, all sacraments. It had the pristine truth of that *womb* which prudish translators of the Bible render as *bowels*, muting the thunder of certain prophetic imprecations. Moreover, this terse simplification of vocabulary was customary in Rosario. When she made mention of certain intimacies which, as a lover, I should know, she employed expressions at once unequivocal and modest, which recalled the "custom of women" that Rachel used to her father, Laban. All *Your woman* asked that night was that I take her with me wherever I went. She picked up her bundle and followed her man without question.

I knew very little about her. I could not decide whether she had a short memory or did not want to talk about her past. She did not hide the fact that she had lived with other men. But these represented phases of her life whose secrecy she maintained with dignity—or perhaps because she felt that it would be indelicate to let me think that anything that had happened before we met was of any importance. This living in the present, without possessions, without the chains of yesterday, without thinking of tomorrow, seemed to me amazing. And yet it was apparent that this attitude must lengthen the lapse of hours from one sun to another. She spoke of days that were very long and of days that were very short, as though they were in different tempos—tempos of a telluric symphony that had its andantes and adagios, as well as its prestos. The astonishing thing was that, now that time was of no concern to me, I noticed in myself different values of the intervals: the prolongation of certain mornings, the frugal elaboration of a sunset, and was lost in wonder at all that could be fitted into certain tempos of this symphony which we were reading backward, from right to left, contrary to the key of G, returning to the measures of Genesis.

At dusk we stumbled upon the habitat of people of a culture much earlier than that of the men with whom we had been living the day before. We had emerged from the Paleolithic—with its skills paralleling those of the Magdalenian and Aurignacian, with stone tools such as I had gazed on many times in collections with a feeling that I was at the very beginning of the night of ages—to enter a state that pushed the limits of human life back to the darkest murk of the night of ages. These beings I saw now with legs and arms that resembled mine; these women whose breasts were flaccid udders drooping over swollen bellies; these children who stretched and curled up with feline gestures; these people still without the primordial shame that leads to the concealment of the organs of generation, who were naked without knowing it, like Adam and Eve before the Fall, were nevertheless men.

It had not yet occurred to them to utilize the power of the seed; they had not stayed in one place, nor could they imagine the act of sowing; they moved forward, without goal, eating palm hearts for which they fought with the monkeys hanging from the roof of the jungle. When the flood waters isolated them for a season in some deltal region, and they had stripped the trees like termites, they ate the larvæ of wasps, munched ants, lice, dug into the earth for worms and maggots, then finally ate the earth itself. They hardly knew the uses of fire. Their skulking dogs, with eyes of foxes and wolves, were pre-dogs.

I looked at the faces of the people, which were meaningless to me, realizing the futility of words, knowing beforehand that we could not even meet in the coincidence of a gesture. Taking me by the arm, the Adelantado led me to the edge of a muddy hole, a kind of stinking pigpen full of gnawed bones, where I saw before me the most horrible things my eyes had ever beheld. They were like two fetuses with white beards from whose hanging lips came sounds resembling the wail of a newborn child; wrinkled dwarfs, with huge bellies on which blue veins traced designs like those of an anatomical chart, and who smiled stupidly, with something fearful and fawning in their look, their fingers between their teeth. My horror of them was so great that I turned my back in disgust and fright. "They are prisoners," said the Adelantado sarcastically, "prisoners of the others, who consider themselves the superior race, the sole rightful owners of the jungle."

A kind of dizziness came over me at the thought of other possible degrees of regression, that these human larvæ, from whose loins hung virile members, like my own, might not be *the lowest.* Somewhere there might exist captives of these captives, who, in turn, had arrogated to themselves the status of a superior species, elect, empowered, who no longer even gnawed the bones left by the dogs, but fought over carrion with the vultures, and, in the rutting season, bellowed like beasts. I had nothing in common with these beings. Nothing. Nor with their masters, the eaters of worms, the swallowers of earth, who surrounded me. And yet, among the hammocks which were hardly hammocks, but rather reed cradles, where they lay and fornicated and procreated, there was a clay object baked in the sun, a kind of jar without handles, with two holes opposite each other in the upper part, and a navel outlined in the convex surface by the pressure of a finger when the clay was still soft.

This was God. More than God, it was the Mother of God. It was the Mother, primordial in all religions. The female principle, genesial, womb, to be found in the secret prologue of all theogonies. The Mother, with swollen belly, which was at one and the same time breasts, womb, and sex, the first figure modeled by man, when under his hands the possibility of the object came into being. I had before me the Mother of the Infant Gods, of the totems given to men so that they would acquire the habit of dealing with the divinity, preparing the way for the Greater Gods. The Mother, "lonely, beyond space, and even time," whose sole name, *Mother*, Faust twice uttered with terror.

Seeing that the old women with wrinkled pubis, the tree-climbers, and the pregnant women were looking at me, I made a clumsy gesture of reverence toward the sacred vessel. I was in the dwelling-place of men, and must respect their Gods. But just then they all started to run. To my rear, under a tangle of leaves hanging from branches that served as a roof, they had just laid the swollen, blackened body of a hunter who had been bitten by a rattlesnake. Fray Pedro said that he had been dead for several hours. Nevertheless, the shaman began to shake a gourd full of pebbles—the only instrument these people know—trying to drive off the emissaries of Death. There was a ritual silence, setting the stage for the incantation, which raised the tension of the spectators to fever pitch.

And in the vast jungle filling with night terrors, there arose the Word. A word that was more than word. A word that imitated the voice of the speaker, and of that attributed to the spirit in possession of the corpse. One came from the throat of the shaman; the other from his belly. One was deep and confused like the bubbling of underground lava; the other, medium in pitch, was harsh and wrathful. They alternated. They answered each other. The one upbraided when the other groaned; the belly voice turned sarcastic when the throat voice seemed to plead. Sounds like guttural portamenti were heard, ending in howls; syllables repeated over and over, coming to create a kind of rhythm; there were trills suddenly interrupted by four notes that were the embryo of a melody. But then came the vibration of the tongue between the lips, the indrawn snoring, the panting contrapuntal to the rattle of the maraca. This was something far beyond language, and yet still far from song. Something that had not yet discovered vocalization, but was more than word.

As it went on, this outcry over a corpse surrounded by silent dogs became horrible, terrifying. The shaman now stood facing the body, shouting, thumping his heels on the ground in the paroxysm of a fury of imprecation which held the basic elements of all tragedy—the earliest attempt to combat the forces of annihilation which frustrate man's designs. I tried to remain outside, to establish distances. And yet I could not resist the horrid fascination this ceremony held for me. . . .

Before the stubbornness of Death, which refused to release its prey, the Word suddenly grew faint and disheartened. In the mouth of the shaman, the spell-working orifice, the *Threne*—for that was what this was—gasped and died away convulsively, blinding me with the realization that I had just witnessed the Birth of Music.

(Saturday, June 23)

XXIV/ For two days we had been crawling along the skeleton of the planet, forgetting History and even the obscure migrations of the unrecorded ages. Slowly, always upward, through stretches of river between cascade and cascade, by quiet channels between one fall and another, forced to portage our boats from level to level to the music of chanteys, we had come to the land of the Great Plateaus. Denuded of their covering—when they had it—by thousands of rainfalls, they were Forms of bare rock reduced to the awesome elementality of a telluric geometry. These were the first monuments that arose upon the surface of the earth before there were eyes to see them, and their age, their ancestry without equal, lent them an overwhelming majesty. Some resembled huge bronze cylinders, truncated pyramids, long quartz crystals poised between the waters. Some were wider at the summit than at the base and were pitted with cavities like gigantic corals. Some had a mysterious solemnity as though they were Gates to Something —Something unknown and terrible—to which the tunnels gouged in their flanks, a hundred feet above our heads, must lead.

Each plateau had its own morphology, consisting of groins, sheer drops, straight or broken edges. The one not

adorned with the incarnation of an obelisk or a basalt head-
land had a flanking terrace, beveled edges, sharp angles, or
was crowned by strange stone markers resembling the figures in a procession. Suddenly, in contrast to this severity,
a stone arabesque, some geological flight of fancy, con-
spired with the water to give a touch of movement to this
land of the unmovable. A mountain of reddish granite
poured seven yellow cascades over the battlements of its
crowning cornice. Or a river hurled itself into space and
became a rainbow on the cutback stairway of petrified
trees. The foam of a river boiled under enormous natural
arches with deafening echo before it divided and fell into a
series of pools emptying into one another. One sensed that
overhead, at the summit, in this series of stairsteps to the
moon, there were lakes, neighbors to the clouds, whose virgin waters had never been profaned by human eye.

There were morning hoarfrost, icy depths, opalescent
banks, and hollows filled with the night before twilight.
There were monoliths poised on the edge of peaks, needles,
crosses, cracks that breathed forth mists; wrinkled crags
that were like congealed lava—meteors, perhaps, fallen
from another planet. We were overawed by the display of
these opera magna, the plurality of the profiles, the scope of
the shadows, the immensity of the esplanades. We felt like
intruders who at any moment might be cast out of a forbidden kingdom. What lay before our eyes was the world
that existed before man.

Below, in the great rivers, were the monstrous saurians,
the anacondas, the fish with teats, the big-headed *laulau*,
the fresh-water dogfish, the electric eels, the lepidosirens,
which still bore the stamp of prehistoric animals, a legacy
from the great reptiles of the Tertiary. Here, though things
slithered beneath the tree ferns, though the bee stored honey
in the caves, nothing recalled living creatures.

The waters have just been divided, the Dry Land has appeared, the green grass has come forth, and, for the first time, the lights to rule the day and the night have been tried out. We are in the world of Genesis, at the end of the Fourth Day of Creation. If we go back a little farther, we will come to the terrible loneliness of the Creator, the sidereal sadness of the times without incense or songs of praise, when the earth was without order and empty, and darkness was upon the face of the deep.

Chapter Five

Thy statutes have been my
songs. . . .—PSALM CXIX, 54

(*Sunday, June 24*)
XXV/ The Adelantado raised his arm, pointing out where
the Gold lay, and Yannes took leave of us to go in search of
the treasure of the earth. Lonely is the miner who does not
want to share his find; avaricious in his dealings, false in his
words, erasing the path behind him like the animal who
wipes out its tracks with its tail. There was a moment of
emotion as we embraced this peasant of the Achæan profile,
reader of Homer, who seemed to be attached to us. Today
his lodestar was covetousness for the precious metal that
made Mycenæ a city of gold, and he took the road of the
adventurers. He wanted to give us a present, and having
nothing but the clothes he wore, he handed Rosario and me
his volume of the *Odyssey*. *Your woman* accepted it with
delight, thinking it was a story of the Bible that would bring
us good luck.

Before I could disillusion her, Yannes was gone, on the way to his boat, his chest bared to the dawn, his oar on his shoulder, a living Ulysses. Fray Pedro blessed him, and we continued our navigation through the waters of a narrow channel that would lead us to the wharf of the City. Because now that the Greek had gone, the secret could be told: the Adelantado had founded a city.

I never wearied of repeating this to myself, ever since this matter of *a city* had been confided to me several nights before, lighting more stars in my imagination than the names of the most coveted gems. To found a city. I found a city; he founds a city—it was a verb that could be conjugated. One could be the Founder of a City. Bring into being and govern a city whose name was not to be found on maps, which was withdrawn from the horrors of the Epoch, which was born of the will of a man, in this world of Genesis. The first city. The city of Enoch, before the birth of Tubal-cain, the worker in brass and iron, or Jubal, the father of all who handle the harp and the organ.

I rested my head in Rosario's lap, thinking of the vast territories, the unexplored lands, the myriad plateaus, where cities could be founded on this continent on which nature had not yet been subdued by man. The rhythmic plashing of the oars lulled me into a pleasant drowsiness, there on the living waters, beside plants beginning to recover the fragrance of the mountains, breathing a thin air which knew nothing of the exasperating tormentors of the jungle. The hours slipped by as we skirted the plateaus, moving from one stream to another through little mazes of quiet waters which had us moving with the sun at our back first, and then, around a point covered with strange ivy, full in our face. The afternoon was falling when we finally tied up the boat and I could look upon the wonder of Santa Mónica de los Venados.

But the truth is that I stood there disconcerted. What I

saw in the hollow of a little valley was a space some two hundred yards wide, cleared by machetes, and at the back a big mud and wattle house, with a door and four windows. Two smaller houses, of construction similar to the first, flanked a kind of storehouse or stable. There were about ten Indian huts from whose hearths a pale smoke rose.

The Adelantado said to me, his voice trembling with pride: "This is the main square. . . . That is the Government House. . . . There's where my son Marcos lives. . . . My three daughters live there. . . . We keep grain and implements in the nave, and some animals. . . . Behind are the Indian quarters. . . ." And he added, turning to Fray Pedro: "Across from the Government House we shall put up the Cathedral."

He was still pointing out to me the gardens, the corn fields, the enclosure where pigs and goats were being raised, thanks to the boars and billy goats that had been brought with greatest difficulty from Puerto Anunciación, when the whole population began to pour out of the houses shouting greetings, and the Indian wives ran up, and the half-breed daughters, and the son who was Mayor, and all the Indians, to receive their Governor, accompanied by the first Bishop.

"It is called Santa Mónica de los Venados," Fray Pedro explained, "because this is the land of the red deer, and Mónica was the name of the founder's mother, Mónica, who bore St. Augustine, *herself a saint who had been the wife of one man and herself had brought up her children.*"

I could not help confessing to him that the word "city" had suggested to me something more imposing. "Manoa?" asked the friar scornfully. It was not that. Neither Manoa nor El Dorado. But I had imagined something different.

"The cities founded by Francisco Pizarro, Diego de Losada, or Pedro de Mendoza were like this at first," Fray Pedro remarked. My silence of consent did not, however, eliminate a series of new questions which the preparations for a feast of haunches roasting over a wood fire prevented me from asking at the moment. I could not understand why the Adelantado, having this unique opportunity to found a city outside the Epoch, should have burdened himself with a church, which carries with it the crushing weight of its canons, interdicts, ambitions, intolerance, especially in view of the fact that his was not a very deeply grounded faith, and the Masses he preferred were those of thanksgiving for dangers overcome.

But at the moment there was small opportunity to ask questions. I was filled with joy at having arrived somewhere. I helped roast the meat, I went for wood, I listened to the songs being sung, and I loosened up my joints with a kind of sparkling pulque tasting of earth and resin, which we all drank in gourds passed from mouth to mouth. Later, when all were gorged, and the Indians were asleep in their village and the daughters of the Founder had retired to their gynæceum, I listened, beside the hearth in the Government House, to a tale that was the tale of routes.

"Well, sir," began the Adelantado, throwing a branch on the fire, "my name is Pablo, and my last name is just as commonplace, and if the title of *Adelantado* smacks of great deeds, you must know that it is only a nickname a group of miners gave me when they saw that I was always ahead of the others in cradling the river sands."

Under the sign of the caduceus, a youth of twenty, racked by a stubborn cough, looked out on the street through the glass jars filled with colored water in an old man's pharmacy. It was a province of matins and rosaries, of convent sweetmeats and pastries; the priest walked past in his shovel hat, and the watchman still called out the hours in the clouded night with a "*María Santíssima.*" Far off lay the Lands of the Horse, leagues and leagues away; close by were the winding roads and the city of big houses where the only trades open to the youth were trades of darkness, of cassocks, of cellars, of sewers.

Discouraged and sick, he had offered his services to the druggist, in exchange for medicines and a roof. There they taught him something about infusions and entrusted to him simple prescriptions whose ingredients were for the most part nux vomica, mallow root, and tartar emetic. At the siesta hour, when nobody walked beneath the shadow of the eaves, the young man sat alone in the dispensary, his back to the street, his hands asleep over grinding slab and mortar, and contemplated as in a reverie the leisurely flow of a great river whose waters came from the lands of gold.

At times, from ships so old that they seemed of another age, came groups of heavy-gaited men who went tapping their sticks upon the rotten planks of the wharf as though even ashore they still feared the pitfalls and quagmires of the earth. They were malaria-shaken miners, rubber-gatherers who scratched their eczema, lepers from the abandoned missions, who came to the pharmacy for quinine, for chaulmoogra oil, for sulphur. And as they spoke of the regions where they had contracted their ailments, they rolled back the curtains of an unknown world before the wondering clerk. The defeated arrived, but there also came those who had wrested from the mud a wondrous stone, and for a week they gorged themselves on women and music. Those who had found nothing came, too, their eyes feverish with prospects. They neither rested nor inquired where there were women. They locked themselves in their rooms, examining the samples they brought back in bottles, and as soon as they were cured of a wound, or their buboes were relieved, they left by night, when all were sleeping, without revealing the secret of where they were going.

The youth felt no envy of those his own age who, every Monday of the year, after listening to the last Mass in the church with the worm-eaten pulpit, set out in their best clothes for the distant city. Between flasks and prescriptions, he learned about new lodes; he knew the names of those who ordered demijohns of orange-flower water to bathe their Indian women; he memorized the strange names of rivers not mentioned in books; obsessed by the ringing sonority of *Cataniapo* or *Cunucunuma*, he dreamed before the maps, never wearying of the bare green-colored areas where no settlements appeared. And one day, at dawn, he climbed out through the window of his laboratory to the dock where the miners were hoisting sail, with a load of medicine that he offered in exchange for his passage.

For ten years he shared the sufferings, disappointments, rages, doggedness of the treasure-hunters. Unfavored by fortune, he pushed farther and farther, always more alone, accustomed now to talking with his shadow. And one morning he found himself before the Great Plateaus. For ninety days he walked, lost among the nameless mountains, eating wasp larvæ, ants, grasshoppers, like the Indians in times of famine. When he came into this valley, a worm-infested wound was rotting his leg to the bone. The Indians of the region—a sedentary people of a culture similar to that of the makers of the funerary jar—cured him with herbs. They had seen only one white man before him, and, like many of the jungle people, they thought us the last survivors of an industrious but weak species, once numerous but now on the way to becoming extinct.

His long convalescence gave him a sense of solidarity with the privations and toil of these people among whom he had come. One night he found some gold at the foot of that cliff which the moon is now turning to quicksilver. When he returned from Puerto Anunciación, where he had sold it, he brought with him seeds, cuttings, and some farm implements and carpenter's tools. On his return from his second trip, he brought back a pair of pigs tied by the feet in the bottom of his boat. Then came the goat with young, the weaned calf, for which the Indians, like Adam, had to invent a name, for they had never seen such an animal before.

Little by little the Adelantado came to identify himself with the life that he had made to flourish there. When he bathed at the foot of a cascade of an afternoon, the Indian maidens threw white pebbles at him from the bank, as a sign that he should choose one of them. One day he took himself a wife, and there was great merrymaking at the foot of the cliffs. It then occurred to him that if he kept returning to Puerto Anunciación with gold dust, it would not take the miners long to pick up his trail and invade this lost valley and destroy it with their vices, their hatreds, and their ambitions. To keep from arousing their suspicions, he passed himself off as a dealer in stuffed birds, orchids, turtle eggs.

One day he realized that he had founded a city. He probably felt the same surprise as I had felt when I realized that the verb "found" could be conjugated when it referred to a city. Inasmuch as all cities came to being in the same way, there was reason to believe that in the future Santa Mónica de los Venados would have monuments, bridges, arcades. The Adelantado laid out the Main Square. He erected the Government House. He drew up and signed a document, and buried it under a stone in a conspicuous place. He laid out the cemetery so that death itself should be an ordered affair.

Now he knew where there was gold, but gold no longer lured him. He had given up the search for Manoa because he was now much more interested in the land and in the power of decreeing its laws. He did not pretend that this was the Garden of Eden, as stated on the old maps. There were diseases here, plagues, venomous serpents, insects, wild beasts that devoured the domestic animals reared with such hardship. There were times of flood and times of hunger and days of impotence resulting from a gangrened arm. But man, through long training, can endure these evils. And when he succumbs, it is in the age-old struggle that is one of the basic laws of existence.

"Gold," remarked the Adelantado, "is for those who go back *there*." And there was a ring of contempt in his tone when he said "*there*," as though the concerns and ambitions of people "*there*" befitted inferior beings.

There was no doubt that the nature surrounding us was implacable, terrible, in spite of its beauty. But those whose life was spent with it found it less evil, more friendly, than the terrors and alarms, the cold cruelties, the never-ending threats of the world back *there*. Here the plagues, the possible sufferings, the natural dangers were accepted as a matter of course; they formed part of an Order that had its severity. Creation is no laughing-matter, and they all knew this instinctively and accepted the role each of them had been assigned in the great tragedy of living. But it was a tragedy with a unity of time, place, and action; in it, death itself operated under the direction of known masters, attired in poison, scale, fire, miasmas, to the accompaniment of the thunder and lightning that the older gods who have long dwelt among us still employ on their days of wrath.

Under the light of the sun or beside the hearthfire the men who lived out their destinies here were content with simple things, and found happiness in the pleasant warmth of a morning, the abundance of fish, the rain that succeeds the drought, in a burst of collective rejoicing, with song and drums, motivated by such simple events as our arrival. "Life must have been like this in the city of Enoch," I thought to myself, and there returned to my mind one of the questions that had perplexed me when we landed.

At this point we stepped out of the Adelantado's house for a breath of air. The Adelantado pointed out to me high on a cliffside certain signs carved by unknown workmen— workmen who had been hoisted to the level of their task by a scaffolding impossible in their state of material culture. The light of the moon made visible figures of scorpions, serpents, birds, among other signs that were meaningless to me, and which may have been astral symbols. A surprising explanation suddenly came to clear up my doubts. One day when he returned from a trip—the Founder related— his son Marcos, who was a boy at the time, amazed him with the story of the Flood. During his absence the Indians had told the boy that those petroglyphs we were looking at had been carved during the time of a gigantic flood, when the river rose to that height, by a man who, when he saw the waters rising, had saved a pair of every kind of animal in a great canoe. Then it had rained during a time that may have been forty days and forty nights, after which, to know whether the flood had ended, he sent out a rat, which came back with an ear of corn in its paws.

The Adelantado had not wanted to teach his children the story of Noah, for he regarded it as a fabrication; but when he discovered that they already knew it, the only departures being the rat instead of a dove and an ear of corn instead of an olive branch, he told the secret of his nascent city to Fray Pedro, whom he looked upon as a man because he traveled alone through unknown regions, and knew how to cure ills, and could tell one plant from another. "Since they are going to be told the same stories anyway, let them learn them the way I did."

Reflecting on the Noahs of so many religions, it struck me that the Indian Noah was better adapted to the reality of these lands, with his ear of corn instead of a dove with an olive branch, here in the jungle where nobody had ever seen an olive tree. But the friar interrupted my train of thought, asking me in a challenging tone if I had forgotten the matter of the Redemption: "There was one who died for those who were born here, and the news must be brought to them." And, making a cross of two twigs fastened with a liana, he planted it with a kind of fury on the spot where tomorrow the building of the round hut that would be the first temple in Enoch was to begin.

"He is going to plant onions, too," the Adelantado informed me by way of excuse.

(June 27)

XXVI/ Dawn rose over the Great Plateaus. The mists of night still lingered between the Forms, spread veils that grew transparent and disappeared as the light was reflected from a cliff of rosy granite and descended to the level of the great sleeping shadows. At the foot of the green, gray, black walls whose summits seemed to melt into the fog, the ferns shook off the light hoarfrost that enameled them. In an opening that could hardly hide a child, I observed a life of lichens, mosses, silvery pigments, and vegetable rust on a minute scale, a world as complex as that of the great jungle. This plankton of the earth was like a patina that thickened at the foot of a cascade dropping from a great height, and whose boiling water had dug a pool in the rock.

It was here we bathed naked, we, the Couple, in water that splashed and flowed, descending from heights already warmed by the sun, and ran below in beds that the tannin of the tree roots turned yellow. There was no Edenic affectation in this clean nakedness, different from that which panted and struggled in our nights in the hut. Here we gave ourselves up to a kind of playfulness, amazed at finding that the breeze and the light fell so pleasantly on parts of the body which people *there* die without ever having exposed to the touch of the air. The sun darkened that strip from hip to thigh which is white among the swimmers of my country, even though they have bathed in sun-drenched seas. The sun got between my legs, warmed my testicles, ran down my backbone, broke against my breast, darkened my armpits, covered my neck with sweat, possessed, invaded me; its ardor hardened my seminal ducts, and I felt once more the tension and the throb that sought the dark palpitations of vitals plumbed to their depths in a boundless desire of oneness which became the longing for the womb.

And then the water again, below whose surface bubbled icy springs in which I buried my face and washed my hands with coarse sand like marble filings. Later on, the Indians would come to bathe naked, their only garment their hands covering their penises. And at noon it would be Fray Pedro, not even covering the whitened hairs of his genitals, bony and gaunt as a St. John preaching in the wilderness.

Today I had made the great decision not to return *there*. I would try to learn the simple crafts followed here in Santa Mónica de los Venados, beginning by watching the building of the church. I would liberate myself from the fate of Sisyphus, which was laid upon me by the world I came from. I would flee the empty callings, the spinning of a squirrel in a cage, the measured time, the trades of darkness. Mondays to me would no longer be Ash Mondays, nor would I need to remember that Monday is Monday, and the stone I had borne would be for whoever wanted to bow beneath its useless weight. I preferred to wield saw and ax rather than go on prostituting music in the announcer's trade.

I told all this to Rosario, who accepted my plan with joyous docility, as she would always accept the will of the man whom she had received as her man. *Your woman* had not grasped the fact that, for me, this decision was much more serious than it seemed, for it meant renouncing everything *back there*. For her, born on the outskirts of the jungle, who had sisters living with miners, it was natural that a man should prefer the open spaces to the congestion of the cities. Besides, I do not think that in accustoming herself to me she had been forced to make as many intellectual adjustments as I had. To her I did not seem very different from other men she had known. Whereas I, to love her—and I realized that I loved her deeply now—had been compelled to establish a new scale of values to make it possible for a man of my formation to establish bonds with a woman who was all woman and nothing but woman.

I was, therefore, clearly aware of what I was doing. And when I told myself again that I was staying, that my lights from then on would be those of the sun and the hearthfire, that each morning I would plunge my body into this cascade, and that a whole and complete woman, without complications, would always be within reach of my desire, a vast happiness came over me.

Lying on a rock while Rosario, her breasts bared, washed her hair in the stream, I took out Yannes's old copy of the *Odyssey*, and as I opened it, I came upon a paragraph that made me smile: the one that speaks of the men whom Ulysses sent to the land of the lotus-eaters and from whose minds, when they had tasted of the fruit they were given, all memory of home faded. "I had to seek them and drag them back on board," relates the hero, "and chain them beneath the thwarts, deep in the well."

In the marvelous tale I had always been irked by the cruelty of Ulysses, tearing his companions from the happiness they had found without offering them other recompense than serving him. I found in this myth a reflection of the irritation always aroused in society by the acts of those who find in love, in the enjoyment of a physical privilege, in an unexpected gift, a way of avoiding the shabbiness, the restrictions, the spying the majority must suffer.

I turned on my side on the warm stone, and this brought into view a group of Indians seated around Marcos, the son of the Adelantado, and weaving baskets. And it seemed to me now that my old theory about the origins of music was absurd. I saw how unfounded were the speculations of those who feel that they can grasp the beginnings of certain of man's arts or institutions without knowing prehistoric man, our contemporary, in his daily life, in his healing and religious practices. My idea of relating the magic objective of the primitive plastic arts—the representation of the animal that gives power over its living counterpart—to the first manifestations of musical rhythm, the attempt to imitate the gallop, the trot, the tread of animals, was highly ingenious. But I was present, a few days ago, at the birth of music. I could see beyond the dirge with which Æschylus revived the Persian Emperor; beyond the rune with which the sons of Autolycus stanched the dark blood that flowed from Ulysses' wounds; beyond the song designed to protect the Pharaoh Unas against serpents' stings in his journey to the other world.

What I had seen confirmed, to be sure, the thesis of those who argue that music had a magic origin. But they had arrived at this conclusion through books, through studies in psychology, building dangerous hypotheses on the survival, in the classical tragedy, of practices deriving from a sorcery already remote. But I *had seen* the word travel the road of song without reaching it; I had seen how the repetition of a single syllable gave rise to a certain rhythm; I had seen how the alternation of the real voice and the feigned voice forced the witch-doctor to employ two pitches, how a musical theme could originate in an extramusical practice. I thought of all the nonsense uttered by those who take the position that prehistoric man discovered music in his desire to imitate the beauty of birdwarblings—as though the song of a bird had any musical-æsthetic value for those who hear it constantly amidst a concert of snorts, screeches, splashing, running, things falling, waters rushing, which for the hunter is a kind of sonorous code, the understanding of which is a part of his craft.

I thought of all the other fallacious theories, and I began to muse on the clouds of dust my observations would stir up in certain musical circles in which ideas all come from books. It would be a good thing to record some of the songs of these Indians, which were very beautiful in their simplicity, with their strange scales, and which would destroy that other widely held belief that the Indians use only the pentatonic scale. But suddenly I grew exasperated at these ideas running through my head. I had made up my mind to stay here, and I had to lay aside, once and for all, these idle speculations.

To rid myself of them I put on the scant clothing I used here, and went to join the group that was completing the building of the church. It was a wide, round cabin, with a pointed roof like that of the huts of palm fronds over a framework of boughs, topped by a wooden cross. Fray Pedro was determined that the windows should have a Gothic air, with pointed arches, and the repetition of two curved lines in a mud and wattle wall was, in this remote spot, a forerunner of the Gregorian chant. We hung a hollow trunk from the bell-tower, and in lieu of bells I had suggested a kind of *teponaxtle*. The idea for that instrument came to me from the drum-rhythm-stick in the hut, and the study of its principle of resonance had given rise to a painful experience.

When, two days before, I had untied the withes that held the protecting mats in place, these, stiffened by the dampness, snapped back, spilling the funerary urn, the rattles, the Panpipes on the floor. Suddenly I found myself surrounded by creditor-objects, which it did no good to stand in the corner, like naughty children, to free myself of their accusing presence. I had come to these forests, shaken off my load, found myself a woman, thanks to the money I had taken for these instruments, which were not mine. By fleeing, I was shackling my creditor. And I

knew I was shackling him, for the Curator without
doubt would take the responsibility for my absconding,
and at any sacrifice would pay back the money given me,
pawning his possessions or perhaps borrowing the money
from some loan shark. I should have been happy, bliss-
fully happy, but for the presence at the head of my hammock of these museum pieces, mutely demanding index
cards and showcase. I ought to have got these instruments out of here, broken them, buried the pieces at the
foot of a rock. But I could not do it, for my conscience
had returned to its deserted post and, after its long exile,
had come back mistrustful and full of complaints.

Rosario blew into one of the reeds of the ritual jar,
and a hoarse bellow echoed, like that of an animal fallen
into the darkness of a pit. I pushed her aside so roughly
that she moved away, her feelings hurt, not knowing what
she had done. To soothe her, I told her the reasons for my
irritation. She came up at once with the simple solution:
I must send these instruments to Puerto Anunciación when
the Adelantado made his regular trip in a few months
to buy needed medicines and to replace some worn-out
tool. There her sister would take charge of seeing that
they got down the river to the post office. My conscience
stopped gnawing at me. The day those bundles were on
their way I would have paid for the keys of my evasion.

XXVII/ I had climbed up the cliff of the petroglyphs
with Fray Pedro, and now we were resting on a floor
of shards, broken by black crags that caught the winds on
all flanks, or had crumbled like ruins, rubble, among
vegetation that seemed cut from gray felt. There was
something remote, lunar, not meant for man, on this terrace that led to the clouds, furrowed by a brook of icy
water that was not spring water, but mist water. I felt

vaguely uneasy—an intruder, not to say a profaner—
at the thought that my presence had torn the veil from
the mystery of a mineral teratology whose arid grandeur,
the work of millenniums of erosion, revealed a skeleton
of mountains that seemed composed of sulphur stones,
lava, chalcedony rubble, plutonic slag. There were gravel
beds that made me think of Byzantine mosaics fallen from
their walls in a landslide and shoveled and heaped up here
like a winnowing of quartz, gold, and carnelian.

To get here we had been traveling for two days by
paths from which the reptiles had gradually disappeared,
paths rich in orchids and flowering trees, through the
Lands of Birds. From sunup to sundown we were escorted
by brilliant macaws and pink parrots and solemn-visaged
toucans, with their greenish-yellow breastplates, their
clacking bills, and their "Go with God" at nightfall when
wicked thoughts have more power over man. We saw the
hummingbirds, more insect than bird, motionless in their
phosphorescent vibration. From overhead came the busy
drill of dark-striped woodpeckers, the noisy confusion of
the whistlers and the warblers in the roof of the forest,
apprehensive of everything, high above the chatter of parrots, and many other birds displaying every color of the
palette, which, Fray Pedro told me, for lack of known
name the conquistadors called "Indian sunflowers." Just
as other cultures were branded with the sign of the horse
or the bull, the Indian with his bird profile placed his
culture under the sign of the bird. The flying god, the
bird god, the plumed serpent were the nucleus of his
mythologies, and everything beautiful was adorned with
feathers. The tiaras of the emperors of Tenochtitlán were
made of feathers, as were the decorations of the flutes, the
toys, the festive and ritual vestments I had seen here.

Struck by the discovery that I was now living in the
Lands of the Bird, I remarked somewhat superficially that

it would probably be difficult to find in the cosmogonies of these peoples myths that paralleled ours. Fray Pedro inquired if I had read a book called the *Popol-Vuh*, of which I did not know even the name.

"In that sacred book of the Quichés," the friar told me, "with tragic intuition the myth of the robot is set down. I would even go so far as to say that it is the only cosmogony that has foreseen the threat of the machine and the tragedy of the Sorcerer's Apprentice." And in the language of the scholar, which must have been his before it became petrified in the forest, he told me how, in the first chapter of Creation, the objects and utensils invented by man, which he used with the help of fire, rose against him and killed him. The water jars, the stone griddles, the plates, the cooking-pots, the grinding stones, the houses themselves, in a horrifying apocalypse, to the accompaniment of the barking of maddened dogs, had turned on him and wiped out the generation of man.

He was still telling me of this when I raised my eyes and found myself at the foot of the gray wall with the rock carvings attributed to the demiurge who, in a tradition that had reached the ears of the primitive inhabitants of the jungle below, triumphed over the Flood and re-populated the world. We were standing on the Mount Ararat of this vast world. This was where the ark had come to rest when the waters began to withdraw and the rat had returned with an ear of corn between its paws. We were where the demiurge threw the stones over his shoulder, like Deucalion, to call into being a new race of men. But neither Deucalion, nor Noah, nor the Chaldean Unapishtim, nor the Chinese or Egyptian Noahs left their signature scrawled for the ages at the point of their arrival. Whereas here there were huge figures of insects, serpents, creatures of the air, beasts of the water and the land, designs of the moon, sun, and stars which *someone* had cut here with a Cyclopean chisel, employing a method we could not divine. Even today it would be impossible to rig up the gigantic scaffolding that would be needed to raise an army of stonecutters to a height at which they could attack the stone wall with their tools and leave it so clearly inscribed. . . .

Now Fray Pedro led me to the other end of the Signs and pointed out on that side of the mountain a kind of crater in whose depths horrendous plants proliferated. They were like fleshy grasses whose morbid shoots were round like tentacles or arms. The huge leaves, open like hands, resembled submarine flora in their texture of coral and seaweed, with bulbous flowers like feather lanterns, birds suspended from a vein, ears of corn of larvæ, bloodshot pistils bursting from their sides without the grace of a stem. And all this, there below, intertwined, tangled, in a grappling, a coupling, monstrous and orgiastic, incests that represent the supreme confusion of forms.

"These are the plants which have fled from man since the beginning," the friar told me, "the rebel plants, those which refused to serve him as food, which crossed rivers, scaled mountains, leaped the deserts for thousands and thousands of years, to hide here, in the last redoubts of Prehistory."

In silent amazement I gazed on what in other places was fossil impression or slept in the petrification of coal, but here continued alive in a timeless spring antedating the days of man, whose season might not be that of the solar year. Perhaps their seeds germinated in hours; perhaps they took half a century. "This is the diabolical vegetation that surrounded the Garden of Eden before the Fall."

Leaning over the devil's caldron, I felt the vertigo of space. I knew that if I let myself come under the spell of what I was looking upon here, this prenatal world, I would end up by hurling myself down, burying myself in this fearful density of leaves which would one day disappear from the planet without having been given a name, without having been re-created by the Word. They might be the creation of gods that came before our gods, gods on trial, clumsy in their works, unknown because they were never named, because they never took on shape in the mouth of man.

With a light blow on the shoulder with his staff, Fray Pedro aroused me from my half-hallucinated gazing. The shadows of the natural obelisks grew shorter as noon approached. We had to start back before evening overtook us on this height and the clouds closed in and we became lost in chill fogs. We passed before the signature of the demiurge once more, to the edge of the crevasse where we began our descent. Fray Pedro paused, took a deep breath, and gazed out upon a horizon of trees above which emerged a dentated slaty range of mountains which stood like a hard, hostile presence over the breath-taking beauty of the valley.

The friar pointed with his gnarled staff: "The only perverse and bloodthirsty Indians of these regions live over there." No missionary had ever returned.

At this point I allowed myself some jocular remark about the futility of venturing into such thankless places. By way of reply two gray eyes, immeasurably sad, were fixed on me with an expression at once piercing and resigned so that I became disconcerted, wondering if I had in some way offended, though the reason escaped me. I can still see the Capuchin's wrinkled face, his long unkempt beard, his ears bristling with hairs, his blue-veined temples like something that had ceased to belong to him and to be a part of his person. At that moment his being was concentrated in those old pupils, reddened by chronic conjunctivitis, which were gazing, as though made of clouded enamel, both inward and outward.

XXVIII/ Sitting behind a board resting on two trestles, almost naked because of the heat, beside his hand a student's notebook on the cover of which was lettered: *"Notebook. Property of . . . ,"* the Adelantado was legislating in the presence of Fray Pedro, the Headman of the Indians, and Marcos, the Keeper of the Garden. Beside his master sat Gavilán, a bone between his hind legs for safekeeping. The purpose of the meeting was to make a number of decisions for the good of the community and to set them down in writing. The Adelantado had discovered that during his absence does had been hunted and killed, and he moved that the killing of what he called the "female deer" and fawns should be absolutely prohibited except in case of famine, and that even then the raising of the ban would have to be treated as an emergency measure subject to the approval of those there present. The migration of certain herds, the thoughtless hunting, the depredations of wild beasts, which threatened the red deer of the region with extinction, were the cause for this measure.

After all had sworn to abide by it and observe it, the Law was inscribed in the Book of the Council, and the next item on the agenda was one of public works. The rainy season was approaching, and Marcos reported that the digging of the beds Fray Pedro had recently ordered had been done against his advice, for they were located in a position that would so channel the waters from a near-by slope that the granary would probably be flooded. The Adelantado frowned at the friar, waiting to hear his explanation. Fray Pedro answered that he had done this as preparation for the planting of onions, which needed well-drained and not too damp soil, which could only be achieved by laying out the beds with their narrow edges toward the slope. The danger, the Keeper of the Garden had pointed out, could be avoided by throwing up a dike of dirt, some three feet high, between the garden and the granary.

It was unanimously agreed that this work should be started the next day, with the help of all the inhabitants of Santa Mónica de los Venados, for the sky was heavily overcast and by midday the heat was almost unbearable, with dense humidity and swarms of flies, come to plague us from nobody knew where. However, Fray Pedro pointed out the fact that the church was not finished, and that this, too, was urgent. The Adelantado cuttingly answered that the safeguarding of the grain was more urgent than services in Latin, and concluded the business of the day with instructions about the cutting and hauling of logs for a fence and the need of posting sentinels to watch for the appearance of certain schools of fish which were coming up the river ahead of time.

Out of the town meeting had come several immediate decisions and a Law—a law whose infraction "will be punished," so read the Adelantado's prose. This disturbed me so much that I asked him if he had already had the disagreeable duty of meting out punishments in the City. "So far," he answered, "the deliquents have been punished by not speaking to them for a time, making them feel the general disapproval; but the day will come when there will be so many of us that more severe penalties will be called for."

Once more I was amazed at the serious problems to be dealt with in these regions, as unknown as the blank *terræ incognitæ* of the old cartographers, in which the men back *there* saw only alligators, vampire bats, deadly serpents, and Indian dances. During the time I had been traveling through this virgin world, I had seen very few snakes—a coral snake, a moccasin, what may have been a rattlesnake—and I had known wild animals only by their roaring, though more than once I had thrown stones at some sly alligator disguised as a rotten log in a treacherously quiet pool. My experience had been meager as far as dangers were concerned, aside from the storm in the rapids. But at every turn I had found stimuli to thought, motives for meditation, forms of art, poetry, myth, more helpful to the understanding of man than hundreds of books written by men who pride themselves on knowing Man. Not only had the Adelantado founded a city, but, without realizing it, he was creating day by day a *polis* that would eventually rest on a code of laws solemnly entered in *Notebook . . . Property of . . .*

And the moment would come when severe punishment would have to be imposed on anyone killing an animal in the closed season, and it was apparent that this little, soft-spoken man would not hesitate to sentence the violator to being driven from the community to die of hunger in the forest, or to establish some spectacular, terrifying penalty like those of certain peoples who condemned parricides to being thrown into the river tied in sacks with a dog and a viper. I asked the Adelantado what he would do if one day a gold-hunter were to appear in Santa Mónica, one of those who spread their fever wherever they go.

"I would give him one day to get out," he answered.

"This is not the place for *those people*," added Marcos, and there was a quiver of resentment in his voice. I learned that the boy had gone *there* some time back against his father's wishes. Two years of bad treatment and humiliation by those with whom he had tried to establish a relationship of friendship and respect had brought him back with a hatred of all he had seen in that world. And he showed me, without offering any explanation, the scars of the fetters that had been welded on him in some remote frontier outpost.

Father and son fell silent; but behind that silence I sensed that they both fully accepted the stern responsibilities engendered by Reasons of State, as in the case of the gold-hunter determined to return to the Valley of the Plateaus, who would never come back from his second trip.

"Lost in the jungle," those interested in his fate would conclude.

This added another subject for thought to the many already filling my mind. What had happened was that after days of absolute mental sloth, during which I had been the physical man, oblivious of all that was not sensation— sunning myself, taking my pleasure with Rosario, fishing, accustoming my palate to totally new taste sensations —my brain had begun to work at an impatient, headlong pace, as though this rest had been essential. There were days when I would wish to be a naturalist, a geologist, an ethnologist, a botanist, a historian, so that I could understand all this, set it down, explain it so far as possible.

One afternoon I learned with surprise that the Indians here preserved the memory of a confused epic, which Fray Pedro was reconstructing bit by bit. It was the account of a Carib migration moving northward, laying waste everything in its path, and filling its victorious march with prodigious feats. It told of mountains moved by the hand of fabulous heroes, of rivers deflected from their courses, of singular combats in which the planets intervened. The amazing unity of myths was borne out by these accounts, which dealt with the abduction of princesses, stratagems of war, memorable duels, animal allies. On nights when in a religious ceremony the Headman of the Indians intoxicated himself with a powder inhaled through a bird's bone, he became a bard, and from his lips came fragments of the epic poem, the saga, which the missionary took down. The poem lived in the memory of the generations of the jungle.

But I knew that I must not think too much. I was not here to think. The daily tasks, the frugal fare—mainly tapioca, fish, and cassava bread—had thinned me down, firming my flesh to my bones. My body had become lean, defined, its muscles girded to its framework. The unnecessary fat I had carried, the pale, flabby skin, the fears, the groundless anxieties, the forebodings of disaster, the throbbings in the solar plexus, had disappeared. My body, adjusted to itself, felt good. When I came into contact with Rosario's flesh, the tension it aroused in me, rather than the stirrings of desire, was the uncontrollable urge of primordial rut, the tension of the taut bow, which, having released its arrow, resumes the laxity of its accustomed form. *Your woman* was at hand. I called her and she came. I was not here to think. I must not think. I must feel and see.

And when from seeing I turned to looking, strange lights sprang up and everything took on meaning. Thus I suddenly discovered that a Dance of the Trees exists. Not all of them possess the secret of dancing in the wind. But those to whom this grace has been given arrange dances of leaves, branches, twigs about their own swaying trunk: the rhythm that begins in the leaves, a restless, ascending rhythm—with the surge and breaking of waves, with gentle pauses, rests—which suddenly becomes a storm of rejoicing. There is nothing more beautiful than a bamboo thicket dancing in the breeze. No human choreography can equal the eurhythmy of a branch outlined against the sky. I asked myself whether the higher forms of the æsthetic emotion do not consist merely in a supreme understanding of creation. A day will come when men will discover an alphabet in the eyes of chalcedonies, in the markings of the moth, and will learn in astonishment that every spotted snail has always been a poem.

XXIX/ It had been raining steadily for two days. There was a prolonged overture of bass thunder rumbling over the ground, between the plateaus, filling the empty spaces, roaring in the caves—and then, suddenly, the water. As the palm-frond roofs were dry, we spent the first night moving our hammocks from place to place, looking in vain for a spot on which it did not leak. Then a torrent of mud began to swirl under us on the floor, and, to save the collection of instruments, I had to hang them from the roof beams. By morning we were all irritable, our clothing was damp, and mud was everywhere. It was hard to light the fire, and the rooms filled with smoke, which made the eyes water. Half the church had collapsed as a result of the downpour on the mud and wattle mixture, which had not yet hardened. Fray Pedro, with his habit girded up around his waist, was trying to shore it up as best he could. He was indignantly upbraiding the Adelantado for not having helped to get the job finished by declaring it an emergency.

Then the rain started up again, and it was rain and more rain until dark, and then it was night once more. I did not even have the consolation of Rosario's embraces: she "couldn't," and when this happened she became nervous, morose, as though every sign of affection annoyed her. I had trouble getting to sleep, what with the incessant drone of the water drowning out every sound not its own, as though the forty days and nights had set in. After finally dozing off—it was nowhere near morning yet—I awoke with the strange feeling that something great had taken place in my mind: something like the ripening and coalescing of chaotic, scattered elements, senseless when dispersed, but suddenly, when ordered, assuming clear meaning. A work had been constructed in my spirit; a "thing" before my eyes, open or closed, which rang in my ears, amazing me by the logic of its order. A work inscribed in me, which could easily be transferred to words, score, something that all could handle, read, understand.

Many years before, I had once yielded to the curiosity of smoking opium. I remembered that the fourth pipe produced a kind of intellectual well-being that brought with it the sudden solution to all the creative problems torturing me at the time. Everything became clear, thought out, measured, complete. When the effects of the drug wore off, I would have only to sit down with staved paper and in no time there would come from my pen, without difficulty or hesitation, the *Concerto* I was trying to work out. But the next day, when I emerged from my lucid sleep and really wanted to go to work, I made the mortifying discovery that nothing of all I had thought, imagined, decided under the influence of the drug amounted to anything. They were stock formulas, ideas without substance, ridiculous inventions, impossible attempts to transfer plastic emotions to sounds that the bubbling pellets had sublimated under the warmth of the lamp.

What was happening to me now, in the darkness, the water dripping all around me, was similar to that other delirious elaboration; but this time the well-being was accompanied by awareness; the ideas themselves were seeking an order, and here, within my head, a hand crossed out, corrected, circumscribed, selected. I no longer needed to wait for the benumbing effects of intoxication to wear off to put my thoughts in order. Now all I had to do was wait for the dawn, which would bring the light I needed to make the first sketches of the *Threnody*, the title stamped on my imagination during sleep.

Before I had become engulfed in the senseless activities that made me forget my composing—at bottom, my laziness, my inability to resist any temptation of pleasure, were nothing but insecurity as to my powers of creation—I had given much thought to certain unexplored possibilities of linking words and music. In order to get a better focus on the problem, I had first reviewed the long and beautiful history of the recitative in both its liturgical and its profane aspects.

But the study of the recitative, of the manners of reciting singing, of singing speaking, of seeking the melody in the inflections of the language, of weaving the word into the accompaniment or, on the contrary, of freeing it from the support of harmony—all this, which has so preoccupied modern composers since Mussorgsky and Debussy, culminating in the exasperated, convulsive achievements of the Viennese school, was not what I was looking for. I was striving for a musical expression that should come from the unadorned word, from the word prior to the music—not the word become music by the exaggeration and stylization of its inflections, after the impressionist manner—which should go from speaking to singing almost insensibly, the poem becoming music, finding its own music in the scansion and prosody, which is probably what takes place in the marvel of the *Dies iræ, dies illa* of plain chant, whose music seems born of Latin's natural accentuation.

I had conceived of a kind of cantata in which a personage taking the role of the coryphæus should step forward and, without a sound from the orchestra, after a gesture to attract the attention of the audience, should begin to *say* a very simple poem, made up of usual words, nouns like *man, woman, house, water, cloud, tree,* and others that because of their inherent eloquence require no adjective. A kind of word-genesis. And, little by little, the repetition of the words themselves, their accents, would give a peculiar intonation to certain successions of words which would be repeated at fixed intervals like a verbal refrain. And a melody would begin to assert itself, a melody which, as I conceived it, would have the simplicity of line, the design concentrated in a few notes, of an Ambrosian hymn—*Æterne rerum conditor*—which I considered music in the state nearest the word. When the words had been transformed into melody, certain instruments would make their discreet entrance, like sonorous punctuation, framing and setting off the normal periods of the recited words, displaying in their participation the vibratile material of which each of them was made: the presence of wood, copper, string, tympanum, like the annunciation of possible combinations.

At the same time, I had been greatly impressed, in those far-off days, by the revelation of a Compostelan trope—*Congaudeant catholici*—in which a second voice is heard above the *cantus firmus*, whose role was to adorn, to give it the melismas, the lights and shadows that would not have been fitting in the liturgical theme—whose purity was thus safeguarded—like a garland upon a bare column, detracting nothing from its dignity, but giving it an ornamental note, flexible and undulant. I saw the successive entrances of the voices of the chorus above the initial chant of the coryphæus—masculine element, feminine element—as in the Compostelan trope. This, naturally, created a succession of new accents out of whose constants a general rhythm emerged, a rhythm to which the orchestra, with its sonorous devices, gave variety and color. In the process of development, the melismatic element shifted to the instrumental group, seeking planes of harmonic variation and the balance of the pure tones, while against it the chorus, finally in unison, could give itself over to a kind of polyphonic invention within the heightened enrichment of the contrapuntal movement.

Thus I hoped to arrive at a combination of polyphonic and harmonic writing, concerted, mortised, in keeping with the most valid laws of music, within the framework of a vocal, symphonic ode, gradually rising in intensity of expression. The general concept, at any rate, was sensible enough. The simplicity of the recitative would prepare the listener to perceive the simultaneous planes which, if they had been suddenly presented, he would have found abstruse and confused. It would allow him to follow a logical process of development, the cell-word in all its musical implications. Naturally, one had to be on guard against a possible anarchy of styles engendered by this attempt to reinvent music—which, from the instrumental point of view, offered dangerous risks. I planned to protect myself by speculating with the pure timbres, and I reminded myself of certain extraordinary dialogues of flute and contrabass, of oboe and trombone, which I had discovered in works of Alberic Magnard. As for the harmony, I hoped to find an element of unity in the skillful use of the ecclesiastical modes, whose untouched resources were beginning to be utilized by some of the most intelligent of contemporary musicians.

Rosario opened the door, and the light of day surprised me in my pleasant reflections. I could not get over my amazement: the *Threnody* had been inside me all the time, but its seed had been resown and had begun to grow in the night of the Paleolithic, on the banks of the river inhabited by monsters, when I heard the medicine man howling over a black, snake-poisoned corpse two paces from a sty where the captives wallowed in their own excrement and urine. That night I was taught a profound lesson by men whom I did not consider men; by those very beings who gave me a sense of my own superiority, and who, in turn, held themselves superior to the two slavering old men who gnawed bones left by the dogs. At the memory of an authentic threnody, the idea of the *Threnody* revived in me, with its statement of the cell-word, its verbal exorcism turning into music when confronted with the need for more than one intonation, more than one note, to achieve its form—a form which, in this case, was that demanded by its magic function, and which, with its alternation of two voices, two ways of growling, was in itself the embryo of the sonata.

I, the musician, who had witnessed the scene, was adding the rest. Obscurely I sensed its potentialities and what it still lacked. I grasped its content of existent and not yet existent music. . . . I rushed out through the rain to the house of the Adelantado to ask him for one of his notebooks, one of those with a label on the cover reading: *Notebook . . . Property of . . .* which he grudgingly gave me, and I began to sketch musical ideas on staves that I myself drew, using the edge of a machete as a ruler.

XXX/ At first, faithful to an old plan of my youth, I thought of working on the *Prometheus Unbound* of Shelley, the first act of which, like the third of *Faust*, Part II, contains a marvelous cantata theme. The liberation of the chained prisoner, which I mentally associated with my flight from *there*, conveyed a sense of resurrection, an emergence from darkness, most appropriate to the original conception of the threnody, which was a magic song intended to bring a dead person back to life. Certain verses I recalled would have fitted in admirably with my desire to work on a text made up of simple and direct words: *"Ah me! alas, pain, pain, pain ever, for ever!"*—*"No change, no pause, no hope! Yet I endure."* And then those choruses of mountains, springs, storms, elements by which I was surrounded and which I felt. That voice of the Earth, at once Mother, clay, and womb, like the Mothers of Gods who still reign in the jungle. And those *hounds of hell* who break into the drama and howl with the accent of mænads rather than furies. *"Ha! I scent life!"* *"Let me but look into his eyes!"*

But no. It was absurd to excite my imagination with this when I did not have Shelley's poem there, and never would. There were only three books there: Rosario's *Genevieve of Brabant*, Fray Pedro's *Liber Usualis* and such texts as his ministry called for, and the *Odyssey* of Yannes. Leafing through *Genevieve of Brabant*, I found to my surprise that the plot, if divested of its execrable style, was not much worse than that of excellent operas, and had points of resemblance to *Pelléas*. As for the religious works, they would not fit in with my idea of the *Threne*, giving a versicular, Biblical style to the cantata. So I was left with the Spanish version of the *Odyssey*.

It had never entered my mind to compose the music for a poem written in this language, which of itself would constitute an obstacle to the performance of a choral work in any important artistic center. I suddenly found myself annoyed by this subconscious confession that I wanted to "hear myself performed." My resignation would never be effective as long as I had such notions. I was the poet of the desert island of Rainer Maria Rilke, and as such I should create out of a deep compulsion. Besides, what was my real tongue? I knew German from my father. With Ruth I talked English, the language of my boyhood education; French, as a rule, with Mouche; the Spanish of my Abridged Grammar—*Estos, Fabio*—with Rosario. But this, too, was the language of the *Lives of the Saints*, bound in purple velvet, from which my mother used to read to me. St. Rose of Lima, Rosario—I took this conjunction for a favorable sign. Without hesitation I returned to Yannes's *Odyssey*.

At first its rhetoric disheartened me. I refused to employ

formulas of invocation like: "Our Father, heir of Kronos, Lord of lords!" or "Kinsman of Zeus and son of Laertes, many-counseled Odysseus." Nothing could be more contrary to the type of text I needed. I read and re-read certain passages, impatient to set to work. I went back several times to the episode of Polyphemus, but finally found it too full of action and incident. I went out of doors and walked around in the rain, to Rosario's horror. I hardly answered *Your woman* when she talked to me, and it upset her to see me so nervous. But she finally stopped questioning me, accepting the fact that a man can have "bad days" and is under no obligation to give the reasons for his scowling brow. To keep out of my way, she went off in a corner, behind me, and started picking the ticks off Gavilán's ears with a pointed bamboo stick.

But in no time I was in a good mood again. The solution to the problem was simple. All I had to do was prune Homer's text down to the needed simplicity. I suddenly discovered the magic, primeval tone, at once clear and solemn, in the episode of the invocation of the dead: "About it I poured the drink-offerings to the congregation of the dead, a honey-and-milk draught first, sweet wine next, with water last of all: and I made a heave-offering of our glistening barley; invoking the tenuous dead, in general, for my intention of a heifer-not-in-calf, the best to be found in my manors, when I got back to Ithaca; which should be slain to them and burnt there on a pyre fed high with treasure: while for Teiresias apart I vowed an all-black ram, the choicest male of our flocks. . . . I took the two sheep and beheaded them across my pit in such a manner that the livid blood drained into it. Then from out of Erebus they flocked to me, the dead spirits of those who had died."

As the text took on the needed consistency, I conceived the musical structure of the speech. The passage from word to music would come as the voice of the coryphæus almost imperceptibly softened into verse when he spoke of the tender girls and the warriors fallen under the brazen spears. The melismatic element would be introduced above the first voice by the lamentation of Elpenor, grieving because he lay unwept and unburied. The poem speaks of his thin wail, which I would vocalize as a prelude to his plea: "Consume my body in fire, with these arms and armor which remain mine, and heap over the ashes a mound at the edge of the sea where the surf breaks white, for a token telling of an unhappy man, and when the rites are completed fix above my mound the oar that in life I pulled among my fellows."

The appearance of Anticleia would bring the contralto note to the vocal edifice, which grew clearer and clearer in my mind, entering as a kind of fauxbourdon in the descant of Ulysses and Elpenor. An open chord of the orchestra, with the sonority of an organ pedal, would herald the presence of Teiresias. But at this point I stopped. The need to write music had become so imperious that I began to work on my outline, seeing the musical signs, so long neglected, come forth at the call of my pencil.

When I had finished the first page of this first draft, I paused in wonder over these rough staves, so unevenly drawn, with lines more converging than parallel, on which I had set down the notes of a homophonic introduction which, in its very configuration, had something of spell, invocation, of music different from any I had written before. In nothing did it resemble the artful writing of that misbegotten *Prelude to "Prometheus Unbound,"* so in the fashion of the day, in which, like so many others, I had tried to revive the health and spontaneity of a craftsman's art—the work begun on Wednesday to be sung at the Sunday service—borrowing its formulas, its contrapuntal devices, its rhetoric, but without recovering its spirit. The dissonances, the misplaced notes, the harshness of the instruments deliberately set in their most difficult and extreme registers would not give permanence to a copybook art that came only from the head, using only the lifeless legacy—the patterns and formulas of "development"—which all too often forgot, and deliberately so, the inspired richness of the slow movements, the sublime inspiration of the arias, substituting sleight-of-hand tricks with the confusion, the haste, the headlong rush of the allegros.

For years a kind of locomotor ataxia had afflicted the composers of *concerti grossi,* in which two movements in eighths and sixteenths—as though there were no such things as half and whole notes—wrenched out of place by a heavy offbeat, which violated all laws of musical breathing, boomed to right and left of a *ricercare* whose paucity of ideas was hidden under the sourest counterpoint that could be imagined. Like so many others, I, too, had been impressed by the slogans of "return to order," the calls for purity, geometry, asepsis, smothering within myself all melody that sought to raise its head. Now, far from concert halls, manifestoes, the unspeakable boredom of art polemics, I was inventing music with an ease that astounded me as ideas, descending from my brain, crowded my hand, falling over one another to reach my pencil. I knew that I should be suspicious of anything brought forth without suffering. But there would be plenty of time to scratch out, weigh, correct. To the relentless sound of the rain, I wrote with feverish impatience, as though driven by an inner dæmon, condensing my script in a kind of shorthand that only I could decipher. When I finally went to bed, the first draft of the *Threnody* had filled the entire *Notebook* . . . *Property of* . . .

XXXI/ I had just suffered a disagreeable shock. The Adelantado, from whom I had requested another notebook, asked me if I ate them. I explained to him why I needed more paper. "This is the last one I'm giving you," he replied tartly, explaining that the notebooks were for minutes, records, and not to be wasted on music. As a sop to my disappointment, he offered me his son Marcos's guitar.

Evidently there was no connection in his mind between composing and writing. The only music he was acquainted with was that of harpists, mandolin-players, the pluckers of stringed instruments, all minstrels of the Middle Ages like those who came to these shores in the first caravels, who had no need of scores, who did not even know that such a thing as staved paper existed. I went to Fray Pedro to complain. But he was in complete agreement with the Adelantado, adding that the latter had evidently forgotten that very soon baptismal, burial, and marriage registers would be needed. Then, all of a sudden, he looked me sternly in the eye, asking if I intended to go on living in my present state of sin the rest of my life.

I was so unprepared for this that I stammered out something that had nothing to do with what he was saying. Whereupon Fray Pedro launched into a tirade against those who, passing themselves off as cultivated, superior persons, made his evangelical tasks more difficult by setting the Indians a bad example. He maintained that it was my duty to marry Rosario, for sanctified and legal unions should be the basis of the order to be established in Santa Mónica de los Venados. Suddenly I recovered my self-assurance, and permitted myself a touch of irony, assuring him that things went very well here without benefit of clergy. All the veins in the friar's face seemed to swell up; he shouted, as though invoking divine wrath upon me, that he would tolerate no reflections on the importance of his ministry, justifying his presence there with the words of Christ about the sheep that were not of his fold and had to be brought in to hear his voice.

Surprised by the wrath of Fray Pedro, who pounded the

ground with his staff as he talked, I shrugged my shoulders and looked the other way, refraining from saying what was in my mind: This is what the church is good for. The shackles hidden beneath the Samaritan's robe have been revealed. Two bodies cannot take their pleasure together without black-nailed fingers wanting to make the sign of the cross over them. The hammocks in which we lie must be sprinkled with holy water some Sunday when we agree to become the protagonists of an edifying scene. This nuptial chromo struck me as so ridiculous that I burst into a guffaw and left the church, which had been temporarily patched up with malanga leaves, on which the rain kept up its persistent drumming.

I went back to our cabin, where I had to confess to myself that my scoffing, defiant laughter was nothing but the cheap reaction of my attempt, in keeping with the best literary formulas, to hide the fact that I was already married. And this would have been of little importance had it not been for the fact that I was truly, deeply, in love with Rosario. At this remove from my country and its courts, the charge of bigamy would carry little weight. I could easily go through with the farce the friar demanded, and everybody would be happy. But the days of deception were over. Just because I had recovered my manhood, I would be a party to no more lies. As I prized above everything in the world the loyalty Rosario put into anything connected with me, the thought of deceiving her revolted me, especially in a matter to which a woman instinctively attaches so much importance, who must be assured of a home to shelter the living home of an always possible pregnancy. I could not bear to think of the farce of Rosario's carrying, tucked away somewhere in her clothes, her "lines," entered in the Adelantado's notebook, declaring us "man and wife before God." The conscience of my conscience made a baseness of this sort impossible.

For this very reason I was worried about the friar's tac-

tics, unswerving in their aim. Pedro de Henestrosa would
work on *Your woman's* feelings until he brought things to
a head. I would be forced into a situation in which I would
have either to confess the truth or lie. If I were to tell the
truth, my position would become difficult as regards the
missionary, and the whole placid, simple harmony of my
life with Rosario would be upset. If I decided to lie, I would
destroy with one act the rectitude of behavior that I had
determined should govern my new life.

To flee this dilemma, this being torn by doubt, I tried to
concentrate on my score, finally achieving it. I was at the
extremely difficult moment when the shade of Anticleia ap-
pears, at which the voice of Ulysses begins a simple descant
beneath the melismatic lament of Elpenor, introducing the
first lyric episode of the cantata, which the orchestra
would take up after the entrance of Teiresias, supporting
the first instrumental development, beneath a polyphony
established on the vocal level. . . . At the end of the day,
in spite of the fact that I had kept my writing as small as I
possibly could, I found that I had filled up one third of the
second notebook.

It was evident that I must quickly find a solution to the
paper problem. There had to be some product there in the
jungle, which was so rich in natural fibers, jutes, leaves,
bark, on which one could write. But there was no let-up
in the rain. There was not a dry thing in the Valley of the
Plateaus. I crowded my writing a little more, utilizing every
millimeter of paper; but this pinching, miserly preoccupa-
tion frustrated the generous proportions of my inspiration,
limiting its flow, keeping my mind on the petty when I
should have been thinking along lines of greatness. I felt
shackled, diminished, foolish, and I finally gave up my task
a little before evening, seething with irritation. It had never
occurred to me that the imagination could founder on anything so stupid as lack of paper.

And when I was at the peak of my indignation, Rosario asked me to whom I was writing letters, inasmuch as there was no post office there. This mistake, the vision of a letter meant to travel, but which could not, suddenly made me aware of the vanity of everything I had been doing since the day before. A score that is not played is utterly valueless. A work of art is meant for others—above all, music, which by its very nature can reach vast audiences. I had chosen the moment of my escape from the places where a work of mine could be heard to begin really to compose. It was foolish, absurd, laughable. And yet, even though I swore to myself that this was the end of the *Threnody*, that it would not go beyond the first third of the second notebook, I knew that the next day, with the dawn, a power beyond my control would make me take up the pencil and work out the entrance of Teiresias, which my ear could already hear, with its mighty organ sonority: three oboes, three clarinets, one bassoon, two horns, one trombone. What would it matter if the *Threnody* were never played? I had to write it, and I would write it, come what may, if only to prove to myself that I was not empty, completely empty, as I had tried to make the Curator believe, one day.

Somewhat calmed, I lay down in my hammock. My mind went back to the friar and his demand. *Your woman* was behind me, roasting ears of corn over a fire she had had trouble getting to burn because of the dampness. From where she sat, she could not see my face in the darkness or observe my expression as I spoke. I finally made up my mind to ask her, in a voice that did not come out very steady, if she thought it would be a good thing for us to get married. And when I thought that she was going to snatch at the opportunity to assign me a role in an edifying Sunday chromo for the use of the new converts, to my amazement she answered that marriage was the last thing she wanted.

Like lightning, my surprise turned to jealous indignation.

I got up and went toward her to find out her reasons. She disconcerted me with arguments employed by her sisters, and probably by her mother, which may account for the secret pride of these women, who feared nothing. According to her, marriage, the legal bond, deprived a woman of all her defenses against man. The arm she always had at her disposal against a bad husband was that she could leave him whenever she liked: he had no rights over her. A legal wife, in Rosario's opinion, was one for whom the husband could send the police when she left the house where he was free to indulge his infidelity, his cruelty, or his drunkenness. To marry was to come under laws drawn up by men and not by women. But in a free union, Rosario sententiously observed, "the man knows that having a person who looks to his pleasure and comfort depends on the way he treats her."

I must confess that the shrewd peasant logic of this concept left me speechless. In her dealings with life, it was clear that *Your woman* moved in a world of ideas, customs, precepts that were not mine. And yet I felt humiliated, reduced to a level of annoying inferiority, because now it was I who wanted her to marry me; I was the one who wanted to play a part in the edifying picture, listening to Fray Pedro perform the marriage ceremony before the assembled Indians. But a signed and sealed paper existed, *back there*, which sapped my moral strength. *Back there* was the paper I needed so badly here, in abundance.

As these thoughts were running through my mind, a terrorized scream from Rosario whirled me around. There, framed in the window, stood leprosy, the terrible leprosy of ancient times, which so many peoples have forgotten, the leprosy of Leviticus, which still existed in those forests. Beneath a pointed cap there was a residue, a mangled scrap of face, offscourings of flesh still clinging about a black hole open in the darkness of a throat, around two expressionless eyes like petrified tears on the point of dissolving in the disintegration of the being who moved them, and from whose trachea came a kind of hoarse whistle, as he pointed to the ears of corn.with an ashy hand. I did not know what to do about this living corpse, gesticulating, moving stumps of fingers, before whom Rosario knelt on the floor, mute with terror.

"Go away, Nicasio," said the voice of Marcos, approaching him without anger. "Go away, Nicasio, go away." And he pushed him gently from the window with a forked stick. He came into the hut laughing, picked up a roasting ear, and threw it to the poor wretch, who put it into his bag and dragged himself off toward the mountains.

I knew now that I had seen Nicasio, a gold-hunter in an advanced state of leprosy, whom the Adelantado had found when he got there, and who lived far away in a cave, waiting for death, which seemed to have forgotten him. He had been forbidden to come near the settlement. But it had been so long since he had done it that there was to be no punishment this time. Horrified at the thought that the leper might return, I invited Marcos to share our dinner. He dashed out through the rain to get his old four-stringed guitar—the same as those which enlivened the caravels—and with a rhythm that put Negro blood into the melody of the ballad, he began to sing:

> *"Soy hijo del rey Mulato*
> *y de la reina Mulatina;*
> *la que conmigo casara*
> *mulata se volvería."*

XXXII/ When the Adelantado discovered that I was trying to write on leaves, bark, a deerskin mat in our hut, he took pity on me and gave me another notebook, warning me that this was positively the last one. He planned to go to Puerto Anunciación for a few days when the rains ended, and would bring me all the notebooks I wanted. But there were still many days of the eight weeks of rains, and before he went the church had to be finished, and all the damage caused by the dampness repaired; also, the crops had to be sowed. So I went on working, knowing that after filling up sixty-four little pages, the first draft would have made little progress. Then I was almost afraid lest the wondrous mental excitement of the beginning should return. So, using the eraser freely—to keep the use of paper at a minimum —I spent my time correcting and paring down.

I had not said anything more to Rosario about marriage; but, if the truth be told, her refusal that afternoon had flicked me on the raw. The days were interminable. It rained too much. The absence of the sun, whose wan disk was visible at noon behind the clouds, which for a few hours turned from gray to white, induced a state of depression there where everything needed the sun to harmonize its colors and cast its shadows on the ground. The rivers were roiled, dragging along trees, masses of rotting leaves, the slag of the forest, drowned animals. Uprooted and broken things piled up in jams, which were broken by the sudden thrust of a tree, wrenched up by its muddy roots, swept down by a cascade.

Everything smelled of water, everything had the sound of water, the hand encountered water everywhere. Every day when I had gone out to look for something on which to write, I had slipped into holes screened by treacherous grass, and had come back covered with mud. Everything that flourished in the dampness thrived and rejoiced. The caladium leaves were never so green and lush, the mushrooms so abundant; the moss was never so high, the frogs were never in such fine voice or the inhabitants of rotten wood so numerous. The outcroppings of the plateaus were streaked in black. Each crack, each fold, each fault in the rock was the bed of a torrent. It was as though these plateaus were carrying out the gigantic task of channeling the waters to the lands below, of providing each area with its quota of rain. It was impossible to pick up a board from the ground without setting the wood lice scurrying. The birds had disappeared from the landscape, and one day Gavilán discovered a boa in the flooded part of the garden.

Men and women accepted all this as one of nature's inevitable crises, keeping to their huts, knitting, twisting rope, unspeakably bored. But suffering the rains was one of the rules of the game, the same as bringing forth their young with travail, and having to cut off the left hand with a machete wielded by the right if the fangs of a poisonous serpent had buried themselves in it. This was a part of life, and many things in life are not pleasant. These were the days for the accumulation of humus, the rotting and decay of the fallen leaves, in keeping with the law decreeing that all generation shall take place in the neighborhood of excretion, that the organs of generation shall be intertwined with those of urination, and that all that is born shall come into the world enveloped in mucus, serum, and blood—just as out of manure comes the purity of the asparagus and the green of mint.

One night we believed the rains were over. There came a kind of truce during which the roofs were silent and the valley took a deep breath. In the distance the flowing of the rivers could be heard, and a thick, white, chill mist filled all the space between things. Rosario and I sought each other's warmth in a long embrace. When we recovered consciousness of the world about us, it was raining again.

"It is in the time of the waters that women conceive," *Your woman* whispered in my ear. I laid my hand on her belly in a propitiatory gesture. For the first time I felt the longing to caress a child born of me, to hold it in my arms, and watch its knees bend over my arm, and see it suck its fingers. . . .

In the midst of these thoughts, with my pencil poised over a dialogue of trumpet and English horn, I was startled by an outcry that brought me to the door of our hut. Something had happened in the Indian village, for they were all milling and shouting around the Headman's house. Rosario, wrapped in her shawl, rushed out in the rain. An atrocious thing had occurred: an eight-year-old girl had just come up from the river dripping blood from her loins to her knees. When they could make out what she was saying through her horrified sobs, they learned that Nicasio, the leper, had tried to rape her, tearing her genitals with his hands. Fray Pedro was stanching the hemorrhage with rags while the men, armed with clubs, were searching the neighborhood.

"I said we ought to get rid of that Lazarus," the Adelantado was reminding the friar, and his words held a latent reproach of long standing. The Capuchin did not answer. With his long experience of forest medications, he was stuffing the wound with cobwebs and rubbing the pubis with mercury ointment. The disgust and indignation I felt at the outrage was unspeakable; it was as though I, a man, all men, were equally guilty of this revolting attempt because of the mere fact that possession, even willing, puts the male in the attitude of aggression.

My fists were still clenched in fury when Marcos slipped a shotgun under my arm; it was one of those long double-barreled guns, bearing the stamp of the gunmakers of Demerara, which perpetuate in those remote spots the techniques of the earliest firearms. Putting his finger to his lips to avoid attracting Fray Pedro's attention, the boy made signs to me to follow him. We wrapped the gun in cloths and set out toward the river. The muddy, rushing waters were dragging along the body of a deer, its white belly so swollen that it looked like a manatee. We reached the place where the attack had occurred, the grass all trampled down and stained with blood. There were deep footprints in the mud, which Marcos, bent low, followed. We walked for a long time. Night was coming on when we reached the foot of the Cliff of the Petroglyphs, and we had not yet caught up with the leper. We were about to turn back when the half-breed pointed to a recent track through the dripping underbrush. We went on a little farther, when suddenly the tracker stopped: there was Nicasio kneeling in the middle of a clearing looking at us with his horrible eyes.

"Aim at his face," Marcos said. I raised the gun, lining up the sights with the gaping hole in the middle of the wretch's face. From his throat came an unintelligible word that sounded like: ". . . fession . . . fession." I lowered the gun. The criminal was asking to be allowed to make confession. I turned toward Marcos. "Shoot," he urged. "It's better for the priest not to get mixed up in this."

I took aim again. But there were two eyes there, two almost extinct lidless eyes, that went on looking. The pressure of my finger would put them out. Put out two eyes. A man's two eyes. He was a horrible thing, a thing capable of the vilest outrage, who had destroyed young flesh, perhaps contaminating it with his own curse. He ought to be eliminated, done away with, left to the birds of the air. But something in me resisted, as though from the moment my finger tightened on the trigger, *something would be changed forever*. There are acts that throw up walls, markers, limits in a man's existence. And I was afraid of the time that would begin for me the second I turned Executioner. Marcos, with an angry gesture, snatched the gun from my hands.

"They can blast a city to pieces from the sky, and can't

do this. Weren't you in the war?" The gun had a bullet in the right barrel and a cartridge in the left. The two reports followed one another almost without interval, and the report echoed from rock to rock, from valley to valley. The waves of the echoes still vibrated in the air when I forced myself to look. Nicasio was kneeling in the same place, but his distorted face had lost all human likeness. It was a bloody mass that was disintegrating, slipping down his chest like melting wax. Finally the blood stopped flowing and the body collapsed on the wet grass. The rain suddenly started up again, and it was dark. Now it was Marcos who carried the gun.

XXXIII/ It was like a prolonged rumble of thunder which came from the north of the valley and passed overhead. I started up from my hammock so violently that I almost turned it over. The men of the Neolithic were fleeing in terror from an airplane that circled and returned.

The Adelantado stepped to the door of the Government House, followed by Marcos. Both stood staring in amazement, while Fray Pedro called out to the Indian women, howling with fright in their huts, that this was a "white man's thing" and would not hurt them. The plane was some five hundred feet off the ground, under a heavy ceiling of clouds on the point of bursting into rain again. But it was not a distance of five hundred feet that separated the flying machine from the Headman of the Indians, who glared at it defiantly, bow in hand; it was one hundred and fifty thousand years. For the first time the sound of the combustion motor was heard in those lands; for the first time the air was churned by a propeller, and this spinning parallel roundness where the birds had their feet introduced them there to nothing less than the invention of the wheel. The plane, however, showed a kind of hesitation in its flight. I noticed that the pilot was watching us as though looking for something or waiting for a signal. So I ran into the center of the square, waving Rosario's shawl. My rejoicing was so contagious that the Indians approached without fear, leaping and shouting, and Fray Pedro had to push them back with his staff to clear the field. The plane turned downriver, descending a little, and then came circling toward us, lower and lower. It touched the ground, taxied dangerously toward the curtain of trees, and with a skillful turn braked to a stop.

Two men leaped out of the cockpit, two men who called me by my name. And my amazement grew as I learned that several planes had been looking for me for more than a week. Somebody—they didn't know the name—had said *back there* that I was lost in the jungle, possibly a prisoner of head-hunting Indians. I had become the hero of a novel, which included the hypothesis that I had been tortured. It was another Fawcett case, and the accounts, published in the newspapers, were a modern version of the story of Dr. Livingstone. An important newspaper had offered a large reward for my rescue. The pilots charted their route on information from the Curator, who pointed out the general area of the musical instruments I had set out to look for. They had been on the point of giving up the search when, that morning, they had had to change their course to avoid a thunderstorm. As they flew over the Great Plateaus, they had been surprised to see a settlement where they had expected only an uninhabited region, and when they saw me waving the shawl, they had thought that I must be the person they were looking for.

I was amazed to learn that this city of Enoch, still without brass- and metal-workers, where I perhaps played the part of Jubal, was only three hours from the city as the crow flies. That is to say, the fifty-eight centuries separating the fourth chapter of Genesis from the current year *back there*, could be spanned in one hundred and eighty minutes, returning to the epoch some identity with the present—as though this were not the present, too—flying over cities that today, at this very time, belonged to the Middle Ages, the Conquest, the Colony, or the Romantic era.

Out of the plane they lifted a bundle wrapped in oil-cloth, which they would have dropped by parachute if they had found me where it was impossible to land, and they handed out medicines, canned goods, knives, bandages, to Marcos and the Capuchin. The pilot unscrewed the cap of a big aluminum jug and made me take a drink. Since the night of the storm over the rapids I had not tasted a drop of liquor. Now, in this all-pervading dampness that surrounded us, the alcohol suddenly produced a lucid intoxication that filled me with forgotten desires. I not only wanted to drink more, and watched with jealous impatience while the Adelantado and his son sampled my liquor, but a thousand taste sensations flocked to my palate. There was the urgent longing for tea and wine, celery and sea-food, vinegar and ice. And that cigarette brought back the taste of the Virginia tobacco I smoked as a boy, when my father could not see me, on my way to the conservatory.

Within me another stirred who was also I, and who did not quite fit his own image; he and I were uncomfortably superimposed on one another, like plates handled by an apprentice lithographer in which the yellows and the reds do not completely coincide, or like something seen through the glasses of a nearsighted person. That burning liquid running down my throat disconcerted and softened me. In that precious moment I became frightened of the mountains, the clouds thickening once more, the trees that the rain had made denser than before. It was as though curtains were closing in around me. Certain elements of the landscape became foreign to me; the planes became confused, the path had nothing more to say to me, and the noise of the cascades became deafening. In the midst of the infinite sound of waters, I heard the voice of the pilot as something distinct from the language he employed. It was something that was fated to happen, an event expressed in words, summons that could not be evaded, that would have caught up with me wherever I might have been. He told me to get ready to leave with them at once, for it was going to rain again, and he was only waiting for the mist to clear from the edge of the plateau to start the motor.

I made a gesture of refusal. But at that very moment something echoed within me with a powerful and joyous sonority: the first chord of the orchestra in my *Threnody*. The tragedy of the lack of paper! And then the thought of the book, the need of a number of books. The desire would soon become irresistible to go to work on *Prometheus Unbound*—"*Ah me! alas, pain, pain ever, for ever!*" Behind me the pilot was talking again. And what he was saying, which was always the same, aroused in me the memory of other verses of the poem: "*I heard a sound of voices: not the voice which I gave forth.*" The language of these men of the air, which was mine for so many years, displaced in my mind the matrix tongue, that of my mother, of Rosario. Then it was hard for me to think in Spanish, as I had managed to do again, confronted by the sonority of words that sowed confusion in my soul.

Yet, I did not want to go. But I admitted to myself that what I lacked there could be summed up in two words: paper, ink. I had managed to dispense with everything I had been accustomed to in other days; I had discarded objects, tastes, clothing, pleasures, like unnecessary ballast, arriving at the supreme simplicity of the hammock, of cleansing my body with ashes, and the pleasure to be found in gnawing ears of corn roasted in the embers. But I could not do without paper and ink, without things expressed or to be expressed by these mediums. Three hours away there was paper and there was ink, and books made of paper and ink, and notebooks, and reams of paper, and bottles, flasks, jugs of ink. Three hours away . . .

I looked at Rosario. There was a cold, detached expression on her face, which was neither anger, anxiety, nor grief. It was evident that she was aware of my struggle, for her eyes, which avoided mine, had a hard, proud expression, as if making it clear to everyone that nothing of what might happen affected her.

Just then Marcos came up with my old suitcase covered with mold. I made another gesture of refusal, but my hand reached out for the *Notebook . . . Property of . . .* The voice of the pilot, who must have been very eager for the offered reward, urged me to hurry. Then Marcos climbed into the plane with the musical instruments that should be in the Curator's hands. I told him no, and then yes, thinking that the rhythm-stick, the rattles, and the funerary jar, once sent off in their fiber mat wrappings, would liberate me from the ghosts that still haunted my sleep in the cabin.

I drank the rest of the contents of the aluminum flask. And suddenly I made my decision: I would go and buy the few things I needed to live a life as full as that of all the others here. All of them, with their hands, their occupation, fulfilled a destiny. The hunter hunted, the friar preached, the Adelantado governed. I, too, would have my calling —the legitimate one—aside from the skills needed in our common effort. In a few days I would be back for good, after sending the instruments to the Curator, and after communicating with Ruth, frankly explaining the situation to her and asking for a quick divorce. I realized that my adaptation to this life might have been a little too abrupt; my past demanded the observance of a last duty, the breaking of the legal tie that still bound me to the world *back there*. Ruth had not been a bad wife, but rather the victim of her unfortunate vocation. She would accept all responsibility when she realized that it was useless to oppose the divorce or to ask the impossible of a man who had learned the paths of evasion. Within three or four weeks I would be back in Santa Mónica de los Venados, with everything I needed for my work for several years.

As for the work I produced, the Adelantado could take it to Puerto Anunciación on one of his trips there and send it off by the river mail. The directors and my musician friends to whom it would be sent could do as they saw fit with it, performing it or not. I felt freed of all vanity in this regard, though I now felt myself capable of expressing ideas, inventing forms, which would cure the music of my time of many errors. Although without feeling vain over what I then knew—without seeking the hollow vanity of applause—there was no reason for me to hide what I knew. Perhaps some young man, somewhere, was waiting for my message, to find within himself, through my voice, the road to freedom. What was done was not completely done until someone else had seen it. But it was enough for one person to see it to bring it to being and accomplish the true act of creation, like Adam, by giving it a name.

The pilot laid his hand on my shoulder with an urgent gesture. Rosario seemed indifferent to everything. I explained to her in a few words what I had just decided to do. She did not answer, shrugging her shoulders with a gesture that had become contemptuous. I held out to her, in proof, the notes of the *Threnody*. I told her that, after her, these were the most valuable things in the world to me. "You can take them with you," she said in an angry voice, without looking at me.

I kissed her, but she eluded me with a swift gesture, escaping from the arms that would embrace her, and moved away without turning her head, like an animal that does not want to be touched. I called to her, I spoke to her, but at that moment the motor of the plane began to turn over.

The Indians burst into a joyous cry. From the cockpit the pilot made one last sign to me. And a metal door slammed shut behind me. The roar of the motors made it impossible for me to think. And then it was taxiing to the end of the square, the half-turn followed by a throbbing motionlessness that seemed to drive the wheels into the miry ground. And then the treetops were beneath us; we cleared the top of the Cliff of the Petroglyphs, and we were circling over Santa Mónica de los Venados, whose square again was filled with its dwellers. I saw Fray Pedro whirling his staff in the air. I saw the Adelantado, arms akimbo, looking up beside Marcos, who was waving his palm-leaf hat. On the path that led to our house, Rosario walked alone without raising her eyes from the ground, and I trembled as I noticed that her black hair, which hung down both sides of her head—divided by a part whose slightly animal perfume came back to me with delectation—had something of the air of a widow's veil.

Far off, where Nicasio fell, a flock of vultures was gathering. A cloud was thickening below us, and, looking for better flying conditions, we flew upward into an opalescent mist that cut us off from everything. We were going to have to fly blind for some time, so I lay down on the floor of the plane and went to sleep, somewhat befuddled by liquor and altitude.

Chapter Six

> And what you call dying is finally
> dying, and what you call birth is
> beginning to die, and what you
> call living is dying in life.
>
> QUEVEDO: *The Dreams*

(July 18)

XXXIV/ We had just emerged from a fleecy bank of clouds still touched with daylight—amid truncated arches, crumbling obelisks, smoke-faced colossi—to descend into the dusk of the city whose lights were just coming on. Some of the passengers amused themselves identifying a stadium, a park, a main thoroughfare in this vast luminous geometry. Some were happy to be arriving, whereas it was with disturbing apprehension that I approached this world I had left a month and a half before by calendar calculation —but the immensity of the six weeks I had lived was incommensurable by the chronology of that climate.

My wife had left the theater for a new role: that of wife.

This was the great novelty that had brought me flying over the smoke of suburbs I never thought to see again, instead of getting ready to return to Santa Mónica de los Venados, where *Your woman* was waiting for me with the outline of the *Threnody*, which could now be developed on reams and reams of paper. To make the situation even more ironic, my traveling companions, for whom I was the great attraction on this trip, seemed to envy me. They all showed me newspaper clippings with pictures of Ruth in our home surrounded by reporters, or standing mournfully and gracefully before the displays of the Museum of Organography, or dramatically examining a map in the Curator's apartment. One night at a performance, I was told, she had a presentiment. She went to pieces and had to leave the stage in the middle of her big scene with Booth, rushing straight to the office of one of the big newspapers, telling them she had had no news of me, that I should have been back at the beginning of the month, and that my old teacher, who had been to see her that afternoon, was really worried.

The reporters' imagination did the rest. There were front-page articles with pictures of explorers, travelers, scientists who had been captured by savage tribes—with Fawcett in the foreground, naturally—and Ruth hysterically begging the newspaper to rescue me, offering a reward to the person finding me in that great green unexplored spot which the Curator had pointed out on the map as the geographical setting of my mission. The next morning Ruth's pathetic figure was in the public eye, and my disappearance, which nobody had known of the evening before, became headline news. Different pictures of me were published, including that of my first communion—that first communion which my father had so reluctantly agreed to —on the steps of the Church of Jesús del Monte, and those in uniform before the ruins of Monte Cassino and outside Villa Wahnfried with the Negro soldiers. The Curator explained to the press, with lavish praise, my theory (which now seemed to me so absurd) of *magic-rhythm-mimetism*, and my wife had drawn a beautiful picture of our happy married life.

But what irritated me most was that the newspaper, which had so generously rewarded the aviators who rescued me, had taken the line that I was an exemplary person. The persistent theme of all the articles was that I was a martyr to scientific research who had been restored to the bosom of his admirable wife; that the domestic virtues were to be found in the world of the theater and art; that talent gave no license to flout the laws of society: *vide* the *Little Chronicle of Anna Magdalena Bach*, remember Mendelssohn's placid home, etc.

As I learned all that had been done to bring me out of the jungle, I felt a mixture of shame and irritation. The country had spent a fortune on me, enough to support several families comfortably for the rest of their lives. In my case, as in that of Fawcett, I was shocked by the contrast of a society that could be completely indifferent to suburbs such as those we were flying over, where the children were packed in under corrugated metal roofs, but which dissolved in pity at the thought that an explorer, ethnologist, or hunter might have got lost or been captured by savages while performing a task he selected of his own accord where such things are normal hazards, like a bullfighter's being gored. For millions of human beings the wars menacing the world's very existence had, for the time being, been crowded out of their mind by the news of me. And those who were prepared to greet me as a hero did not know that they would be applauding a liar. For everything about that flight, then coming in for a landing, was a lie.

I was in the bar where the *Kappellmeister* had been laid out when, from the other end of the earth, Ruth's voice reached me over the telephone wires. She was crying and

laughing, and there were so many people around her that I
could hardly hear what she was trying to tell me. Then
suddenly there came words of endearment and the information that she had left the theater to be with me always, and
that she was taking the first plane to join me. Terrified by
this plan, which would bring her into my territory, to the
very antechamber of my evasion, there where divorce is
extremely long-drawn-out and difficult because of His-
panic laws that include laying the case before the Rota, I
shouted to her that she was to stay home, and that I was the
one who would take the first plane. In her confused
good-by, interrupted by extraneous noises, it seemed to me
that I heard her say something about wanting to become a
mother. Afterwards, mentally reviewing what I had been
able to make of the conversation, I asked myself if she had
said she wanted to become a mother or was going to be a
mother. Unfortunately, this latter possibility was not to be
discounted, for we had had our last routine Sunday rites
less than three months before.

It was at this moment that I accepted the considerable
sum offered by the newspaper that had arranged my rescue
for the exclusive rights to a pack of lies—fifty pages of
them. I would not describe the wonders of my journey,
for that would have put Santa Mónica and the Valley of
the Plateaus at the mercy of the most undesirable visitors.
Fortunately the pilots who found me had alluded only to a
"mission" in their reports, following the custom of calling
any remote spot where a friar has erected a cross a "mission." And as the public was not particularly interested in
missions, I could keep many things to myself. What I
would sell was a tall story to which I had been putting the
finishing touches during the trip: I was held prisoner by a
tribe that was suspicious rather than cruel; I finally managed to escape, crossing, all alone, hundreds of miles of
jungle; finally, lost and hungry, I reached the "mission"

where they found me. I had in my suitcase a famous novel by a South American writer, giving the names of animals, trees, native legends, long-forgotten events, everything needed to lend a ring of authenticity to my narration.

With what I was to be paid for it, which would guarantee Ruth about three years of comfortable living, I should feel less remorse at asking for a divorce. There was no doubt that my situation was now worse, from a moral point of view, with this matter of her pregnancy—which would explain her sudden abandonment of the theater and her desire to join me. What I would have to face was the worst of all tyrannies: that exercised by those who love over the person who does not want to be loved, abetted by a tenderness and humility that disarm violence and silence the words of repudiation. There is no worse adversary in the kind of fight that confronted me than one who shoulders all the blame and begs forgiveness before he can be shown the door.

I had barely stepped down from the plane when Ruth's mouth had come to meet mine, and her body to seek mine in that unexpected intimacy created by the unbuttoned coats brushed aside. I recognized her breasts and belly beneath their thin covering—and then came the weeping on my shoulder. I was blinded by a thousand flashes like broken mirrors in the twilight of the airport. Then it was the Curator, who threw his arms about me; there came the delegation from the university, headed by the Chancellor and the deans of the faculties; several high government and city officials; the managing editor of the newspaper—weren't Exteeaych and the painter of ceramics and the dancer there, too?—and, finally, the staff of my studio, with the president of the company and the public-relations agent, who was already completely drunk. Out of the confusion and bewilderment that lapped me around, I saw many faces emerge, as though from a great distance, which I had forgotten, faces of so many who had been close associates for years, working together, or meeting at the same places, and who, after I had not seen them for a time, had disappeared with their names and the sound of the words they spoke.

Escorted by these wraiths, I set out for the reception at City Hall. I watched Ruth under the chandeliers of the portrait gallery, and it seemed to me that she was playing the best part she ever had in her life. Treading the measures of an endless arabesque, little by little she became the center of the stage, its focal point, and, stealing the show from the other women, she assumed the functions of the mistress of the house with the grace and agility of a ballerina. She was everywhere; she disappeared behind the pillars, to appear somewhere else, ubiquitous, intangible; she adopted the right gesture for the photographer snapping her; she relieved an important headache, finding the needed tablet in her purse; she came toward me with a tidbit or a glass in her hand, gazed raptly at me for a moment, brushing against me with a gesture of intimacy which each of those present thought that he alone had noticed; she came, she went, adding the sparkling comment when someone quoted Shakespeare, made a brief statement to the press, said that she would go with me on my next trip to the jungle; stood slenderly erect before the newsreel camera—and her performance was so subtle, so varied, so suggestive, surrendering while keeping her distance, arousing admiration while showing her utter devotion to me, employing a thousand skillful devices to convey the picture of connubial bliss, and all so perfectly staged that I felt like applauding.

At this reception Ruth displayed the tremulous joy of the bride about to embark—this time without the pain of deflowering—on a second honeymoon; she was Genevieve of Brabant back in the castle; she was Penelope listening to Ulysses speak of the conjugal couch; she was Griselda ennobled by faith and patience. Finally, when she sensed that her repertory was wearing thin, and that repetition might take the bloom off this Leading Lady act, she referred touchingly to my fatigue, to my desire for rest in the intimacy of the home after so many and such cruel tribulations, and they let us leave. The men winked knowingly as they watched my wife, in her clinging dress, descend the stairway of honor on my arm. I had the impression as we left City Hall that the curtain was about to be lowered and the footlights turned off.

I felt remote from all this. I was so far from all this. When, a few moments before, the president of the company, had said to me: "Take yourself a few more days of rest," I had looked at him strangely, almost in indignation at the thought that he felt he had any rights over my time. And then I found myself in what was my house, as though I was stepping into that of another. None of the things I saw there had the meaning for me they once had had, nor had I the least desire to repossess any of them. Among the books lined up on the shelves of the library, there were hundreds that were dead as far as I was concerned. An entire literature that I had considered the most intelligent and subtle of the epoch had toppled with all its false wonders. The special smell of this apartment took me back to a life I did not want to live a second time. . . .

As we walked in, Ruth bent over to pick up a newspaper clipping that someone, a neighbor no doubt, had slipped under the door. Its contents seemed to cause her mounting surprise. I gave thanks for this distraction, which would delay the dreaded gestures of affection, giving me time to collect my thoughts for what I wanted to say to her, when with a violent gesture she turned to me, her eyes flashing with anger. She handed me the clipping, and I shivered at the sight of a picture of Mouche talking with a reporter of one of the scandal sheets.

The title of the article spoke of "revelations" about my

trip. The writer told of a conversation he had had with my former mistress, who had coolly informed him that she had been my collaborator in the jungle. According to her, while I was studying the primitive musical instruments from the point of view of organography, she was observing them from the astrological angle, because, as was well known, many nations of antiquity related their musical scales to the order of the planets. With the most unabashed boldness, with errors that would have provoked the mirth of any specialist, Mouche spoke of the "rain dance" of the Zuñi Indians, with its species of elemental symphony in seven movements; dragged in the Hindustani *ragas*, referred to Pythagoras with examples that she had clearly picked up from Exteeaych. And it was not without skill, this display of phony erudition, designed to justify her presence on the trip in the eyes of the public, completely covering up the real nature of our relations. She presented herself as a student of astrology who had taken advantage of this mission entrusted to a friend to acquaint herself with the cosmogonic concepts of the most primitive Indians. She wound up her tale by stating that she had been forced to give up her undertaking when stricken by malaria, and had returned in Doctor Montsalvatje's canoe.

That was all she said, knowing that it would suffice for those who could read between the lines. This was her revenge for my flight with Rosario and for the fine publicity my wife was getting in this great hoax. And what she did not say, the reporter managed to convey with vicious sarcasm: Ruth had stirred up the whole country to rescue a man who, if the truth were told, had gone off to the jungle with his mistress. The equivocal aspect of the story was borne out by the silence of the one who had reappeared out of the shadows with the sliest opportunism.

Suddenly the conjugal drama my wife had put on fell from the sublime to the ridiculous. She looked at me with unspeakable fury; her face seemed the papier-mâché of a tragic mask, and her mouth, contracted in a sardonic grimace, showed her set teeth. Her tense hands were clenched in her hair, as though looking for something to tear to pieces. I realized that I had better forestall the rage that was on the point of exploding, so I precipitated the crisis by blurting out what I had planned to hold off for several days, when I could employ the coarse but undeniable argument of money.

I laid the blame on her theatrical ambitions, on the vocation that she had put ahead of everything else, our bodily separation, the impossibility of a married life reduced to fornicating every seventh day. And, swept along by the vengeful need of adding the knife-edged detail to what I had already said, I told her that, one fine day, her flesh had become indifferent to me, that her body had turned into the mere image of a duty performed because of the unwillingness to face the problems involved in an apparently unjustified rupture. Then I told her about Mouche, about our first meetings, about her studio with its astral *décor*, where at least I had found a kind of youthful abandon, a gay shamelessness, with that touch of the animal which for me was indispensable to physical love. Ruth, sunk to the carpet, panting, all the veins of her face traced in green, kept repeating in a kind of hoarse moan, as though to bring to an end an unbearable operation: "Go on . . . go on . . . go on."

But I was now up to my break with Mouche, my disgust with her vices and lies, my contempt for all her misguided ideas about life, for her profession, which lived by deceit, and the eternal confusion of her friends taken in by the deceptive ideas of others equally deceived, ever since I had seen things with new eyes, as though I had returned, my sight restored, from a long sojourn in the house of truth. Ruth had risen to her knees to hear me better. And I saw in her eyes the spark of too facile a pity, of a generous tolerance that was the last thing I wanted. Her face was softening into an expression of understanding at the thought of weakness so severely punished, and in a moment a hand would be held out to the strayed sheep—and then tearful, magnanimous forgiveness. Through an open door I saw her bed all decked out with the best sheets, flowers on the dresser, my slippers standing beside hers, in anticipation of the foreordained embrace, which would undoubtedly be followed by a delicate dinner that was probably ready somewhere in the apartment, with its white wines already chilling.

Forgiveness was so close that I felt the moment had come for the *coup de grâce*, and I brought Rosario out of her hiding-place, presenting this new *dramatis persona* to Ruth's astounded eyes as something rare, remote, exceptional, incomprehensible for those *back here*, for a special code was necessary to understand her. I painted her as a being who had no point of contact with our values, whom it would be impossible to hope to comprehend through the usual approaches; she was an arcanum made flesh who had set her seal upon me after trials whose secret must never be revealed, like those of the knightly orders. In the midst of the drama that had this familiar room for its setting, I was taking a perverse delight in further disconcerting my wife by the Kundry-like air my words were lending Rosario, surrounding her with the props of a Garden of Eden, the boa that Gavilán had tracked playing the part of the serpent. I was so carried away by this verbal invention that my voice acquired so firm and steady a ring that Ruth, in the face of a real threat, drew closer to give more attention to what I was saying. Suddenly I let fall the word "divorce," and, as she did not seem to grasp it, I repeated it calmly several times in the resolute, unruffled tone of one who states an irrevocable decision.

This was the great tragedienne's cue. I cannot recall what she said during the half-hour she held the stage of our room. The thing that most impressed me was her gestures, the gestures of her slender arms, which moved from her rigid body to her masklike face, underscoring her words with pathetic restraint. I now suspect that all Ruth's dramatic inhibitions, her having had to play the same role year after year, her never-achieved desire to flagellate herself, living the sorrow and the fury of Medea on the stage, suddenly found their outlet in that monologue, which rose to a paroxysm. But all at once her arms fell, her voice descended to the lower register, and my wife personified the Law. Her language became that of the bench, the prosecuting attorney. Cold and implacable, assuming the attitude of accusation, stiff in the blackness of the dress that no longer molded her figure, she warned me that she had it in her power to keep me chained to her for a long time, that she would put every obstacle in the way of a divorce, that she would lay every kind of legal snare for me, dragging out the proceedings endlessly to prevent my return to the side of the woman to whom she applied the ridiculous name of *Your Atala*. She seemed a majestic statue rather than a woman, standing there on the green carpet like an inexorable Power, like the personification of Justice.

I finally asked her if it was true that she was pregnant. At that moment Themis became a mother: she clasped her arms about her with a desolate gesture, bending over the life that was coming to being in her womb as though to protect it from my contaminating presence, and began to cry quietly, almost like a child, without looking at me, so hurt that her deep sobs emerged as gentle moans. Then, calmer, she fixed her eyes on the wall as though seeing something in the distance, rose to her feet with a great effort, and went to her room, closing the door after her.

Wearied by the scene, feeling the need for air, I went down the stairs and into the street.

(Later)

XXXV/ As I had acquired the habit of walking in time to my breathing, I was amazed to see how the people around me came, went, passed one another on the wide sidewalk, in a rhythm that had nothing to do with their organic wills. If they walked at one pace rather than another, it was because their walking was linked to the idea of getting to the corner in time to see the green light go on to tell them they could cross the avenue. At times the crowd that welled up from the mouth of the subway with the regularity of a pulsation seemed to upset the prevailing rhythm of the street; but in a little while the regular tempo between semaphore and semaphore was restored. As I now found myself unable to adjust to these laws of collective motion, I decided to walk very slowly, close to the store windows, since beside the shops there was a kind of protected zone for old folks, invalids, and those who were not in a hurry.

It was then I discovered in the narrow spaces to be found between two show windows, or two houses not tightly joined together, beings who stood quietly, as though bemused, with the air of erect mummies. A kind of niche sheltered a woman far gone with child, whose face had a waxy look; in a red brick recess a Negro, huddled in a frayed overcoat, tried out a new ocarina; in an excavated hole a dog shivered between the legs of a drunk who had fallen asleep on his feet.

I reached a church and was attracted to its incensed shadows by the notes of an organ gradual. The Latin of the liturgy echoed through the arched vault of the ambulatory. I looked at the faces turned toward the officiant, on whom the yellowness of the candles was reflected: not one of those whose devotion had brought them to this evening service understood a word the priest was saying. The beauty of the language was alien to them. Now that Latin had been dropped from the schools on the grounds that it was useless, what I saw here was the presentation, the staging, of a growing misunderstanding. Between the altar and the faithful from year to year a moat was widening, filled with dead words.

The Gregorian chant was heard: *"Justus ut palma florebit:—Sicut cedrus Libani multiplicabitur:—plantatus in domo Domini—in atriis domus Dei nostri."* To the unintelligibility of the text there was now added that of a music which had ceased to be music for most people; a song listened to but not heard, like the dead language that accompanied it. And as I now observed how strange, how foreign to these men and women congregated here was a thing said and sung to them in a language they did not understand, I realized that the lack of awareness which they brought to this mystery was typical of nearly all their acts. When they married here they exchanged rings, they threw handfuls of rice, without any realization of the age-old symbolism of what they were doing. These people prided themselves on preserving traditions whose origins had been forgotten, the expression, for the most part, of a collective reflex, like collecting objects whose use is unknown, covered with inscriptions that fell silent forty centuries ago.

In the world I would now return to, on the contrary, not one gesture was made without cognizance of its meaning: the food set out upon the grave, the purification of the house, the masked dance, the herb bath, the pledge of alliance, the dance of defiance, the veiled mirror, the propitiatory drum, the devils' dance of Corpus Christi, were practices whose effects were weighed in all their implications.

I raised my eyes to the frieze of that public library set in the middle of a square like an ancient temple; between its triglyphs was carved the bucrane that some hard-working architect designed without remembering, in all probability, that this ornament out of the night of the ages was nothing but the emblem of a trophy of the chase, still slippery with coagulated blood, which the head of the family hung at the entrance of his dwelling.

On my return I found the city covered with ruins that were more ruins than those considered as such. Everywhere I saw sickly columns and dying buildings, with the last of the classic tablatures employed in this century, and the final acanthus of the Renaissance, which had withered in the styles the new architecture had turned its back on, without substituting new ones or a grand manner. A beautiful detail of Palladio, a bold thrust of Borromini, had lost all meaning on façades that were a patchwork of earlier cultures which the invading cement would soon efface. From these cement mazes emerged, exhausted, men and women who had sold another day of their time to the enterprises that fed them. They had lived another day without living, and would now restore their strength to live another day tomorrow which would not be lived either, unless they fled—as I used to do, at this same hour—to the din of the dance hall or the benumbment of drink, only to find themselves the next sunrise more desolate, wearier, sadder than before.

My steps had led me to the Venusberg where Mouche and I so often came to drink, with its electric sign in Gothic letters. I followed those in search of amusement and went down to the basement, on whose walls were painted scenes of desert wastes, which seemed airless, strewn with skeletons, fallen arches, bicycles without riders, crutches that supported what seemed stone phalluses, and, in the foreground, as though overwhelmed with despair, a number of half-flayed old men who seemed to ignore the presence of a bloodless Gorgon, her ribs pierced above a belly devoured by green ants. Farther off, a metronome, an hourglass, and a snail rested on the cornice of a Greek temple whose columns were the legs of a woman wearing black stockings with a red garter as astragal. The orchestra platform was mounted on a construction of wood, stucco, pieces of metal, indented with small lighted grottoes holding wax heads, hippocampi, anatomical plates, and a mobile consisting of two wax breasts mounted on a revolving disk, whose nipples were brushed, in their interminable whirl, by the middle finger of a marble hand.

In a slightly larger grotto there were greatly enlarged photographs of Louis of Bavaria, the coachman Hornig, and the actor Joseph Kainz as Romeo, against a background of the rococo Wagnerian castles of the King whose madness had made him fashionable among certain circles —now old hat, though Mouche had remained faithful to them until very recently, as a protest against everything she dubbed "the bourgeois spirit." The ceiling imitated the roof of a cavern irregularly blotched with mold and damp.

Now that I had recognized the setting, I gave my attention to the people around me. The dance floor was a jigsaw puzzle of bodies fitted into one another, with myriad legs and arms, blending in the darkness like the ingredients of some amorphous mass, of heaving lava, swaying to blues reduced to their basic rhythmic patterns. The lights went out, and the darkness, which encouraged certain futile embraces, certain contacts frustrated by thin barriers of silk or wool, lent a new sadness to this collective movement which had something of a subterranean ritual, of a dance to stamp down earth not there to be stamped. . . .

Once more I found myself in the street, dreaming monuments for these people which should be great rutting bulls covering their cows in masterly manner upon plinths ennobled with turds in the middle of the public squares. I paused before a picture gallery where dead idols were on exhibit, devoid of all meaning for lack of worshippers, in whose enigmatic or terrible faces many contemporary painters were seeking the secret of a lost eloquence with that same desire for instinctive energies which made many of the composers of my generation strive for the elemental power of primitive rhythms in the abuse of percussion instruments. For more than twenty years a weary culture had been seeking rejuvenation and new powers in the cult of the irrational. But now I found ridiculous the attempt to use masks of Bandiagara, African *ibeyes*, fetishes studded with nails, without knowing their meaning, as battering-rams against the redoubts of the *Discourse of Method*. They were looking for barbarism in things that had never been barbarous when fulfilling their ritual function in the setting for which they were designed. By labeling such things "barbarous" the labelers were putting themselves in the thinking, the Cartesian, position, the very opposite of the aim they were pursuing. They were trying to bring new life to Western music by imitating rhythms that had never had a musical function for their primitive creators.

These reflections led me to the conclusion that the jungle, with its resolute inhabitants, with its chance encounters, its accidental meetings, its not yet elapsed time, had taught me far more of the essence of my art, of the profound meaning of certain texts, of the ignored grandeur of certain trends, than the reading of so many books that lay dead forever on the shelves of my library. The Adelantado had taught me that the greatest challenge a man can meet is that of forging his destiny. Because here, amidst the multitude that surrounded me and rushed madly and submissively, I saw many faces and few destinies. And this was because, behind these faces, every deep desire, every act of revolt, every impulse was hobbled by fear. Fear of rebuke, of time, of the news, of the collectivity that multiplied its forms of slavery. There was fear of one's own body, of the sanctions and pointing fingers of publicity; there was fear of the womb that opens to the seed, fear of the fruits and of the water; fear of the calendar, fear of the law, fear of slogans, fear of mistakes, fear of the sealed envelope, fear of what might happen.

This street had brought me back to the world of the Apocalypse where all seemed to await the opening of the Sixth Seal—the moment when the moon would become as blood, the stars of heaven fall even as a fig tree casteth her untimely figs, and the islands be moved from their places. Everything foretold this: the covers of the books in the windows, the titles, the inscriptions above the cornices, the phrases launched into space. It was as though the time of this labyrinth and of other similar labyrinths was already weighed, numbered, divided. And there came to my mind, as a relief, the memory of the inn at Puerto Anunciación where the jungle came to me in the person of the Adelantado. My mouth recovered the flavor of the hearty brandy that tasted of hazelnuts, with its lemon and its salt, and there emerged behind my forehead the letters with their shading and wreaths that spelled out the name of the place: *Memories of the Future.*

I was here tonight as a bird of passage, remembering the future, the vast land of possible Utopias, the possible Icarias. Because my trip had upset my ideas of past, present, future. This could not be the present, which would be yesterday before man had been able to live and contemplate it; this chill geometry without style, where everything grew weary and old a few hours after birth, could not be the present. Now I believed only in the present of the intact; in the future of that which was created face to face with the planets of Genesis. I no longer accepted the condition of Man-Wasp, of No-Man, nor did I admit that the rhythm of my existence could be set by the mallet of the Galley Master.

(October 20)

XXXVI/ When, three months before, the manuscript of my experiences in the jungle had been returned to me without any explanation, my knees shook with fear. The news of my divorce suit had sprung the trap on me. The newspaper could not forgive me for the money it had spent on my rescue, or for its having made me the object of a great publicity campaign, only to have the gentlemen of the cloth denounce me as a transgressor of the Law, an object of abomination. I had to sell my story for almost nothing to a third-rate magazine, and, fortunately, an international incident came along in time to relegate me to the back pages.

Then my battle with Ruth began, a Ruth dressed in black, wearing no make-up, who was determined to go on with her role of offended wife and mother-to-be before the public bar of justice. The pregnancy turned out to be a false alarm. But this, instead of simplifying matters, only made them worse, for her shrewd lawyer played up for all it was worth the fact that my wife had been prepared to give up her stage career the moment she thought herself pregnant. I became, therefore, the unworthy man of the Bible, the one who builds a house and does not dwell in it, who plants the vine and does not harvest its fruits. Moreover, that setting of the Civil War which had so tortured Ruth because of its treadmill automatism now suddenly became a shrine of art, the royal road to a career, which she had not hesitated to leave, sacrificing fame and glory to the sublime task of creating a new life—a life that the amorality of my behavior denied her. I had everything to lose in this mess which my wife was spinning out indefinitely, feeling that, with time on her side, she could make me return—my escape but a memory—to my previous existence. When all was said and done, she had taken the stellar role in this improvised drama, and Mouche had been crowded off the boards.

For three months, every afternoon, I turned the same corners, rode from floor to floor, opened doors, waited, talked to the secretary, signed whatever I was told to sign, and then found myself on the same sidewalks again, lighted up by the same electric signs. My lawyer now received me with visible ill humor, fed up with my impatience and warning me that I was going to have more and more trouble meeting the expenses of the divorce. And the fact of the matter was that I had moved from a first-class hotel to a student's hotel, and from there to a rooming-house on Fourteenth Street, where the carpets smelled of margarine and rancid fat. Nor did my publicity agency forgive my delay in returning to work: Hugo, my former assistant, had been made head of the studios. I tried unsuccessfully to find work of some sort in this city where one thousand hunt for every job. I was going to leave here, divorce or no divorce. But to reach Puerto Anunciación I had to have money, money that grew in amount and importance with the passing of time. And all I found was insignificant orchestration commissions, which I worked on without interest, knowing that a week after I was paid, I would be penniless again.

The city would not let me go. Its streets wove a web around me like a net, a seine, that had been dropped over me. Week after week I came closer to those who wash their one shirt at night, whose shoes let in the snow, who smoke the butts of cigarette butts, and cook in the closet. I had not quite come to this, but the Sterno stove, the aluminum saucepan, and the package of oatmeal now formed part of the furnishings of my room, foretelling a state of affairs that filled me with horror. I spent whole days in bed, trying to forget the threat that hung over me by reading the wondrous pages of the *Popol-Vuh*, the Inca Garcilaso, and the travels of Fray Servando de Castillejos. At times I opened the volume of the *Lives of the Saints* bound in purple velvet with my mother's initials stamped in gold, and looked up the section on St. Rose of Lima which had mysteriously fallen open the day of Ruth's departure—a day on which so many routes were silently changed by the strange convergence of chance incidents. And each time I felt a greater bitterness as I came upon the tender verses that seem charged with painful allusions:

> *Ah me! My beloved,*
> *Who detains him?*
> *The hour is past, noon strikes.*
> *But he comes not.*

When the memory of Rosario gnawed at my flesh like an unbearable pain, I took interminable walks that always brought me to Central Park, where the smell of the trees, rusty with autumn, drowsing in the mists, afforded me a little relief. The touch of their bark, damp with rain, recalled the wet wood of our last hearthfire, with its acrid smoke bringing tears to the laughing eyes of *Your woman*, as she went to the window to catch her breath. I watched the Dance of the Firs to see if I could discern some favorable omen in the movement of their needles. My inability to think of anything but my return to what was waiting for me there made me look for auguries each morning in the first things I saw. A spider was bad luck, like the snakeskin displayed in a show window, but the dog that came over and let me pat it was a favorable sign. I read the daily horoscope in the paper.

One night I dreamed that I was in a prison whose walls were as high as the nave of a cathedral, between whose pillars swung the bodies that were to be stretched on the rack; there were thick arched roofs, repeated in the distance, with a slight upward deflection to each, as when an object is seen in two reflecting mirrors. At the end there were shadowy underground vaults where the muted gallop of a horse could be heard. The quality of a mezzotint about the whole thing made me think, when I opened my eyes, that some museum memory had made me a prisoner of the *Invenzioni di Carceri* of Piranesi. I could not get it out of my mind all day. Then, as night approached, I went into a bookstore to leaf through a volume on the interpretation of dreams. "*Prison. Egypt:* a strengthened situation. *Occult sciences:* prospect of the love of a person from whom one neither expects nor desires affection. *Psychoanalysis:* linked to circumstances, objects, and persons from whom one must free oneself."

I caught a whiff of a perfume I knew, and a woman's figure joined mine in a near-by mirror. Mouche was standing beside me, looking ironically at the book. And then her voice: "If you're looking for advice, I'll make you a special rate."

The street was close at hand. Seven, eight, nine steps, and I would be outside. I did not want to talk to her. I did not want to listen to her. I did not want to argue. She was to blame for everything that was happening to me. But at the same time there came that familiar weakness in my legs and loins and a prickling that spread to the back of my knees. It was not clearly felt desire or excitation, but rather a kind of muscular acquiescence, a weakness of the will, which, in my youth, had dragged my body to the brothel while my spirit was struggling to prevent it. At such times I had undergone a kind of personality split, the recollection of which later caused me untold suffering. While my mind clung to the thought of God, the memory of my mother, the menace of disease, repeated the Lord's Prayer, my feet moved slowly, unswervingly, toward the room with its bedspread trimmed with red ribbon, knowing that at the smell of certain cosmetics on the marble-topped dresser, my will would succumb to sex, leaving the soul defenseless in the darkness. Afterwards, my spirit was angry with my body, refusing to have anything to do with it until the night when the need for rest united us in a prayer, making ready for the repentance of the following days as I awaited the appearance of the ulcers and pus that were the punishment of the sin of lust.

I sensed the revival of these struggles of adolescence as I walked along with Mouche, past the brick wall of the Church of St. Nicholas. She was talking a blue streak as though to quiet her conscience, insisting that she had had no part in the scandalous newspaper accounts, that she had been the victim of an abuse of trust on the part of the reporter, etc.—not having lost, naturally, her inveterate ability to lie with wide-open eyes, looking one straight in the face. She did not reproach me for what I had done to her when she had come down with malaria, magnanimously attributing it to my zeal to acquire the authentic musical instruments. As she had been in the grip of a high fever that first time I had embraced Rosario in the Greeks' cabin, I was left wondering whether she had really seen us.

I endured her company that night for the sake of having someone to talk to, not to be alone in my dimly lighted room, walking from wall to wall amidst the reek of margarine. And as I was determined to frustrate her attempts at seduction, I let myself be led to the Venusberg, where my credit was still good. In that way I would not have to confess that I was completely broke, and I would take care not to drink too much. But in spite of everything, the liquor maliciously managed to undermine my firm intentions, and before long I found myself in the studio for astrological consultations, whose paintings were now finished. Mouche filled up my glass several times, and then excused herself to get into something more comfortable, and when she had done so she called me a fool for depriving myself of a pleasure that would have no consequences. She said that what I did now would not compromise me in any way, and she used her body to such advantage that I gave in with a lack of protest caused in large measure by several weeks of unwonted abstinence.

After a few minutes I experienced the depression and disillusion of those who return to a flesh that no longer holds any surprises, after a separation that might have been final, when there is no link to the being this flesh envelops. I was sad, angry with myself, more alone than before, beside a body I once more regarded with contempt. Any streetwalker I had picked up in a bar, to whom I had paid a fee, would have been better than this.

Through the open door I saw the paintings in the consultation room. "This trip was written on the wall," Mouche had said the evening before we left, giving a prophetic sense to the presence of Sagittarius, the Ship *Argo*, and Berenice's Hair in the motifs of the decorations, personifying herself in the third of these figures. Now, the prophetic implications of all that—if it had any—took on noonday clarity in my mind: Berenice's Hair was Rosario, with her virgin hair, which had never been cut, while Ruth became the Hydra that completed the mural, poised threateningly behind the piano, which could be interpreted as the instrument of my profession.

Mouche sensed that my silence, my indifference, were not favorable to her. To change the direction of my thoughts, she picked up a publication lying on the night-table. It was a little religious journal to which a black nun, who shared her plane seat for several hours, had persuaded her to subscribe. Mouche explained to me laughingly that, as she was going through a bad time, she had taken the subscription on the off-chance that Jehovah might be the true God. Opening up the modest missionary bulletin, printed on cheap paper, she put it in my hands. "I think it mentions that Capuchin we knew; there is a picture of him."

In an ornate black frame there really was a photograph of Fray Pedro de Henestrosa taken many years before, for his face was still young in spite of the fact that his beard was already graying. I learned, with growing emotion, that the friar had undertaken a mission to the lands of the savage Indians he had once pointed out to me from the top of the Cliff of the Petroglyphs. From a gold-hunter—the article went on—who had recently reached Puerto Anunciación, it had been learned that the body of Fray Pedro de Henestrosa had been found horribly mutilated in a canoe sent downstream to the white man's lands by his killers as a grim warning. I put on my clothes without answering Mouche's questions and rushed out of her house, knowing that I would never go back.

All night until dawn I walked past empty warehouses, banks, dark funeral parlors, sleeping hospitals. Unable to rest, at daybreak I took a ferry, crossed the river, and went on walking past the warehouses and customs buildings in Hoboken. I thought how the Indians had undoubtedly stripped Fray Pedro after shooting him with arrows, and then had cut through his gaunt ribs with a stone knife and torn out his heart in keeping with an ancient ritual. Perhaps they castrated him; perhaps they skinned and quartered him and cut him to pieces like a steer. I could imagine the most cruel possibilities, the bloodiest surgery, the worst mutilations carried out on his old body. But his terrible death did not arouse in me the horror of the death of other men who did not know why they were dying, calling for their mothers, trying to hold back with their hands the further mutilation of a face already devoid of nose or cheek. Fray Pedro de Henestrosa had found the supreme reward a man can confer on himself: that of going to meet his death, defying it, and falling in a combat which, for the vanquished, is the arrowed victory of St. Sebastian, the rout and final defeat of death.

(*December 8*)

XXXVII/ I had a painful surprise when the boy who was acting as my guide pointed the house out to me, saying it was the new inn. Behind those thick walls, beneath that roof covered with grass swaying in the wind, we had sat up one night with Rosario's dead father. There, in the vast kitchen, I had drawn near *Your woman* for the first time with a dim sense of her future importance to me.

Now one Don Melisio came forward to meet us, and his "lady," a dwarf Negress, took three suitcases from the boys following me and piled them on her head as though the papers and books with which they were stuffed weighed nothing. The rooms were just as before except that the ingenuous adornment of the old pictures was gone. The same plants were still growing in the patio; in the kitchen stood that round tub which gave our voices the resonance of a cathedral nave. The big front room, however, had been turned into a combined dining-room and general store. There were great coils of rope in the corners, and shelves containing cans of black powder, balms and oils, and medicines in bottles of shapes no longer seen, as though intended for ailments of another age.

Don Melisio explained to me that he had bought the house from Rosario's mother, and that she had gone, with all her unmarried daughters, to live with a sister on the other side of the Andes, some ten or twelve days distant. Again I was struck by the naturalness with which these people accepted the size of the world, setting out to sail or ride for long weeks with their hammocks in a roll on their shoulder, without all the worries of the cultivated man confronted by distances that the precarious methods of transportation made immense. Besides, setting up their tent elsewhere, going from the estuary to the headwaters of a river, moving to the other side of a savanna that it took days to cross, formed part of the innate concept of freedom of beings to whom the earth was not an affair of fences, boundary stones, or limits. The earth, here, belonged to the person who took it; a river bank was cleared with machete and fire, a shelter was raised on four posts, and this was a ranch, which bore the name of the one who titled himself the owner, reciting the Lord's Prayer and tossing a few branches to the wind, like the old conquistadors. It did not make him any richer; but in Puerto Anunciación the one who did not possess the secret of a gold vein felt himself a landowner.

The aroma of *sarrapia* and vanilla that filled the house put me in a good humor. And this presence once more of fire on the hearth where a tapir haunch sputtered its grease that smelled of unfamiliar acorns. This return to the fire, to the living blaze, the flame that danced, the spark that shot out and found, in the hot wisdom of the embers, a glowing old age beneath the wrinkled gray of the ashes. I asked the dwarf Negress, Doña Casilda, for a bottle and glasses, and my table was open to anyone who remembered that I had been here six months before; in a little while I had guests. Here, bringing news from upstream and downstream, sat the Tuna-Fisher, the hunter of manatees, the carpenter who could take the measurements for a coffin at one glance, and a slow-moving lad, with an Indian profile, by the name of Simon, who got tired of being a shoemaker in Santiago de los Aguinaldos, and now sailed the less-traveled rivers with a canoe full of merchandise for barter.

The answer to my first question confirmed the death of Fray Pedro. His body, pierced by arrows and with the thorax split open, had been found by one of the Yannes brothers. As a warning to all who might think of profaning their dominions, the Indians had put his mutilated corpse in a canoe, which the waters carried downstream to where the Greek found it, covered with buzzards, aground in a channel. "He's the second to die that way," observed the carpenter, adding that among these bearded friars there were those who were real men.

It was my bad luck to learn that the Adelantado had been in Puerto Anunciación not more than two weeks before. Once more the tales were repeated of what he owned or was seeking in the jungle. Simon informed me that at the headwaters of unexplored rivers he came upon people who were settled and had built houses and planted the fields, and were not looking for gold. Another told of someone who had founded three cities, and called them St. Inés, St. Clara, and St. Cecilia for the patron saints of his three oldest daughters. By the time Doña Casilda brought us our third bottle of hazelnut brandy, Simon had offered to take me in his canoe to where I found the Curator's instruments.

I told him that I was looking for another collection of drums and flutes, not wishing to give the real reason for my trip. From there I would go with the Indian rowers who took us the other time, and who knew the way. The lad had never been that far and had only caught a glimpse on rare occasions of the first outcroppings of the Great Plateaus. But he promised to guide me past the Greeks' old mine. After rowing upstream three hours, we would have to find that palisade, that wall of treetrunks, which hid the entrance to the channel. I would look for the carved sign that marked the branch-arched passage. Farther ahead, always bearing east by the compass, we would come to the other river, where the storm had caught us one memorable afternoon of my life. When we got to where I had found the instruments, I would think up some way of getting rid of my traveling companion and staying on with the villagers. . . .

Now that I was sure of leaving the next day, I went to bed with a delightful feeling of relief. Those spiders spinning their webs between the roof beams would not bring me bad luck any more. When everything seemed lost *back there*—and how far *back there* everything seemed now—the legal bond was cut, and a successful, falsely romantic concerto for the movies opened the gate of my labyrinth. Here I was at last on the threshold of my chosen land, with everything I needed to work for a long time. As a measure of precaution against myself, in observance of a vague superstition that consisted in admitting the worst in order to conjure and ward it off, I had accepted the possibility that some day I might get tired of what I was seeking here; some work of mine might make me want to go *back there* for the time needed to publish it. But then, even though I knew I was pretending to admit what I did not admit, I was gripped by a real fear, fear of all I had just seen and suffered, which weighed on my life. Fear of the fetters, fear of the circles of hell. I did not want to write bad music, knowing that it was bad. I was fleeing from the useless professions, from the people who talked so they would not have to think, from the hollow days, from the meaningless gesture, and from the Apocalypse gathering over it all.

I longed to feel the breeze blow across my thighs once more; I was impatient to plunge into the cold streams from the Great Plateaus, and to turn myself over under the water, to see how the living crystal that would surround me would take on a pale green tint in the infant light. And above all I yearned to measure Rosario with my whole body, to feel her warmth glow against my trembling flesh; when my hands recalled her thighs, her shoulders, the softness beneath the short, coarse hairs, the surge of desire became almost painful in its urgency. I smiled, thinking that I had escaped from the Hydra, set sail in the Ship *Argo*, and that the one who displayed Berenice's Hair was at the foot of the Marks of the Flood, now that the rains were over, gathering the herbs she macerated in jars of bubbling curatives, fortified by moon dew or the white of the morning hoarfrost. I was coming back to her stronger than I was before I loved her, for I had undergone new Trials; because I had seen farce and pretense everywhere. Besides, here the most important question of my sojourn in the Kingdom of this World would be decided—the one question, when all was said and done, that admitted of no dilemma: whether I was the master of my time, or whether it was ruled by others, trying to make me pull the right oar or the left oar of the galley. The answer depended on the determination I put into not living for them or serving them. In Santa Mónica de los Venados, while my eyes were open, my hours would belong to me. I was the master of my steps, and I would set them where I chose.

(December 9)

XXXVIII/   The sun was just rising above the trees when we tied up near the Greeks' abandoned mine. Their house was deserted. Barely six months had elapsed since I had been here, and the jungle was once more lord of all. The hut where Rosario and I knew each other for the first time had been literally burst apart by the force of the plants that had grown into it, pushing up the roof, cracking the walls, turning to dead leaves, rot, what once had been the mate-

rials of which a home was made. Besides, as the last rise of
the river had been very high, the ground was swamped. It
had rained out of season, the waters had not receded to their
normal level, and a strip of wet land fringed the river, covered with the slag of the jungle, above which myriads of
yellow butterflies fluttered, flying wing to wing, so that if
one hit at them with a stick it came away yellow. At the
sight of them I understood the origin of the migrations I
had witnessed in Puerto Anunciación, when the skies had
been blotted out by seemingly endless wings. Suddenly the
water began to bubble, and a school of fish surrounded our
boat, leaping, colliding, turning the stream into a swish of
lead-colored fins and tails which slapped the waters with a
sound of applause.

Above us a triangle of herons flew and, as though in response to a conductor's baton, all the birds of the woodland
broke into song. This omnipresence of the bird, which
spread the sign of the wing over the terrors of the jungle,
brought to my mind the transcendence and plurality of the
Bird in the mythologies of this world. From the Bird-Spirit
of the Eskimos, the first to caw beside the Pole at the stem
end of the continent, to those heads which flew with the
wings of their ears in the regions of Tierra del Fuego, all
the coasts display birds of wood, birds painted on rock,
birds drawn on the ground—of such a size that they must
be viewed from the mountains—in an iridescent parade of
monarchs of the air: the Thunder Bird, the Eagle of the
Dews, the Sun Birds, the Condor Messengers, the Macaw
Meteors launched across the wide Orinoco, the *zenzontles*
and the *quetzales*, all presided over by the great trinity
of plumed serpents: Quetzalcoatl, Gucumatz, and
Culucán. . . .

We sailed on down the river, and when the noon sun on
the muddy, yellow waters became too overpowering, I
pointed out to Simon the wall of trees to the left, which

covered the entire bank. We pulled over and slowed down, watching for the sign marking the entrance to the connecting channel. With my eyes riveted on the trees, I watched for the three *V*'s one above another, at the height of a man's breast if he were standing on the water. From time to time Simon inquired if we had reached the spot. We moved ahead. But I was watching so closely, my anxiety not to miss the sign was so great, that my eyes became weary of seeing the same tree. I began to wonder whether I had seen it without realizing it; I asked myself whether my attention might not have faltered for a minute; I ordered him to turn back, and all I found was a spot on the bark or a ray of sunlight. Simon, unruffled, followed my instructions without a murmur. The canoe rubbed against the tree roots, and at times we had to push off with the tip of a machete.

This search for the sign on this endless succession of tree-trunks was beginning to make me dizzy. Yet I told myself that this could not be wrong, that I had not seen anything resembling the three superimposed *V*'s. We sailed on for another half-hour, when suddenly a spur of black rock jutted out from the jungle. It was so irregular, of such strange design, that I was sure that if we had seen it before I would have remembered it. I made a sign to Simon to turn the boat around and backtrack. I had a feeling that he was looking at me ironically, and this annoyed me as much as my own impatience. I turned my back on him and went on observing the trees. If I had missed the sign, I would have to make sure of it this second time. There were two trunks, like the jambs of a narrow door. The lintel was of leaves, and the sign was halfway up the left trunk.

When we had started out, the sun had been in our faces. Now, going back, we were rowing in a shadow that stretched farther and farther across the water. My anxiety was heightened by the thought that it might get dark before we found what we were looking for, might have to wait until the next day. This in itself would not be serious. But under the circumstances, it seemed a bad omen. Everything had gone so well of late that I could not accept the thought of such an absurd contingency. Simon kept looking at me with ironic meekness. Finally, just to say something, he pointed to some trees, asking if they might not be the entrance.

"It is possible," I answered, knowing that there was no sign there.

"*Possible* is not a legal term," he remarked sententiously, and at that moment I fell against the side of the boat, which had just struck a network of lianas. Simon got to his feet and with the pole felt for bottom to push the canoe off. At that moment, in the second the pole took to sink into the water, I realized why we had not found the sign, were not going to find it: the pole, which was some three yards long, did not touch bottom, and my companion had to cut us loose with his machete. When we started off again and he looked at me, my expression was one of such distress that he came over to me, thinking I had been hurt. What had happened was that I had remembered that when we came here with the Adelantado, *the oars touched bottom all the time*. This meant that the river was still high, and that *the sign we were looking for was under water*.

I told Simon what I had just realized. Laughing, he told me that that was exactly what he had thought, but that "out of respect" he had not wanted to say anything. Besides, he had thought that I was taking the rise of the river into account. Now I asked him, haltingly, fearful of his answer, if he thought that the waters would soon recede enough so that we could find the sign. "Not before April or May," he answered, bringing me face to face with a reality that admitted of no appeal. So until April or May the narrow door of the jungle would be closed to me.

I realized now that after having successfully passed the

trial of the nocturnal terrors, of the tempest, I had to submit to the acid test: the temptation to return. It was Ruth, at the other end of he world, who had sent the Messengers that had dropped from the sky one morning, with their eyes of yellow glass and their earphones around their necks, to tell me that the things I needed to express myself were only three hours' flying time away. And I had taken off into the clouds, to the stupefaction of the Neolithic men, to find myself a few reams of paper, without suspecting that I was being kidnapped by a woman mysteriously aware of the fact that only the most drastic means would give her one last chance to bring me back to her terrain.

During these last days I had felt the presence of Rosario close at hand. There were times at night when it seemed that I heard her quiet breathing. Now, with the sign covered and the entrance closed, this presence seemed to withdraw. Winnowing the bitter truth from words my companion listened to without understanding, I told myself that the discovery of new routes embarked upon without realization, without awareness of the wonder of it while it is being lived, is so unique, so defies recapture, that man, puffed up with his vanity, thinks he can repeat the feat whenever he wishes, master of a privilege denied to others. One day I had made the unforgivable mistake of turning back, thinking that a miracle could be repeated, and on my return I found the setting changed, the landmarks wiped out, and the faces of the guides new. . . .

The sound of the oars filled me with anxiety. Night was sifting through the jungle; the swarms of buzzing insects were growing thicker around the roots of the trees. Simon, no longer listening to me, had moved to the center of the stream to return as quickly as possible to the Greeks' abandoned mine.

(*December 30*)

XXXIX/ I was working with Shelley's text, cutting certain passages, to give it a more authentic cantata quality. I had left out part of Prometheus' long lament at the magnificent beginning, and I was now trying to fit in the scene of the Voices—where some of the verses are irregular—and the dialogue between the Titan and the Earth. This task, it goes without saying, was merely an attempt to curb my impatience, to relieve the obsession, the one idea that had kept me paralyzed there in Puerto Anunciación for the past three weeks. I had been told that there was a guide on the point of returning to Río Negro who knew the passage I was looking for, or, at any rate, other waterways that would take me to my final destination.

"He'll be back. . . . He'll be back," Doña Casilda told me in response to my questions about the guide as she served me my early morning coffee. I also had the hope that the Adelantado, in need of medicines or seed, might suddenly show up, and for that reason I stayed on in the town, turning a deaf ear to Simon's tempting suggestion that we try the northern channels. The days rolled by with a slow monotony that would make me happy in Santa Mónica de los Venados, but which here, unable to concentrate my thoughts, I soon found unbearably tedious. Besides, what I was interested in now was the *Threnody*, and I had left the first draft with Rosario. I could have started it all over again, but what I had done there so satisfied me in its spontaneity of accent that I did not want to begin again cold, with a heightened critical sense, drawing on my memory, and nagged by impatience to continue my journey.

Every afternoon I walked down to the rapids and lay on the rocks shaken by the rushing of the waters. I found a kind of surcease from my irritation when I was alone amid that thunderous roar, isolated from the world by the sculpture of that foam which boiled and still preserved its form

—a form that swelled and diminished in keeping with the varying force of the current, without losing a design, a volume, and a consistency that transformed its perennial, dizzying mutation into something alive and fresh, as caressable as the back of a dog, with the roundness of an apple to the lips resting on it. The island of Saint Prisca became one with its inverted reflection, and the sky drowned in the depths of the river.

Under the leadership of a dog that always barked in the same high-pitched key, all the dogs of the neighborhood intoned a kind of chant, made up of howls, which I listened to with closest attention as I walked back from the rocks, for I had noticed, on repeated afternoons, that its duration was always the same, and that it invariably ended as it began, on two barks—never one—of the mysterious dog-shaman of the pack. The dances of the monkey and of certain birds having been discovered, it occurred to me that systematic recordings of the noises of animals that live with man might reveal a certain obscure musical sense in them, not too far removed from the chant of the medicine-man which had so impressed me one afternoon in the Jungle of the South. For five days the dogs of Puerto Anunciación had been howling the same way, entering in a set order, and ending on an unmistakable signal. Then they returned to their homes, went to sleep under the stools, listened to what was said to them, and licked the bowls, without begging for more until the paroxysmal days of being in heat would return, when man must resign himself to waiting patiently until the animals of the Alliance had concluded their rites of reproduction.

I was thinking all this as I came to the outer street of the town, when suddenly two powerful hands were clapped over my eyes, and a knee in the middle of my spine bent me backward so brutally that I let out a screech of pain. The joke seemed so stupid that I tried to wrench myself loose and let fly with my fists. But a roar of laughter that I recognized quickly turned my anger to joy. Yannes threw his arms about me, enveloping me in the sweat of his shirt. I grabbed him by the arm as though afraid he might run away and took him back to my lodging, where the dwarf Doña Casilda served us a bottle of hazelnutted brandy.

At first I feigned a flattering interest in what he had been doing, the quicker to establish a climate of friendship and thus arrive, on the basis of affection, at the only thing that interested me. Beyond doubt Yannes knew the secret entrance; he had been with us the other time we went there; besides, with his long experience of the jungle, he would be able to open the Door without need of looking for the triple *V*. Probably, too, the water had gone down somewhat in those last weeks. But I observed that there had been a change in the Greek's expression; his eyes, once so penetrating and steady, now seemed restless, suspicious, never coming to rest anywhere. He had a nervous, impatient air, and it was hard to carry on a coherent conversation with him. When he was telling something, his words rushed out in a torrent, or he hesitated, but without pausing to turn over an idea, as he had before.

Suddenly, with a conspiratorial air, he asked me to take him to my room. Once there, he turned the key in the door, tried the windows, and showed me, by the light of the lamp, a quinine tube from which the tablets had been removed and which now contained small crystals that looked like smoked glass. He explained, almost in a whisper, that these quartzes were something like the advance guard of diamonds; not far from them one always finds the object of his search. He had buried his pick in a certain place and found a fabulous deposit. "Diamonds of fourteen carats," he confided to me in a hoarse voice. "And there are probably bigger ones there."

He was dreaming of the recently discovered hundred-carat gem that had turned the head of all the seekers of El Dorado still roaming the continent, who had not given up hope of finding the treasures sought by the dreamer Felipe de Utre. Yannes was upset by his discovery; he was on his way to the capital to file a claim to the mine, haunted by the fear that during his absence someone might stumble on his remote find. It seemed that there had been cases of the miraculous coincidence of two hunters on the same little acre of the vast map. But none of this interested me. I raised my voice to get his attention and told him the one thing I wanted.

"All right, on the way back," he answered, "on the way back."

I implored him to put off his trip so that we could leave that very night, before daybreak. But the Greek answered that the *Manatí* had just arrived, and was sailing the next day at noon. Besides, it was impossible to reason with him. He was thinking of nothing but his diamonds, and when he stopped talking about them it was because he was afraid that Don Melisio or the dwarf might overhear. In helpless rage, I resigned myself to this new delay. I would wait until he came back—which would be soon, spurred as he was by greed. And to make sure that he would not fail to come for me, I offered to advance him money to begin his diggings. He gave me a smothering embrace, calling me brother, and dragged me off to the tavern where I had met the Adelantado. He ordered another bottle of brandy, and to make sure of my interest in his discovery he pretended to give me confidential information about the place where he found the quartz, forerunner of his strike. And in this way I learned something I should never have suspected: *he discovered the mine on his way back from Santa Mónica de los Venados*, after having come upon the hidden city and spending two days there.

"Stupid people," he said, "imbeciles! They have gold

close by and don't mine it. I wanted to work it; they said shoot me with gun."

I grabbed Yannes by the shoulders, and shouted at him that I wanted news of Rosario, how she was, how she looked, what she was doing.

"Wife of Marcos," the Greek answered. "Adelantado happy because she with child. . . ."

It was as though I had been hit over the head. My skin felt as though a thousand cold needles were coming through it. With an immense effort I reached for the bottle, and the touch of it seemed to burn me. I slowly filled my glass, poured the liquor into a throat that could no longer swallow, and broke into an agonizing cough. When I recovered my breath, I looked at myself in a mirror, black with fly specks, in the rear of the room, and what I saw was a body sitting at a table, looking hollow, empty. I was not sure that it would move and walk if I ordered it to. But the being that moaned within me, lacerated, flayed, its wounds filled with salt, finally dragged itself to my throat, and I began a stuttering protest.

I don't know what I said to Yannes. What I heard was the voice of another talking of prior rights to *Your woman*, explaining that the delay in returning was due to reasons beyond his control, trying to justify himself, appealing his case, as though he was on trial before a court determined to destroy him.

Aroused from his diamonds by the broken, imploring timbre of a voice that was trying to turn back time and undo what had been done, the Greek looked at me in surprise that turned to pity. "She no Penelope. Young, strong, handsome woman needs husband. She no Penelope. Nature of woman here needs man . . ."

The truth, the crushing truth—now I realized it—was that these people had never believed in me. I was there on loan. Rosario herself must have looked on me as a Visitor

incapable of staying on indefinitely in the Valley where
Time had Stopped. I recalled now the strange way she had
looked at me when she saw me writing feverishly for days
on end, there where writing fulfilled no useful purpose.
New worlds had to be lived before they could be analyzed.
Those who lived there did not do so out of any intellectual
conviction; they simply thought this, and not the other,
was the good life. They preferred this present to the present of the makers of the Apocalypse. The one who made
too much of an effort to understand, the one who under-
went the agonies of a conversion, the one whose idea was
that of renunciation when he embraced the customs of those
who forged their destinies in this primaeval slime in a hand-
to-hand struggle with the mountains and the trees, was vulnerable because certain forces of the world he had left behind continued to operate in him.

I had traveled through the ages; I had passed through the
bodies and the times of the bodies, without realizing that I
had come upon the hidden straitness of the widest door. But
association with the miracle, the founding of cities, the lib-
erty encountered among the Inventors of Callings on the
soil of Enoch, were realities whose grandeur was perhaps
not scaled to the puny dimensions of a contrapuntalist, always ready to employ his leisure in seeking a victory over
death in an arrangement of neumes. I had tried to make
straight a destiny that was crooked because of my own
weakness, and a song had welled up in me—now cut short
—which had led me back to the old road, in sackcloth and
ashes, no longer able to be what I had been.

Yannes offered me passage on the boat in which he was
sailing the next day, the *Manatí*. I would sail toward the
burden awaiting me. I raised my burning eyes to the flowery sign of *Memories of the Future*. Within two days the
century would have rounded out another year, and this
would be of no importance to those around me. There

the year in which we live can be forgotten, and they lie who say man cannot escape his epoch. The Stone Age, like the Middle Ages, is still within our reach. The gloomy mansions of romanticism, with its doomed loves, are still open. But none of this was for me, because the only human race to which it is forbidden to sever the bonds of time is the race of those who create art, and who not only must move ahead of the immediate yesterday, represented by tangible witness, but must anticipate the song and the form of others who will follow them, creating new tangible witness with full awareness of what has been done up to the moment. Marcos and Rosario were ignorant of history. The Adelantado stood at the first chapter, and I could have remained at his side if my calling had been any except that of composing music—the calling of a scion of the race. It remained to be seen whether I would be deafened and my voice stilled by the hammer strokes of the Galley Master who waited for me somewhere. Today Sisyphus' vacation came to an end.

Somebody behind me said the river had fallen a great deal these last days. Many of the submerged stones had reappeared, and the rapids bristled with rocky spurs whose fresh-water algæ died in the light. The trees along the bank looked taller now that their roots would soon feel the warmth of the sun again. On one scaly trunk, a trunk of ochre streaked with pale green, there would become visible, when the waters settled, the Sign carved on its bark with the point of a knife some three handspans above the level of the waters.